THOMAS MANN

JOSEPH AND HIS BROTHERS

I · JOSEPH AND HIS BROTHERS

II · YOUNG JOSEPH

III · JOSEPH IN EGYPT

Translated from the German by H. T. Lowe-Porter

THESE ARE BORZOI BOOKS, PUBLISHED BY

ALFRED A. KNOPF

JOSEPH IN EGYPT

✳

THOMAS MANN

JOSEPH IN EGYPT

[VOLUME ONE]

Translated from the German for the first time by H. T. Lowe-Porter

NEW YORK · ALFRED · A · KNOPF

1938

CONTENTS

VOLUME ONE

A map of Joseph's journey into Egypt, prepared by C. E. Riddiford, will be found at the end of this volume.

JOSEPH IN EGYPT

✵

1

THE JOURNEY
DOWNWARDS

"Where are you taking me?" Joseph asked Kedema, one of the old man's sons, as they were setting up the sleeping-huts, in the rolling, moonlit lowland at the foot of the mountains called Fruitlands.

Kedema looked him up and down.

"Thou'rt a good one!" said he, and shook his head in token that he did not mean good at all but various other things such as pert or queer or simple. "Where are we taking thee? But are we taking thee anywhither? No, not at all. Thou art by chance with us, because our father hath purchased thee from harsh masters, and thou goest with us whither-ever we go. But taking thee that cannot be called."

"No? Then not," responded Joseph. "I only meant: whither doth God lead me, in that I go with you?"

"Thou art and remainest a funny fellow," countered the Ma'onite, "and thou hast a way of putting thyself in the centre of things till one knoweth not whether to wonder or be put out. Thinkest thou, thou 'Come-hither,' that we are a-journeying in order that thou mayest arrive somewhither where thy God will have thee to come?"

" Not that do I think," Joseph replied. " For I know that you, my masters, journey whither you will and on your own affairs and of a certainty no question of mine meaneth any wrong to your dignity or power. But lo, the world hath many centres, one for each created being, and about each one it lieth in its own circle. Thou standest but half an ell from me, yet about thee lieth a universe whose centre I am not but thou art. Therefore both are true, according as one speaketh from thy centre or from mine. And I, on the other hand, stand in the centre of mine. For our universes are not far from each other so that they do not touch; rather hath God pushed them and interwoven them deep into each other, so that you Ishmaelites do indeed journey quite independently and according to your own ends, whither you will, but besides that you are the means and tool, in our interwovenness, that I arrive at my goal. Therefore I ask whither you are leading me."

" Well, well! " said Kedema, and kept looking him up and down, his face turned away from the peg he was driving. " All that thou thinkest out and thy tongue runs on like a lizard's tongue. I will tell the old man my father how thou — son of a dog as thou art — takest leave to riddle and stick thy nose into such high wisdom as that thou hast a universe to thyself and we are destined for thy guardians. Take care, I'll tell him! "

" Do so," responded Joseph, " it will do no harm. It will make thy father careful not to sell me too cheap to the first comer, if he thinketh of making trade with me."

" Are we chattering here," asked Kedema, " or are we setting up a hut? " And he motioned him to lend a hand. But as they worked he said:

"Thou askest too much, when thou wilt know from me whither we journey. I would have naught against telling thee, if I knew. But it is the old man my father's business, he keepeth all in his own head how it will go and afterwards we see how it cometh to pass. So much is clear, that we keep on, as the shepherds thy harsh masters counselled us, and go not into the interior but are bound toward the level shore; there shall we travel day by day and come into the land of the Philistines, the cities of the seafaring traders and the pirate strongholds. Perhaps thou wilt be sold there somewhere to the galleys."

"That would I not have," said Joseph.

"No use to wish. All will be as the old man hath thought, and whither we journey at the end, that he himself perhaps knoweth not. But he would like us to think that he knoweth all quite precisely, beforehand, and so we all act as though we thought so — Epher, Mibsam, Kedar, and I. . . . I tell thee this because we happen to be setting up the huts here together; otherwise I have no reason to say it to thee. I could wish the old man would not exchange thee too soon for purple and cedar oil but that thou wouldst remain here with us for a spell that one might hear more from thee about the universes of men and their interwovenness."

"As thou wilt," answered Joseph. "You are my masters and have bought me for twenty silver pieces, including my tongue and my wits. They are at your service; and to that about the universe of the individual I can add something about God's not quite flawless wonder-working with numbers, so that man must improve His calculations; and further about the pendulum, the year of the dog star, and the renewal of life — "

"But not now," Kedema said. "The huts must absolutely be set up now for the old man my father is tired, and so am I. I fear that I could not follow thy tongue any more for today. Art thou still ailing from thy fast and are thy limbs still sore where thou wast bound with cords?"

"Scarcely at all," responded Joseph. "After all it was only three days that I spent in the pit, and your oil with which I might anoint myself has done my limbs great good. I am now whole, and nothing detracteth from the value and usefulness of thy slave."

He had, in fact, had opportunity to cleanse and anoint himself, had received from his masters a loincloth and for cooler hours a rumpled white hooded cape such as the thick-lipped camel-boy wore. Probably the expression " to feel as one new-born " may have fitted him more precisely than it has any human being since the creation of the world — for had he not actually been born again? It was a deep cleavage and abyss that divided his present from his past, it was the grave. Since he had died young his vital forces reassembled themselves quickly and easily beyond it; but that did not prevent him from distinguishing sharply between his present existence and that earlier one which had ended in the grave, nor from considering himself not the old Joseph but a new one. If to be dead and perished means to be quite inseparably bound to a state which permits no looking back, no gesture, no smallest resumption of relations with his previous life; if it means to be vanished speechless from that former life without leave or thinkable possibility of breaking the silence with any whatsoever sign — then Joseph was dead; and the oil with which he might anoint himself after cleansing from the dust of the grave had been no other than that which one gives the dead into the grave for his anointing in another life.

I stress this point, for it seems to me urgent to defend Joseph, now and later, from a reproach which has often historically been levelled against him. For certainly a reproach lies in the query: why, after escaping from the pit, had he not bent all his strength to get in touch with Jacob in his pitiable state, to let him know that he still lived? The opportunity must early have presented itself; yes, as time passed it would surely have been more and more possible for the son to send to that father in his error some word of the truth. Proportionally strange, even offensive must it seem that he did nothing of the kind.

But the reproach confuses the outwardly with the inwardly possible, and leaves out of consideration the three black days which preceded the rising of Joseph. They had driven him, amid severest anguish, to an insight into the deadly error of his former life and to a renunciation of it; they had taught him to accept his brothers' conviction of his death. His resolve and purpose not to betray their belief was the firmer because it was not voluntary but as involuntary and logically necessary as the silence of the dead. A dead man is silent about his love, not out of lovelessness but necessity; and not in cruel wise was Joseph silent to his father. Indeed it became very hard to him, and the longer it lasted the harder it grew, that we may believe; not easier than on the dead lies the earth which covers him. Pity for the old man who he well knew had loved him more than himself, whom he too loved with grateful, natural love, and together with whom he had brought himself down to the grave tempted him sore and would have made him glad to act contrary to his better sense. But there is something strange about a pain felt by others for our own fate. Our sympathy with it is of a peculiar kind, distinctly harder and colder than that we feel with a stranger sorrow. Joseph had passed through frightfulness, he had received cruel instruction; and it eased for him his compassion for Jacob, yes, the consciousness of their common burden made his father's woe seem somehow in the nature of things. His bond to death prevented him from cancelling the bloody sign which the other must have received. Jacob, he knew, could not fail to take the blood of the kid for his son's blood; and that this must be so worked upon Joseph until it practically obliterated the distinction between " This is my blood " and " This represents my blood." Jacob held him for dead; and since he did so irrevocably, unalterably — then was Joseph dead or was he not?

He was. The proof lay in the compulsion to keep silence to the father. The kingdom of the dead received him — or rather would receive him; for he soon learned that he was still on the way thither, being led in that direction by the Midianites who had bought him.

TO THE MASTER

" Thou'rt to come to the master," a boy named Ba'almahar said one evening to Joseph as the latter was busy baking pancakes on hot stones. They were now some days distant from Mount Kirmil, having come along the sandy shore close to the open sea. Joseph had asserted that he made uncommonly good pancakes. And actually by God's help he succeeded in making excellent ones, though he had never made or been asked to make them before. They had camped at sunset at the foot of the rushy and grassy line of dunes which had for days monotonously accompanied their course on the land side. It had been very hot; now mildness descended from a paling sky. The beach extended, violet-hued. The retreating sea rustled silkily, sending broad, shallow waves to the wet margin of the shore, where they were gilded with red-gold splendour by the scarlet rays of the parting sun. The camels rested beside their pegs. Not far from the shore a clumsy freight boat, worked by two men and seemingly laden with wood, was being towed southwards by a sailing-ship propelled by oars. The sail-boat had a short mast and a long yard, many cables, and an animal's head on the prow high above the water.

" To the master," repeated the camel-boy. " He summons thee through my mouth. He is sitting on the mat in his tent and he says thou art to come before him. I was passing and he called me by my name, Ba'almahar, and spake: ' Send to me him lately bought, that son of the swamps, that " Come-hither " out of the depths, I would question him.' "

" Aha! " thought Joseph, " Kedema hath told him about the universes, that is very well." " Yes," said he, " he expressed himself thus because he knew not how otherwise to make thee comprehend whom he meant. He must speak to thee, my good fellow, according to thy understanding."

" Indeed," retorted the other, " what else should he have said? For wanting to see me, he would say: ' Send to me Ba'almahar.' For that is my name. But with thee it is harder, for to thee one can but whistle."

"I suppose he would see thee always," said Joseph, "though thou art but a scaldhead! Go now. Thanks for thy message."

"What thinkest thou?" cried Ba'almahar. "Thou must come straightway with me, that I bring thee before him, for if thou comest not I shall suffer."

"But first," answered Joseph, "I must just finish this pancake before I go. I will take it with me, that the master may try my excellent baking. Be quiet and wait." And with the slave emitting cries of impatience he baked the pancake brown, then rose from his squatting posture and said: "I come."

Ba'almahar accompanied him to the old man, who sat contemplatively on his mat in the low entrance of his travelling tent.

"To hear is to obey," said Joseph, saluting. The old man, gazing into the fading glow of eve, nodded and then lifted one of his hands from his lap with a sidewise wave in sign that Ba'almahar should disappear.

"I hear," he began, "that thou hast said thou art the navel of the world."

Joseph shook his head with a smile.

"What could that mean," answered he, "and what may I have chanced to utter and turn-a-phrase that they have so bungled it to my lord's ears? Let me see. Yea, truly, I said that it hath many centres, the world, as many as there are men on earth to say 'I say.' For each a centre."

"That is the same in the end," said the old man. "It is true, then, that thou didst give tongue to such a folly. Never have I heard the like, in all my wanderings, and I see too well thou art a blasphemer and ill-doer, just as thy former masters said. What should we be coming to if every gawk and gaby in all the tribes were to consider himself the centre of the world wherever he standeth? And what should we do with so many centres? When thou wast in the well, whither thou camest, as I now see, only too justifiably, was then this well the sacred centre of the world? "

" God hallowed it," answered Joseph, " in that He kept an eye on it and let me not be destroyed therein but sent you by that way that you might save me."

" ' So that '? " questioned the merchant, " or ' in order that '? "

" ' So that,' and ' in order that,' " responded Joseph, " both, or as one will."

" Thou art a prattler. Up to now there was at least question whether Babel was the centre of the world and its tower or perhaps the city of Abdu on the river Hapi, where he lieth buried, the First of the West. Thou multipliest the question. To what god belongest thou? "

" God the Lord."

" Adon, then, and thou lamentest the going down of the sun. To that I agree, it is at least a statement worthy of a hearing, and better than if one were to say: ' I am a centre,' as though he were gone mad. What hast thou there in thy hand? "

" A pancake, which I baked for my lord. I can make uncommonly good pancakes."

" Uncommon? Let me see."

And the old man took the cake out of Joseph's hand, turned it about, and then bit a piece off with his side teeth, for he had none in front. The pancake was as good as could be and not better; but the old man gave judgment:

"It is very good. I will not say uncommonly, since thou hast said it first; thou shouldst have left it to me. But good it is. Capital, indeed," he added, as he chewed. "I commission thee to bake them often."

"It shall be done."

"Is it true or not, that thou canst write and keep a record of stocks?"

"With ease," answered Joseph. "I can write human and divine writing, with reed or graver, at will."

"Who taught thee?"

"He did who was set over the house. A wise steward."

"How many times goeth seven into seventy-seven?"

"But twice, as written. But in sense I must take the seven first once, then twice, then eight times to reach seventy-seven, for seven, fourteen, and fifty-six make it up. One, two, and eight are, however, eleven and thus I have it: eleven times doth seven go into seventy-seven."

"So quickly findest thou a hidden number?"

"Quickly or not at all."

"Thou hast probably learned from practice. But suppose I have a piece of meadow that is three times as large as the field of my neighbour Dagantakala, but he buyeth a yoke of land in addition and now mine is only twice as large as his. How many yoke have both fields?"

"Together?" asked Joseph and reckoned.

"No, each one."

"Hast thou a neighbour named Dagantakala?"

"I only call so the owner of the second field in my sum."

"I see and understand. Dagantakala — that must be a man from the country of Pelesheth to judge by the name, from the land of the Philistines, whither we seem to be going down according to the decree of thy mind. There is no such person; but he is named Dagantakala and he tills in contentment his little ploughland, now increased to three yoke, incapable of envy of my lord and his six yoke, since after all he hath increased from two to three yoke and besides, because he doth not exist at all nor yet the ploughland which all together maketh up nine yoke — that is the joke of it. There is only my lord and his busy brain."

The old man blinked uncertainly, for he did not quite see that Joseph had already solved the problem.

" Well? " asked he. . . . " Ah, yes, yes. Thou hast said already and I scarce marked it, so hast thou woven and fabled it into thy prattle that I almost failed to hear it. It is right, six, two, and three, those are the figures. They were concealed and hidden — how then hast thou so quickly brought them out while prattling? "

" One must fix the unknown quantity clearly in one's eye, then the concealments fall away and it becometh known."

" I must laugh," the old man said, " because thou madest the answer run all in together so and made nothing of it when thou gavest it. I really must laugh heartily at that." And so he did, with his toothless mouth, his head on one side, and shaking it to boot. Then he grew serious again and blinked with eyes yet moist.

" Now hearken, Come-hither," said he, " and answer honestly and in accordance with the truth. Tell me, art thou really a slave and a nobody's son, a rascal and under-servant of the basest sort, heavily punished for heaped-up crimes and moral transgressions as the shepherds said? "

Joseph veiled his eyes and rounded his lips in a way he had, making the under one protrude.

" My lord," said he, " hath given me unknown problems to try me, and not given me the answer at once, for then there would be no trial. Since now God trieth thee with riddles — wilt thou have the answer at once and shall the questioner answer for the asked? So doth it not go in the world. Hast thou not drawn me out of the grave where I had fouled myself like a sheep with its own filth? What sort of under-servant must I then be and how gross my moral breach! I have moved the double and triple to and fro in my brain and weighed their relations until I saw the solution. Reckon thou too, if thou wilt, to and fro between punishment, guilt and baseness and of a certainty thou wilt come from the two to the three."

" My example was in words and bore the answer in itself. Figures are clear and final. But who giveth me warrant that life too can be solved like them, not deceiving the known about the unknown? For many things speak here against a clear conclusion."

" Then one must take that into consideration: if life cannot be solved like figures, on the other hand it is spread before thee so that thou seest it with thine eyes."

" Whence hast thou the precious stone on thy finger? "

" Perhaps the base servant stole it," suggested Joseph.

" Perhaps. But thou must know whence thou hadst it."

" I have had it so long that I no longer remember when I did not have it."

" So then thou hast brought it with thee out of the swamps and reeds where thou wast conceived? For thou art truly a son of the swamps and child of the rushes? "

" I am the child of the well, out of which my lord drew me and brought me up with milk."

" Hast thou known no mother but the well? "

" Yes," said Joseph. " I did know a sweeter mother. Her cheek smelt like the rose-leaf."

" Thou seest. And hath she not named thee with a name? "

" I have lost it, my lord, for I have lost my life. I may not know my name as I may not know my life, which they thrust into the grave."

" Tell me thy transgression, which brought thy life down to the grave."

" It was culpable," answered Joseph, " and is named confidence. Criminal confidence and blind, unreasoning presumption, that is its name. For it is blind and deadly to test men beyond their strength and require of them what they neither will hear nor can. Before such love and respect their gall runneth over and they become like ravening beasts. Not to know this, or not to want to know it, is fatal. But I did not know or I flung it to the winds, so that I did not hold my tongue and told them my dreams, in order that they might marvel at me. But ' in order that' and ' so that' are sometimes two different things and go not together. The ' In order that' did not come to pass and the ' So that' was called the grave."

" Thy presumption," said the old man, " with which thou madest men mad, that was of course arrogance and pride, I can well believe it, and it doth not surprise me in one who sayeth: ' I am navel and centre of the world.' But I am much travelled between the rivers that take different courses, the one from south to north, the other the other way, and I know that many a mystery obtaineth in the apparently so manifest world, and behind loud rumour the hidden things pursue their silent way. Yea, often it hath seemed to me as though the world is full of such loud rumours to the end that it may better hide the hidden beneath them and out-talk the secrets that lie behind men and things. Much I came on without looking, much thrust itself on me unsought. Yet I heeded not, for I am not so curious that I must get to the bottom of everything, rather it sufficeth me to know that mystery encompasseth the garrulous world. I am a doubter as I sit here; not because I believed nothing, rather because I hold everything for possible. Such am I, an old man. I know of fables and happenings which count not as probable and yet come to pass. I know of one, come from the nobility and of lofty rank, wherein he clothed himself with royal linen and anointed himself with the oil of gladness, who was driven into desert and misery — "

Here the merchant interrupted himself and blinked, for the necessary and given conclusion of his speech, the continuation which was now due, without his having thought in advance that it would be due, put him in thoughtful mood. There are deeply chamferred trains of thought out of which one does not escape, once in them; associations cut and dried from old time, which fit into each other like rings in a chain, so that he who has said A cannot help saying B or at least thinking it; and like links in a chain they are, too, in that in them the earthly and heavenly are so interlocked one into the other that one passes willy-nilly, and whether speaking or silent, from one to the other. True it is that man for the most part thinks in set phrases and fixed formulas; not such as he himself searches out but as he remembers the traditional. Even as the old man spoke of one driven from high estate into darkness and misery, he had fallen into a pattern. And to continue with the pattern was inevitably to arrive at the resurrection of the abased to be the saviour of man and bringer of the new time; and thus the old man paused, in silent perplexity.

But more than mild perplexity it was not — only the decent and reverent restraint of the self-respecting practical man before the metaphysical or the sacred. If it became more — a sort of disquiet, a deeper dismay, yes, an alarm, if only passing and half unconscious — that could only be due to the encounter between the old man's blinking gaze and the eyes of the youth standing before him. Hardly did it even deserve the name of encounter — not so much; for Joseph's eyes did not " encounter " the other's gaze, did not actually respond to it or return it. They only received it, only offered themselves, in silence and candour, to be looked at: a mystery, equivocal, intriguing, obscure. Others before now had blinked and been startled as they tried to pierce this mute provocation to its depths, as now the old Ishmaelite tried, in face of the question: what had he done, what not quite canny business had he been about when he bargained with the shepherds for his possession?

But after all, that and nothing else had been the subject of the whole conversation; and when it suddenly showed signs of shifting into the unearthly and fabulous, the old man had to tell himself that many things on this earth could be regarded in the same uncanny light; it was for a sensible man to make distinctions and to shift back again as soon as possible to the practical side.

He cleared his throat to facilitate the process.

"H'm," said he. "All in all, thy master is travelled and full of experience between the rivers and hath knowledge of affairs. He needeth not to be instructed therein by thee, child of the swamps and son of the well. I have bought thy body and what thou displayest of dexterity, but not thy heart, that I could force it to reveal thy thoughts. Not only is it unnecessary that I should urge thee, it is not even advisable and might be to my harm. I have found thee and given thee again the breath of life; but to buy thee was not my purpose; for I did not even know thou wast for sale. I thought of no advantage save perhaps a finder's reward or a ransom, as might be. However, it came to a bargain for thy person, and I made a test. I said: 'Sell him to me,' and the test seemed decisive to me and it was so decided, for the shepherd men entered into it. I have won thee by hard and prolonged bargaining, for they were stubborn. Twenty shekels of silver according to weight, as is customary, have I weighed out for thee and have not remained in their debt. How is it with the price and how do I stand? It is a medium price, not too good, not too bad. I could lower it, on account of the errors which, as they said, brought thee to the pit. According to thy parts I could sell thee higher than I bought thee and enrich myself at will. What should I gain from prying into thy antecedents and perhaps learning that it standeth with thee the gods know how, so that thou wast not at all for sale and art not, so that I have lost mine own, or if I sell thee again it is a wrong and a trade with stolen goods? Go to, I will know naught of thy affairs nor their details, that I may remain innocent and in the right. It is enough that I suspect that they are something out of the common and belong to things which I am doubter enough to consider possible. Go, I have already talked longer with thee than needful and it is time for sleep. But bake such pancakes often, they are right good, if yet not so out of the common. Further I command thee that thou procure from Mibsam, my son-in-law, writing tools, sheets, reed, and ink, and make for me in common writing a list of the wares we are carrying, each after its kind: the balsams, salves, knives, spoons, canes, and lamps, as well as the footgear, the burning-oils, and the glass-paste, according to count and weight; the items in black, the weight and quantity in red, without blunder or blot, and shalt bring me the list within three days. Is it understood? "

" Commanded is as good as done," said Joseph.

" Then go."

" Peace and sweetness to thy slumbers," spoke Joseph. " May blithe and easy dreams be woven from time to time among them."

The Minoan smiled. And he followed Joseph with his thoughts.

TALK BY NIGHT

THREE days they had gone on by the margin of the sea and it was evening once more and time of rest in the tents, and as they rested, it looked just as it had three days before; it might have been the same place. As the old man sat on his mat at the door of his tent, Joseph appeared before him, with pancakes and a written scroll in his hands.

"The least of his slaves," he said, "bringeth to the master according to his commands."

The Midianite put the bake-stuff to one side; the list he unrolled, and studied the script with his head on one side. He did so well pleased.

"No blots," said he, "and that is well. But one can tell likewise that the signs are drawn with pleasure and a sense of beauty and are an adornment. It is to be hoped that the content agrees, so that it is not only decorative but also practical. It is a pleasure to see one's own so cleanly set down and the various items listed in order. The goods themselves are greasy or they are sticky with gum; the merchant does not willingly soil his hands, he deals with them as they are written. They are there, but they are also here; clean, not stinking, easy to see. A list like this is like the Ka or the spiritual body of things, alongside the real. Good, then, Come-hither, thou knowest how to write and canst also reckon somewhat, as I saw. And in thy station it lacketh thee not for readiness of speech, for it hath pleased me, the way thou gavest thy lord good-night three days past. What were thy words again?"

"I know them no more," replied Joseph. "But it may be that I wished peace to thy slumbers."

"No, it was pleasanter than that. But no matter; likely there will come more occasion for such a phrase. But what I could say is this: when I have naught more important to think of, then at the third and fourth remove I think of thee. Thy lot may be hard, since in any case thou hast seen better days and now thou servest the travelling merchant as baker and clerk. Since, then, I purpose to dispose of thee, and innocent of the knowledge of thy origins to enrich myself further as much as I can, I will see to it that I look out for thee."

" That is most gracious."

" I will bring thee to a house that I know, where I have sometimes done a service to mine own and its advantage; a well-kept house, a house of honour and distinction. It is a blessing, I say to thee, to belong to such a house, be it only as the least of servants, and if there be one wherein a servant may display the finer gifts it is this. If thou hast fortune and I bring thee to this house, then is thy lot as favoured as in view of thy guilt and culpableness it could possibly fall."

" And to whom belongeth the house? "

" Yea, to whom? To a man — and a man he is, or rather a lord. A great among the great, gilded with gold of favour, a man good, stern, and holy, for whom his grave waits in the West, a shepherd of men, the living image of a god. Fan-bearer on the right hand of the king is his title, but dost thou think he beareth the fan? No, the man leaves that to others, he himself is too exalted for it, he only beareth the title. Thinkest thou I know the man, the gift of the sun? No, for I am a worm before him, he seeth me not at all, and also I saw him but once from afar in his garden on a lofty seat, as he stretched forth his hand to command, and I made myself small that he take not offence at me and be distracted from his commanding, for how could I answer for it? But the upper high steward of his house I know from face to face and word to word, who is over the stores and domestics and tradesmen and governeth all. He loveth me and greeteth me in blithe words when he seeth me and sayeth: ' Well, old man, so we see thee again and thou comest with thy pack before our house to over-reach us? ' That he sayeth in sheer jest, thou perceivest, thinking to flatter the merchant by calling him a cheat and we chuckle together. To him will I show thee and propose thee and if he be in good mood and can use a young slave for the house, so art thou provided for."

"What king is that," asked Joseph, "whose golden rewards the master beareth? "

He wanted to learn whither he was being taken, and where the house lay for which the old man destined him; but it was not this alone made him ask. He did not know it; but his thinking and asking were controlled by traditions which worked hither from the beginnings and the times of the forefathers. Abraham spoke out of him; he who in his arrogance toward man held the view that he could serve the Highest and Him alone, and whose thinking and doing had excluded with contempt all lower and lesser gods to address itself to the Most High. The grandson's voice was pitched in a lower, more worldly key; yet the question was Abraham's question. Joseph heard with indifference of the house steward, on whom after all, according to the old man, his immediate fate depended. For the Midianite he felt contempt because he knew only the steward and not even the nobleman to whom the house belonged. But even about the latter he troubled himself little. Above him was a higher, a highest, of whom the old man spoke; and he was a king. Toward him alone and urgently went Joseph's thoughts and the speech of his tongue, unaware that it was guided not by chance or choice but by inheritance and tradition.

"What king? " repeated the old man. " Neb-mat-Re-

Amun-hotpe-Nimmuria," he said in liturgical accents as though repeating a prayer.

Joseph was startled. He had stood there, his arms folded across his back, but now he quickly released them and seized his cheeks in both palms.

" That is Pharaoh! " he cried. How could he not have understood? The name which the old man chanted was known to the ends of the earth and to the stranger people of whom Eliezer had taught him, to Tarshish and Kittim, to Ophir and Elam closing in the east. How could it have been meaningless to the instructed Joseph? Some names of the title pronounced by the Midianite: " Lord of truth is Re," " Amun is satisfied," were incomprehensible; but the Syrian addition " Nimmuria " (" He goes to his fate ") must have enlightened him. There were many kings and shepherds, every town had one, and Joseph had stood quietly as he put his question expecting to hear the name of some ruler of a fortified city by the sea, some Zurat, Ribaddi, Abdasherat, or Aziru. He had not been prepared to interpret the title in its most splendid and regal sense, in the most godlike and glorious signifi-cance which the word commands. Written inside a long-ish, upstanding annulet, guarded by falcon wings spread over it by the sun itself, it stood last of a glorious row of such names, losing themselves in the mist of the past, each similarly ringed and each illustrious. With each was associated the history of victorious campaigns, of far-extended boundary-stones and buildings world-fa-mous for their magnificence; so that this last name itself connoted such a heritage of awe, such enhancement of the single life, as justified any homage and made quite comprehensible the involuntary start which Joseph gave.

" Certainly," said the old man. " That is the great house that hath made great the house to which I will bring thee and will offer thee to my friend the overseer to try thy fortune."

" Then wilt thou lead me down to Mizraim into the land of mud? " asked Joseph and felt his heart beat.

The old man, his head bent on one shoulder, gave it a shake.

" The question is like thee again. I know already from Kedema, my son, that out of childish conceit thou imaginest we lead thee hither or thither, though in truth we are taking our way where we take it, even without thee, and thou only comest thither where our way leadeth us. I do not travel to Egypt that I may bring thee thither, but because I have business there which will enrich me: I will buy things there which they are skilful in producing and are much sought after, such as glazed collars, camp-stools with pretty little legs, head-rests, draught-boards, chess-boards, and pleated linen aprons. These I will buy in the workshops and in the bazaars as cheap as the gods of the land will let me and take them back over the mountains of Canaan, the Retenu and Amor, into Mitanniland on the Euphrates and to the country of King Hattusil, where they have an eye for them and will spend money recklessly. Thou speakest of the ' land of mud ' as though it were a land of filth, baked out of excrement like a bird's nest and like an uncleaned stall. And yet it is the land whither to travel again I am resolved and where I shall perhaps be able to leave thee; the finest land in all the round of earth, with such exquisite customs that thou wilt seem to thyself like an

ox before whom one plays the lute. Thou, wretched
Amu, wilt make great eyes when thou seest the country
beside the river of God, which is called there ' the lands '
because it is two lands, and double-crowned, but Mempi,
the house of Ptah, holds the balance between them.
There range unthinkably vast spaces that antechamber
the desert; there crouches the lion in the head-cloth,
Hor-im-akhet, created before time, the mystery of the
ages, at whose breast the king fell asleep, the child of
Thoth, and in dreams had his head lifted up with most
exalted promise. Thine eyes will stand out of thy head
when thou seest the marvels and all the splendour and
choiceness of the land that is called Kemt, because it
is black with fruitfulness, not red like the poverty-
stricken desert. But from what is it fruitful? Because of
the river of God and from that alone. For it hath its
rain and its fructifying semen not in heaven but on
earth and it is the god, Hapi, the Strong Bull, who spreads
himself out above it and stands over it full of blessing
the space of a year, leaving behind the blackness of his
power, wherein one may sow and harvest a hundredfold
fruit. But thou speakest as though it were a dunghill."

Joseph hung his head. He had learned that he was
on his way to the kingdom of the dead; for the habit of
regarding Egypt as the underworld, and its inhabitants
as a people of Sheol, was born with him, and never had
he heard otherwise, especially from Jacob. So then he
was to be sold into the melancholy nether world, the
brothers had sold him down thither, the well had been
its appropriate entrance. It was very sad, he could have
wept. Yet joy in the appropriateness balanced the sadness, his view that he was dead and the blood of the

beast had been in truth his blood being so neatly confirmed by the old man's disclosures. He had to smile — however near to tears on his own and Jacob's account. Precisely down thither should he go, into the land which was the object of his father's pronounced aversion, Hagar's home, the monkey-land of Egypt! He recalled the prejudiced description with which Jacob had sought to make this land intolerable to his son, regarding it, without any actual knowledge, in the light of his own hostile and horrified principles, as the seat of worship of the past, of dalliance with death, of insensibility to sin. Joseph had always been inclined to a blithe mistrust of the justice of the picture, to that sympathetic curiosity which is regularly the consequence of parental moralizing and warning. If the good, worthy, and didactic man had known that his lamb was travelling Egyptwards, to the land of Ham, the bare, as he called it, because it was black on account of the black fruitful soil, which its god gave it! The confusion of thought was right indicative of the pious prejudice of his judgment, Joseph said to himself with a smile.

But the bond between son and father was not one of opposites alone. True, it was a diabolic joke that he should be travelling toward the utterly taboo; it was a youthful triumph thus to coquet with the moral terrors of the underworld. Yet with it, in his blood, was a mute resolve which must have gladdened the father's heart: the resolve of the child of Abram not to let his eyes run over at sight of the elegance and the marvels so praised by the Ishmaelite; quite definitely not to admire too warmly the splendid civilization which awaited him. A deep and native spirit of mockery drew down the corners of his mouth at the mere thought of that elegance; and his contempt was to be a shield and buckler against the timidity which results from too great reverence.

He asked, looking up: " Is the house to which thou wilt bring me at Mempi, the dwelling of Ptah? "

" Oh, no," the old man replied, " we must go farther up, that is down, I mean up the river, out of the land of the serpent into the land of the vulture. Thou askest in thy simplicity; for when I said to thee that the master of the house is fan-bearer on the king's right hand, of course that means he must be where His Majesty the good god is, and whose house is at Wese, the city of Amun."

Joseph learned much that evening by the sea, hosts of information thronged upon him. So he was going to No, No-Amun, the city of cities and talk of the world, a subject of conversation amongst the remotest populations, where rumour said that it had a hundred gates and more than a hundred thousand inhabitants. Would Joseph's eyes then not run over, after all, when they caught sight of the metropolis? He saw that he must firmly resolve beforehand not to fall prey to vacant admiration. He stuck out his lips disdainfully. But despite his efforts to compose his features, to the honour of his own God, he could not quite escape a certain embarrassment. For he felt somewhat afraid of No, more particularly the name of Amun alarmed him: that mighty name, intimidating to everybody and having a domineering ring even in regions strange to the god. Trepidation seized him at the thought of entering the throne of the god's cult and seat of his power. The sovereign of Egypt, ruler of the two lands, king of the gods, that was Amun. Joseph knew it well, and confusion dwelt in the thought of that unique power. Amun was the Highest — if indeed only in the eyes of the children of Egypt. It seemed it would be useful to speak of Amun and practise himself in talk of him. He said:

"Wese's lord in his chapel and in his bark, that is one of the more exalted gods hereabouts?"

"The more exalted?" answered the old man. "Truly thou speakest not better than thy understanding. What thinkest thou that Pharaoh hath set before him of bread and cake, beer, wine, and geese, for his consuming? That is a god without compare, I tell thee; what treasures he calleth his own, movable and immovable, my breath would give out would I tell the tale of them, and the number of his scribes who administer all is like to the stars."

"Wonderful," said Joseph. "A very important god indeed according to all thou relatest. Only I asked, to be precise, not about his importance but about his nobility."

"Bow down before him," advised the old man, "since thou wilt live in Egypt, and make not too many distinctions between important and noble, as though one could not stand for the other and both were not all the same. For Amun's are all the ships of the seas and rivers, and the rivers and seas are his. He is the sea and the land. He is also Tor-Neter, the cedar mountain, whose trunks grow for a barge called Amun's-Front-is-Mighty. In Pharaoh's shape he goeth in unto his first and true wife and begets Hor in the palace. He is Baal in all his members, doth that impress thee? He is the sun, Amun-Re is his name — doth that satisfy thy demands as to nobility, or not quite?"

"But I heard," Joseph said, "he is a ram in the darkness of the innermost chamber."

"I heard, I heard. . . . As thou hast understood, so speakest thou and not a doit better. Amun is a ram, just as Bastet in the land of the Delta is a cat, and the great writer of Schmun an ibis and an ape. For they are sacred in their animals and the animals sacred in them. Thou must learn much if thou wilt live in the land and wilt live before him, be it only as the lowest of his youthful slaves. How wilt thou see the god if not in the beast? The three are one: god, man, and beast. For if the divine wed with the beast, then it is the man, as Pharaoh when he is at the feast puts on a beast's tail, according to ancient custom. And if on the other hand the beast wed with the man, then it is a god, and the divine is not otherwise to be regarded and understood than in such a marriage; thus you see Heqet, the great midwife, like a toad on the wall, to judge from her head, and Anpu, the Opener of the Way, dog-headed. Lo, in the beast man and god find themselves, and the beast is the sacred place of their meeting and their union, sacred and honourable in its nature as such. And very worthy of honour among feasts is that one in which the ram cohabits with the pure virgin in the city of Djedet."

"I have heard of it," Joseph said. "Doth my lord approve of the practice?"

"I?" asked the Ma'onite. "Leave an old man in peace! We are travelling merchants, middlemen, at home everywhere and nowhere, and for us the word holdeth good: 'Nourish thou my belly, I honour thy customs.' Heed it in the world, for it will behove thee too."

"Never," answered Joseph, "will I in Egypt in the

house of the fan-bearer say a word against the honour of
the feast of the covering. But between thee and me, let
me point out that in this word ' honourable ' lieth a snare
for the unwary. For easily doth man hold the old for
honourable, simply because it is old, and imagineth they
are the same. But the catch is that sometimes we do
reverence to the old when it is simply worn out and rotted
with age. Then its honourableness is but seeming, and is
in fact an abomination and indecency before the Lord.
Just between you and me, the presentation of the human
virgin at Djedet seems more like an indecency."

" How wilt thou distinguish? And where should we be
if every booby were to set himself up as the navel of the
world and as a judge of what is sacred and what merely
old, what still worthy of reverence and what an abomination? Soon there would be nothing sacred! I do not
believe that thou wilt hold thy tongue and hide thy impious thoughts. For it is peculiar to such thoughts as
thou hast that they must be uttered — I know that."

" In thy presence, my lord, it is easy to learn to hold
age and honour as the same."

" Flatter me not with sweet words, for I am but a
travelling merchant. Heed rather my warning, that thou
run not up against the children of Egypt and speak to
thy undoing. For certainly thou canst not keep thy
thoughts; therefore must thou take care that thy thoughts
are just, and not only thy words. Certainly nothing is
more holy than the union of god, man, and beast in the
sacrifice. Reckon to and fro between these three with
reference to the sacrifice and they are resolved therein.
For in the sacrifice are all three and each represents the

other. And therefore Amun moves as sacrificial ram in the darkness of the furthermost chamber."

"I know not rightly how I feel, my lord and purchaser, reverend merchant. It is so dark, while thou instructest me, and scattered sparkles of light trickle down like dust of precious stones from the stars. I must rub my eyes, pardon me for doing it, for I am dazed, and as thou sittest before me on thy mat, it is to me as though it were the head of a green frog that thou wearest, and as though thou squattest there wise and wide and comfortable, like a toad."

"Seest thou that thou canst not hold thy thoughts, however offensive they may be? Why wilt thou and wouldst thou see a toad in me?"

"My eyes ask not if it is my will. Just like a squatting toad thou seemest to me under the stars. For thou wast Heqet, the great midwife, when the well bore me, and thou didst lift me from my mother."

"Ah, chatterer! That was no great nurse that helped thee to the light. Heqet, the she-frog, is called great because she was by at the second birth and resurrection of the mangled one, when the lower world fell to him, but to Hor the upper, according to the belief of the children of Egypt, and Osiris became the First of the West, king and judge of the dead."

"I like that. So then if one is going toward the west, one must at least become the first of those there. But instruct me, my lord: Is then Osiris, the sacrifice, so great in the eyes of the children of Kemt that Heqet became a great frog because she was midwife at his rebirth?"

"He is great entirely."

" Great above the greatness of Amun? "

" Amun is great by reason of his kingdom, his renown affrights stranger peoples so that they cut their cedars for him. But Osiris, the mangled one, is great in the love of the people, all the people from Djanet in the Delta up to Heb, the elephant island. There is not one among all, from the coughing pack-slave of the quarry, who liveth millionfold, to Pharaoh, who liveth once and singly and worshippeth himself in his temple — I say to thee there is not one who did not know and love him and wish to find his grave in Abdu his city, at the grave of the mangled one, were it possible. And since it is not possible, yet they all hang fervently on him, trusting in the hope of becoming like him at their hour and to live for ever."

" To be like God? "

" To be as the god and to be like him; that is, one with him, so that the dead man is Osiris and so is called."

" What all thou sayest! But spare me, my lord, in thy teaching and help my poor understanding as thou helpedst me out of the womb of the well. For it is not for everyone's understanding, that which thou wilt teach me here in the night by the slumbering sea, of the beliefs of the children of Mizraim. Shall I then understand that it would be in the power of death to change nature and for the dead to be a god with the beard of a god? "

" Yes, that is the confident belief of all the folk of the land and they all as one love it so fervently from Zoan to Elephantine for that they have had to wrest it for themselves in prolonged struggle."

" They have wrested the belief for themselves in prolonged struggle and held out for it until the dawn? "

" They have won it. For in the beginning and originally it was only Pharaoh, he alone, Hor in the Palace,
who when he died came to Osiris and became one with
him so that he was like a god and lived for ever. But all
those who cough, as they drag the heavy statues, all the
brick-makers, the pot-drillers, those behind the plough
and those in the mines, they have not rested and have
struggled till they achieved it and made it good, so that
they too now at their hour become Osiris and are called
Osiris-Khnumhotpe, Osiris Rekh-mi-re after their death,
and live for ever."

" Again it pleaseth me, that which thou sayest. Thou
hast chidden me for the view that every child of earth
hath his own universe about him for himself alone and is
the centre thereof. But in one way or the other it seemeth
to me the children of Egypt shared the view, since each
would be Osiris after his death, as in the beginning only
Pharoah, and have brought it to pass."

" That is and remaineth foolishly spoken. For not
the child of earth is the centre point, Khnumhotpe or
Rekh-mi-re, but rather their faith and confident belief;
they are all one in that, up the water and down, from
the Delta to the sixth rapid: the belief in Osiris and his
resurrection. For thou must know: not only one single
time hath this very great god died and risen; rather he
doth it ever anew in even ebb and flow before the eyes
of the children of Kemt — he goeth down and cometh
forth again mightily to stand as blessing over the land,
Hapi, the Strong Bull, the river of God. Countest thou the
days of the winter time, when the river is small, there are
seven-and-twenty of them and they are the seven-and-

twenty who were forsworn with Set, the wicked ass, and brought the king to his coffin. But at his hour he goeth forth, the growing, swelling, flooding, the increasing, the lord of bread, who begetteth all good things and maketh all life, by name Nourisher of the Land. They slaughter the oxen before him; but seest thou then that god and sacrifice are one, for he himself is a bull and an ox before them on earth and in his house: Hapi, the black, with the sign of the moon on his flank. But when he dieth he is preserved with balsam and swaddled and put away and is called Osiris-Hapi."

"Lo then!" exclaimed Joseph, "hath he also brought it about, like Khnumhotpe and Rekh-mi-re, that he becometh Osiris when he dieth?"

"I think that thou mockest?" queried the old man. "I see thee little in the glimmering night, but I hear thee and it seemeth to me very much as though thou mockest. I tell thee, mock not in the land whither I am taking thee because simply I am travelling that way, and presume not in thy folly against the beliefs of its children, thinking that thou knowest better with thy Adon, rather adapt thyself piously to its customs; otherwise thou wilt be grievously disappointed. I have taught thee somewhat and initiated thee, and turned a few phrases with thee this evening to my amusement and to pass the time; for I am already old, and sometimes sleep faileth me. I had no other ground to speak with thee. Thou mayest say good-night now, that I may try to sleep. But pay heed to thy phrases."

"Commanded is as good as done," replied Joseph. "But how should I mock, since my lord hath so graciously instructed me this evening that I may hold out and not come to grief in the land of Egypt, and hath taught the culprit things of which I, a child of the masses, dreamed not, so new are they to me and not to be understanded of all. Might I know how I could thank thee I would. But since I know not, I will do something yet this evening for my benefactor, do that which I would not do, and answer a question before I leave thee, which thou askedst me. I will tell thee my name."

"Wilt thou do that?" asked the old man. "Do so or rather do not so; I have not urged thee to it, for I am old and cautious and would rather not know what are thy connections, because I must take care not to involve myself therein and be guilty of wrong-doing through the knowledge."

"Not at all," Joseph replied. "Thou runnest no such danger. But at least thou must know how to call the slave, if thou wilt pass him on into this house of blessing in the city of Amun."

"Then what is thy name?"

"Usarsiph," answered Joseph.

The old man was silent. Though only a distance of respect was between them, they were aware of each other but as shadows.

"It is well, Usarsiph," spoke the old man after a while. "Thou hast named me thy name. Take thy leave now, for with the sunrise we shall set forth."

"Farewell," Joseph saluted him in the dark. "May night cradle thee in softest arms and thy head slumber on her breast as thy childish head on thy mother's heart."

THE TEMPTATION

AFTER Joseph had told the Ishmaelite his name in death and had shown him how he wished to be called in the land of the dead, they all passed on down for some days, several and many, with the greatest placidity and in entire indifference to the time, which some day, as they were aware, by adding to itself, would have done with space, and this the more securely if one did not trouble about it at all but left it to time quietly and unobservably to heap up its progress to large quantities the while one lived on and only held in the direction of the goal.

Their direction was given them by the sea, which spread endlessly away on the right of their sandy route, under a sky fading into mystic distance; now in silver-shot blue calm, now hurling great waves aglitter with foam like strong bulls roaring against the peopled coast. And in the sea the sun went down, the changing-unchangeable, the Eye of God, sometimes a clear-glowing and solitary orb, which made as it sank a gleaming path across the endless water to the shore and to passers-by who worshipped as they went; but sometimes too in the heart of a splendour of gold and rose, that worked still more adoring conviction in the soul of the worshipper. But his soul might sometimes be saddened too or oppressed by fears, when the deity enveloped himself in threatening mists or clouds suffused with lurid light. He rose, however, not on an open horizon but behind the heights and hills that hid the view on their left. Between shore and mountains spread the immediate inland, with cultivated fields, wells scattered through the rolling expanse, and orchards adorning the terraced hills. Often our travellers took their way through it, at a distance from the sea and some half a hundred ells above its glassy surface; passing through the federation of fortified hill-cities. Gaza in the south, Khadati, the strong citadel, was head of the league.

The walled white cities, fringed with palm, crowned the hill-tops, the mother cities, refuge of the inhabitants of the land, the citadels of Sarnim. And on the level ground before the village and at its heart, the square before the gate of the crowded city with its temples, the Midianites spread out their wares and offered to the people of Ekron, of Jabne, of Asdod, their merchandise from beyond the Jordan. Joseph performed the office of clerk. He sat and set down with his brush countless petty transactions with the hard-bargaining children of Dagon; fishermen and boatmen, tradefolk and mercenaries from the citadels, in their copper armour. Usarsiph, the literate young slave, laboured to pleasure his good master. The heart of the young chattel beat higher day by day — not hard to guess why. He was not formed to drift content with sensuous impressions alone, but must make a mental picture of the place where he was and its relation to other places. He knew that he was taking, in leisurely, time-consuming fashion, a parallel route, some field-lengths farther west and in reverse direction, the same journey which he had covered riding on poor Hulda to meet his brothers. He was going toward, if also past, his home; soon the point must be reached where he had covered the distance and was separated from the paternal hearth by a space not more than half the length of the whole journey. Somewhere not far from

Asdod it would be: seat of Dagon the fish-god whom they worshipped hereabouts; a busy settlement, two hours from the coast and connected with it by a road crowded with people, ox-carts, and teams of horses, all making terrific din. The coast road down to Gaza, as Joseph knew, curved more and more westwards, so that the distance from the mountainous interior increased with each day they travelled; he also knew that they would be passing by noon under the heights of Hebron.

Therefore it was his heart beat so anxiously as temptation knocked; here, and on the slow road beyond to Askalona, the rocky citadel. He knew the contours of the countryside: they were entering Sephala, the lowland, running along the coast. But his Rachel-eyes sought out and dwelt pensively on the mountain ranges, which looked down on the east and formed the second, higher, valley-furrowed level of the land of the Philistines. Behind again and ever steeper the world rose toward the east and into the highlands above sea-level, rougher, harsher ground, to pastures unpeopled by the lowland palm, and upland meadows on whose short grass grazed sheep, grazed Jacob's sheep. . . . Could it be? Up there Jacob was sitting, despairing, dissolved in tears, in God-sent, God-suffering agony, in his hands the blood-spotted sign of Joseph's death and mangling — while down here, under his feet, from one city of the Philistines to the next, marched Joseph, the stolen one, dumb, making no sign, past his own place with strangers, down to Sheol, into the house of bondage and death. How near lay the thought of flight! How the urge to it pulled and tugged at his limbs, how his thoughts worked in him to half-resolves and even to visions of their tempestuous realization.

They came, these visions, especially at evening, when he had bade the good old man his owner good-night, for that he had daily to do, it was one of his duties, he had to wish the Ishmaelite pleasant dreams at the day's end and always in choice and varied phrases, otherwise the old man would say he knew that one already. Especially then in the darkness when they lay camped before a city of the Philistines and his companions were wrapped in slumber, the boy who had been ravished away was ravished anew by longings to be off up the orchard-clad hills, in the dark, on over heights and gullies, eight miles and furlongs of ground, for more it probably was not, and Joseph would easily find the right direction as he climbed — on into the mountain land, into Jacob's arms, to dry his father's tears with the words " Here am I! " and once again to be his darling.

But did he carry all this out and flee? We know that he did not. He reconsidered — sometimes just on the verge; put away temptation, gave up the idea, stopped where he was. When all was said and done, it was at the moment more sensible. Flight in itself meant great perils; he might perish, might fall among robbers and murderers, be devoured by wild beasts. Yet it is not doing justice to his renunciation to attribute it to our human tendency to indolence instead of action. In his career we know that Joseph renounced a physical act far sweeter than a wild escape over the mountains would have been. No, the renunciation which in both cases followed on the violent temptation came from a point of view quite peculiar to Joseph. Put into words, it was something like this: " How could I commit such a folly and sin against God? " In other words, he had insight into the mad and sinful error that would lie in escape: the clear and intelligent perception that it would have been a clumsy blunder to try to destroy God's plan through flight. For Joseph was penetrated by the certainty that he had not been snatched away to no purpose, that rather the planning intelligence which had rent him away from the old and led him into the new had plans for him in one or another way; and to kick against the pricks, to shrink from the affliction, would have been a great sin and error — these being one and the same in Joseph's eyes. The conception of sin as blunder, as clumsy offence against God's wisdom, was right native to him, and life so far had extraordinarily strengthened him therein. He had made mistakes enough — he learned that in the pit. But now he had escaped from the pit and was obviously being taken away according to plan; so the mistakes committed up to now might be considered as lying in the plan itself, as purposeful and God-guided in all their blindness. But any more of them — as now for instance escape — would be very distinctly evil; it would literally mean to wish to be wiser than God — which according to Joseph's shrewd insight was quite simply the height of folly.

The darling of his father once again? Ah, no, for he was always that; but now it would be so in a new sense — one he had always longed for and dreamed of. Now, since the experience of the pit, it was his to live in a new and higher state of being chosen and preferred in the sense and the bitter savour of the myrtle wreath, which was set apart for the set-apart and reserved for the reserved. The torn garland, the adornment of the whole sacrifice, he wore it anew — no longer in prophetic play but in very truth and in the spirit. Should he now for the sake of the blind urge of the flesh betake himself to his own? So foolhardy, so lacking in all divine wisdom Joseph was not — in the last moment he was not so blind as to fling away the advantage of his state. Did he know, or did he not, the feast in all its hours? The centre of the present and of the feast, was he or was he not? The garland in his hair, should he run from the feast to be once more with his brothers a shepherd of the flocks? The temptation was strong in his flesh, but weak in his spirit. Joseph resisted. He went on with his owners, on past Jacob and out of his neighbourhood — Usarsiph the swamp-born, Joseph-em-heb, to speak Egyptian, which is to say: Joseph in the Feast.

A MEETING

SEVENTEEN days? No, it was a journey of seven times seventeen — not in actual numbers, but in the sense of a very long time indeed; and at the end of it nobody knew how much of its length was due to the Midianites' tarrying progress and how much to the extent of the ground they covered. They went through a populous, busy, fruitful land, crowned with olive orchards and palms, set thick with walnut and fig trees, planted with corn, watered from deep springs where camels and oxen gathered. Little royal fortresses lay sometimes in the open fields, called stations, with walls and battle-towers; bowmen stood on their battlements and charioteers drove snorting steeds forth from their gates. The Ishmaelites did not hesitate to enter into trade, even with the soldiers of the kings. Villages, farms, and Migdal settlements everywhere invited them to stop, and they lingered for weeks without a thought. Before they reached the spot where the low land along the coast rose to the abruptly towering rocky wall on whose top lay Ascalon, summer was already waning.

Sacred and strong was Ascalon. The four-square stones of its ring walls, which ran down to the sea in a half-circle and included the harbour, seemed borne up by giants, its temple of Dagon was square and full of courts, very lovely its grove and the pond of its grove, abounding in fish, and its dwelling of Ashtaroth was renowned as older than any shrine of Baalat. A spicy sort of little onion grew wild in the sand here under the palms. Derketo vouchsafed them, the lady of Ascalon, and one could sell them abroad. The old man had them gathered into sacks and wrote thereon in Egyptian characters: " Finest Ascalon onions."

Thence they went on among gnarled olive groves in whose shadow flocks were pastured, and by the time they had reached Gaza, called Khadati, they were certainly come very far. Almost within the Egyptian sphere of influence. For in times past Pharaoh had come up from Egypt with wagons and foot-soldiers, to thrust through the barren lands of Zahi, Amor, and the Retenu to the ends of the earth that his gigantic image might be graven deep above the temple walls, holding clutched in his left hand the topknots of five barbarians at once and with his right swinging his club over their dazzled heads. And in such enterprises Gaza had always been the first stage. Nowadays in its reeking streets one saw many Egyptians. Joseph observed them attentively. They were broad-shouldered, white-clad, and high-nosed. Excellent wine grew here very cheap on the coast and far inland on the way to Beersheba. The old man traded for numerous jugs, two camel-loads of them, and labelled the jugs: " Thrice-excellent wine from Khadati."

But however much ground they had covered to reach the strong-walled city of Gaza, the worst part of the journey still lay before them, compared to which the leisurely progress through the land of Philistia had been but child's play. For beyond Gaza to the south, where a sandy road ran along the coast toward the Brook of Egypt, the world, as the Ishmaelites well knew, having covered the ground several times, was inhospitable in the extreme. Between them and the rich plains where flowed the branches of the Nile there extended a melancholy underworld, a frightful expanse, nine days in breadth, accursed and perilous, the dreaded desert, where could be no loitering, rather it was imperative to cross it as fast as possible and get it behind one. Gaza therefore was the last halting-place before Mizraim, and the old man, Joseph's master, was in no hurry to leave it. There would be far too much time hereafter to hurry, he said. He lingered at Gaza for several days, partly to make careful preparations for the desert journey; provision for water, the engaging of a special guide and opener of the way. Actually, weapons were needed to protect the train against roving bands and robber dwellers in the desert. Our old man, however, made no such provision. Firstly because he in his wisdom thought it useless. Either, he said, one had luck and escaped the marauders — then one needed no weapons — or else one did not; and then however many of them one killed, enough were left to steal one bare. The merchant, he said, must trust to luck, not to spears and crossbows, they were not for him.

But in the second place the guide whom he had engaged, at the gateway, where they congregated for engagements, expressly reassured him about the roving bands and said he would need no arms under his conveyance, he was a perfect guide and opened the safest way through the dreaded region, so that it would be quite absurd to secure his services and then carry arms to boot. How Joseph started, pleased and incredulous at once, when he recognized in the man who came in the dawning to the little caravan and put himself at its head the officious and annoying youth who had guided him from Shechem to Dothan, so short and so crowded a time before!

He it was beyond a doubt, although he was changed by the burnous he wore. The small head and swelling throat, the red mouth and round fruity chin, and especially the weariness of his gaze and the peculiarly affected posture were unmistakable. Joseph was amazed to see or think to see the guide wink at him, shutting one eye with an otherwise wholly immovable face. It seemed at once to recall their former acquaintance and to suggest discretion on the score of it. That reassured Joseph a good deal; for this meeting led further back into his former existence than he wanted the eye of the Ishmaelite to penetrate, and he interpreted the wink as a sign that the man understood.

Yet he sorely wanted to exchange a word with him, and when the little troop, amid the ringing of camel-bells and the songs of the drivers, had left the green country behind them and faced the parching desert before,

Joseph asked the old man, behind whom he rode, if he might once and for all make certain from the guide that he was quite sure of his task.

" Art thou afeard? " asked the merchant.

" For all of us," responded Joseph. " But I now ride for the first time into the accursed land and I am near to tears."

" Ask him, then."

So Joseph guided his beast abreast of the foremost animal and said to the guide:

" I am the mouthpiece of our master. He would know if thou art certain of thy road."

The youth looked at him in his old way over his shoulder with half-opened eyes.

" Thou shouldest be able from thy experience to re-assure him," he answered.

" Hush! " whispered Joseph. " How comest thou here? "

" And thou? " was the answer.

" Yes, of course. Not a word to the Ishmaelites that I went to my brethren," whispered Joseph.

" Have no fear," the other answered as softly; and therewith the matter was closed for the time.

But as they pressed farther into the desert, a day and then another day — the sun had set sombrely behind dead mountain chains, and hosts of cloud, grey in the centre and with a sunset glow at the rim, covered the sky above a waxen-yellow sandy plain, while far and wide in front of them were visible scattered hummocks with tufts of withered grass — there was a chance to speak again un-observed with the man. Some of the troop were camped about one of the tussocks of grass on which they had kindled a brushwood fire against the sudden cold; among them the guide, who for the most part associated little either with masters or servants, scorned exchange of talk, and only spoke briefly with the old man from day to day about the route. Joseph finished his tasks, wished the old man a good night's rest, and then mingled with the group by the fire. He lay down near the guide and waited till the monosyllabic exchange among them died down and they were falling visibly into a doze. Then he gave his neighbour a little nudge and said:

"Hearken: I am sorry that I could not keep my word that time and had to leave thee in the lurch as thou waitedst for me."

The man only looked at him idly over his shoulder and stared again into the embers.

"So, thou couldst not?" he answered. "Well, let me tell thee, so faithless a chap as thou I have never seen in all the world. I might have sat guarding thy ass seven jubilees long, if it had depended on thee, who came not again as thou hadst promised. I am surprised that I will speak with thee again at all, I am surprised at myself."

"But I am explaining, as thou hearest," murmured Joseph, "and I have truly an excuse, that knowest thou not. Things turned out other than I had thought, and went as I could not have guessed. I could not return to thee, however much I wished."

"Yes, yes, yes. Idle talk. Seven jubilee years might I have sat and waited for thee. . . ."

"But thou hast not sat seven jubilee years for me, but hast gone thy way when thou sawest I was not coming. Exaggerate not the trouble which I unwillingly made for thee; tell me rather what became of Hulda after I left."

" Hulda? Who is Hulda? "

" 'Who' is a little too much," said Joseph. " I am asking thee news of Hulda, the ass that carried us, my white ass out of my father's stall."

" Ass, ass, white ass for a journey! " mocked the guide in a murmur. " Thou hast a way of speaking of thine own, so tenderly that one may guess at thy self-love. Such people behave then so faithlessly — "

" Not so," Joseph contradicted him. " I speak not tenderly of Hulda on my own account, but on hers, she was so friendly and careful a beast, entrusted to me by my father; when I think of her mane on her forehead, and the way it hung down in curls to her eyes, my heart melteth within me. I have not ceased to feel troubled about her since I lost her, and even asked after her fate in moments and long hours which for my own fate were not lacking in perils. Thou must know that since I came to Shechem ill luck hath not ceased to follow me and heavy oppression hath been my lot."

" Impossible," said the man, " and unbelievable. Oppression? My understanding standeth still and I am stoutly convinced I have not heard aright. But thou wentest after all to thy brethren? And with all the folk thou hast passed thou hast not ceased to exchange smiles, for thou art beautiful and well favoured as a carven image and hast dear life to boot! Whence came then thy ill luck? I ask myself and am not answered."

" None the less it is so," replied Joseph. " And through it all, I tell thee, not a moment have I ceased to think of the fate of poor Hulda."

" Good," said the guide, " very good." And Joseph recognized that curious movement of the eyeballs which he had noted before: a rapid squinting and rolling right round. " Good, then, young slave Usarsiph, thou speakest and I hear. One might think indeed that it were idle to waste so many words on an ass, for what sort of rôle doth an ass play in these things and of what importance could it be in them? Yet I think it possible that thy care shall be reckoned to thee for a virtue, that thou thoughtest of the little creature in thine own need."

" Then what became of her? "

" Of the beast? Verily, it is somewhat annoying for the likes of us to have to play the part of ass-herd for nothing and be asked to give account of what happened besides. One would like to know why one should. But set thy heart at rest. My impression is that the creature's pastern was not so bad as we thought in our first dismay. It seems it was sprained, and not broken — that is, apparently broken and actually only sprained, dost thou understand? Waiting for thee I had only too much time to tend it, and when at last I lost my patience thy Hulda too was so far along that she could amble, even though mainly on three legs. I rode on her myself as far as Dothan and put her in a house there where I had often done a good turn to advantage both sides. It is the first in the place, belonging to a farmer, where she will be as well off as in the stall of thy father, the so-called Israel."

" Is that true? " cried Joseph, low and rejoicingly. " Who would have thought it? So she got up and could walk and thou hast cared for her so that she is well off? "

" Very well," confirmed the other. " She can count herself lucky that I took her to the farmer's house and her lot has fallen well for her."

"In other words," Joseph said, "thou hast sold her in Dothan. And the price?"

"Thou askest after the price?"

"Yea, herewith."

"I have paid myself for my guidance and my service as watchman."

"So. Well, I will not inquire the amount. And all the good eatables that hung round the saddle?"

"Is it really true that thou thinkest of those tidbits in thy difficulties and findest that they have comparative importance?"

"Not so much; but they were there."

"With them too I have reimbursed myself."

"Indeed," Joseph said, "thou hadst early begun to repay thyself behind my back, by which I mean certain quantities of onions and fruit-bread. But never mind, perhaps it was well meant and I will always and everywhere extol the good side thou showest. That thou gottest Hulda once more on her legs and madest her full in the land, for that I reckon my thanks are due, and I thank the good fortune that made me meet thee unexpectedly to learn it."

"Yea, have I again to guide thee, thou windbag, that thou mayest come to thy goal," replied the man. "Whether it be so fitting and proper for me, I do ask myself that, in passing; yet in vain, for no one else payeth any heed."

"Now thou art vexing again," responded Joseph, "just as in the night on the way to Dothan when thou unasked didst help me to find my brethren and did it with such ill grace. Well, this time I need not reproach myself

for molesting thee; for thou hast bargained with the Ishmaelites to guide them through the desert and I am only
among them by chance."

" It mattereth not if I guide thee or thy Ishmaelites."

" Say not that to the Ishmaelites, for they keep themselves on their dignity and self-independence and do not
like to hear that in a way they journey that I may come
hither where God will have me."

The guide was silent and dropped his chin into his
mantle. Did his eyes roll round again after their wont?
Very like, but the darkness prevented one from telling.

" Who liketh to hear that he is a tool? " said he with a
certain effort. " And particularly who would hear it
from a brat like thee? Coming from thee, young slave
Usarsiph, it is shameless, but on the other hand that is
just what I say, that it cometh to the same thing and even
so it might be the Ishmaelites who are coming with thee,
and it is really thou to whom I must open the way — it
is all one. Moreover, I had a well to watch down there,
to say nothing of the ass."

" A well? "

" I always had to reckon with such a job, as far as the
well was concerned. It was the emptiest hole I ever saw,
could not be emptier; and the more absurd was its emptiness, by that measure may be judged the dignity and
fitness of my task. Yet perhaps it was the very emptiness
that was the important thing about this well."

" Was the stone rolled away? "

" Of course. I sat on it; and I remained sitting however much the man wanted me to go."

" What man? "

" Why, he who in his folly came secretly to the well.

A man of towering stature, with legs like the pillars of a temple, and inside this husk a poor thin voice."

"Reuben!" cried Joseph, almost forgetful of caution.

"Call him as thou wilt, it was a blundering tower of a man. Came back there with his rope and his coat to such a proper empty hole."

"He wanted to save me!" Joseph affirmed.

"As thou wilt," said the guide and yawned like a woman, putting his hand affectedly before his mouth and giving a dainty little sigh. "He too played his role," he added. His voice was indistinct, for he had tucked his chin and mouth farther into his mantle and seemed to want to go to sleep. Joseph heard him still muttering disconnectedly and irritably: "Trifling and folly — words of a young brat. . . ."

There was nothing more pertinent to be got out of him. Even in their further journey Joseph did not succeed in getting more speech with his guard and guide.

THE FORT OF THEL

DAY by day they plodded patiently through the bad lands, to the sound of the bell on the leading camel, from well-station to well-station, until nine days had passed; and they counted themselves lucky. The guide had not boasted when he said he knew his business. He did not lose his way nor get off the road even when it passed through wild mountain country where there was no good going, but merely a confusion of frightful sandstone boulders, grotesque shapes and towering masses, that glistened blackly, more like bronze than stone. Their sombre gleam suggested a tall city built of iron. The guide held on his way all day long, even when there could be no talk of a road in any upper-worldly sense at all. For it was like a country of the damned, like the illimitable floor of the sea, shutting them in with corpse-coloured sand up to the hot bleached horizon, and they rode over mounds of dune with ridges ruffled by the wind into unpleasant sharp-edged patterns. Across the plain the heat vibrations looked as though near to bursting into tongues of flame, and sand whirled in the air so that the men wrapped their heads before this evil dance of death and tried not to look, but rode blindly on to get past these horrors.

Bleached skeletons often lay by the way, the ribs and thigh-bones of a camel and the parched limbs of a human being stood up out of the waxen-coloured dust. They looked at it dazed and kept on trying to hope. Two half-days long, from midday to evening, a pillar of fire went on before and seemed to guide them. They well knew the nature of the phenomenon, but their attitude toward it was not conditioned by their knowledge. These fiery pillars were, as they were aware, small cyclones in which the whirling dust was turned flame-coloured by the sun. But to each other they said with due awe: " A pillar of fire leadeth us on." If the sign were suddenly to collapse before their eyes it would be frightful; for in all probability a dust Abubu would follow. But the pillar did not collapse, only changed its shape like a jinnee and slowly flickered away on the north-east wind, which prevailed throughout the nine days. Their good luck banned the south wind that it was quiet and could not parch their water-skins and drink away the moisture on which their lives depended. But on the ninth day they were already out of danger, escaped from the horrors of the desert, and could count themselves fortunate; for the region now before them was colonized and administered by Egypt. Bastions, breastworks, and watch-towers by the wells extended for some distance into the desert, with little companies of soldiery, Nubian bowmen wearing ostrich feathers in their hair, and Libyan axe-bearers with Egyptian captains, who called out harshly to the oncomers and questioned them whence they came and whither they went.

The old man had a shrewd and cheery way of talking with the military to put beyond doubt the innocence of his designs; and of giving them little presents out of his pack, knives, lamps, and Ascalon onions to win their goodwill. So they passed well pleased through all the formalities from watch to watch; for it was much better to be exchanging jokes with the guards than to be going through the brazen city and across the bleached sea-floor. Our travellers, however, knew that only the preliminaries were over with the passing of these frontier stations and that they had still to prove their harmlessness and their innocence of any designs against civilized society. The real test would come at the mighty and ineluctable barrier which the old man called the sovereign's wall, which had been built ages before across the neck of land between the Great and Little Bitter Lakes, as a protection against the savages of Shosu and the sand-dwellers who thought to drive their cattle upon Pharaoh's soil.

From the rising ground where they halted at sunset they overlooked these menacing precautions and arrogant measures of defence. The old man had succeeded several times, by dint of his harmless garrulity, in pass-

ing them in both directions; wherefore he did not now
fear them all too much. Tranquilly he lifted his hand
and pointed them out to his train: a long marching wall,
notched with battlements, broken by towers and running behind canals which connected a chain of lakes
great and small. Somewhere about the middle a bridge
crossed the water, but at this point, on either side of the
passage, rose the sternest barriers of all: castellated forts
enclosed in their own ring walls, two-storeyed, massive
and tall, whose sides and ajutments rose in ingenious
broken lines to the parapets to make them yet more secure
against siege. They bristled with square battlemented
towers, bastions, sally-ports, and ledges for defence on
all sides; narrower structures had grated windows. This
was the fort of Thel, the powerful offensive and defensive
structure set up by the refined and fortunate and vul-
nerable land of Egypt against the poverty and rapine of
the East. The old man named it to his followers by name
and was not afraid before it. But yet he said so much
about it, asserting how easy it would be for his utter
harmlessness to get past once more, that one might have
thought he was talking to keep his courage up.

"Did I tell you I have a letter from a business friend
at Gilead across the Jordan," he said, "to his business
friend in Djanet, also called Zoan, which was built seven
years after Hebron? Well, I have; and you will see, it
will open for us gate and door. The great thing is to have
a document to show and that the people of Egypt have in
their turn to write something and send it somewhere to be
copied down again and keep the record. For without
something written you do not get through; but if you can
show a potsherd or a roll and document, then they

brighten up. They say, of course, that Amun is the highest, or Osiris, the Eye Enthroned; but I know better, at bottom it is Thoth, the writer. Believe me, if only Horwaz comes on the wall, the young officer-clerk who is an old friend of mine, and I can get speech with him, then there will be no trouble at all and we can pass. Once we are inside, nobody tests our innocence again and we can go freely through all the districts up the river as far as we like. Let us set up huts here and pass the night, for my friend Hor-waz will not come on the wall any more today. But tomorrow before we go thither and beg for entrance at the fort of Thel we must wash ourselves and dust the desert from our garments and wipe it out of our ears and scratch it out from our nails that we seem to them like men and not like sand-rabbits; also you young ones must pour oil on your hair and paint your eyes and make yourselves look wanton; for to them misery is suspect and lack of elegance an abomination."

Thus the old man, and they did after his words, stopped where they were for the night and made themselves beautiful in the morning as well as they could after so long a journey through the waste. During these preparations, however, they were surprised to find that their guide, whom the old man had hired at Gaza and who had guided them so safely, proved to be no more among them, without anyone being able to say when he had gone: whether back in the night or while they were adorning themselves for Thel. Anyhow, when they looked round for him he was no more there, though the bell-camel was, on which he had ridden; nor had the guide collected his pay from the old man.

That was no cause for lamenting, but only for surprise,

since they no longer needed a guide, and the man had
been a distant creature at best, and chary of speech.
They wondered awhile, and the old man's satisfaction
over the saving of money was diminished by his lack of
understanding and the disquiet caused by unfinished
business. He concluded that the man would turn up
again some time to get his pay. Joseph thought it possible that the guide had privately taken to himself goods
instead of pay and instigated an examination of the
stock; but it proved him in the wrong. It was Joseph who
wondered the most, especially over the inconsistency in
the character of his acquaintance and the indifference in
money matters which seemed not to fit with the covetous
nature. For services voluntarily offered he had paid
himself extravagantly. Now it seemed he heedlessly let
slip a covenanted wage. But Joseph could not talk with
the Ishmaelites about these discrepancies, and words that
are not uttered are soon forgotten. They all had other
things to think of besides the guide and his caprices;
for when they had washed their ears and painted their
eyes they advanced toward the water and the sovereign's
wall and came before midday to Thel, the fort on the
bridge.

Ah, it was even more alarming from near by than at a
distance, double and unassailable by force, with its irregular line of walls, towers, and defence platforms, the
battlements filled all round with warriors of the heights,
clad in jerkins with shields of hide on their backs, who
stood with lances folded in their fists and on their fists
their chins, looking down right contemptuously on the
little caravan as it approached. Officers were there in
half-long wigs and white shirts, with leather stomachers

in front over their skirts, and little canes in their hands; they moved to and fro behind the men. The latter paid no heed to the advancing train; but the foremost posts raised their arms, curved a hand round their mouths, their lances lying in the hollow of their arms, and cried out:

"Back! Turn back! Fort of Thel! No passage. We will shoot!"

"Pay no heed," said the old man. "Only be quiet. It is not half so bad as it looks. Let us give evidence of peace by advancing slowly but undisturbed. Have I not the letter of my business friend? We shall get through."

Accordingly they moved straight up to the gap in the walls where the entrance was, and behind it the great bronze gate which led to the bridge. Here they indicated by signs their peaceful intentions. In the wall above the gate, graven deep in the masonry and painted in glaring colours, was a huge figure of a bare-necked vulture with pinions spread, the ring of the cartouche in its claws. Right and left of it out of the brick structure sprang a pair of stone cobras on sockets, four feet high, with spread hoods, erected on their bellies, horrible to see, the symbol of defence.

"Turn round!" cried the watch on the wall above the outer gate, above the vulture. "Fort of Thel! Back, sand-rabbits, into the desert! Here is no road."

"You mistake, Egyptian warriors," answered them the old man from his camel, among his group of retainers. "Just here is the entrance and not elsewhere. For where else could it be in this bottle-neck? We are well-informed people, who come not to the wrong quarter but know exactly where one enters into the land, for we have already been across your bridge and back again."

"Yes, back!" cried those above. "Always back and nothing but back with you into the desert, that is the order. No rabble shall be let into the land."

"To whom say you that?" countered the old man. "To me who not only know it well but also expressly approve it? I hate rabble and sand-rabbits as much as you and praise you highly in that you prevent them from profaning your land. But look well at us and study our faces. Do we look like thieves and vagrants and rabble from Sinai? Do our looks awake the idea that we want to spy out the land with evil intent? Or where are our flocks that we thought to drive on Pharaoh's pasture-lands? Nothing like that cometh in question even for a moment. We are Minæans from Ma'on, travelling trad-ers, proud of our rank; and bring from abroad attractive wares which we would offer you, and would sell them in exchange with the children of Kemt, that we may carry in turn the gifts of Jeor, which here is called Harri, to the ends of the world. For it is the season of trade and barter and we travellers are its servants and priests."

"Fine priests! Dust-covered priests! All that is a lie!" the soldiers shouted back.

But the old man did not lose courage, he only shook his head forbearingly.

"As if I did not know," he remarked aside to his people; "they always do this on principle, and make difficulties till one would be glad to turn round and go away. But I have never turned back and I will get through this time too."

"Hearken, ye stout brown warriors of Pharaoh," he called up again. "Gladly speak I here with you, for your words are blithe. But actually would I speak with one who is the youthful commander of the troops, Horwaz, who let me in the last time. Call him, if you will be so good, to the wall. I will show him the letter which I am bearing to Zoan. A letter! " he repeated. " A written letter, a document. Thoth, Djehuti, the ape! "

He smiled as he called out the words.

And indeed it often happens, in speaking to those who are not known to us as individuals but representatives of some well-known nation, that we thus half tease, half flatter them by invoking some phrase or symbol by which they are labelled in popular fancy. The soldiers on the wall laughed too. Perhaps they were simply amused at the obsession of every foreigner, that all Egyptians were quite daft about writing and the written word. At the same time they were probably impressed with the old man's knowledge of the name of one of their leaders. For they consulted among themselves and then called down to the Ishmaelites that the troop leader Horwaz was away on duty in the town of Sent and would not be back for three days.

" What a pity! " said the old man. " How badly it falls out, ye Egyptian warriors! Three black days, three new-moon days without Hor-waz, our friend! That means waiting. We will wait here, dear warriors, till his return. Only call him, if you will, to the wall at once on his return from Sent, with the news that the famous Minæans from Ma'on are on the spot and bring written papers."

And actually they set up their tents in the sand before the fort of Thel and remained three days awaiting the lieutenant, keeping on good terms with the people on the wall, some of whom came down to them to see their wares and drive bargains. Their numbers were increased by another party of travellers who came from the south, probably from Sinai, along the Bitter Lakes. They too would enter into Egypt. They were a right ragged crew and little polished by civilization. They waited with the Ishmaelites, and when the hour came and Hor-waz was back, all the applicants were let in through the wall into the court in front of the bridge gate. Here they had again to wait a few hours until the young officer came springing down the stair on his spindling legs and stood on the lower step. With him were two men, one of whom had his writing tools, the other a standard with a ram's head. Hor-waz beckoned the petitioners to advance.

His head was covered with a light brown wig cut straight on the forehead and lying smooth as glass as far as the ears; behind them it consisted of tiny curls that fell down on his shoulders. The mailed doublet he wore, with an order in the shape of a bronze fly, went ill with the delicate folds of the snow-white, short-sleeved linen garment that showed underneath it, and not better with the snowy pleated skirt that hung diagonally to the hollow of his knee behind.

The travellers greeted him with circumstance; yet not more courteously — however poor they were in his eyes — than he returned their greetings. It was a foppish politeness. He arched his back like a cat, throwing back his head with a sickly-sweet smile, kissed the air, as it were, with his pursed lips, and raised toward them out of his pleated sleeve a very thin brown arm adorned at the wrist with a bangle. He did it so simply and easily that only for a brief moment did he give this picture of a graceful, fastidious, and over-expressive pose. It went as it came. But one realized — at least Joseph did — that it had nothing to do with them but proceeded from his own self-respect and his reverence for the civilization he represented. Hor-waz had the face of an elderly child, short, with a pug nose, the eyes lengthened by cosmetics, and sharp furrows graven at the sides of his still pursed and laughing mouth.

" Who are ye? " he asked in rapid Egyptian. " Men of wretchedness in such great numbers, who would enter the country? "

With the word " wretchedness " he did not mean exactly a criticism; he meant simply foreigners. But in the " great numbers " he included both groups of travellers, making no difference between the Midianites and the people from Sinai, who indeed cast themselves on the ground before his feet.

" There are too many of you," he went on reproachfully. " Every day come some from here or there, from the land of God or from Shu, the mountain, and want to set foot inside; if daily is saying too much, then almost daily. Day before yesterday I let some come in from the land of Upi and the mount User, for they had letters. I am a scribe of the great gate, who renders reports upon the affairs of the lands, well and good for him who sees it. My responsibility is great. Whence come ye and what would ye? Do ye design good things or not so good or even quite evil, so that you must either be driven back or else pale your cheeks in death? Come ye from Kadesh and Dubakhi or from the city of Her? Let your leader speak. If from the port of Sur, that wretched spot is known to me, to which water is brought in boats. We know foreigners too well in all conscience, for we have conquered them and taken their tribute. . . . Above all, know ye how to live? I mean, have ye to eat and can be at your own cost so that ye come not as burden on the state or be driven to steal? But if the first be the case, where then is the evidence and the written guarantee that ye know how to live? Have ye letters to a citizen of the country? Then out with them. Else there is naught but turning back."

The old man approached him with studied mildness. " You are here as Pharaoh," he said, " and if I fear not the influence you wield and stammer not in amazement before your authority, it is only because I stand not for the first time before you and have already known your kindness, O wise lieutenant! "

And he recalled to him about such a time it had been, perhaps two years ago, or four, that he, the Minæan merchant, trod the gate for the last time and for the first was passed by the troop leader Hor-waz on the ground of the purity of his intentions. Hor-waz seemed faintly to recollect; to remember the little beard and drooping head of this old man, who spoke Egyptian as though he were a human being. He listened amicably as the other answered to the questions put, that not merely had he no evil designs, not merely fair ones, but quite definitely the best; that he was come across Jordan on a business trip, through the land of Pelesheth and through the desert; and with his followers well knew how to live and to pay, as the valuable wares on the backs of his pack-animals bore witness. But as to his connections in the country: here was a letter — and he unrolled before the lieutenant the piece of polished goatskin on which the business

friend at Gilead had written some phrases of recom-
mendation in Canaanitish script to the business friend at
Djanet in the Delta.

Hor-waz's slim fingers — all ten of them, indeed —
reached with a fastidious gesture for the document. He
could not gather much from it, but so much he saw from
his own visa in the corner, that this parchment had already lain before him.

"You bring me always the same letter, old friend,"
said he. "That will not do, you cannot come in on it
for ever. This paper crackles with age, I would see it no
more; it is out of date, you must show something new."

The old man retorted that his connections were not
limited to the man in Djanet. They extended, he said, as
far as Thebes itself, the city of Amun, whither he had it
in mind to go, to a house of honour and distinction, with
whose overseer, called Mont-kaw, son of Ahmose, he
had been on terms of close acquaintance for many years,
and often been permitted to supply him with foreign
goods. The house, however, belonged to one great above
the great, Petepre, fan-bearer on Pharaoh's right hand.
This mention of a connection with the court, however
second-hand, obviously made an impression on the young
officer.

"By the king's life!" said he. "According to that
you would amount to something, and if you lie not with
your Asiatic mouth, that would indeed alter the matter.
Have you nothing written concerning your connection
with this Mont-kaw, son of Ahmose, who is set over the
house of the fan-bearer? Nothing at all? What a pity,
for that would have simplified matters no little! But
still, you know this name to tell me, and your peaceable

countenance gives your words a satisfactory warrant of good faith."

He beckoned for his writing materials and the attendant hastened to hand him the sharpened rush and the wooden tablet on whose smooth clay surface the lieutenant was used to scribble notes. Hor-waz dipped the rush in an inkwell of the palette held by the soldier next to him, shook off a few drops, carried his writing hand in a wide curve to the surface, and wrote down the old man's record as it was repeated to him. He wrote standing beside the standard, the tablet on his arm, bent slightly forward, with his mouth pursed, squinting a little — charming, self-satisfied, and with obvious enjoyment.

" Pass! " he said, handed back tablet and pen, saluted again in his absurdly fastidious way, and sprang up the stair by which he had come. The Sinai sheik, with the dishevelled beard, who had spent the whole time on his face, was not interrogated at all. Hor-waz had included him and his among the old man's train, and the information, written out on beautiful paper and sent to the officials at Thebes, would be most incomplete. But there would be no wailing in Egypt on that account nor would any confusion come to the land. To the Ishmaelites the main point was that the soldiers of Thel pushed back the bronze wings of the gate that gave access to the floating bridge, across which they might move with beasts and burdens and enter the plains of Hapi.

Least among them, noted by none and named by no name in Hor-waz's official protocol, Joseph, son of Jacob, came into Egypt.

2

THE ENTRANCE
INTO SHEOL

WHAT part of it did he see first? That we know with
some precision; the circumstances show it. The route
which the Ishmaelites took him was dictated to them in
more than one way, and by the lie of the land besides:
it is as certain as it is ever little commented on that the
part of Egypt to which Joseph first came was one which
is known and even famous, not because of the rôle it
played in the history of Egypt but on account of its connection with the story of Jacob and his family. It was
the land of Goshen. It was called Gosen or Goshen,
indifferently, according to the speaker's enunciation, and
belonged to the district of Arabia, the twentieth of the
land of Uto the serpent, that is to say, Lower Egypt. It
lay in the eastern part of the Delta, wherefore Joseph and
his guides entered it so soon as they had left the salt inland
seas and frontier fortifications behind. There was certainly nothing great or remarkable about it — Joseph did
not find himself in any danger of losing his head or being
hampered by awe at the importunate marvels of Mizraim.

Wild geese flew across a mild, dull, rainy sky above the monotonous marshland, threaded with ditches and dikes, out of which here and there rose a single blackthorn or a mulberry-fig-tree. The travellers went on causeways, following the watercourses where long-legged birds, storks and ibises, stood in the cane-brake that choked the streams. Whole villages mirrored the cone-shaped clay roofs of their storehouses and the shade of their doum-palms' fan-shaped leaves in the green duck-ponds beside them. They were not different to the eye from villages in the homeland and not a very reward-ing sight after a journey of seven times seventeen days. It was simple earth-land that Joseph saw, without any sur-prising features; it was not even the " granary " of the well-known phrase. For what he saw was simply grass-land and pasture-land far and wide, though, to be sure, the pasturage was lush and well watered — and the son of shepherds looked with interest at it. Many flocks grazed over it, cattle white and red, either hornless or with upstanding lyre-shaped horns; there were sheep too; their shepherds had made shelters from the drizzling rain by stretching papyrus mats above their crooks, and squat-ted underneath with their jackel-eared dogs.

The cattle, the old man instructed his followers, were mostly not from these parts. They came from far up-stream and belonged to the landowners and the overseers of the temple stables in regions where there was hardly anything but arable land and the cattle would have had to feed on the clover-fields. So at the right time of year the herds were sent down into the fenny districts of north-ern Lower Egypt to batten on the meadows made luxuri-ant by these very fresh-water canals along which our little train was now passing. They led it straight to Per-sopd, the original holy city of the district. For there the ditch branched off from the Delta arm of Hapi and connected the river with the Bitter Lakes. These, as the old man knew, were in turn united by a canal with the Sea of the Red Earth, otherwise the Red Sea; so that one could pass straight on through from the Nile and sail from the city of Amun to the incense land of Punt, as had once the bold ships of Hatshepsut, the woman who had been Pharaoh and worn the beard of Osiris.

As they went on, the old man continued to prattle about all these traditional matters, in his shrewd and easy-going way. But Joseph listened uncomfortably and had no ear at all for the doings of Hatshepsut, that woman whose sex had been changed by the dignity of the king-ship so that she had worn the beard. Shall I be saying too much if I set down how his fancy flung an airy bridge between the gay meadows here and his kin at home, his father and little Benjamin? Surely not — even though his thinking may not have been of the same kind as ours, but played about a few dream-motifs which formed, as it were, the musical fabric of his mental life. One of these had always been closely related to the thoughts of being " snatched away " and " lifted up ": the motif of being " followed after." Then there was another, contradictory one, in his changeful play of thought, which concerned Jacob's dislike of the country whither he was snatched. He harmonized the two contrapuntally, by telling himself that this peacefully primeval pasture-land here might indeed be already Egypt but after all was not the real Egypt, therefore not utterly abhorrent; and that it might appeal to Jacob, the king of many flocks who found it hard to sustain them at home. He looked at the grazing herds sent hither by Upper Egyptian proprietors to feed on the fat of the land, and had a lively feeling that the motif of being " snatched away " needed completion by that of being " lifted up," before the flocks of the lords of the upper river would make way for other flocks in the land of Goshen; in other words, before the motif of being " followed after " could come in. He weighed afresh his conviction and strengthened himself mightily in it, that if one were indeed going to the West, at least one must become the first of those who were there.

For the present, however, he went with his masters along the flat, clayey margin of the beneficent water-course dotted here and there with spindling palms. On the smooth water a flotilla of boats was slowly gliding eastward with monstrously tall sails on swaying masts. By this route they could not miss the holy city Per-sopdu, which, when they reached it, proved to be a huddled settlement surrounded by disproportionately high walls with but little life inside them. For almost the whole population consisted of the presiding " field judge " and " privy bearer of the king's command," who bore the good Syrian title of Rabisu, together with his officials and the shorn priesthood of the regional god Sopd, called " Scourge of the Dwellers of Sinai." Among the rest of the inhabitants the coloured Asiatic dress and the language of Amor and Zahi were much more in evidence than the white Egyptian garb and the Egyptian tongue. The narrow streets of Per-sopd smelt so strong of carnations or clove-pinks that at first it was pleasant and then painful; for this was the incense most favoured of Sopdu in his temple, and every offering reeked of it. This

Sopdu was so old, so ancient a god that his own priests
and prophets, who wore lynx-skins on their backs and
went about with their eyes cast down, no longer knew for
a certainty whether his head was that of a pig or a hippopotamus.

He was a god rejected and obscure; embittered
thereby, to judge from the mood and language of his
priests. For a long time now he had not been the scourge
of the dwellers in Sinai. His image — only hand-high
— stood in the remotest part of his primitive and very
clumsy temple, whose courts and antechambers were
adorned with extremely ungainly seated images of the
early Pharaoh who had built the temple. The foremost
gatehouse, with its buttressed, picture-covered walls, had
little niches in each of which stood a gilded flag-pole
flying a gay pennant; but all this strove in vain to give
blitheness to the house of Sopd. It was poorly endowed,
the treasuries and storehouses round the main court
stood empty, and not many people waited on Sopdu with
offerings — only the Egyptian inhabitants and none
from elsewhere; and there was no feast of general observance to draw zealous pilgrims down-river and within
the crumbling walls of Per-sopd.

The Ishmaelites, as a business gesture, laid on the
offertory in the square hall a few nosegays which they
found for sale in the open court, also a duck spiced with
cloves. They talked to the shiny-pated priests with long
fingernails and for ever downcast gaze; and from them
heard, in heavy accents, of the fallen state of their aboriginal lord and his city. They complained of the times,
which brought great injustice with them and heaped all
the power, splendour, and precedence in one side of the

balance of the lands — namely, in the southern or upper part, since when it was that Wese had grown so great; whereas originally they had piously weighed down the northern or lower land of the Delta, as was right and just. For in the good old times, when Mempi had been the brilliant city of kings, the Delta region had been the real and true Egypt, and the upper parts, including Thebes, had ranked almost with the wretched Kush and the Negro countries. Then the south had been poor in culture and enlightenment, as well as in beauty of life. From the ancient north these blessings had spread fruitfully southwards up the river. Here were the sources of knowledge, civilization, and prosperity; here the most venerable gods of the land had had their birth, as, for instance, Sopd, the Lord of the East in his chapel, whom now a wrong adjustment of the balance had put quite in the shade. For Theban Amun, up there near the Negro lands, set itself up today as a judge of what was to be considered Egyptian and what not — convinced that its name spelled Egypt and Egypt Thebes. A little time ago, said the embittered " temple-treaders," people of the west living near the Libyans had even sent to Amun and represented to him that it seemed to them they were Libyans too and not Egyptians; for they lived outside the Delta and agreed in nothing with the children of Egypt, either in service of the gods or otherwise: they loved, so they said, the flesh of cows and wanted freedom to eat it as did the Libyans, whose like they were. But Amun had answered and reproved them: there could be no talk of the flesh of cows, for all that land was Egypt which was fertilized by the Nile, up and down stream, and all were Egyptians who dwelt this side of the city of elephants and drank from the river.

Thus Amun's judgment; the priests of the lord Sopdu lifted their long-nailed hands as they strove to make clear to the Ishmaelites the arrogance of it. Why then, they scornfully asked, this side of Shab and the first cataract? Just because Thebes lay this side? If Sopd, their lord, down here in the north, in the first and genuine land of Egypt, were to declare that everything was Egyptian that drank from the river, it would be a broad and high-minded thing to say. But when Amun said it, a god who, to speak mildly, stood under suspicion of Nubian origin and of being originally a god of the wretched Kush; who had achieved primacy in the mind of the peoples only by arbitrarily putting himself on a par with Atum Re — then there was something lacking in his broad-mindedness and you could not call it high-minded at all.

In short, the prophets of Sopd suffered from jealousy and peevishness at the eclipse of their god through time and events. And the Ishmaelites, the old man at their head, humoured them like the good men of business that they were. Also they increased their offerings with sundry loaves of bread and jugs of beer and showed the neglected Sopd all due attention before they went on to Per-Bastet close by.

THE CITY OF CATS

AND here it smelt so strong of catnip that it almost turned a stranger's stomach. For the odour is offensive to everybody, save only to the sacred animal of Bastet, namely the cat, which is well known to love it. Numerous specimens of the animal were kept in Bastet's shrine, the

city's mighty core; black, white, and coloured, they
frisked with the stealthy and persistent charm of their
species among the worshippers in the court and were
flattered with offerings of the hateful herb. But cats
were everywhere in Per-Bastet — in all the private
houses as well — and the smell of valerian pervaded
everything; it even flavoured the food and lingered in
men's garments, so that when they went as far as On
and Mempi they were greeted with laughter and the
words: " You come from Per-Bastet, don't you? "

The laughter had not to do with the smell alone, but
with the cat-city itself and its associations, which were
matter enough for mirth. For Per-Bastet, unlike Per-
Sopd — which it exceeded in size and population —
had a reputation for gaiety. It even looked jolly, although lying so deep in the ancient Delta, its jollity
being of a primitive, coarse-fibred kind which made all
Egypt laugh whenever it thought of it. This city — also
therein unlike the shrine of Sopd — had a feast of general observance; its citizens boasted that " millions,"
that is certainly tens of thousands of people, came down-
river by land or water to attend it. Even on the way
thither they got very jolly; the women especially,
equipped with rattles, behaved with roguish abandon,
according to all accounts; and words and gestures of a
decidedly primitive character were flung across from the
decks of their boats to the villages on the shore. The
men too were jolly; they whistled, sang, and clapped;
and all of the visitors held great press of popular meetings
in Per-Bastet, camping in tents for a three days' feast,
with sacrifices, dances, and mummery to the dull rolling
of drums; with a fair, story-telling, juggling, snake-

charming, and more grape wine than was drunk otherwise in Per-Bastet in all the rest of the year. We are
told that the mood of the people so passed over into the
primitive that they even flagellated themselves, or rather
beat themselves till it hurt with a sort of thorny club,
amid general bawling. And this bawling was an insepa-
rable feature of the primitive feast; indeed, it was what
made people laugh when they thought of Bastet, for it
sounded just like the nocturnal caterwauling of the female at the visit of the male cat.

With all these matters, then, the inhabitants regaled
the strangers and boasted of the profitable crowds which
enlivened once every year an otherwise uneventful life.
The old man, on business grounds, regretted that he had
not come at the right time of year for the feast. His
young slave Usarsiph listened to the narration with apparently respectful eyes, nodded politely, and thought of
Jacob. Of him he thought, and of the templeless God of
his fathers, as he stood at the highest part of the city
and looked down through its middle depth where two tree-
shaded branches of water embraced the sacred peninsula,
into the dwelling of the female idol, enclosed in towering walls. The main building lay inside a hedge of old
sycamore trees; its pylons were thick with images, its
courts were shaded by awnings, and the roofs of its
colourful halls were borne by columns whose capitals
imitated the open and closed calyxes of the byblus reed.
It lay there, spacious and extended, accessible by the
stone-paved road from the east, by which he had come in
the Ishmaelite train. He continued to think when later
he entered the temple halls and looked at the pictures
graven on the walls and painted deep red and sky-blue:

Pharaoh burning incense before the cat goddess, among incredibly clear inscriptions of eyes, mouths, arrows, beetles, and birds; while red-brown deities, with tails, wearing loincloths and brilliant arm-bands and collars, high crowns on their animal heads and the cross-ring of the symbol of life on their hands, laid a friendly touch on the shoulders of their earthly son.

Joseph, a tiny figure among giants, gazed up at all this with calm young eyes. Young he was, and it was weighty with age. Yet he was aware that he opposed it with his youth not only according to the measure of his years but in a larger sense; he stiffened his back against the weight of the ages; and when he thought of the ancient crying by night with which the folk at the feast filled the courts of Bastet he gave his shoulders a shrug.

EDIFYING ON

How well we know the route by which the " snatched away " was taken! — up or down according as you choose to put it. For, like so much else here, the up and the down were confusing. For Joseph — probably for Abram too — the road to Egypt went down; but in Egypt it went up — that is, against the river, which flowed from the south, so that as you went southwards you went, not down, but up. It seemed like a deliberate confusion, like a game in which one turns a blindfold person two or three times round till his head whirls and he no longer knows hind from fore. And not only with direction but also with time and the calendar things were confusing down here below.

It was in the twenty-eighth year of the reign of Pharaoh; and, as we should say, in the middle of December. The people of Kemt said and wrote the " first month of the flood," called Thoth, as Joseph learnt with pleasure, or Djehuti, as they called the moon-friendly ape. But nature and the calendar did not agree: the current year almost always conflicted with reality; only at enormous distances of time did the New Year's Day of the calendar coincide with the natural one, when the dog-star appeared again in the morning sky and the waters began to rise. In short, between the conception of a year and the seasons of nature confusion reigned. Even practically there could be no sense in saying that they were now at the beginning of the flood season; the river had so abated as almost to be back in its old bed; the land had emerged, the sowing had been largely finished, the crops were up. Indeed, the journey of the Ishmaelites had been so leisurely that half a year had passed since Joseph, at the time of the summer solstice, had lain in the pit.

Somewhat dazed, then, as to time and space, he moved on in his stations — and which were they? We know precisely; the circumstances show us. For his guides, the Ishmaelites — who still gave themselves plenty of time, or rather, after their old wont, troubled about time not at all, only taking care that their slow progress kept more or less the right direction — went with him along the branch from Per-Bastet south to the point where it flowed into the river at the apex of the triangle of the Delta. And so they came to golden On, lying at the apex, a most extraordinary city, the house of the Sun, the largest place which Joseph had ever seen. It seemed to his dazzled eyes to be built chiefly of gold.

But thence they would some day reach Mempi, likewise

called Menfe, unique and æon-old royal city, whose dead did not need to take the water journey, as it lay already on the western bank. This they knew beforehand about Mempi. And from that point they meant to travel no farther by land but to charter a boat and sail to Pharaoh's city, No-Amun. Thus the old man had planned, according to whose planning everything proceeded, and so they went on for the present, with halts for trade, along the bank of the Jeor, here called Harri. The stream had gone brown in its bed, and lay in isolated pools on the fields, which were beginning to green, as far on both sides, between desert and desert, as the fertile land extended.

Where the bank was steep, men were drawing up water in leather bottles at well-curbs, with a lump of clay at the other end of the sweep to serve as balance. Drawing up the muddy seminal fluid from the river and pouring it into channels, that it might flow down into the ditches below and prosper the corn against the coming of Pharaoh's scribes. For this was the Egyptian house of bondage so frowned upon by Jacob; the tax-gatherers were accompanied by Nubian lictors carrying palm rods.

The Ishmaelites did business among the labourers in the villages, trading their lamps and resin for necklaces, head-rests, and the linen which the peasant women made out of field flax and turned over to the tax-gatherers. They talked with the people and they saw the land of Egypt. Joseph saw it too and breathed in its vital air as they took their trading way. It was strange enough; the customs, beliefs, and forms of the country were sharp-flavoured like the taste of its spices. Yet we must not conclude that what he thus took in with mind and senses was utterly foreign and unheard-of to him. His fatherland — if we take in that sense the region of the Jordan, the mountains, and the mountainous country where he grew up — was a region of passage and transit. On the south accordingly it took character from Egyptian influence, on the east from the Babylonian sphere. Pharaoh's campaigns had passed through and left behind garrisons, governors, and buildings. Joseph had seen Egyptians and the clothes they wore; the look of Egyptian temples was not strange to him; all in all he was not only the child of his mountains but the child of a larger territorial unit, that of the eastern Mediterranean, within which nothing could impress him as quite outlandish or absurd. Still more, he was a child of his age, that time now submerged in which he lived and moved, into which we have gone down to him as Ishtar went down to her son. Time and space worked together to create a unity and community in the physical and the mental world. So that probably the one actual novelty which Joseph perceived on his travels was just this: that he and his were not alone in the world, not quite unique; that much of the thinking and doing of the fathers, their outlook and their anxious speculation anent the nature of God, had not been altogether a peculiar personal advantage of theirs, but rather it was a property of the unifying time and space — aside of course from considerable differences in the amount of the blessing and their adroitness in the use of it.

When for instance Abram had argued so long and ardently with Melchisedec about the degree of unity which subsisted between his own Adon and El Elyon, the Shechemite god of the league of Baal, their discussion had been quite typical of their world and time; as regards not only the problem they discussed but also the importance they attached and the feeling they brought to its discussion. At the very time when Joseph came to Egypt the priests of On, the city of Atum-Re-Horakhte, the sun lord, had just made a pronouncement on the relation of their sacred bull Merwer to the Dweller on the Horizon, designating it a " repeating birth " — a formulation in which the idea of proximity and identity came more or less to its own. Wherefore also it occupied the thoughts of all Egypt and even at court had made a lively impression. Everybody talked about it, great and small; the Ishmaelites could not exchange five deben of labdanum against a corresponding quantity of beer or a good bullock hide without hearing mentioned in the preliminaries to the bargain the capital new definition of the relation of Merwer to Atum-Re and being asked what the strangers thought of it. The questioner could reckon, if not on their agreement, at least on their interest; they came indeed from afar, but not from outside his unit of space; though, above all, it was the time they had in common which made them listen with a certain excitement to the new thing.

On, then, the dwelling of the sun, the dwelling, that is, of him who in the morning is Kheper, at midday Re, and Atum in the evening; who opens his eyes and the light arises, who closes his eyes and darkness comes; of him who had named to Eset his daughter his name; On in the land of Egypt, thousands of years the same, lay on our travellers' southward route. Over it glittered the gilded four-sided top of the enormous obelisk of highly polished granite, which stood on the projecting foundation before the great temple of the sun. Here was the alabaster table of Re-Horakhte, covered with lotus-crowned wine-jugs, laden with cakes, dishes of honey, birds, and all sorts of vegetable produce. And here the " treaders" of the sanctuary, in stiffly starched kilts, panther-skins on their backs with the tails dangling, were burning incense before that very bull Merwer: the great bull, the " repeating birth" of the god, with a brazen neck just behind the lyre-shaped horns, and powerful hanging testicles. This at least was a city such as Joseph had never seen; different not only from the cities of the rest of the world, but also from the other cities of Egypt. Its very temple — with the adjacent lofty-built " Ship of the Sun " made of gilded bricks — was also entirely different in ground-plan and appearance from other Egyptian temples. The whole city glittered and glistened with gold, like the sun; in such wise that all its citizens had permanently enflamed and weeping eyes and strangers mostly drew hood or mantle over their heads against the glare. The roofs of its ring wall were gold, golden rays quivered and darted everywhere from the tips of the phallic sun-lances with which they were lined — all these golden symbols of the sun in the shape of beasts, all these lions, sphinxes, goats, bulls, eagles, falcons, and sparrow-hawks. And it was not enough that even the poorest house, built of bricks made of Nile mud, bore a gilt symbol of the sun — a winged disk, a hooked wheel or wagon, an eye, an axe, or a scarab, or showed on its roof a golden ball or apple. For the dwelling-houses, granaries, and buildings in the outlying villages of Greater On were the same: each reflected the rays of the sun in some such

emblem — a copper shield, a snaky spiral, a gilt beaker
or shepherd's crook; for this was the domain of the sun
and precinct of the blinking.

A city to make one blink was On, the thousand-year-
old. Yet not only in outward appearance; it was so in
its inward kind and spirit as well. Age-old doctrinal
wisdom was here at home, as the stranger perceived at
once — it came in through his pores, one might say. But
it was a doctrinal wisdom solely and simply concerning
the measurement and structure of bodies conceived as
in three-dimensional space, and the surfaces bounding
them; bounded by equal angles, meeting in sharp edges
that came together at a point which although it existed
had no extension and occupied no space — and more
mysteries of the kind. All this interest in abstract figure
which prevailed at On, the sense for the theories of space,
characterized this ancient city and obviously had to do
with its local cult, the worship of the day-star. It be-
trayed itself even in the structure of the place. Situated
just at the apex of the triangular region of the diverging
river-mouths, it formed with its houses and streets an
equilateral triangle, whose tip — ideally and also more
or less in fact — coincided with the apex of the Delta;
and on this very spot there reared itself from a mammoth
rhomboidal base the four-sided obelisk of flame-coloured
granite, covered with gold where its surfaces met in a
point. Daily it kindled in the first gleam of the rising
sun; and with its surrounding courtyards it formed the
culmination of the temple precincts, which extended as
far as the middle of the triangular city.

The temple gate was hung with banners and gave access to passages painted with the most delightful repre-

sentations of the seasonal activities on the land and their
fruits. In front of the gate was an open square planted
with trees; and here the Ishmaelites spent nearly the
whole day, for all the weak-eyed people of On came
hither to do business and strangers from other parts as
well. The servants of the god came out to the market too,
their eyes running with much gazing into the sun; with
heads reflecting it on their shiny surfaces, and wearing
only the short aboriginal kilt and priest's garland. They
mixed with the people and had nothing against convers-
ing with such as would learn from their wisdom. It appeared indeed that they were kept here to that end and
only waited to be asked to testify for their venerable cult
and the ancient learning which their temple possessed.
Our old man, Joseph's master, availed himself freely of
the unspoken but obvious willingness and conversed at
length with the sun-instructed teachers on the square;
Joseph at his side listened too.

The power of thinking on God and the gift of giving
laws to the faith were, they said, hereditary in their order.
They had possessed for ages a faculty of religious insight. They, or rather their forerunners in the service,
had first divided up and measured time and contrived
the calendar; all which, as well as that fruitful understanding for abstract figure, was connected with the
nature of the god at the opening of whose eye the day began. Up to that time men had just lived on in blind time-
lessness, without measure or mark. But He, who made
the hours — from which then the days were born — had
through his wise men opened the people's eyes. That
they — that is to say, their forbears — had discovered
the sun-dial, went without saying. The tradition was not

so clear with regard to the apparatus that measured the hours of the night, the water-clock. But probably it was made through the circumstance that Sobk, the crocodile-shaped water-god from Ombo, like so many other objects of veneration was, when one fixed it with one's watering eyes, nothing but Re under another name and in token bore the serpent and the disk.

That sort of general survey, in fact, was the special line and learning of these shiny-pated priests. They were, by their own account, very strong at generalization and at equating any and every regional and local protecting deity with Atum-Re-Horakhte of On — a complex himself and representing a constellation of originally single numina. To make out of many one: that was their preferred activity, yes, according to them there were at bottom only two great gods: one the living, that was Hor in the Mount of Light, Atum-Re; and one the dead, Osiris, the Eye Enthroned. But the eye also was Atum-Re, it was the disk of the sun; and so to the penetrating mind Usir was lord of the nightly bark into which, as everybody knew, Re mounted after his setting, to travel from west to east and to light the underworld. In other words, even these two great gods were at bottom one and the same. But if the shrewdness of such a general survey was admirable, not less so was the art these teachers displayed of avoiding offence; for in the midst of their assimilating activities they took care to leave intact the actual multiplicity of the gods of Egypt.

This they achieved by means of their science of the triangle. Were their hearers, asked the teachers of On, at all versed in the nature of this glorious symbol? To its width, they said, corresponded the deities many-named and many-shaped, invoked of the people, served by the priests in all the cities of the lands. But above it rose and strove to a meeting the two legs of the beautiful figure, and the unique space which they bounded might be called " the space of conspectus," distinguished by the fact that it narrowed as it went up and the hypothetical bases drawn through it became shorter and shorter until they had a very narrow extension and finally none at all. For the legs met in a point, and this terminus and point of intersection, beneath which all the varying widths of the symbol remained equilateral — that was the lord of their temple, that was Atum-Re.

Thus the theory of the triangle, the beautiful figure of the conspectus. The priests of Atum plumed themselves no little on it. They had, they said, made a school with it; conspectus and comparison were going on everywhere. But only in a clumsy and uninstructed way, not in the right spirit — without intelligence, crudely and by force. Amun, for instance, the " Rich in Bulls," at Thebes in Upper Egypt, had had himself made equal to Re by his prophets and would now be called Amun-Re in his shrine. All very well, but not in the sense of the triangle and reconciliation; rather in the sense that Amun had conquered Re, had consumed him and lived in him — as though Re, so to speak, had had to name him his name! That was a brutal misuse of the doctrine, a narrow-minded effrontery quite contrary to the meaning of the triangle. Atum-Re for his part was not called the " Horizon-Dweller " for nothing; his horizon was wide and all-embracing, and all-embracing was the triangular field of his conspectus. Yes, he was world-wide, and world-friendly the nature of this ancient god; long ago it had matured into blitheness and benevolence. He was ready, so said the shiny-pated priests, to find himself not alone in the changeful shapes which the people worshipped in the regions and cities of Kemt. No, for he was also complaisantly inclined to come to terms of a far-reaching and general kind with the sun-gods of other peoples. How different from young Amun in Thebes, who lacked every speculative faculty and whose horizon was in fact so narrow that he not only knew and realized nothing but the land of Egypt, but even here had no thought but to consume and incorporate instead of giving free rein — in all of which, so to speak, he saw no farther than his own nose.

But, said the blear-eyed ones, they would not dwell upon conflict with young Amun at Thebes; conflict was not the nature or affair of their god, but rather complaisance and harmony. He loved the stranger as himself, and thus they his priests delighted in converse with strangers — namely, with the old man and his companions. Whatever gods they served and whatever name they called them, they might without disloyalty and with good heart approach the alabaster table of Horakhte and offer doves, bread, fruit, and flowers, according to their power. One glance at the mild and smiling countenance of the fatherly head priest, as he sat on a golden chair at the foot of the great obelisk, a golden cap on his bald pate with its aureole of white hair, the white robe flowing wide about him, a winged sun's disk at his back, and presided with benignity over the offerings — a single such glance would convince the strangers that in offering to Atum-Re they offered to their own domestic gods, to whom satisfaction was given within the triangle.

The servants of the sun embraced and kissed the old man and his companions, including Joseph, one after the other, in the name of the fatherly great prophet. Then they turned to other visitors to the market, to make further propaganda for Atum-Re, lord of the far horizon. But the Ishmaelites departed, very pleasantly impressed, from On at the apex of the triangle, and bent their steps farther down — or up — into the land of Egypt.

JOSEPH AT THE PYRAMIDS

THE NILE rolled its slow course along between flat reedy banks; where many a palm tree still stood half-submerged and mirrored its trunk in the subsiding flood. There were plots of land in the blessing-zone between desert and desert where the corn and barley were already green; on others cattle and sheep were being driven by white-aproned brown bearers across the level land, that they might tread the seed into the soft moist earth. Vultures and white falcons peered and hovered under a clearing, sunny sky; they swooped down toward villages half-hidden by towering date-palms with crowns of fan-shaped leaves. There were many such settlements along the irrigation canals; their dung-roofed dwellings had walls made out of Nile mud and buttressed like pylons. And everything bore the stamp of the characteristic, all-pervading spirit of the land of Egypt: its forms and its gods conditioned the picture of men and things. Heretofore, and in his own country, Joseph had only seen it in single manifestations, as for instance some characteristic building. Here it confronted him in all its typicality and in great and small.

At the village landing-places naked children were playing among farm-yard fowl; shelters made of poles and withies stood along the bank, and people returning from their necessary occasions came poling along the canal and landed from their high-backed osier barks. The river, dotted with sails, divided the land into two parts from north to south; but everywhere the fertilizing watercourses ran east and west and made it into islands like oases of fan-shaped green. You walked on the road as on a causeway among ditches, reservoirs, and groves. Thus the Ishmaelites passed on southwards, amid all the people of the land, riding on asses, driving loaded wagons drawn by oxen and donkeys, or going on foot, apron-wearers carrying ducks and fish on yokes to market. A lean, reddish, flat-bellied folk, square-shouldered, in-offensive in bearing, ready to laugh. They had thin-boned faces with projecting jaws; little noses broad at the end, and childish cheeks; a rush blossom in their mouths, behind one ear, or stuck in the much-washed apron, which had a diagonal hem and was higher back than front. Their hair fell smooth over the brow and was cut off straight under the ear-lobes. Joseph liked these wayfarers. Considering what they were — people of Sheol and the land of the dead — they were pleasant to look at, and they laughed as they shouted greetings to the Shabirite dromedary-riders, for anything foreign to them was a joke. Joseph tried his tongue on their speech by himself and trained himself by listening, that he might soon be able to talk readily with them in their own idiom.

The land of Egypt was narrow at this point, the strip of fertility small. To the east, on their left, the arid Arabian ranges ran close by, matched by the sandhills of

Libya on the west, their deathly desolation masked in purple loveliness as the sun sank behind them. But at the edge of the desert, in front of this chain and near the greening fields, the travellers saw straight ahead of them a symmetrical and very singular elevation, composed of triangular surfaces, whose huge planes met in sharp corners and ran together to a point at the top. These were mountains not created by nature but made by the hand of man; they were the world-famous erections — the old man pointed them out to Joseph as they went — the monuments of Khufu, Khefren, and other kings of the early time, built through decades by the sweat of hundreds of thousands of slaves coughing under the lash; built out of granite blocks weighing millions of tons which they dug in the Arabian quarries and dragged to the river, ferried over, and, groaning, sledged to the border of Libya, where they hoisted them with some kind of incredible lifting apparatus and piled them into pointed mountains. They fell and died, their tongues hanging out with their superhuman effort on the blazing desert — all in order that Khufu, the king and god, might lie far beneath them, shut off by a tiny chamber from the perpetual weight of millions of tons of heavy stone, a little twig of mimosa on his heart.

It was no work for human beings that the children of Kemt had there performed. And yet it was the work of the same little folk who trotted and poled along the causeways; the work of their bleeding hands, lean muscles, and panting lungs — won from the human, if surpassing the human, because Khufu was a god-king, the son of the sun. But the sun which struck down and consumed the builders might be satisfied with the superhuman human achievement — Ra-hotep, the satisfied sun. For in their abstract form they represented him, they were his pictographic symbols; these great piles of death and resurrection stood there sun-monument and sun-tomb at once; and their vast triangular surfaces, polished and glittering from base to apex, lay piously adjusted to the four quarters of the heavens.

Joseph looked up wide-eyed at these three-dimensional tomb-mountains, heaped up by slave-labour in the Egyptian house of bondage so misprized by Jacob. As he looked he listened to the old man, who expended himself in tales of King Khufu. Even today sinister tales of that superhuman master builder were on the lips of the people. These thousand years and more the folk of Kemt had preserved a grudge against the memory of that evildoer who had got from them the impossible for that he had been a bad and self-seeking god and closed all the temples that no one should steal time from him with sacrifices. And he had kept all the people harnessed in toil for the building of his marvellous tomb and for thirty years had not granted even one little hour for their own life. Ten years, that is, had they to drag and chisel and on top of that build for twice ten, expending every ounce of strength they had and more besides. For reckoning all their strength together it would not have been quite enough to build the pyramid. The necessary remainder had come to them from the divinity of King Khufu, but they had not been glad. The building had cost great treasures; and when the treasure of that majestic godhead had been exhausted, he exposed his own daughter in the palace and gave of her body to every man who paid the price. By such means he replenished his treasury.

So went the legends, the old man said. It is quite possible that they were for the most part fairy-tales and falsehoods, which were told these thousands of years after Khufu's death. But so much was clear, that the people were even now more terrified than grateful to him for wringing out of them their utmost and more, and insisting on the impossible.

As our travellers came nearer, the peaks stood up separate in the sand, and they saw that the surfaces of the triangles were damaged, their polished planes had begun to crumble. Desolation reigned between the giant tombs, as each by itself, and all too massive for time to have done more than nibble at their surfaces, they stood there on the shelving rubble and sand of the desert plain. They alone had come off victorious in the frightful struggle with time, which had long since destroyed and buried the splendours with which piety had once filled the spaces between their mammoth forms. Temples of the dead had once leaned against their sides, where services in honour of those dead in the sun had been set up " for ever "; covered passages thick with pictures had once led thence and broad-based gates on the eastern side near the fertile zone had once formed the entrance to the closed passages which led into the enchanted kingdom of immortality. All of this Joseph in his day saw no more and did not even know that not seeing was actually a no-more-seeing, a beholding of destruction. He came on them early of course by comparison with his relation to us. But from another point of view he was late and green indeed; his gaze encountered this great rubbish-heap of death, this bald survival of a mathematic of giants, as one's foot will stub against a pile of rubble. Astonishment and awe did move

him, of course, at sight of these triangular domes; but the
frightful endurance which made them, forsaken of their
time, stand here, survivals into God's present day, gave
them among their other aspects something awesome and
accursed in his eyes; he thought of the tower.

Then there was that riddle in the head-cloth, Hor-im-
akhet, the great sphinx, which lay somewhere hereabouts
residual, flat on the sands which were drifted over so as
almost to cover it. Pharaoh's predecessor, Thutmose IV,
had rescued it out of them, obedient to the promise-dream
which he dreamed when he took his midday nap. That
was not so long ago; but the sand was already mounting
again about the enormous creature, which had lain there
so long that no man could say when and how it had come
out of the rock — drifts of sand slanted up to its breast
and hid one of the paws. The other, still free, was the size
of three houses. At the breast of this mountain the son of
the king, like a doll compared to the immense god-beast,
had lain asleep while his servants at some distance
guarded his hunting-wagon. And high above the manikin
rose the inscrutable head, with the stiff neckcloth, the im-
mortal brow, the eroded nose which lent it a somewhat
roguish air, the rocky vault of its upper lip, the wide
mouth which seemed to be shaping a sort of calm and
primitive and sensual smile. The clear, wide-open, intelligent eyes, intoxicated from deep draughts of time, gazed
eastwards as they had ever done.

And thus it lay there now, the unpreconceivable Chi-
mera, in a present whose distance and difference from
times of yore were doubtless negligible in its eyes; and
gazed steadfastly, sensually, unchangeably away eastwards above the heads of Joseph and his owners. An in-

scribed tablet more than a man's height leaned against its breast, and the Minæans read it with refreshment and strengthening of the heart. For this recent stone afforded a firm basis of time; it was like a narrow platform which gave a foothold above the abyss; it was the commemorative tablet which Pharaoh Thutmose had erected here in memory of his dream and the moving of the sand. The old man read the text and the pronouncement to his people: how the prince, lying in the shadow of the monster, was overcome by sleep at the hour when the sun was at its height and saw in his dream the majesty of this glorious god, his father, Harmakhis-Khepere-Atum-Re, who spoke fatherly to him and called him his dear son. " It is already a long time in years," he said, " that my countenance is directed upon thee and my heart the same. I will give thee, Thutmose, the royal sovereignty, the crowns of the two lands shalt thou wear upon the throne of Geb, and to thee shall the earth after its length and breadth belong with all that the radiant eye of the all-lord shineth upon. The treasure of Egypt and the great tribute of the people shall be thine. But meanwhile the sands of the desert where I lie weigh heavy upon me, all worthy of adoration as I stand. My justified wish groweth out of this weight. I doubt not that thou wilt accede to it as soon as thou canst. For I know thou art my son and my deliverer. But I will be with thee." When Thutmose awoke — so the story went — he still knew the words of the god and kept them in mind until the hour of his elevation. And in that very hour his command went forth that they should at once remove the sand which rested heavy on Harmakhis, the great sphinx, at Mempi in the desert.

Thus the tale. And Joseph, who listened as the old man

his master read it, took care to add not even one little word. For he heeded the old man's warning to hold his tongue in this land of Egypt, and wished to show that in case of need one could conceal even such thoughts as he had. But in secret he was vexed on Jacob's account at this dream of the promise, and in his vexation found it arid and meagre. Pharaoh, so he thought, made altogether too much of his tablet. What after all had he been promised? Nothing more than that which had been his destiny from birth; that at a certain hour he would become king and reign over the two lands. This definite prospect the god had confirmed to him, in case, that is, Pharaoh rescued his image from the sands that threatened it. And here one saw the folly of making to oneself an image. The image fell into danger from the sand, and the god into such a pass as to implore: " Save me, my son! " And to enter into a bond wherein he promised in exchange for a petty benefaction something that would most likely happen anyhow. Joseph found that offensive. It had been a different and higher bond that God the Lord had concluded with the fathers, likewise out of need, yet mutual need: that they should save each other out of the sands of the desert and become holy the one in the other. In any case, the king's son had become king at his hour, but the desert sand had already encroached again upon the image to a considerable extent. For such passing relief probably only a redundant return-gift was in place, thought Joseph. He expressed his thought to Kedema, the old man's son, when they were alone; and Kedema was amazed at such a critical spirit.

But let Joseph carp as he would and mock out of respect to Jacob, yet the sight of the sphinx made on him in one way or another more impression than all he had hitherto seen in the land of Egypt. It set his young blood in an unrest, against which mockery did not avail and which did not let him sleep. Night had fallen while they lingered by these great things of the desert; and so they set up their tents that they might sleep and go on to Mempi in the morning. But Joseph, who had already lain down in the hut with Kedema, his bedfellow, strolled out once more under the stars. He heard in the distance the jackals howling as he approached the giant idol, to look at it quite by himself, without witnesses, in the brightness of the night and question its uncanny vastness.

For uncanny it was, that monster of old time, in its regal rock head-dress, and uncanny not only for its size or even for the darkness of its origins. How did the riddle run? Ah, it ran not at all, it lay there, or crouched, consisting but in the silence, that rapt-drunken silence in which the monster gazed out with its wide wild eyes above the questioning and questioned. And its want of nose had an effect as when a man sets his cap crooked over one ear. Yes, if this had been a riddle like the good old man's about his neighbour Dagantakala's plot of land — then, however the numbers were hidden and concealed, one might have shifted the unknown quantity hither and thither and weighed the proportions so as not only to find the answer but to enjoy the game and be arrogant at one's own skill. But this riddle was nothing but silence, and its was the arrogance, to judge from its nose; and if it had a human head it was nothing for such as he, let him be ever so clear-headed.

To begin with: what sex was it, male or female? The people called it Hor in the Mountain of Light and took it for an image of the sun lord, as Thutmose had done not long before. But that was a modern interpretation, it had not always obtained, and even if it were the sun lord who manifested himself in the recumbent figure — that proved nothing as to its sex. As it lay there, one could not tell. Suppose it got up, would it then have majestic dangling testicles like Merwer at On — or would it reveal itself as female, as a lion virgin? There was no answer. For if at some time or other it had produced itself forth out of the rock, it had been as an artist makes a lying picture, or actually not makes but represents it, so that what was not visible was not there; and let a hundred masons come with hammer and chisel to question the monster of its sex, there would be no answer still.

It was a sphinx, in other words a mystery and a riddle — and certainly a savage one, with lion's paws, thirsting after young blood, dangerous to the child of God and a snare to the descendants of the promise. Alas for the tablet of the king's son! At this rocky breast, between the claws of the dragon-woman, one dreamed no promise-dreams — or at least very meagre ones came to pass. It had nothing to do with promise; wide-eyed and cruel, with time-gnawn nose, fixed in vacant immobility, it gazed across at its river, and its menacing riddle was not of such a kind. It endured drunkenly on into the future, but that future was wild and dead for that it was mere endurance and false eternity, bare of expectancy.

Joseph stood there and tried his heart upon the voluptuously smiling majesty of that endurance. He stood quite close . . . would not the monster lift its paw from the sand and snatch the youth to its breast? He armed his heart and thought of Jacob. Curiosity is a shallow-rooted

weed; it is but youth triumphing in freedom. Eye to eye
with the forbidden, one knows the sonhood of the spirit
and holds with the father.

Joseph stood long under the stars before the giant
riddle, leaning on one leg, his elbow in one hand, his chin
in the other. When he lay again with Kedema in the hut,
he dreamed of the sphinx, that it said to him: " I love
thee. Come to me and name me thy name, of whatever
sex I am! " But he answered: " How shall I commit such
a deed and sin against God? "

THE HOUSE OF THE SWADDLED ONE

THEY had gone along the western bank, the one on their
right as they faced south and the right one in any case.
For they needed not to cross over to reach Mempi the
great, which itself lay in the west — the hugest sheep-
fold of men that Rachel's first-born had ever seen. Above
it towered the heights where stone was quarried and
where the city buried its dead.

Bewilderingly ancient was Mempi, and venerable in so
far as the two ideas coincide. Meni, the first king, he
who stood at the beginning of all memories and dynasties,
had fortified the city to keep out the subjugated lower
land. The mighty dwelling of Ptah, built out of eternal
stone, was Meni's work; accordingly it had stood here
much longer than the pyramids — had stood here since
days behind which no man could look.

But there was no rigidity nor torpor here; the primitive and ancient presented itself in Mempi's image as
a scene of bustling life and alert modernity; a city of
more than a hundred thousand souls and composed in its

great extent of many variously named quarters — a confusion of narrow winding streets going uphill and down,
all sloping toward their centres, where waste water ran
in a drain. They reeked and seethed with trade and traffic, and hordes of grubbing and garrulous little men.
There were the smiling quarters of the rich, where villas
with beautiful gates lay enclosed in lovely gardens; there
were green temple precincts, where pennants fluttered and
halls bright with delicate colour were mirrored in sacred
pools. There were sphinx-avenues fifty ells broad, and
tree-bordered drives on which the wagons of the great
rolled along, drawn by fiery steeds crowned with bunches
of feathers. They were heralded by panting runners who
cried out: " Abrek! " " Take thy heart to thyself! "
"Take care! "

Yes, " Abrek! " Joseph too might well say it to himself and take heed to his heart so as not to fall victim to
idle admiration before all that elegance and distinction.
For this was Mempi or Menfe, as the people said here,
pertly abbreviating the name from Men-nefru-Mire,
which signified " The beauty of Mire abides." Mire was
a king of the sixth dynasty, who in his time had extended
the temple fortress about his royal quarters and built
close by the pyramid wherein his beauty was to abide. It
had actually been the tomb that had been called Men-
nefru-Mire; but the whole city overlapping it had taken
over the name of the burial place: Menfe, the balance of
the lands, the royal city of the dead.

How strange it was that the name Menfe was an im-
pertinent abbreviation for a place of tombs! The idea
occupied Joseph's mind a good deal. It was these little
people thronging the narrow streets, with the gutters in

the middle, who had run it all together like that; these
lean-ribbed dwellers in the crowded poorer quarters of
the town. In one such quarter was the caravanserai where
the Ishmaelites lodged. It was crammed with strange
specimens of the human race, Syrian, Libyan, Nubian,
Mitannic, and even Cretan; its dirty brick court was full
of the bleating of animals and the squealing and whining
of blind beggars playing on musical instruments. If
Joseph issued forth, the street scene was like that in the
cities of the homeland as well, only Egyptian and much
magnified. On either side of the gutter barbers were
shaving their customers, and cobblers pulling straps with
their teeth. Potters turned their whirling vessels and
shaped them with practised and earthy hands, singing the
while songs to Khnum the creator, goat-headed lord of
the wheel. Coffin-makers planed coffins in human shape
with chin-beards; drunken men staggered out of noisy
pot-houses and were jeered at and mocked by little boys
whose youth-locks still hung over their ears. What hordes
of people! They all wore the same linen apron and the
same hair-cut; had the same square shoulders and thin
arms and lifted their brows in one and the same naïve and
unabashed way. They looked quite capable of shortening
the pomp and circumstance of death into the brisk and
sprightly " Menfe." Joseph, when he heard it, recalled
the feelings that possessed him when once, from his hill-
top home, he looked down on Hebron, the burial-place
of his ancestors, and piety, whose source is death, had
mingled in his heart with the appeal made by the sight
of the bustling town. A complex and delightful mixture,
and one peculiarly his own. He felt its mysterious fitness
in the light of the double blessing whose child he was.

And also in the light of the jesting spirit which might be regarded as the link and messenger between them. To this latter, then, corresponded the popular name for the city of the dead; as a message from the jesting spirit; he felt his heart warm toward its inventors, those lean-ribbed little people along the gutters. He wanted to joke with them in their own tongue, to laugh and lift his eye-brows with their unconcern — that would not be hard.

Likewise he saw with sympathy that their love of the jest did not come from numbers alone, nor did it direct itself entirely outwards. The people of Menfe were making fun of themselves when they laughed about what their city once had been and was no longer. And their joke was an expression of the same sullenness which Joseph had felt in Per-Sopd when he listened to the bitter carping of the temple priests. It was the mood of the outmoded and the superseded; but here it turned into a mockery which misdoubted all the world, including itself. For the fact was, Menfe, the balance of the lands, thick-walled, had been the royal city at the time of the pyramid-builders. Menfe had been world-famous for endless years, and Thebes, in the upper southlands had not been known at all. But after the accursed epoch of confusion and foreign domination, it was from Thebes that liberation came, and reunion under the now ruling dynasty of the sun. It was Wese that now wore the double crown and bore the sceptre; while Menfe, though bursting with population and no smaller than before, was a former queen, the grave of her own greatness, a capital whose name was an impudently abbreviated name of death.

Not that Ptah, in his chapel, was a god rejected and

impoverished, like Sopd in the east. No, great was his name among the regions, and rich in foundations, lands, and cattle was the god in human shape. So much was plain, from the treasuries, granaries, stalls, and hayricks included in the complex of his temples. The lord Ptah was seen of no one — for even when he made a progress in his bark and visited one or other local divinity, his little image was hidden behind golden curtains and only the priests who performed his service knew his face. He dwelt in his house, together with his wife, called Sakhmet or the Mighty, who was depicted lion-headed on the temple walls and who was said to love war, and their son Nefertem, whose name signified "the beautiful," but who was even more obscure than Ptah the human-formed and Sakhmet the grim. He was the son, more one knew not, nor did Joseph learn more by questioning than this: that Nefertem the son wore a lotus blossom on his head. It was even asserted that he himself was nothing else than a blue water-lily. This vagueness, however, did not prevent the son from being the most popular person of the Triad of Menfe. Since all that was certain about him was his preference for the sky-blue lotus, that became the essence of his being, and thus his dwelling was always richly adorned with bunches of that beautiful flower. The Ishmaelites did not hesitate to honour his popularity, in the way of trade, by bringing him offerings of the blue lotus.

Never had Joseph been so much among forbidden things as here, those things to which his tradition referred when it said: "Thou shalt make to thyself no graven image." For Ptah was the god who created works of art, the protector of masons and craftsmen, of whom it was said that the plans of his heart were realized and his thoughts carried out. Ptah's great dwelling was nothing but pictures; full of images his house and the courts thereof. Hewn out of the hardest, or out of lime and sandstone, wood and copper, the thoughts of Ptah peopled his halls; columns thick with shining scenes, resting on bases like millstones, elephant-like, and crowned with capitals like bundles of reeds, rose up to the gold-dusted beams. Statues were everywhere, standing, sitting, striding, embraced on thrones with their diminutive children; single images of kings with caplike crowns and crooked staves, the pleated front piece of their kilts spread out on their laps; head-cloths with wings falling on the shoulders, on the front of which their ears stood out. These broad-shouldered, narrow-hipped lords of the earth had tender breasts, their hands lay flat on their thighs, their mien was high and grave. And their muscular upper arms were held by the clumsy little fingers of a tutelary goddess, while a falcon spread its wings in the nape of their necks. King Mire, who had made the city great, paced on his staff, a figure in copper, with his disproportionately small son at his side. He was fleshy of nose and lips; and like the other images was reluctant to lift from the ground the sole of his rear foot, but trod on both soles, standing in his walk and walking in his stance. They trod on sturdy legs, with heads erect, away from the stone pilasters at the back of their pedestals, and let their arms hang down from their square shoulders. In their clenched fists they held short, cylindrical cones. Or they were represented as scribes, legs tucked under them, hands busy with the work spread out in their laps, looking out over it with shrewd eyes. Sometimes

there was a man and wife, sitting beside each other with
knees together, with their skin, hair, and garments painted
in the most natural colours, so that they were like the
living dead. Often Ptah's artists had made them eyes
to frighten the beholder — not out of the material of
their faces, but separately put in: a little black stone set
in vitreous paste, with a little silver peg inside that which
caught the light and glittered until one felt impelled to
escape that flashing gaze and hid one's face in one's
hands.

Such were the thoughts of Ptah. For ever fixed and
rigid they dwelt there in his house, along with him, the
lion mother, and the lotus son. He himself appeared in
his human shape a hundred times over, in his chapel
shrine, not an inch on whose walls but was covered with
the magic of art. Yes, certainly in human shape, yet
oddly doll-like and as it were in abstract form, a side
view, with one leg and one long eye; his head covered
with a close-fitting cap, on his chin the artificially attached wedge of the kingly beard. His whole figure was
curiously undeveloped, sketched in outline as were
his fists, which held the staff of power before him. He
seemed to be sheathed in a close, formless upper garment, or rather, quite frankly, he looked swaddled and
embalmed. . . . What was it about the lord Ptah? How
did it stand with him? Did the ancient great city deserve
its name, not only on account of the pyramids after
which it was called, and not only because its glory was
of the past, but further and finally, even solely, as the
house of the lord Ptah? Joseph had understood whither
he was bound when his purchasers led him down into
Egypt, the land of Jacob's misprision. He had fully

recognized that in consequence of his own estate he belonged thither and that the forbidden was not forbid to him, but even oddly appropriate. Indeed, had he not betimes given himself a name which should characterize him as native-born? And yet he had constantly felt a grudge against his new surroundings, in the sense of his father, and always he itched to try the children of the land with questions about their gods and about the land of Egypt itself, that they might betray it to him who knew and also themselves when they seemed not to know it rightly.

So was it with master baker Bata of Menfe, whom they met at the Apis-sacrifice in the temple of Ptah.

For besides the formless one, the lioness, the obscure son, and the concrete thoughts of Ptah, there abode in the temple Hapi, the great bull, the " repeating birth " of the lord, begot by a light-ray from the sky upon a cow which afterwards never bore again; and his testicles dangled as massive as those of Merwer at On. He lived behind bronze doors at the back of a roofless columned hall where wainscotings filled with magnificent stonework ran between the pillars and fine mouldings at half their height. A dense crowd thronged the flag-paven court, when Hapi was brought forward by his servants some paces out of the lamplit twilight of his chapel stall that the people might see that the god lived and bring him offerings.

Joseph with his owners witnessed one such ceremony: it was an extraordinary abomination and an amusing one as well, thanks to the good nature of the folk of Menfe, men and women and sprawling children. They were excited by the festival and their expectation of the god;

chattered and laughed, " kissed " (as they said for ate)
sycamore figs and onions; water dripped from the corners of their mouths from the watermelon slices they ate;
and they chaffered with the hucksters who lined the court
selling consecrated bread, sacrificial fowl, frankincense,
honey, and flowers.

A fat-bellied man in bast sandals stood next the
Ishmaelites, and as the crowd squeezed them together,
they spoke with each other. He wore a knee-length apron
skirt of coarse linen with a three-cornered turnover;
about his arms and rump he had wound all sorts of ribbons in which he tied knots with pious intent. His hair
lay short and smooth on his round pate, he had a good-natured face, and his glassy protruding eyeballs protruded
still more when his well-formed shaven mouth moved
as he talked. He measured the old man and his company
from one side for a long time before he addressed them
and questioned them, curious of their strangeness, whence
they came and whither they went. He himself was a
baker, he explained; that is, he did not bake with his
own hands and stuck not his head in the oven, but employed half a dozen journeymen and distributors who
carried his excellent rolls and crescents in baskets on
their heads through the city. Woe to these if they did
not take pains to wave their arms above their wares so
that the birds of the air did not pounce down and steal
out of the basket! The bread-carrier to whom this happened " got a lesson," as master baker Bata expressed
himself. That was his name. Also he possessed some
ground outside the city where he grew the corn he baked.
But it was not enough, for his business was considerable
and he had to buy as well. Today he had come out to

see the god, which was profitable in so far that it was not profitable to omit it. His wife, meanwhile, was visiting the Great Mother in the Eset-house and taking her flowers, being especially affected to that goddess; while he, Bata, got more satisfaction from coming here. And as for them, the baker asked, they were visiting the country for their business interests?

That was it, the old man responded. And they were, so to speak, at their goal, in that they were at Menfe, mighty in gates, rich in dwellings and enduring monuments; and might just as well now turn round again.

" Thanks very much," said the master baker. They could, but probably they would not; for like everybody else they would more likely regard this old hole as a stage where to set their feet that they might pass on to the splendours of Amun. They would be the first to do otherwise, the first travellers whose goal was not Weset, the brand-new, Pharaoh's city — might he live, thrive, and be healthy! — where men and treasure streamed together and where Menfe's weather-beaten name was good enough to be used for titles by Pharaoh's courtiers and head eunuchs; for instance the head baker of the god, he who had oversight over the palace baking, was called Prince of Menfe, and perhaps with some justice. At least so much was true, that at Menfe fine cakes in the shape of cows and snakes were carried round and sold when the Amun-city was still content to bolt down roasted corn.

The old man replied that, well, yes, they would probably go to Weset after a considerable sojourn at Menfe: to cast an eye and see how far it had come on since then in the refinements of life and the development of bake-stuffs.

He was interrupted by a roll of drums; the rear gate opened and the god was led into the court, only a few paces forward from the open doors. The excitement of the crowd was great. " Hapi! Hapi! " they shrieked, as they hopped on one leg, and whom the crush permitted threw himself on his face and kissed the earth. Many backs were so bent, the air was full of the throaty mewing of the sound with which the hundredfold utterance of the god's name began. It was likewise the name of the river, which had made the land and which preserved it. It was the name of the sun-bull, the abstract of all the powers of fertility, on which these people knew themselves to depend, the name of the continued existence of land and folk, the name of life. They were deeply moved, light and garrulous though they might be, for their adoration was compact of all the hope and anxiousness with which narrowly conditioned existence fills the breast. They thought of the flood, which must not be an ell too high or too low if the land was to survive; of the industry of their wives and the health of their children; of their own body and its functions subject to reverses, which gave them comfort and pleasure when all went well but caused hard suffering when they gave out, and which must be safeguarded by magic against magic. They thought of the enemies of the land, south, east, and west; of Pharaoh, whom also they called the "Strong Bull" and who they knew was cherished and preserved in the palace at Thebes just as Hapi here, for that he protected them and formed in his transitory person the bridge between them and him on whom all depended. " Hapi! Hapi! "

they cried in anxious jubilation, oppressed by the sense
of their narrowly conditioned, precarious lives. Hope-
fully they stared at the square forehead of the beast-god,
the brazen horns, the compact neck-line, without a curve
from back to skull; at his sex organs, that pledge of fruitfulness. " Security! " was what they meant by their cry.
" Protection and permanence! " " Up Egypt! "

Vastly beautiful was Ptah's " repeating birth." And
no wonder; for experts spent years searching for the
finest specimen between the marshes of the Delta and the
Elephant Isle. He was black; and his blackness set off
in great, not to say godlike splendour the scarlet *sha-
bracke* on his back. A bald-headed servitor, in an apron
of pleated gold stuff which left the navel free in front
and reached behind half-way up the back, held him on
either side by a gold cord. The one on the right hand
lifted the cover a little before the eyes of the people to
display the white spot on Hapi's flank, in which one was
supposed to recognize the sign of the crescent moon. A
priest, down whose back hung a leopard-fell together
with the claws and tail, came and made obeisance. Then
he stood with one leg before the other and held out the
incense vessel on a pole toward the bull, who lowered
his head, sniffed, and blew out his thick moist nostrils
as the smoke tickled them. He sneezed mightily; the
crowd redoubled its acclaim and hopped still more joyously on one leg. Harp-players knelt, with their faces
turned heavenwards, sang and played, while behind them
other singers clapped out the time, during the offering
of the incense. There were women too, temple maidens
with unbound hair. One of them always naked and with
a girdle for all covering above the swelling hips; the

second in a long garment, fine like a veil, that stood open in front and likewise showed all her youth. Pacing the scene in dance, they shook sistra and tambourines above their heads, stretching and lifting their legs astonishingly high from the hips. A priest-reader sitting at the feet of the bull with his face to the crowd began to chant a text out of his roll, nodding his head in time, while the people joined in the refrain: " Hapi is Ptah. Hapi is Re. Hapi is Hor, the son of Eset! " After that appeared another priest, bald-headed and of haughty mien, obviously of high rank for he was escorted by bearers holding feather fans and wore a wide batiste apron held on with shoulder-straps. He came on in a sort of dextrous crawl, one leg far out behind him, the other, balanced on its toes, tucked up beneath.

Hapi paid no heed. He was used to all these ceremonial offerings; to an existence of stately boredom which, thanks to a certain bodily constitution, was become his melancholy lot in life. He stood there straddle-legged, and looked loweringly with his little bloodshot bull-eyes out over the ministrant's head at the populace, skipping and hopping, one hand on their breasts, the other stretched toward him, as they cried out his holy name. They were so glad to see him held with golden strands, in the safe custody of the temple, hemmed round by ministering guardians. He was their god and their prisoner. And it was his imprisonment, the security it afforded them, that gave rise to their exultation and made them jump about; and perhaps he looked so lowering and evilly upon them because he realized that despite all the honours and ceremony they did not mean so well by him after all.

Master-baker Bata did not jump about, on account of his corpulence. But he joined in the responses with a powerful voice and repeatedly saluted the god, prostrating himself and raising his arm, visibly pleased by the spectacle.

"The sight of him does one good," he declared to his neighbour. "It strengthens the spirits and restores one's confidence in life. My experience is that I need to eat nothing more the whole day when I have seen Hapi, for it is like a hearty meal of beef in all my limbs. I am full and sleepy; I take a nap and awake as one new-born. He is a very great god, the living representative of Ptah. You must know that his grave awaits him in the West, the command hath gone out that in death he shall be swaddled and embalmed in the most costly manner with good resin and bands of royal linen and laid to rest in the city of the dead according to custom in the eternal house of the god-bull. So it is commanded," he said, "and so it will be. Already two Usar-Hapis rest in stone coffins in their eternal home in the West."

The old man gave a glance at Joseph which the latter took as encouragement to test the man with a question. He said:

"Ask the man to explain to you why he says that Usar-Hapi's eternal home awaits him in the West; because it is not the West where it waits, but Menfe, city of the living, itself lies on the west bank, and no dead ferries across the water."

"This youth," the old man turned to the baker, "asks thus and thus. Will you give him answer?"

"I spoke as they speak," responded the Egyptian, "and took no thought of the phrase, and so do we all.

The West, that is the city of the dead, according to our speech. But it is true that Menfe's dead travel not across the river as elsewhere, but the city of the living lies also and already in the West. According to reason your youth is right with his objection. But according to our speech I spoke correctly."

"Ask him this too," said Joseph. "If Hapi, the beautiful bull, is the living Ptah for the living, what then is Ptah in his chapel?"

"Ptah is great," answered the baker.

"Tell him I do not doubt that," Joseph replied. "But Hapi is called Usar-Hapi when he has died; and again Ptah in his bark is Usir and called in human form because the figure has the form with the chin-beard, on which the joiners work, and he seems swaddled. What is he then?"

"Instruct your youth," said the baker to the old man, "that the priest enters daily to Ptah and opens his mouth with a powerful instrument that he may eat and drink, and renews daily for him the paint of life upon his cheeks. That is the service and the cherishing."

"And now I would ask, with all due politeness," Joseph continued, "what about the dead before his burial, when Anpu stands behind him, and wherein for instance the service may consist which the priest practises on the mummy?"

"Does he not even know that, your youth?" answered the baker. "It is plain that he is a sand-dweller, wholly foreign and a new-comer in the land. The service, so I would have him told, consists in the so-called opening of the mouth, above all. It is called that because the priest therewith opens the mouth with a special staff that the god may eat and drink again and enjoy the edible offerings. Therefore is it that the priest of the dead, in sign that the dead like Usir will live again, puts the blush of rouge on the mummy for a consolation to the hearts of the mourners."

"I hear with gratitude," Joseph said. "This then is the difference between the service of the gods and that of the dead. But now ask the lord Bata wherewithal one builds in the land of Egypt."

"Your youth," answered the baker, "is good to look upon but somewhat stupid. We build for the living with Nile bricks. But the abodes of the dead are of everlasting stone."

"I hear," Joseph answered again, "with many thanks. But if of two things the same holds, then they are like and one may interchange them unreproved. The graves of Egypt are temples, but the temples — "

"Are houses of God," finished the baker.

"You have said it. The dead of Egypt are gods; and your gods — what are they?"

"The gods are great," replied Bata the baker. "I feel it in the fullness and fatigue which steal over me now I have seen Hapi. I will go home and lay myself down to the sleep of new birth. Also my wife will have come back from waiting on the Great Mother. Be healthy, ye strangers. Rejoice and rest in peace!"

With that he went. But the old man said to Joseph:

"The man was worn out with God; thou shouldest not have pressed him through my mouth with petty questionings."

"But must not," the other justified himself, "thy slave inform himself that he may find himself with understanding of life in Egypt, where thou wilt leave him and he will abide? Strange and novel enough is everything here for the youth. For the children of Egypt worship in tombs, whether they be called temples or eternal dwellings; but we at home worship after the custom of our fathers beneath the green trees. Shall not one laugh and ponder at thought of these children? They call Hapi the living form of Ptah, and such, it seems to me, Ptah can use, as he himself is certainly embalmed and is a corpse. But they rest not until they have also wrapped up the living form and made out of it an Osiris and godmummy; until then there is something wrong about it. But I like Menfe itself, whose dead need not to travel across the water because it already lies in the West — this great city so full of people, who so blithely make a nickname of its solemn form. It is a pity that the house of blessing before which you will bring me, Petepre the fan-bearer's house, lieth not at Menfe, for it pleaseth me among the cities of Egypt."

"Thou art much too unripe," the old man answered him, "to distinguish what is good for thee. But I know, and procure it for thee like a father. For such I evidently am to thee, assuming that thy mother is the grave. Tomorrow early we take ship and sail nine days long through the land of Egypt, southwards up the river, that we may set our feet on the shining shore of Weset-per-Amun, the royal city."

3

THE ARRIVAL

RIVER JOURNEY

" SHINING in Swiftness " was the name of the boat on which the Ishmaelites embarked with their animals, after providing themselves from the booths at the landing-place with food for nine days' travel. The name was written on both sides of its goose-head prow. And the empty boast was characteristic of the country, for it was the clumsiest freighter to be found anywhere on Menfe's landing-places; with a bellying hold built for cargo space, latticed wooden weather-boards, a cabin consisting only of a mat-covered shelter opening forward, and a tiny but very heavy rudder fastened perpendicularly to a pole at the stern.

The pilot was named Thot-nofer. He was a man from the north, in ear-rings, with white hair on head and breast. The old man had made his acquaintance at the hostel and covenanted with him for a cheap passage. Thot-nofer's ship carried lumber, one bale of royal and one of coarse linen, papyrus, neatskins, ship's rope, twenty sacks of lentils, and thirty casks of dried fish. " Shining in Swiftness " also had on board the portrait statue of a rich burgher of Thebes, standing quite forward at the peak, done up in slats and sacking. It was for the " good house " — in other words, for the grave — of the man who had ordered it, west of the river. It would be set up as issuing from an imitation door to behold his ever-lasting goods and the representations of his daily life painted on the walls. To be sure, the eyes by which he might do this were not yet set, the figure was not yet coloured with the tints of life, and the stick was lacking that should go through the fist extended along the slant-wise front of his projecting skirt. But its model had set store by having at least his double chin and his thick legs executed in the rough under the eyes of Ptah and by the hand of Ptah's artists; the last touches might be given in some workshop in Thebes, the city of the dead.

At midday the crew untied the ship from the pile and raised the patched brown sail, which at once filled with the strong north wind. The pilot sitting on the slanting beak in the stern of the boat began to operate the rudder with the perpendicular lever; a man at the goose-head in the prow tested the channel with a pole; while Thot-nofer, the ship-master, propitiated the gods by burning in front of the cabin some of the resin with which the Ishmaelites had paid their fares. Thus the boat bearing Joseph moved upstream, curving fore and aft and cutting the water only with the middle of her keel; while the old man, sitting with his party on the lumber piled behind the cabin, extended himself in observations on the wis-dom of life; how almost always the advantages so equal-lized and cancelled each other that the result was a moderate perfection, not too good and not too bad. Thus one travelled upstream against the current; but on the other hand the wind came regularly from the north and swelled the sail to advantage so that the two contrary forces resulted in moderate progress. Of course, it was all very fine, sailing downstream, for one could let oneself be borne by it. But it was easy for the boat to get out of hand, it might go crosswise of the stream and give no end of trouble with the steering to avoid accidents. Thus in life the advantages were always balanced by the disadvantages and vice versa, and the result, mathematically, might seem to be nil; but in practice it was a wise balance and an average felicity; in view of which neither jubilation nor cursing but real satisfaction was in place. For perfection consisted not in one-sided heaping up of advantages until life became impossible on the other. Rather it consisted in the mutual cancellation of disadvantage and advantage, and the result was called contentment.

So the old man, with uplifted finger and head on one side. His people listened open-mouthed, but exchanged abashed and sulky looks, as ordinary people do when listening unwillingly to the claims of the higher life. Nor did Joseph give more than half an ear to the old man's prosing; for he was rejoicing in the new experience of the water journey, the fresh wind, the melodious chuckling of the waves against the bow, the gentle rocking and gliding on the wide river, whose tide came sparkling toward him as once to Eliezer the earth, upon his travels. The shore afforded a changing succession of gay or luxuriant or sacred scenes; pillared halls often stood on the banks, sometimes with palm groves before them, but just as often stone roads built by men, belonging to the temples of the city. Villages glided past, with high dove-cotes and green orchards; and again gay and splendid cities with spires glittering golden to the sun, and pennanted gates. Pairs of statues of enormous size sat stately and rigid with their hands on their knees and gazed from the bank across the river and the land, into the desert. Sometimes it was all quite close, and then far away; for they moved at times in the centre of a river whose waters had widened to a lake; or again wound in curves behind which new scenes of Egypt unfolded. But life on the sacred river itself, the great highway of Egypt, was hugely diverting. How many sails, fine and coarse, swelled in the wind, how many rudders stemmed themselves in its flood! The carrying air was full of voices: the jokes and halloos of sailors, the warning cries of the polesmen at the prow as the boat approached eddies and sandbanks; the chanting calls of seamen on the cabin roofs to sailors and pilots below. Common boats like Thot-nofer's there were in hordes; but also fine slender barks met and hailed " Shining in Swiftness " or overtook her. They were painted blue, with a short mast and a broad dove-coloured sail, which bellied in a charming swell; their beaks were shaped like the lotus flower and they had dainty pavilions instead of a rude board cabin. The temple barks had purple sails and large pictures painted on the side; the private yachts of the great and mighty boasted twelve oarsmen on a side, and on the deck a pillared pleasure-house with the owner's luggage and chariot stowed on the roof. Its walls were formed by splendid carpets, and in it sat the lordly owner, hands in his lap, fixed, as it were congealed, in beauty and richness and looking neither right nor left. They even met a funeral procession of three ships fastened together, and on the rear one, a white bark without rudder or sail, the bright-coloured Osiris, head to the prow, lay amongst his mourners, on a lion-footed bier.

Yes, there was much to see, on river and shore. Joseph, on whom the joys of a water journey had never smiled before, on such a one as this now found the days pass like hours. He was to grow used indeed to this kind of travel and to this very stretch between Amun's house and grave-jesting Menfe! Very like these mighty ones in their carpet-hung chapels he himself would one day sit, with the prescribed and stately immobility which he would have to learn because the common folk expected it from gods and great ones. For he was to bear himself so shrewdly and prove himself so skilled in his dealings with God as to become the first among those of the West and entitled to sit there looking neither right nor left. This was reserved for him. But meanwhile he looked right and left all he could round about in the land and the life of the land, to take it into his spirit and senses, always mindful lest his curiosity should express itself in amazement and futility instead of keeping a certain due and blithe reserve for the father's sake.

Thus the evening and morning were another day and so the days increased. Menfe lay behind them, and the day when they sailed hence. The sun sank down, the desert distance turned violet-blue; the Arabian sky on their left gave back a softened glow from the extravagant orange of the western, Libyan sky. Where they found themselves at nightfall they tied up and slept, to float on next day. The wind favoured them, with exception of the days when it fell. Then they had to row, and the slave Usarsiph, also the younger Ishmaelites, helped at the

oars; for the boat had no large crew, and Thot-nofer was
anxious not to lose time, for he had promised to deliver
the statue by a certain date. They were in fact not greatly
delayed; for when the wind blew, it filled the sails the
fuller, and thus advantage and disadvantage were resolved in satisfaction. On the ninth evening they saw
some jagged heights rising rosy and translucent in the
distance. They looked like red corundum, and very
beautiful, though, as everyone knew, they were barren
and accursed like all the mountains of Egypt. The pilot
and the old man recognized them as Amun's mountains,
the heights of No; and when they had slept and sailed
again and even taken in sheer impatience to the oars —
at last they saw it, it came nearer, Pharaoh's famous city,
glittering with gold, greeting their eyes with shimmering
rainbow colours. They entered it while still on the boat
and without going on shore, for the river became a
splendid boulevard and flowed between rows of celestial
structures, of temples and palaces amid green gardens of
delight; all this both right and left, on the shore of life
as well as on the shore of death. There were papyrus
colonnades and lotus colonnades, gold-tipped obelisks,
colossal statues, turreted gates with sphinx avenues leading to them from the bank. Their doors and flag-poles
were gilded, and light flashed from them that dazzled
the eyes, till the painted scenes and inscriptions on the
buildings, the cinnamon red, the plum-colour, the emer-
ald green, the ochre yellow, and the azure blue all swam
together into one confused sea of colour.

"That is Ipet-Isowet, 'Amun's Great House,'" said
the old man to Joseph, pointing with his finger. "It has
a hall fifty ells wide, with fifty-two columns and pillars

like tent-poles, and the hall itself, if it please thee, is paved with silver."

"Surely it pleaseth me," Joseph answered. "I knew, of course, that Amun is a very rich god."

"Those are the shipyards of the god," said the old man again, pointing to the basins and dry-docks on the left, where numerous apron-wearers, the god's carpenters, were at work with drills, hammers, and picks on skeletons of ships. "There is Pharaoh's temple of the dead and there his house of life," said he and pointed here and there westwards into the land to various blocks of buildings in character both magnificent and charming at once. "That is Amun's southern house of women," turning toward the other side to point out an expanse of temple precincts on the bank. The sun glared against their façades, the shadows cast by their projections were sharp and black. Hordes of men were bustling about, engaged in building-activities.

"Dost thou see this beauty? Dost thou see the shrine of the mystery of the kingly conception? Dost thou see where Pharaoh buildeth another hall in front of the hall and the court, with taller columns than all the rest? That, my friend, is Nowet-Amun, the proud, which we see. Observe then the ram avenue that runneth from the southern house of women to the great house. Five thousand ells long is it, let me tell thee, bordered right and left with Amun-rams bearing Pharaoh's image between their legs."

"All very nice," said Joseph.

"Nice!" said the old man, firing up. "Thou choosest me words out of the treasury of speech so inept as to be comic, I must say. Thou hast pleased me little indeed with thy response to the marvels of Weset."

" I did say *very* nice," replied Joseph. " As nice as thou wilt. But where is the house of the fan-bearer before which thou wilt bring me? Canst thou show it to me from here? "

" No, that one cannot make out from here," responded the elder. " It lieth toward the western desert, where the city thinneth out, losing itself in villas and lordly gardens."

" And wilt thou take me even today before the house? "

" Thou canst not well expect that I shall take thee thither and sell thee? Dost thou know then that the steward of the house will take thee and offer enough for thee that I am paid for my outgo and get a little just profit therefrom? It is some changes of the moon since I released thee out of thy mother the well and some days that thou hast baked me pancakes and fetched new words out of thy storehouse to wish me good-night. So that it may be the time has grown long to thee and thou weariest of us and would seek new service. Yet it might as well have been that the many days had made habit with thee, so that thou couldst not lightly part from thy rescuer, the old Minæan from Ma'on, but be content to wait the hour till he goeth away and leaveth thee in the hands of strangers. Either of these might issue out of the many days of our wandering together."

" The latter," answered Joseph, " quite incontestably the latter is the reality. Of a surety I am in no haste to part from thee, my deliverer. My only haste is that I may arrive whither God will have me."

"Content thyself," replied the old man. "We will land and submit ourselves to the troublesome formalities which the children of Egypt lay upon us, and which will take a long time. After that we will go to a hostel that I know in the city's heart, and there spend the night. But tomorrow I will bring thee before the house of blessing and offer thee to my friend the house-steward, Mont-kaw."

﹐While they were talking they had come to port, or rather to the place where the boat should tie up, crossing over from the middle of the stream while Thot-nofer burned more balsam in front of the cabin, as a thank-offering for their safe journey. The landing was as troublesome and time-consuming as only such journeys anywhere ever were or are. They came into the noise and bustle of the landing-stage and the water in front of it, where there was a congestion of ships native and foreign either already tied up or looking for a landing-place to fling their rope when a post was free. "Shining in Swift-ness" was docked by the port authorities and customs officials, who began to make entries of great and small, of mice and men, and every piece of freight, while on shore the servants of the owner of the statue stretched out their arms and shrieked their demands for its delivery. There were many pedlars of sandals, caps, and honey cakes; their cries mingled with the bleating of herds being un-shipped close by and the music of jugglers trying to call attention to themselves on the quay. It was a vast con-fusion; Joseph and his companions sat still and shrinking on the lumber at the stern of their boat and awaited the moment when they could get off and seek their hostel. But it was still remote. The old man had to come before the customs in person, to vouch for himself and each of his party and pay the harbour dues for his wares. He was shrewd enough to establish human relations instead of official ones; so that the authorities laughed and joked, accepted small presents, and were not too precise about the landing rules for stranger merchants. A few hours after they had tied up, the owners of Joseph were able to lead their camels across the gang-plank and, quite unnoticed by a crowd used to the sight of any and every complexion and costume, to make their way through the mingled tumult of the port quarter.

JOSEPH GOES THROUGH WESE

THE EGYPTIAN city whose name the Greeks later adapted for their own convenience and called it Thebai was, when Joseph landed and lived there, by no means at the height of its fame, although already famous, as can be gathered from the way the Ishmaelites spoke of it and the feelings Joseph entertained when he found himself at his journey's end. From dark and small beginnings in the long-ago, it had waxed and was on the way to full splendour. Yet much still lacked before its glory was complete and it paused perfected, one of the seven wonders of the world. It was this as a whole; but also and indeed principally in one of its parts, the unique and marvellous vast columned hall which a later Pharaoh, named Ramessu, or " The Sun hath begotten him," added to the group of buildings which composed the great Amuntemple in the north, at an expense commensurate with the renown of the god. Of this hall, then, Joseph's eyes beheld as little as they had of the departed glories in the environs of the pyramids, only on contrary grounds.

The hall had not yet achieved any presentness and no one
had yet had courage to imagine it. To make it possible,
something had to precede it, which then as men tired of it
and it could no longer satisfy their difficult imaginations
would be superseded by something else. There was, for
instance, the silver-paved hall of Ipet-Isowet, built by the
three predecessors of the present god. The old man knew
it, with its fifty-two columns like tent-poles. Or there was
the hall which Pharaoh himself, as Joseph had seen, was
having added to Amun's southern house of women, the
beautiful temple on the river; it excelled all the rest.
And this beauty must first be imagined and then realized
in the faith that it was the uttermost man could perform,
before man's insatiable imagination could use it as a
spring-hoard for the actually uttermost, the unsurpassable beauty of a final achievement — in other words, the
wonder of the world, the Great Hall of Rameses.

This, then, in Joseph's and our time, was not yet present, but only, as it were, on the way. None the less, Weset,
also called Nowet-Amun, chief city on the river Nile, was
even at this time a marvel to all the world both near and
far, wherever it was known. Report even exaggerated
the marvel, making it a point of honour and a convention,
as men love to do, if only by hearsay; so that a man
would have been looked at askance and considered outside the pale who had dared to doubt in public that No
in the land of Egypt was beautiful beyond word or measure, the abstract of all architectural magnificence and
simply a dream of a city. We come down to her, down in
a spatial sense — that is, with Joseph up the river — but
down in a temporal sense as well: namely, into the past
where at moderate depth Wese still lies, still glitters, still

resounds with the busy tumult of her streets, still mirrors
her temples clear and sharp in the stirless surface of her
sacred lakes. And coming thus, we must feel about Wese
a little as we did about Joseph himself when we first
glimpsed beside the fountain that form so besung and
belauded in saga and psalm. We traced back the fantastic legend of his loveliness to its source in the opinion
of his own time and found that, even discounting all
trumped-up exaggerations, quite enough remained of
beauty and of charm. So too with No, the heavenly city.
It was not compact of any supernal stuff, but built of
painted bricks mixed with straw, like any other city; its
streets, as Joseph noted with satisfaction, were as narrow,
crooked, foul, and ill-smelling as the streets of any man-
made city large or small ever have been and will be in
this part of the world. At least, they were so in the poorer
quarters, which as usual were much more numerous than
the richer sections, these indeed being most spacious and
charming. True, it was said and sung, even to the uttermost isles and the coasts beyond, that Wese's houses
" were rich in treasure," and in the temples they measured their gold with a scoop. But of such houses there
could be but a few, those which Pharaoh had enriched;
the great majority held no treasures at all, but were as
mean as those of the very island-dwellers and denizens
of the further coasts, who sunned themselves in the leg-
endary glory of Wese's fame.

As for the size of No, it passed for enormous, and it
was. That is, if we add that the word " enormous " has
not one simple, unequivocal meaning, but is a relative
conception, depending on who applies it and to what it is
applied. For instance, the chiefest monument of Wese's

greatness is a good example of the kind of misunder-standing which can arise. I refer to her reputation as the "city of a hundred gates." On Cyprus-Alashia, on Crete and places yet more remote, she was called in extrava-gant awe the "hundred-gated"; and it was related that forth from each of these hundred gates two hundred men with steed and harness might ride abreast to battle. Such prattle as this took for granted a ring wall so large round that it could be broken not by four or five but by a hundred city gates, an utterly childish conception, only possible to those who had never seen Wese with their mortal eyes but known it only from legend and hearsay. The Amun-city might with some justice have been called the "many-gated," for it had in fact many "gates." But these were not gates in the sense of sally-ports in the wall. The word referred to the pylons with which the wearers of the double crown had on the occasions of jubilees and great progresses from time to time adorned and comple-mented the shrines of the gods. For indeed of these there were very many, and mighty they were, shining and bright with the colours of their high reliefs and wonder-working inscriptions, blithe with pennants that fluttered above their gilded flag-staffs. And more were added, be-tween the time of which I write and the epoch of Wese's full and incomparable bloom. A hundred there were not, either now or later. But a hundred is only a round number; even on our own lips it often means no more than simply "very many." Amun's great dwelling in the north, Ipet-Isowet, had at this time six or seven such "gates" and the smaller temples near it, the houses of Khonsu, Mut, Mont, Min, and the hippopotamus-formed Ipet, had several. The other large temple on the river-

bank, known as Amun's southern house of women, otherwise simply the harem, had towered gates too, and still
others belonged to the smaller shrines of deities not actually indigenous here, yet settled and provided with nourishment: the houses of Usir and Eset, Ptah of Menfe,
Thoth, and many more.

These temple precincts, with their gardens, groves,
and lakes, formed the kernel of the city; they were the
city itself, and the dwellings of the profane and human
simply filled the spaces between, extending, that is, from
the port quarters on the south and Amun's house of
women to the temple complex in the north-east. Across
it lengthwise ran the great triumphal road of the god,
the ram-sphinx avenue which the old man had pointed out
to Joseph from the boat. It was a considerable area, and
five thousand ells in length. To the north-east the triumphal avenue curved landwards and the residential city
filled the widening space between it and the river; while
on the other side it spread out toward the eastern desert,
where it lost itself in fine gardens and villas — where indeed " the houses were rich in treasure." So that in actual fact the city was large, enormous if you like; more
than a hundred thousand people were said to live in it.
If a hundred was an exaggerated figure for the gates,
a sort of poetic licence, certainly on the other hand a
hundred thousand for the population of Wese erred on
the low side. If we may trust our own estimate and Joseph's, it was not only larger but very much larger, even
possibly double and treble that figure. Quite definitely
so, if one include the inhabitants of the city of the dead
over in the West, across the river, called " opposite their
lord "; not the dead, of course, but those living who

dwelt there for professional reasons, having some serious task, either ritual or mechanical, connected with the service of the departed who had gone over the water. These, then, and their dwellings were a city in themselves, which, added to the size of Wese, made the whole exceedingly large. And among them was Pharaoh himself, who did not live in the city of the living, but without in the West; on the edge of the desert, under its red rocks, there lay his palace in all its airy grace and there the pleasure-gardens of his palace, with their lake and pleasure-waters, which earlier had not been there.

A very great city, then — great not alone in its extent and the number of its inhabitants, but even more in the intensity of its inner life and the racial variegations which made it gay and lively like a country fair. Wese was great as kernel and focus of the world. It considered itself the navel of the world — a piece of presumption in Joseph's eyes, and even otherwise debatable. After all, there was Babel on the Euphrates, that flowed the other way; in Babel they were convinced that Egypt's stream flowed the wrong way; and they had no doubt that round about Bab-ilu the rest of the world was grouped in an admiring circle. Though there, too, in respect of building-activities they had not yet reached the fullness of beauty. But it was not without reason that they liked in Joseph's home to say of the Amun-city that " Nubians and Egyptians without number were their strength and folk from Punt and Libyans were their auxiliaries." Even on his way with the Ishmaelites from the port to the hostel which lay in the heart of the narrow inner city, Joseph received a hundred impressions which confirmed the legend. Nobody looked at him and his; strangers were the daily fare, and his companions were not crass enough in their strangeness to cause remark. He might gaze undisturbed, his only care being lest his spiritual pride be encroached upon by the sight of so great a world; fear of falling prey to diffidence made him look with reserve on what he saw.

And what all did he not see, on the way from the harbour to the inn! What treasures of merchandise swelled the bazaars! How the streets teemed and seethed with every kind and breed of the children of Adam! All the citizenry of Wese seemed to be on their legs, to be impelled to move from one end of the city to the other and back; while with these natives mingled human types and costumes from the four corners of the earth. By the landing-stage there had been a noisy crowd about a group of ebony-black Moors with incredibly thick, swollen lips, and ostrich feathers on their heads: men and animal-eyed women with breasts like wineskins and absurd children in baskets on their backs. The men were leading animals on chains: horribly whining panthers and baboons walking on all fours; a giraffe towered up, tall as a tree in front and like a horse behind. There were greyhounds too. And the Moors carried bundles covered with cloth of gold, whose contents doubtless corresponded to the value of the wrapping. Probably it was gold and ivory. These, Joseph learned, were a tribute-bearing mission from the land of Kush, southwards beyond the land of Wewet, far up the river. Only a very small, non-compulsory, and irregular tribute, sent by the governor of the southern lands, viceroy and prince of Kush, as a surprise for Pharaoh and to rejoice his heart, that he might be favourably mindful of the prince and not take it into his head to recall him and replace him by one of the gentlemen in the royal entourage who had been dinning in Pharaoh's ears at every levee that the holder of the valuable office up the river was quite unworthy of his charge. The strange thing was that these harbour hands who gaped at the embassy, these street gamins who laughed at the palm-tree neck of the giraffe, were perfectly informed about the inner history, the viceroy's anxiety and the carping of Pharaoh's courtier. Joseph and the Ishmaelites heard them comment on these things in loud and certain tones. A pity, thought Joseph, that sophistication must mar their pure and simple pleasure in the picturesque spectacle. But perhaps it only added spice. He himself was glad to hear their talk. It was good to get a side-light on such matters; to learn that the prince of Kush trembled for his office; that the courtiers intrigued against him; and that Pharaoh liked to be surprised. The knowledge strengthened his confidence and armed him against humility.

The Negroes, in charge of Egyptian officials, were ferried over the river to stand before Pharaoh; Joseph watched them go. More of their colour he saw as he made his way with his owners; but in fact he saw every shade of skin, from obsidian-black through all the tones of brown and yellow to cheese-white. He saw even yellow hair and bright blue eyes, faces and garments of every cut; he saw the human race. For the foreign ships with which Pharaoh traded very often did not stop in the ports of the Delta region but sailed with the north wind up-river to unload their tribute of freight and goods for exchange on the spot whither everything came at last: namely, Pharaoh's treasure-house, that he might there-

with enrich Amun and his friends, enabling the former
to enlarge his demands in respect of building-activities
and surpass anything previously built. As for the friends,
the gifts of Pharaoh refined their lives to the last degree,
making them so fastidious that from refinement they fell,
indeed, into foppery.

These things the old man explained to Joseph. And
thus it was Joseph saw, among the people of Wese, Moors
from Kush; Bedus from the land of God this side the Red
Sea; pale-faced Libyans from the oases of the western
desert, in gay woven skirts and plaits standing out
straight from their heads; Amu people and Asiatics like
himself in coloured woollens with the beards and noses
of his own land; Hattite men from beyond the Amanus
range, in tight shirts and with their hair in bags; Mitanni
traders in the dignified fringed and draped garb of
Babel; merchants and seafarers from the islands and
from Mycenæ, in white woollen robes with beautifully
falling folds, wearing bronze rings on their bare arms.
So much he saw, even though the old man modestly led
his troop as much as possible through the poorer streets
and avoided the finer quarters in order not to offend their
beauty. But it was not possible to spare them quite.
There was the beautiful street of Khonsu, which ran
parallel to the triumphal avenue of the god, "the Street
of the Son," as it was called. Khons, related to the moon,
was son of Amun and Mut, his Baalat; he was in Thebes
what Nefertem the blue lotus was at Menfe, and with his
exalted parents he made up the Triad of Weset. The
street of Khons, then, was a main artery; a real Abrek
avenue, where it was always well to take heed to one's
heart. The Ishmaelites had to traverse it, for a distance

long enough to expose them to the full danger of its
splendours. Joseph saw the ministries of the treasury
and the granaries and the palace where the sons of Syrian
city princes were brought up; wonderful and spacious
erections of brick and fine woods, brilliant with colours.
He saw chariots roll past, covered all over with ham-
mered gold, wherein the lords of the earth stood and
swung the lash over the backs of steeds prancing and
rolling their eyeballs, snorting fire from their nostrils
and foam from their jaws. Their legs were like deer's
legs, their heads were drawn in on their chests and
crowned with ostrich feathers. He saw sedan-chairs pass,
carried on shoulder-poles, in easy swinging tread, by tall
youths wearing gold aprons. The chairs were carven,
gilded, and canopied and men sat in them with their
hands hidden in their garments, their lacquered hair
stroked back from brow to neck, their eyelashes cast
down; condemned by rank to immobility. At their backs
a screen of reeds and painted linen sheltered them from
the wind. Who was it who one day should sit like that
and be borne before his house, which Pharaoh had enriched? That lies in the future; our narrative has not
yet reached that hour and feast, though where it lies it
is already present and known of all. For the time Joseph,
of course, only saw what he once would be; gazed upon
it with eyes as large and strange as those which would
rest on him or cringe before him, the foreign great man
— young slave Osarsiph, son of the well, stolen and sold
hither, in ragged shirt and hood, with dirty feet, pushed
to the wall by soldiers who came dashing by in even,
shining ranks, amid blare of trumpets, armed with
shields, bows, and clubs, bristling with lances, down the

Street of the Son. He took these grim ranks for Pharaoh's soldiery; but by the standards and the insignia on the shields the old man recognized that they were troops of the gods, temple soldiery, the strength of Amun. What, thought Joseph, had then Amun armies and bodies of soldiers like Pharaoh? He did not like it; and not wholly because the squad had pinned him to the wall. He was conscious of jealousy on Pharaoh's account; on account of the question who was the greatest here. The proximity of Amun's pride and fame in any case oppressed him. He took comfort in the presence of another Highness, namely Pharaoh's own; and the thought that this idol rivalled him in his own field, that he even kept an army, angered him. He thought to guess that it angered Pharaoh too and took his side against the arrogant deity.

But soon they left the Street of the Son, not to mar it any longer, and by narrow lanes came to the inn called Sippar Court because its owner and host was a Chaldæan from Sippar on the Euphrates and took by preference Chaldæan folk to lodge, though all sorts of other folk as well. It was called a court because it was almost nothing but a well and courtyard, quite as full of dirt, noise, and smells, bleating of herds, quarrelling of men, and squealing of mountebanks as the inn at Menfe; and even that very evening the old man struck up a little trade and had a run of customers. They slept under their mantles, and had to take turns, all except the old man, in standing watch lest valuables be stolen from the packs and treasures by their very doubtful fellow-lodgers. They had to wait their turn to wash themselves at the well, then they breakfasted on a sort of pap which was served to them, a Chaldæan dish prepared from sesame, called pappasu.

At last the old man said, not looking at Joseph as he spoke:

"Now then, my friends — thou, Mibsam, my son-in-law, Epher, my nephew, and Keder and Kedema, my sons — we will leave here toward sunrise with our goods and offerings in the direction of the desert where the city leaves off among the dwellings of the great. For I have acquaintance there and folk with needs, who I hope will be ready to buy from our packs this and that for their storehouses and to pay us so that we come not on our own cost but pocket a good advantage and enrich ourselves conformably to our rôle as traders on this earth. Load, then, our goods upon the beasts and saddle me mine that I may lead the van."

Thus it came about. And they drew out of Sippar Court toward the gardens of the rich. In front Joseph led the old man's dromedary by a long rein.

JOSEPH COMES BEFORE PETEPRE'S HOUSE

THEY went toward the desert and the hot desert hills where Re rose in the morning; and their road lay into the land of God, in front of the Sea of the Red Earth. It was a level road and they went along it just as they had entered into the Vale of Dothan, only that now it was not the thick-lipped youth named Jupa but Joseph who led the old man's beast. They came on a buttressed ring wall, long and embracing, out of whose inner precinct towered beautiful trees, sycamores, honey-locusts, date-palms, figs, and pomegranates, and the tops of buildings, shining white or gay with colour. Joseph looked over at them and then at his master to learn from his face whether this was the abode of the fan-bearer, for it was obviously the house of one with the blessing. But the old man was looking straight before him, with his head on one side; they went along the wall and he showed nothing until it rose to a tower and a covered gateway; there he stopped.

In the shadow of the gateway was a brick bench on which sat boys in aprons, four or five, playing a game with their fingers. The old man looked down on them awhile from his beast, till they began to heed. They dropped their hands in their laps and looked at him, raising their brows in pretended amazement, to put him out of countenance.

" Be of good cheer," said the old man.

" Rejoice," answered they, shrugging their shoulders.

" What sort of monkey-shines may they have been," asked he, " which you broke off because I came? "

They looked at each other and laughed in turn.

" Because you came? " one repeated. " We stopped out of distaste at your own monkey-shines, old pedlar! "

" Must you improve your knowledge here, old sand-rabbit," cried a second, " on this very spot and nowhere else, that you ask about our game? "

" I have indeed something to peddle," responded the old man, " only not monkey-shines, however complete my pack, for I know not the ware, but take it from your distaste that you have a superfluity of it yourselves. Hence then probably your need of diversion, which, if I be not mistaken, you satisfy by the amusing game of ' How many fingers? ' "

" Well, then? " they asked.

" I only inquired in passing and by way of preliminary," he went on. " Is this, then, the house and garden of the noble Petepre, fan-bearer on the right hand? "

" Whence know you that? " they asked.

" My memory instructs me," he answered, " and your answer confirms it. But you, as it seems, are set as watchers at the gate of the exalted man to announce the familiar guests? "

" Then you are familiar guests? Bush-rangers and snappers-up from the desert! You would sell us a sell, old man! "

" Young guardian of the gate and bringer of tidings," retorted the Ishmaelite, " you deceive yourself, and your knowledge of the world is unripe as green figs. We are no snappers-up and fly-by-nights, but hate all such and are their true opposite in the scheme of things. For we are travelling traders, who go here and there between kingdoms and make fine connections so that we are well received, as everywhere else so here too and in this house, whose storehouses gape for our wares. For the moment we stand rebuffed by your lack of manners. But I counsel you, become not guilty before Mont-kaw, your head, who is over the house and calls me his friend and treasures my treasures. Rather fulfil the service which is vouch-safed you in the scheme of things and run to announce to the steward the well-known travelling traders from Ma'on and from Mosar — in short, the Midianite merchants are once more at hand with good things for the house's chambers and barns."

The watchers had exchanged looks at hearing him name the name of the steward. Now said he whom the Ishmaelite had addressed, a chubby-cheeked, narrow-eyed lad:

"How then shall I announce you to him? Bethink yourself of that, old man, and go your ways. Can I come running to him and say: 'The Midianites from Mosar are at hand, therefore have I left the gate where at midday the lord will enter, and run to disturb you'? He will call me the son of a dog and take me by the ear. He is settling accounts in the bakery and speaking with the scribe of the buffet. He has more to do than to haggle with you about your wares. Therefore go hence."

"It is pity for you, young door-keeper," said the old man, " that you make yourself a hindrance between me and my years-long friend Mont-kaw, standing between us like a river full of crocodiles and a mountain of impassable steepness. Are you not called Sheshi? "

"Sheshi! Ha ha! " laughed the gate-keeper. "I am called Teti."

"It is all the same," responded the old man. "It is only my pronunciation and because in my old age some teeth are lacking me that I spoke it otherwise. Well then, Tshetshi — though that is no better, alas! — let me see if a dry ford does not lead through the river and mayhap a curving path round the steepness of the mount. You have made a blunder in calling me a snapper-up, but here " — he put his hand in his garment — " is something of the sort, and very pretty too, that belongs to you if you will run and announce me and bring hither Mont-kaw. There, take it from my hand. It is but a small example of my treasures. Look, the sheath is of hardest wood, finely etched, and has a slot out of which you push the diamond-sharp blade, and lo, there is the knife. But if you press the blade down to the handle again, it snaps into its bed and rests secure in its sheath so that you can hide the thing in your apron. What do you say now?"

The youth came forward and tried the spring of the knife.

"Not bad," said he. "Is it mine?" and he pocketed it. "From the land of Mosar?" he asked. "And from Ma'on? Midianite traders? Wait a little."

And he went through the gate.

The old man looked after him, laughed and shook his head. "We have forced the stronghold of Thel," he said, "and passed through Pharaoh's border watches and military scribes. We shall pass here too and win to my friend Mont-kaw."

And he gave a little cluck which was a sign to his beast to lie down. Joseph helped him to dismount. The other riders got down too; and they waited.

After a while Teti came back and said:

"You are to come in into the court. The overseer will come."

"Good," replied the old man, "if he has the wish to see us we will take time and oblige him, although we must still go on."

And led by the young keeper they passed through the covered gateway, which echoed to their tread, into a court covered with hard clay. They faced an open double gate flanked by shady palm trees; it stood in the brick wall of the square inner court, and through slits in the wall they could see the house, with its fine mouldings, its entrance between painted columns, and on the roof its three-cornered ventilators opening to the west. It lay in the centre of the grounds, surrounded on west and south by the green depths of spacious gardens. The court was large, with many open spaces among the buildings which stood facing westwards, without any wall, on the north side of the property. The largest building extended on their right, long, gay, and charming, guarded by watchmen. Through its doors went maidservants with tall jugs and platters of fruit. Other women sat on the house roof, spinning and singing. Farther westwards, against the northern wall, was another house from which steam was rising and before which people were busy beside vats and grain mills. Yet another house lay farther west behind the orchard, and workmen were busy in front of it. At the back, in the north-west corner of the ring wall, lay cow-stalls and corn granaries with ladders against them.

An estate rich in blessing, beyond a doubt. Joseph glanced over it quick-eyed, seeking to penetrate everywhere. But he had little time, for his help was needed in the task which his master undertook as soon as they entered: they unloaded the camels and set up shop on the clay pavement between the gate and the master's house, spreading out their wares that the overseer, or whoever else among his people desired to buy, might be tempted by the alluring contents of their packs.

THE DWARFS

AND actually they were soon surrounded by an inquisitive crowd of people who had seen the Asiatics come in, and though the event was nothing unusual, found in it a welcome diversion from their work or even from mere idling. There were Nubian guards from the house of women and maidservants whose female forms, after the custom of the country, shone clear and plain through the

sheer batiste of their garments; domestics from the main
house dressed according to their place in the hierarchy of
servants, in the short apron or with a longer one over it and
with the short-sleeved upper garment; people from the
cook-house with half-plucked fowls in their hands; stable-
boys, workmen from the servants' house, and gardeners;
they all came up, looked and chattered, bent over the
wares, took this or that in their hands and inquired after
its price in weight of silver or copper. There were two
tiny men, dwarfs, included in the fan-bearer's household.
Neither of them was more than three feet tall; but they
were very different in bearing, for the one was quite a sim-
pleton and the other most dignified of mien. The latter
came first from the main house, on little legs which seemed
still more crooked by comparison with his body; with
careful and circumspect gait, very upright or even somewhat bent backwards, looking importantly about him and
paddling rapidly with his stumpy arms, the palms turned
backwards. He wore a starched apron which stood out
in a slanting triangular plane in his rear. His head was
relatively large, and bulbous behind, covered with short
hair which grew low on brow and temples; he had a
powerful nose and a manner equable, even settled.

" Are you the leader of the caravan? " he asked, standing before the old man, who had squatted down near his
goods, a position gratifying to the dwarf since he could
thus speak to him as man to man. His voice was hollow;
he pitched it as low as possible, sinking his chin on his
chest and drawing his under lip over his teeth. " Who
let you in? The outside guards? With permission from
the overseer? Then it is well. You may stop and await
him, although it is doubtful when he will find time for

you. Do you bring things of use and beauty? It is more likely to be trumpery. Or are there objects of value among them, solid, sensible things? I see balsams, I see walking-sticks. I personally could use a stick if it is of the hardest wood and solid in its make-up. Above all, have you ornaments, chains, necklaces, rings? I am the care-taker of the master's wardrobe and trinkets, the chief steward of the robing-room. Dudu is my name. And I should enjoy giving my wife Djeset a good piece of jewellery, as a reward for child-bearing. Are you provided with such things? I see vitreous paste, I see knick-knacks. But I should want gold, electrum, good stones, lazuli, cornelian, crystal. . . ."

While the little man talked in this wise, the other dwarf came running from the direction of the harem, where he had probably been amusing the ladies with jests. He had just heard of the arrivals, it seemed, and, full of childish zeal, he hastened to be on hand — running as fast as his fat legs would carry him and now and then interrupting his trot to hop on one; in a thin, sharp, short-winded voice, in a sort of ecstatic outburst, he was saying:

" What's this, what's this? What is happening in the world? An uproar, a great hubbub? What is there to look at? What to stare at in our court? Merchants — even wild men — men of the desert? The dwarf is frightened, the dwarf is eager for new things. Hop, hop, hop, here he comes a-running — "

A rust-coloured long-tailed monkey sat on his shoulder, and he held it there with one hand, while it stretched its neck and glared wild-eyed from its perch. The costume of this wight had a comic effect, consisting, as it seemed to do, of a gala garment worn every day. His little, finely pleated apron reached down to his calves, with a fringed turnover; the transparent little camisole had finely pleated sleeves; but all this pleating was crumpled and draggled from long wear. About his diminutive wrists were gold spiral rings; round his little neck a dishevelled garland of flowers, with other flowers sticking in it and standing out round his shoulders. On his wig, made of brown woollen curls, sat a cone of ointment, which, however, was not made of scented fat, but consisted of a conical felt hat soaked in fragrant grease. His face, in contrast to the other dwarf's, was like an elderly child's, elfish, shrivelled, wizened.

Dudu, the guardian of the wardrobe, had been greeted with respect by the crowd, but it burst into laughter at sight of his partner in pettiness and brother dwarf.

"Vizier!" they shouted at him, as in mockery. "Bes-em-heb!"

That was the name of a comic dwarf god imported from foreign parts, with the addition of the designation "in the feast," by which they played on the little man's gala attire.

"Will you buy, Bes-em-heb? How he takes his legs under his arms! Run, Shepses-Bes, mighty Bes, magnificent Bes! Run and buy, but first get your breath! Buy yourself a sandal, vizier, and make little ox-legs under it, then you will have a bed to stretch in; but you must put a step to climb up!"

They shouted at him as he came up, and he answered in his wheezing, cricket voice which sounded as though it came from far away:

"Plying your jokes, are you, long-legs? And think they hit the mark right well? But your vizier can but yawn, so do they bore him, as does of a truth this whole weary world whereon a god has set him and where all is made for giants: not only the sandals, but the jokes as well — and even the time! For if the world were made after my measure and for me to dwell in, time would be much shorter too and I should not have to yawn! There would be yare little years and double hours, nimble night-watches would there be! Tick tock, tick tock, the clock of the heart would hurry away, so swiftly running down that a generation would pass in a trice and scarcely find time to make one good jest on earth ere it were gone and another see the light. How merry would that short life be! But the dwarf is set here in this long-legged, long-winded world and so must yawn. I will not buy your gross wares, and your rude wit will I neither take for a gift. I would but see what there is new in the giant's world of time and space here in our court. Here are strange men, men of wretchedness, men of the desert and wild nomads, in clothes such as men do not wear them. . . . Fie! " He broke off, and his gnome-like face contracted in angry wrinkles. He had seen Dudu, his partner dwarf, where he stood before the squatting old Ishmaelite, gesticulating with his stumpy arms, as he demanded full value for his money.

"Fie! " said the so-called vizier. "There is His Honour, to be sure! What a pity the old gaffer must get in my way when I want to satisfy my desire for the new. Stands there ahead of me his worship the ol'-clo'-man and makes as ever his dull and edifying talk. . . . Good morning, worshipful Dudu," chirped the little wight, ranging himself by the other's side. " A right good morning and very good health to your substantial person!

May one be so bold as to inquire after the health
of the lady Djeset, who embraces you with her arms?
And after that of your towering scions, stout Esesi and
Ebebi? "

Very contemptuously Dudu turned his head over his
shoulder and did not so much seek the mock-vizier with
his eyes as let his gaze fall to the ground somewhere in
front of the other's feet.

" You midge! " he said, shaking his head, as it were
at the sight. He drew in his lower lip so that the upper one
stood out over it like a thatch. " What, are you crawling
and piping down there? I heed you no more than I
would a crab, or an empty nut full of wind and dust. You
are no more than that in my eyes. How dare you ask
after Djeset, my wife, mocking as you speak, and fleering
at my aspiring sons, Esesi and Ebebi? Your inquiry is
unfitting, it is not proper or becoming for you even to
ask after them, minimus and cipher as you are! "

" Hark at him! " retorted he whom they called
Shepses-Bes, and his little visage wrinkled even more.
" Wants to exalt himself above me, who knows how high;
his voice issues as out of a tun, for sheer pomposity —
when you cannot see over a mole-hill yourself and are
no match for your brood, let alone for her who embraces
you with her arms. A dwarf you are and a dwarf you
remain, no matter how you puff yourself out; and ill it
beseems you to scorn my polite inquiries after your
family, on the score that it does not befit a dwarf to make
them! But you yourself — truly it befits you well and
becomes your stature to play the married man and father
of the family, wedding with one of the big folk and deny-
ing your dwarfish kind — "

The courtyard people laughed uproariously; the wrangling and mutual dislike of the manikins seemed to be a familiar source of merriment. They egged them on: " Give it him, vizier! " " Pay him out, Dudu, spouse of Djeset! " But he whom they called Bes-em-heb had stopped scolding and lost interest in the fray. He was standing near his enemy, who in his turn stood next the old man. But on the old man's other hand was Joseph, and thus Bes found himself confronting the son of Rachel. As he became aware of him he ceased to speak and gazed steadily, while his dwarfish face, but now so full of petty rage, smoothed itself out and assumed an expression of self-forgotten inquiry. His mouth remained open, and if he had had brows — but he had none — they would have risen high. Thus he looked up at the young Shabirite, and the little ape on his shoulder did the same, as though fixed by magic; with neck thrust out, with wide-staring eyes, it gazed up into the face of the descendant of Abram.

Joseph submitted to the scrutiny. Smiling he returned the gnomish gaze, and thus they stood, while the solemn Dudu resumed his chaffering with the old man and the attention of the other courtyard folk veered again to the strangers and their wares.

At length the manikin, pointing with dwarf finger to his breast, said in his strange, remote little voice:

" Sa'ankh-Wen-nofer-Neteruhotep-em-per-Amun."

" What did you say? " Joseph inquired.

The dwarf repeated his words, still pointing to his breast. " Name," he explained. " The little one's name. Not vizier. Not Shepses-Bes. Sa'ankh-Wen-nofer — " and he whispered it for the third time, his full name, as long and resounding as he himself was insignificant. Its meaning was " May the Favouring Essence (in other words, Osiris) preserve the beautified of the gods in the house of Amun." And Joseph understood it.

" A fine name! " said he.

" Fine, yes, but not true," came the murmuring voice. " Me not beautiful, me not favoured of gods, me little frog! You beautiful and favoured, you Neteruhotep, so is fine and true too."

" How can you know that? " Joseph asked with a smile.

" See," came the subterranean accents. " See very clear." And he carried his small finger to his eye. " Wise," he added. " Small and wise. You not of the little race, yet wise too. Good, wise, and beautiful. Do you belong to him? " He pointed to the old man, who was busy with Dudu.

" I belong to him," said Joseph.

" From a child? "

" I was born to him."

" He is your father? "

" He is a father to me."

" What is your name? "

Joseph did not answer at once. He smiled before he spoke. At length: " Osarsiph," said he.

The dwarf blinked. He pondered the name.

" Are you born from the reeds? " he asked. " Are you an Usir in the rushes? Did the mother search and find you in the water? "

Joseph was silent. The little man went on blinking.

Then they heard the voices of the people in the yard: " Mont-kaw is coming! " They began to disperse to their tasks, that he might not find them idle and chattering.

Mont-kaw was standing or moving about near the open courtyard in front of the buildings in the north-west corner of the estate. You could see him by looking between the harem and the master's house: an elderly man, beautifully dressed in white, accompanied by scribes, who, with reed pens behind their ears, bowed before him and wrote down his words on tablets.

He approached. The servants had scattered. The old man had got to his feet. But through all the sound of these movements Joseph heard, as though a voice, a little voice, whispered up to him from under the earth, the words:

" Stay with us, young sandman! "

MONT-KAW

THE OVERSEER had arrived at the open gate in the crenellated wall before the master's house. Half turned toward it, he looked back over his shoulder at the group of strangers and the wares exposed for sale.

" What is this? " he said rather gruffly. " What men are these? "

It seemed as though he had forgotten, in the press of other affairs, that he had sent for them to come in. Nor did the exhaustive salutations of the old man help matters much. A scribe reminded him, pointing to his tablet, upon which he had obviously noted the incident.

" Yes, yes, the pedlars from Ma'om or Mosar, " said the overseer then. " Good, good; but I need nothing except time and that they have not for sale. " And he approached the old man who came bustling up to him. " Well, old man, how are you, after all this time? "

asked Mont-kaw. " So we see you at our door with your
goods, all ready to swindle us once more? "

They laughed together. Both of them had only the
lower canines left in their jaws, sticking up solitary like
posts. The steward was a stocky, powerfully built man
of fifty, with an expressive head. The decided bearing
which his office brought with it was softened by benevolence. He had very prominent tear ducts under his eyes,
giving the latter a swollen, slit-like look beneath heavy,
still black eyebrows. From the well-formed though wide-
nostrilled nose deep furrows ran down to the corners of
the arched and outstanding upper lip, which like the
cheeks was shaven so that it shone. On the chin sat a
club-shaped beard sprinkled with grey. The hair had
already retreated from brow and temples, but grew in a
bush at the back of the head, standing out like a fan behind the ears, in which he wore gold rings. Mont-kaw's
features had something traditionally shrewd and peasant-
like about them, and withal a twinkle that suggested
the seafaring man. His dark red-brown complexion con-
trasted with the florid white of his clothing — that in-
imitable Egyptian linen which lent itself to such exquisite folds and pleating as those in the front flap of his
apron kilt, the stiffly starched flaring folds of which began
below his navel and reached down nearly to the ankle-
length hem. His body-garment was tucked into the apron,
and its wide, half-length sleeves were likewise pressed
into fine diagonal folds. The fine batiste revealed his
muscular, hairy torso.

The two dwarfs had taken leave to remain in the
court, and Dudu now came up to Mont-kaw, paddling importantly and rowing with his stumpy arms.

"I fear, overseer, it is time lost to deal with these people," he said, and notwithstanding his stature he spoke as an equal. "I have looked over their stock. I see trumpery. I see gimcrackery. What lacks is good, solid, high-class stuff, suitable for an aristocratic house and estate. The master will scarcely be grateful to you for purchasing trash."

The old man was cast down. He indicated by a gesture his distress that the overseer's hopeful and cordial greetings should have aroused in him expectations which now were destroyed by Dudu's severity.

"But I have valuable goods too," he said. "Maybe not valuable to you upper officials, nor of course to your lord, I have not said that. But how many servants are there not in the courtyard — cooks and bakers, gardeners and water-bearers, runners and waiters-on! Countless like the sands of the sea! Yet not so many that they are enough or too many for such a great lord as Petepre, His Grace, the friend of Pharaoh, or that one could not always add one or another well-built and clever slave, let him be native or a foreigner, if only he be useful. But why do I prattle of what is not to the point instead of saying simply: You, great steward, buy for the many and their use; you stand as their head, and it is the business of the old Minæan, the travelling pedlar with his popular wares, to suggest to you. Look at these well-painted, earthenware lamps from Gilead beyond the Jordan — they cost me little, so should I value them high to you, my patron? Take some of them as a present, and if I may see your favour therefor, I am rich. On the other hand these little pots of eye-paint with cow-horn tweezers and spoons of cow-horn — their value is considerable, but not their price. Here are hoes, an indispensable tool; I will give one for two pots of honey. More costly, indeed, are the contents of this little bag, for there are onions from Ascalon in it, from Ascaluna, rare and hard to come by as they are savoury. But the wine in these jugs is eight times good wine from Khadati, in the land of Phœnicia — as it stands written. Lo, I grade my offers, I go from the lower to the higher, and from them to the very choice, that is my considered practice. For the balsams here, and incense-resins, the goat's-thorn gums, the brownish labdanum, they are the pride of my business, and the speciality of my house. We would be praised and renowned between the rivers, because we are stronger in sudorifics than any merchant, be he travelling trader or a settled man of the bazaar. 'There are the Ishmaelites from Midian,' they say of us; ' they carry spices, balsam, and myrrh from Gilead down toward Egypt.' So is it in the mouth of the people — precisely as though we did not carry and bring much else, as doth in truth happen, dead and alive, the created or the creature, so that we are the men not only to provide a house but also to increase it. But I am silent."

"What, you are silent?" the overseer pretended amaze. "Do you ail, then? For when you are silent I know you not, but only when your mild prattle of speech wells out from beneath your beard — I can still hear it from the last time and know you by it again."

"Is not," responded the old man, "speech the pride of mankind? Who knows how to set his words well and hath a gift of expression, upon him gods and men nod with applause, and he findeth inclined ears. But your servant is little gifted with expression, and not master of the treasure of speech, I say it openly. So then he must substitute persistency for speech and duration of flow for what it lacks in choiceness. For the merchant must be of ready tongue, the which must know how to flatter his clients, or he cannot earn his living and doth not bring the seven gifts to the man — "

" Six," came the whispering of little Bes, as from afar off, although he stood quite near. " Six gifts, old man, you offered: lamps, salve, hoes, onions, wine, and myrrh. Where is the seventh? "

The Ishmaelite laid his left hand like a mussel-shell round his ear and the right to his eyes to peer.

" What," he asked, " was the remark of this middle-sized, gaily clad gentleman? "

One of his party repeated it to him.

" Oh," he replied, " the seventh likewise is to be found among all the things which we have brought down to Egypt, besides the much-talked-of myrrh. For it, too, will I let my tongue run on, with persistency, if not with chosen words, that I may bring the ware to the man and the house, and that the Ishmaelites of Midian may make for themselves a name on account of all that which they bear and bring to Egypt."

" Spare me," said the overseer. " Do you think I can stand here and hear you chatter all the days of Re? He is already almost at his midday, may the gods keep us! Any minute the master may come home from the west and be here again from the palace. Shall I then leave it to the slaves and trouble not myself whether all is right in the dining-room, with the roast ducks, the cakes, the flowers; and the master find his meal as he is used to, likewise the mistress and the exalted parents from the upper storey? Make haste, or else make off! I must go. Old man, I cannot well use you or your seven gifts — scarcely at all, to be frank — "

" For they are but beggarly trash," interpolated Dudu, the married dwarf.

The overseer gave a downward glance as he heard the harsh judgment.

" But you have need of honey, it seems," he said to the old man. " I will give you a few pots against two of these hoes, that I may not offend you or your gods. Give me five bags of the little onions too, in the name of the Hidden One, and five measures of your Phœnician wine, in the name of the Mother and the Son! Tell me the cost — yet give me not first the triple price, as a haggler does so that we sit down and bargain, but at most the double one, so that we may come more quickly to the just one, and I can go in. I will give you writing-paper in exchange, and some of our linen. If you like, beer and bread as well. Only make haste that I may go! "

" You are served," said the old man, loosing the hand scale from his girdle. " You are served in a trice, and without conditions, served by your servant. What am I saying, without conditions? With conditions, of course, but only of the best. Had I not to live, the things were yours without price. But even so I will make you a price that may indeed cut me short, yet keep myself in your favour, for that is my chief concern.

" Hallo," said he to Joseph over his shoulder, " take the list of wares which you have made, the things in black but the weight and quantity in red. Take and read to us the weight of the shallots as well as the wine, that is their price, but translate as you stand and in your head into the values of the country, in deben and lot, that we may know what the goods are worth in pounds of copper and the high steward may give us, for just so much copper, linen and writing-paper of the house. But I, my patron, if you allow, will weigh out the goods once more for test and proof."

Joseph had the roll ready and stepped forward as he unrolled it. Next him stood Master Bes, who, indeed, was far from being able to look at the list, but gazed up attentively at the extended hands.

" Doth my lord command me to read the just price or the double one? " asked Joseph discreetly.

" The just one, of course; dost thou dote? " the old man scolded.

" But the high steward commanded that thou shouldest name the double price," responded Joseph with the most charming seriousness. " If now I name the just one he might take it for the double and offer but the half; and how then couldst thou live? Better would it be if he took the double price for the real one; and if he drive it down, even so thou comest not short."

" He he! " the old man laughed. " He he! " he went again, and looked at the overseer to see how he took it. The scribes, with the reed pens behind their ears, laughed. The thumbling " Beauty " clapped his knee with his little hand, drawing it up to his chest and hopping on the other. His goblin face was flawed into a thousand little wrinkles of dwarfish delight. But Dudu, his brother manikin, only shook his head and stuck out the thatch of his upper lip more disdainfully than ever.

As for Mont-kaw, he had so far of course given no heed to the knowing young scribe with the roll. But now

he looked at him, with a surprise which at once turned
to perplexity, and presently to something very like
admiration — save that it betokened indeed a far, far
deeper feeling. Perhaps — I will not venture an asser-
tion — perhaps at this moment, upon which so much
depended, the planning God of his fathers did a little
something extra for Joseph. Perhaps He let fall upon
him a light calculated to produce the desired effect upon
the hearts of all beholders. For He, in truth, has given
us all our senses for our pleasure; yet reserved to Himself their use as medium and avenue for His larger purposes to play upon our minds. Hence my suggestion —
which, however, I am willing to withdraw if it seem too
supernatural an element to be introduced into our very
natural tale.

Indeed, the more natural and practical our interpre-
tations, the better, since Mont-kaw himself was a practical and natural man. Besides he belonged to a world
already remote from any in which the idea of meeting
a god unexpectedly, in broad daylight and, so to speak,
on the street, would have been a familiar thing. Yet
even so his world stood nearer than ours does to such
possibilities and expectations; though in his they might
only have been held with half one's mind, no longer in
a real, positive, and unequivocal sense. It came to pass
that Mont-kaw looked at Rachel's son and saw that he
was beautiful. But beauty of so striking and arresting
a kind was associated in the steward's mind with one
immediate order of ideas: it belonged to the moon, which
was the planet of Djehuti of Khmunu, Thoth's heavenly
manifestation — Thoth, who was master of measure and
order, the wise man, scribe and magician. And now

Joseph stood there before him, a roll in his hands, and in his mouth words which for a slave, even an educated one, were unusually subtle and shrewd. The combination was upsetting. The young Bedouin and Asiatic had no ibis-head on his shoulders; he was, of course, a human being, not a god, not Thoth of Khmunu. But he had, by association, to do with him. He seemed ambiguous, in the way that a word can be ambiguous, for instance the epithet " divine." Compared with the august substantive from which it derives, it conveys indeed a weakening, a derogation of the idea; it is not absolute, but only suggestive, and thus it is partly unreal and derivative, but partly too lays claim to absoluteness, in that the word " divine " is a description of the perceptible attributes and form of the god.

Some such equivocal associations came to Mont-kaw's mind and gave him pause when he saw Joseph for the first time. It was indeed a recurrent event; others before him had felt the same, still others would yet feel it. But we must not suppose that Mont-kaw was very powerfully moved. He felt no more than what we might express by the exclamation: " What the devil! " He did not say that. He asked:

" What is that? "

He cautiously — likewise somewhat contemptuously — said " what " instead of " who "; and thus the old man's answer came very pat:

" That," he replied with a smirk, " is the Seventh Gift."

" It is a habit of the uncivilized," the Egyptian retorted, " to speak in riddles."

" Does my patron not love riddles? " responded the

old man. " 'Tis a pity! I could tell him so many. But this one is quite simple: they have said that I offered only six gifts and not seven, as I had boasted and as it is proper to do. Well, then, this slave who keeps my list is the seventh gift — a Canaanitish youth whom, besides my much praised myrrhs, I have brought down to Egypt and who is for sale. Not that I must sell him or would do so because he is no good to me. For he can bake and write and hath a clear head for accounts. But to a good house, a house like yours, in short, is he for sale, if you will pay me a living price, no more. For I would have a good place for him."

" Our numbers are full," the steward said hastily, shaking his head. For he had no liking for riddles, either in the usual or in a higher sense, but spoke like a practical man, anxious to protect his business interests against importunity from anything out of the usual order — the divine, in short.

" There is no vacancy here," he said, " and the house is full. We need no baker nor writer; nor any clear heads, for mine is clear enough to keep things in order. Take your seventh gift with you on your way and may it find you profit."

" For it is beggarly trash and a beggar and the trash of a beggar," Dudu, husband of Djeset, concluded sententiously. But another little voice answered his heavy one, the cricket-like chirp of " Beauty," the fool:

" The seventh gift is the best — buy it, Mont-kaw! "

The old man took up his tale:

" The clearer one's own head, the more vexing the dullness of the others', for one suffereth impatience on their account. A clear head at the top needeth clear heads below. I had already in mind this servant for your house when great space yet lay between me and it, and brought him down before you to make you an advantageous and friendly offer. For the young one is clear of head and eloquent of tongue so that it is a pleasure, and bringeth before you adornments out of the treasure-house of speech so that it is a mere delight. Three hundred and sixty times in the year he sayeth good-night to one in a different phrase and still has something left for the other five days. But if ever he says it twice the same, you may give me him back again and I will refund the purchase money."

"Hearken, old man," replied the overseer. "All that you say may be true. But whilst we speak of patience I am wellnigh at the end of mine. In my good nature I was ready to take a few gew-gaws from your pack, of the which I have no need at all, but not to disoblige your gods and so as to be able to go into the house. And lo, you would talk me into buying your good-night-saying slave and makest as though he were destined for the house of Petepre since the foundation of the land."

Here Dudu, scribe of the wardrobe, gave vent, from his lowly station, to a burst of deep round laughter: "Ho, ho, ho, ho!" he went, and the overseer cast him a quick angry look.

"Where did you get it, then, this seventh gift with the gift of tongues?" he asked. He did not look toward Joseph, but stretched out his hand for the roll which the latter gracefully presented. Mont-kaw unrolled it and held it away from his eyes, for he was already very long-sighted. Meanwhile the old man answered:

"A pity it is indeed that my patron does not love

riddles. Else I could tell him one in answer to his question whence I have the lad."

"A riddle?" repeated the overseer absently, for he was looking at the roll.

"Guess it if you will," said the old man. "It runs: 'A barren mother bore him to me.' Can you solve the riddle?"

"Did he write this list?" Mont-kaw asked, still reading. "H'm. Step back, you. It was done with thoroughness and with pleasure and executed with a sense for adornment, that I will not dispute. It might serve as an inscription to decorate a wall. Whether it is correct as well, that I cannot judge, for it is gibberish. 'Barren'?" he asked, for he had heard the old man's words with half an ear. "A barren mother? What does that mean? A woman is barren or else she bears. Both cannot be true."

"It is a riddle, my lord," explained the old man. "I took the liberty to dress my reply in the garment of jest. If it please you, I will supply the answer. Far from here, I came on a dry well, out of which sounded a whimpering. And I drew up to the light of day this which had been three days in the well's belly, and gave it milk. Thus the well became a mother and yet was barren."

"H'm," said the overseer. "Your riddle is passable, more one cannot say, or laugh very heartily at it. If I smile, it is out of pure politeness."

"Mayhap," replied the old man, rather hurt, "you might have laughed more readily if you had been able to guess it."

"Solve me," the steward gave back, "another riddle, and a harder one: namely, that I should stand here prattling with you, and why. Solve it better than you have your own; for, so far as I know, there are no monsters that breed in wells to give birth to such as this. How, then, did the child come into the belly and the slave into the well? "

" Hard masters and former owners, of whom I bought him, had cast him in, by reason of slight misdemeanours which do not lessen his value, because they had to do only with subtle matters and fine distinctions like that between the ' so that ' and the ' in order that ' — matters not worth talking about. But I bought him, having taken him be-tween thumb and finger, as it were, and found the boy to be fine in thread and grain, notwithstanding the darkness of his origins. Also he had already rued his errors while in the well, and punishment had so purged him that he was a valuable servant to me; and he can not only read and write but bake uncommonly relishable pancakes on stones. I well know that a man should not boast of his own, but leave it to others to call it extraordinary. Yet indeed, for the dexterity and the understanding of this youth, purified as they are by chastisements, there is in the language but one word: they are extraordinary. And now since your eyes have fallen upon him and I owe you a debt for my folly in plaguing you with riddles, receive him as a present from me for Petepre and his house over which you are set! Though of course I well know that you would contrive a recompense for me out of the riches of Petepre so that, and in order that, I may live to supply your house and ever increase it."

The overseer looked at Joseph.

" Is it true," said he, with suitable gruffness, " that you have the gift of speech and can say such things as are pleasant to hear? "

Jacob's son gathered all his Egyptian together.

" ' Servants' speech is no speech,' " he answered, using a popular phrase. " That the lowly shall be silent when the masters speak together stands at the beginning of every book of precepts. Besides, my name, by which I call myself, is a name of silence."

" How so? How are you called, then? "

Joseph hesitated. Then he lifted up his eyes.

" Osarsiph," he said.

" Osarsiph? " repeated Mont-kaw. " I know not the name. It is not foreign; indeed, it is comprehensible, since he from Abodu occurs in it, the lord of the eternal silence. But it is not customary in the land, no one is so called in Egypt, either now or under any earlier kings. But even if you have a name of silence, Osarsiph, yet your master says that you can utter pleasant wishes and say good-night in a variety of ways at the end of the day. Well, I too shall go to bed tonight and lie on my bed in the special room of trust. What will you say to me? "

" Rest gently," answered Joseph with feeling, " after the toil of the day. May your soles, that are scorched from the heat of your path, move blissfully over the mosses of peace, and your languid tongue be refreshed from the murmuring springs of night! "

" Yes, that is really moving," said the steward; the tears stood in his eyes. He nodded to the old man, who nodded back, rubbing his hands and smiling. " When one has troubles in the world, like me, and sometimes feels not too good about the kidneys, one is moved by things like that. Can we then, in the name of Set," he turned back to his scribe, " use a young slave — as a lamplighter, perhaps, or as a floor-sprinkler? What do you say, Kha'ma't? " he said to a tall, stoop-shouldered man who carried several reed pens behind each ear. " Do we need one? "

The scribes made gestures of indecision, seeming to debate. They stuck out their lips, drew their heads down between their shoulders, and flapped their hands in the air.

" Need? " answered he who was called Kha'ma't. " Is ' need ' to need, to lack the indispensable? Then no. But even the unnecessary may be made useful. It depends on the cost. If the man of the desert would sell you a scribe, then drive him away, for we are writers enough and neither need nor can use one. But if he offer you a baser slave, for the dogs or for the bathing-room, then inquire of him his price."

" Well, old man," said the steward, " hasten, then, and say what you would ask for your son of the well."

" He is yours! " replied the Ishmaelite. " Since we speak of him at all and you ask me about him, he already belongs to you. Truly it is not fit that I decide on the worth of the present in exchange which, as it would seem, you will make me. But since you command — the ape sits beside the scale! Who sins in measure and weight is convicted by the power of the moon. Two hundred deben of copper the slave must be reckoned at, considering his extraordinary properties. But the little onions and the wine from Khadati I will throw in, as a gage of friendship."

The price was high. It was a clever stroke to make extras of the shallots and the much-liked Phœnician wine, and to charge only for the young slave Osarsiph. But high it was, even granted that of all the old man's stock-in-trade, not excepting the famous myrrhs, only this single thing paid for the transportation to Egypt. It was high even from the point of view that the Ishmaelites' entire business was only an extra, and their sole and single significance consisted in the fact that they were bringing the boy Joseph down to Egypt in order to fulfil the ordained. We may not venture to think that any such idea entered the old Minoan's head; certainly it was remote from the overseer Mont-kaw's, and probably he would have protested against the overcharge if the dwarf Dudu had not forestalled him. From under the thatch of the little man's lip a full-mouthed protest rolled out; the tiny hands at the end of his stumps of arms gesticulated before his breast.

" It is absurd! " he said. " Utterly fantastic and not to be borne. Turn your back on him, show your disgust to this shameless old thief and vagabond who dares to speak of friendship, as though there could be anything of the kind between you, an Egyptian overseer to the great, and him, a wild man from the desert. His business is pure swindle — asking two hundred copper deben for this lout here — " and he gestured palm upwards at Joseph as he stood beside him — " for such worthless trash, a snot-nosed sand-rabbit! It is all highly suspicious to me; he may be able to prattle about moss and murmuring streams, but who knows what sort of abandoned vices brought him to acquaintance with the pit that the old rascal is supposed to have got him from? I say you shall not buy the lout; my advice is not to acquire him for Petepre; he will not thank you for it."

Thus Dudu, overseer of the wardrobe. But hard upon his voice came a little pipe like a cricket's out of the grass, the voice of " Beauty " in the gala attire, the vizier who stood at Joseph's other side — for they had taken him between them.

" Buy, Mont-kaw," he whispered, standing on his tiptoes. " Buy the sand-boy. Of all the seven gifts buy him alone, for he is the best. Trust me, I have the use of my eyes. Good, beautiful, and wise is Osarsiph. Blessed is he and will be a blessing to the house. Hearken to the voice of wisdom."

" Take not the advice of the base, but of the worthy," cried the other in his turn. " How can this dried-up nothing give you anything of worth, being himself without worth and like a rotten nut with nothing but dust and wind inside? He has no weight in the world, no social value, but bobs on the surface of things like a cork. How can a clown and court fool speak anything of value, or have judgment of human folk and their goods, or of human goods? "

" Oh, you stuck-up little busybody, you! " shrieked Bes-em-heb, his gnome-face crumpled into a thousand wrinkles with sheer rage. " How can you have judgment or give counsel, you backslider and turncoat? You threw away your wisdom when you denied your dwarfdom and wived yourself with a tall woman and gave life to long, lathlike children called Esesi and Ebebi! You pompous ass! You have remained a dwarf according to your stature and cannot see over the boundary-stone of the field. But as for your stupidity, that is full-size; and it has entirely blunted your judgment of men and wares and human wares! "

Dudu was brought by these epithets and this description of his mental state to a pitch of almost incredible fury. He got white as cheese, the thatch quivered on his upper lip, and he burst out in venomous invective, which Beauty was not slow in repaying with even more malicious allusions to Dudu's loss of finer intelligence, his renegade state and ridiculous pretensions. The two little men stood, hands on knees, on Joseph's either side as though he were a tree, scolding and spitting at each other round him. The crowd, Egyptians and Ishmaelites together, and the overseer with them, roared with laughter at the petty war going on at the level of their knees. But suddenly everything came to a stop.

POTIPHAR

FROM afar in the street, sounds came and swelled: the trampling of horses, the rolling of wheels, the thud of running feet, and many-voiced cries of warning. It all came on so fast that in no time it stood before the door.

"There we are," said Mont-kaw. "The master. And the arrangements in the dining-hall? Great Triad of Thebes, I have wasted my time in sheer folly! Quiet, ye underlings, or ye shall have a taste of the lash! Kha'ma't, conclude the bargain, I must go with the master into the house. Take the goods and pay a proper price for them. Keep well, old man! And come back again — in six or seven years' time!"

He hastened away. The gate-keepers, from the benches, shouted into the court, and from all sides servants came running, in zeal to line up before the master with their foreheads to the ground. The trotting feet of the runners and the rattle of the car came from the gateway: Petepre drove in. Before him went his panting, shouting runners, among and behind them his fan-bearers came. Two proud and glossy chestnuts in fine trappings, with ostrich plumes on their heads, drew the little two-wheeled car, a sort of gala chariot, with prettily curved rails. In it was just room for himself and his driver; but the driver did nothing save to add to the splendour of the equipage, for Pharaoh's friend drove himself — it was plain, from his bearing and his attire, that it was the master who held reins and whip. He was an extremely tall, fat man, with a little mouth, Joseph remarked; but only at a glance, for his eyes went rather to the wheels of the chariot, which had bright stones let into the spokes and sparkled like fireworks as they whirled round in the sun. Joseph wished that little Benjamin might see it. The same splendour, though not whirling, repeated itself on Petepre's person; for he wore a jewelled collar, a magnificent piece of workmanship, set with stones and enamel in all colours; their countless facets, arranged in rows with the narrow sides together, flashed like a rain of sparks in the strong white light which the sun-god at his zenith was pouring down on Weset and upon this very spot.

The ribs of the runners panted in and out. The shining steeds came to a halt, pawing the ground, rolling their eyes and snorting; a groom held them by the bridle, patted their foaming necks, and murmured soothing words. The chariot had stopped by the palm trees, just between the group of merchants and the gate in the ring wall which led into the inner court. And at the gate stood Mont-kaw, bowing and smiling and gesturing his delight. His head was quivering with sheer admiration as he stepped up to the car and offered his hand to help the master alight. Petepre handed reins and whip to the driver, keeping in his small hand only a short staff made of cane and gilded leather, thick at the end and looking like a kind of reduced bludgeon. " Wash them off with wine, cover them well, and lead them about! " he commanded in a thinnish voice, lifting his staff and pointing to the animals with that elegant survival of a savage weapon, become in his hands merely a symbol of his power. He waved back the hand offered by Mont-kaw and sprang down, with a movement agile for one of his weight — though he might as easily have stepped.

Joseph saw and heard clearly, especially after the car moved slowly off toward the stables and the master and his steward stood gazing after it, in full view of the group of Ishmaelites. The great man might be perhaps forty years old, or less; and like a tower for size — Joseph could not help thinking of Reuben as he looked at the columnar legs showing through the royal linen of the outer garment, which came not quite to the ankles and revealed the pleats and ribbons of the skirt through its thin weave. But this massiveness was not heroic like brother Reuben's, for it was fat: fat everywhere, especially on the breasts, which stood out like two hillocks under the thin batiste. They had shaken not a little with the man's unnecessarily active jump from the car. His head was quite small in proportion to his height and breadth; but nobly shaped, with short hair, short, aristocratically hooked nose, delicate mouth, pleasantly prominent chin, and long-lashed eyes with a veiled and haughty gaze.

Standing with the steward in the shade of the palms,

he looked well pleased after his horses as they were led off.

" They are very fiery," he was heard to say. " User-Min even more than Wepwawet. They were unruly, they tried to bolt. But I got the better of them."

" As only you can do," answered Mont-kaw. " It is amazing. Your driver, Neternakht, would not dare cope with them. Nor any of the others here, the Syrians are so wild. They have fire, not blood, in their veins. They are not horses, but demons. Yet you have conquered them, they feel the master's hand, and their pride is subdued, they are tamed and run in harness for you. And you, after triumphing in the struggle with them, are not even tired; you spring like a lad from your car, my lord."

The deep corners of Petepre's mouth deepened more in a fleeting smile.

" I have further intent," said he, " to pay homage to Sebek this afternoon and go hunting in the marshes. Make all ready and rouse me betimes should I fall asleep. Put throw-sticks and fishing-spears in the boat. And harpoons as well, for I hear that a hippopotamus of great size has strayed into the backwater where I mean to hunt, and I am minded most of all to kill it."

" The mistress," answered Mont-kaw, his eyes cast down, " the mistress Mut-em-enet will tremble with fear when she hears. Be persuaded at least not to attack the brute single-handed — leave the struggle and the danger to your servants. The mistress — "

" That gives me no pleasure," Petepre responded. " I will myself hurl the spear."

"But the mistress will be afraid."

"Let her be afraid. — But," he asked, turning with a swift movement toward the steward, "is all well in the house? Naught untoward has befallen? Nothing? And what people are those? Travelling merchants — very good. The mistress is happy? Is all well with the exalted parents in the upper storey?"

"Order and well-being reign," Mont-kaw gave answer. "Our gracious mistress went in her litter toward noon to visit the lady Renenutet, wife of the head steward of the bulls of Amun, to practise hymn-singing with her. When she returned she sent for Tepem'ankh, scribe of the house of the secluded ones, to read fairy-tales to her, the while she felt desire to kiss the sweetmeats which your servant sent her. As for the exalted parents from the upper storey, it pleased them to cross the river, to make sacrifice in the tomb of Thutmose, father of God united with the sun. Returned from the west, the exalted brother-sister pair, Huia and Tuia, have spent the time sitting peacefully hand in hand in the pleasure-house by the pond, awaiting your return and the hour of the evening meal."

"You may tell them too, and let it come privily to them," the master said, "that I mean to hunt the hippopotamus this very day. They may as well know it."

"But on that account," replied the steward, "they will, alas, fall into anxiety and great distress."

"No matter," retorted Petepre. "It seems," he added, "that life here today has gone to everybody's liking; whereas I had annoyance at court and vexation in the palace Merimat."

"You?" Mont-kaw questioned in dismay. "But how

can that be, for the good god in the palace . . ."

"Either a man is captain of the guard," the master was
heard to say, shrugging his massive shoulders as he
turned away, "and head executioner, or else he is not.
But if one is only — and there is a man there . . ." The
rest of his words were lost as he passed through the gate
and toward his house through the rows of slaves standing with uplifted hands. Mont-kaw moved a little behind
him, bent over, listening and replying to what he said.
And thus Joseph had seen Potiphar, as he pronounced
the name to himself — that great man of Egypt to whom
he had been sold.

JOSEPH IS SOLD FOR A SECOND TIME
AND FLINGS HIMSELF UPON HIS FACE

FOR the bargain was now made. Khamat, the tall scribe,
concluded it with the old man in the overseer's name, the
dwarfs looking on. But Joseph scarcely listened, nor did
he hear the price he fetched, so intent was he on his
thoughts and so busy with his first impressions of the
person of his new owner. The collar glittering with jewels, the gold of favour, the proud, over-fleshy form; the
spring from the car, the flatteries uttered by Mont-kaw
about his master's prowess as a tamer of steeds; his in-
tention of fighting the wild hippopotamus single-handed,
heedless of his consort's fears or those of Huia and Tuia,
his parents (and even the word "heedless" seems in-
adequate to characterize his mood); on the other hand
his hurried inquiry about the order and well-being of
the household; even the disconnected words he had let
fall about the annoyances he suffered at court — all this

gave the son of Jacob most urgently to think, to consider, to examine; he laboured within himself to probe, to interpret and fill in the blanks, like one who, placed by chance in a certain set of circumstances, and having to reckon with them, tries to master them as quickly as he may.

Would he, his thoughts ran on, stand some day in the chariot beside Potiphar and be his driver? Would he go with him to hunt in the backwaters of the Nile? That seems incredible, but so it was: scarcely had he come before the house when his thoughts flew to such an hour. Scarcely had his quick appraising eye taken in men and things when he considered how — sooner or later, but certainly as soon as possible — he would win to the master's side, to the side of him highest in this sphere if not the highest in Egypt. If not the highest: the words betray that whatever unforeseeable difficulties lay in the way of attaining his immediate though still very distant goal, these did not prevent him from looking beyond it to where hovered other, yet more conclusive incorporations of the highest.

Yet so it was; we know our man. And would he, with lesser pretensions, have gone so far in this country as he did? He was in the nether world, to which the pit had been the entrance. He was no longer Joseph, but Usarsiph; lowest among these below, but that could not last for long. Advantage and disadvantage he scanned with rapid eye. Mont-kaw was good. Tears had come in his eyes at Joseph's gentle greeting, because he often did not feel too well. The dwarf jester was good too, and obviously minded and ordained to help him. Dudu was a foe — for the present; perhaps there were ways to get around him. The scribes had shown some jealousy, because he too was a scribe; he must pay heed to their natural grudge and treat it gently. Thus he went on, weighing his immediate prospects — but it would be wrong on that account to chide him and call him a place-hunter. That Joseph was not; such is not a just judgment upon his thoughts. He mused and pondered upon a higher duty. God had put an end to his life, which had been one of folly, and resurrected him to a new one. He had used the Ishmaelites to lead him to this land; and in so doing He had, as in all else, undoubtedly great purposes. Never did He do aught that brought not great things in its train; it behoved Joseph, then, to lend himself trustfully to His design and use all his spiritual gifts in its service, instead of weakening it by idle lack of ambition. God had sent him dreams, which the dreamer had done better to keep to himself: the dream of the sheaves, the dream of the stars. For such dreams were less a promise than a guide. They would be fulfilled, in one way or another — in what way actually, God alone knew, but that he had been snatched away into this land was the beginning of the fulfilment. But in the meantime nothing would happen of itself — one had to help. That was no base ambition: to live in the light of the silent conviction that God had unique designs regarding him. Ambition is not the right word for it; for it was ambition for God, and that deserves a higher name.

Thus Joseph paid little heed to the chaffering that went on at his second sale, and thought little about the price he fetched, in his zeal to master his present situation and prospects. Lanky Khamat — with reed pens behind his ear, so astonishingly balanced that they lodged as though stuck on, no matter how much his head shook as he bargained — insisted stoutly on his distinction between needing and being able to use, as an argument to bring down the price. The old man produced his former strong plea: namely, that he must receive a present large enough that he might still exist to serve the illustrious house; and he knew how to make the necessity seem so inevitable that the scribe was taken at a disadvantage and could not refute it. Yet he was supported by Dudu, chamberlain of the wardrobe, who denied all claims, the needing and the being able to use as well, and in respect of all the wares in question, the wine and the onions no less than the slave. The other part was taken by Shepses-Bes, who vaunted his penetration in a chirping voice and demanded that Osarsiph be purchased at the price of first asking, without any haggling at all. Only at the end and quite incidentally did the object of the chaffering take any hand in the deal: saying offhand that he thought a hundred and fifty deben too low, and that they should agree on a hundred and sixty at the least. He said this out of sheer respect for God, and was brushed aside by the scribe Khamat, in high excitement, he considering it most improper that the chattel should have a voice in his price. Joseph then dropped the point and fell silent once more.

At length he saw a young spotted steer brought from his stall into the court by order of Khamat. He had a strange sensation at seeing, outside of himself and in animal form, the estimated value of his own person. That was strange, yet not offensive; for in this country nearly all the gods could recognize themselves in animal shape, and great respect was paid always to the idea that being near to a thing and being a thing were closely related conceptions.

But it did not stop at the young steer, for the old man sturdily refused to value him at more than a hundred and twenty deben, which was much less than what Joseph was worth. So various goods were added: a neat's-leather breast-plate, several bales of writing-paper and the cheaper sort of linen, a few wineskins of panther-fell, a quantity of natron for embalming, a bundle of fish-hooks, and some hand-brooms. All this had to be laid beside the steer before the scale with the ape was brought to a balance in the time-honoured way. Even then the bargain was concluded more by agreement than by calculation, for in the end they gave up reckoning and each side contented itself with the feeling that it had not been too grossly swindled. The whole amount had come to perhaps a copper weight of one hundred and fifty or sixty deben; for which sum Rachel's son, together with the wine and the onions, became the property of the great Egyptian, Petepre.

It was done. The Ishmaelites from Midian had accomplished the purpose of their existence: they had delivered that which they had been chosen out to bring down to Egypt; they might vanish from the scene, it needed them no more. But their self-satisfaction was untroubled by the state of things; they took themselves as seriously as ever they had, packed up their wares, and never dreamed that they were now superfluous. The desire and fatherly concern of the old man to protect his foundling and provide for him in the best place he could — had it not its full value in the moral world, though from another point of view one might consider his whim a means and tool to ends he knew not of? True and obvious it was that he sold Joseph, as though he could not do anything else — for a price, indeed, which " let him live that he might further serve the house "; and knew how to state his necessity in such a way that the scribe, to his disadvantage, could not gainsay it. Thus he satisfied his mercantile conscience; yet plainly he did not do it for profit, and — unless I am mistaken — he would gladly have kept the son of the well, to bake him pancakes and bid him good-night. He did not act to his own advantage, while being at pains to safeguard his business interest. But then, what is self-interest? Interest urged him to look after Joseph and advance his lot in life; for in so doing he got satisfaction, of whatever sort, and from whatsoever source it came.

Joseph, moreover, was quite the youth to respect the dignity of freedom which humanly animates the inevitable. The old man, on concluding the bargain, addressed him, saying: " Lo, now, ' Come-hither,' or Usarsiph, or however thou callest thyself, now thou art no more mine, but belongest to this house; and I have made good my purposes." So then Joseph willingly paid him due meed of gratitude, kissing many times the hem of his garment and calling him his saviour.

" Farewell, my son," the old man said, " and show thyself worthy of my kindness. Be tactful and obliging to all, and bridle thy tongue when it twitches to criticize and to practise itself on injurious distinctions like that between the honoured and the outworn. For suchlike bringeth one to the pit. Sweetness is given to thy mouth; thou knowest how to bid a soothing good-night and turn a phrase with charm. Keep to such, then, and rejoice mankind, instead of winning their abhorrence for thy carping, for it doeth no good. And now farewell. Those errors which brought thee to thy grave — culpable self-confidence and blind presumption — of them I need not to warn thee, for I think thou art taught of experience to shun them. I have not pried into the details of thy history or thy antecedents. It sufficeth me to know that much mystery lurketh in this blustering world; and I am taught of experience that strange things are possible. If it be true, as thy manners and gifts sometimes make me sus-pect, that thou comest of the best and didst anoint thy-self with the oil of gladness before thou camest unto the body of the pit — well then, here is a life-line thrown to thee, a prospect that thou mayest raise thyself to better conditions by my having sold thee to this house. For the third time, fare thee well! For I have said it twice al-ready, and what one says three times must come to pass. Old am I, and know not if I shall see thee again. May Adon thy God — who, so far as I know, may be like the setting sun in power — keep thee and guard thy steps, that they stumble not. And blessings on thee!"

Joseph knelt down on the ground before this father of his and once again kissed the hem of his robe, as the old man laid a hand upon his head. Joseph took leave also of Mibsam, and thanked him for pulling him out of the pit; from Epher, the nephew, and Kedar and Kedema, the old man's sons, and more informally from Ba'al-mahar, the pack-boy, and Jupa, the thick-lipped lad, who was holding by a rope the animal representative of Joseph's value — in other words the young steer. Then the Ishmaelites went off across the court and through the echoing gateway, as they had come — only without

Joseph. He stood looking after them; not without pain at the parting and some sinking at the pit of his stomach as he thought of the new and uncertain prospects before him.

When they were out of sight he turned round and saw that everybody was gone from the court, that he was alone save only for the mock-vizier, Sa'ankh-Wen-nofer-Neteruhotep-em-per-Amun, who stood with the red monkey on his shoulder and looked up at him with a wrinkled smile.

" What do I do now, and whither do I go? " Joseph inquired.

The dwarf did not reply, only nodded and went on smiling. But suddenly he turned his head with a start and whispered:

" Throw yourself on your face! "

And at once he did as he had bade the other, lying with his forehead to the earth in a fat little heap, with the monkey atop. For the little creature had cleverly parried his master's abrupt movement by leaping from shoulder to back and squatting there with uplifted tail and staring eyes directed to the point where Joseph also took leave to look. He had followed the dwarf's example, but yet lifted his head a little on his hands that he might see before whom or what he thus abased himself.

A train was passing across from the women's to the master's house: in front five servants in aprons and narrow caps; behind, five maidservants with flowing hair; and between them, swaying on the bare shoulders of Nubian slaves, a sort of gilded carrying-chair adorned with the heads of gaping beasts. Leaning among the cushions, with crossed feet, was an Egyptian lady, exquisitely got up, glittering ornaments in her curling locks, gold about her neck, with beringed fingers, and arms like lilies, one of which — very white and lovely — hung idly down at the side of the chair. Beneath the wrought-gold garland on her head Joseph saw her profile: that peculiar and personal, despite all adherence to the fashion quite unique and individual profile, with its eyes lengthened toward the temples by cosmetics, its flattened nose, its shadowy cheeks, its mouth at once thin and soft and sinuous as a snake between its two deep corners.

It was Mut-em-enet being borne to her evening meal; the lady of the house, consort of Petepre — a personality big with fate.

4

THE HIGHEST

HOW LONG JOSEPH STAYED WITH POTIPHAR

ONCE there was a man who had a refractory cow, that would not bear the yoke for the plough, but always shook it from her neck. The man took her calf from her and brought it to the field which was to be ploughed. When the cow heard the lowing of her calf she let herself be driven to the field and submitted her neck to the yoke.

The calf is on the field, the man has brought it hither; yet it lows not, rather makes no sound as it looks about in the strange field, which it thinks to be a field of the dead. It is too soon, thinks the calf, to let its voice be heard. But it has a clear idea of the man's purpose and long-distance calculations, this calf Jehosiph or Osarsiph. Knowing the man, it assumes at once and understands, though as in a dream, that its transportation to this field, so rebelled against at home, is no isolated fact or half-measure, but part of a plan, in which one thing follows upon another. This theme, of the "following on" or the "drawing after" is one of those which presented themselves contrapuntally in his intelligent and dreamy soul, in which, as one may say, the sun and the moon, as we sometimes see them, are in the sky at the same time, and the moon comes into play as the leading motif, making a gleaming path for its brothers the constellations across the sky. Joseph, the calf — had he not had his own thoughts at sight of the bright meadows of the land of Goshen, quite irrespective of the man's plans, though even so in harmony with them? Premature thoughts they were, and wide-ranging into the future — he saw that himself, and for the present they should remain unuttered. For much was yet to be fulfilled before they could come to fulfilment, and the mere coming hither was by no means enough. Something more must be added, to which there was need of the quietest waiting and the most childlike and secretive caution, withal no speculation at all as to the how. For that lay with the Man who brought the calf to the field — that lay with God.

No, Joseph was not unmindful of the old man at home, benumbed by his grief. His silence — the silence of so many years — must never lead us to reproach him. Least of all at this moment, the events of which I relate with emotions precisely like his own — for they are his own. I feel indeed as though I had once already reached this point in my story and told it once before; the special feeling of recognition, of having been here before and dreamed the same dream, moves me and challenges me to dwell upon it — and such precisely were the feelings, such the experience of my hero. For all which there is probably very good reason. What I am tempted to call his bond with his father — a bond the stronger and deeper in that, thanks to far-reaching associations, it was also a bond with God — was in particular strength at this moment, as indeed how could it not have been, when it subsisted in him, with him, and outside of him? What he felt was imitation and succession; with slight differences, his father before him had experienced the same. It is uncanny to see the mixture of free will and guidance in the phenomenon of imitation. In the end it is hard to tell whether it is the individual or the destiny that actually follows the pattern and insists upon the repetition. The inward and the outward play into each other, and materialize apparently without act of will into the event which was from all time bound up with and one with the individual. For we move in the footsteps of others, and all life is but the pouring of the present into the forms of the myth.

Joseph played with many forms of imitation and artlessly deluding self-metamorphoses, knowing how to make an impression with them and win men to himself, even if temporarily. But just now he was entirely preoccupied with the return of the father-idea and its resurrection in him. He was Jacob the father, a refugee from home, fleeing before fraternal hate, stolen to the kingdom of Laban to escape from the Red One's jealousy of the first-born blessing. This time, to be sure, there was not one Esau but ten, and Laban's present form was quite other than the old one: he was Potiphar, tamer of horses, arriving in a chariot with fiery wheels, arrayed in royal linen, fat and heavy, and so brave that one must tremble for his life. But Laban he was all the same, no doubt of that, however much life changed its forms. And once more, as the past had foretold, had the seed of Abram come a stranger into the land that belonged not to him, and Joseph was to serve a Laban who in his present form bore an Egyptian name and a high-flown title like " Gift of the Sun." But how long should he serve him?

Thus did we ask in the time of Jacob, and made the

matter clear to the light of reason. Now we ask it with
regard to the son, again with intent to clarify the matter
and establish the dream within the reality. In Joseph's
story the question of time and age have always been very
laxly dealt with in the field of reality. Dreamy and super-
ficial fantasy ascribes to his figure an unchangeableness
untouched by time, such as it had in Jacob's eyes when he
believed him to be dead and mangled. But that is an
unchangeableness only conferred by death; actually the
lad, immortalized to the father's eye, lived on and increased in years. We need to realize that the Joseph before whose chair the famine-stricken brethren stood and
made obeisance was a forty-year-old man; and that they
failed to recognize him not only on account of his dress
and his dignity of rank but also because of the changes
wrought by the years in his person.

Twenty-three years had passed since the Esau-brethren
had sold him into Egypt — almost as much time as
Jacob, all in all, spent in the land of never-more-return.
And the same name might with even more justice be
given to the country where now Abram's seed was once
more strange; for the years which Joseph remained in
it were not fourteen and six and five, or seven and thirteen
and five, but actually the whole of his life; and only
with his death did he return home. But it has remained
uncertain and has been little considered in what proportion the years of his underworld life were divided into
the two plain and clear epochs of his blessing-life: the
first and decisive period of his sojourn in Potiphar's
house, and the period spent in the pit whither he once
more came.

The two periods came together to thirteen years — the

same number that Jacob took to rear up his twelve Mesopotamian children — supposing that Joseph was thirty when his head was lifted up and he became the first among those below. Certainly we are nowhere told that that was his age — or at least nowhere where the statement would be authoritative. Yet it is a generally accepted fact none the less, an axiom, requiring no evidence and simply speaking for itself — begetting itself, as it were, like the sun, from its own mother, and with the clearest claims to a simple " So it was." For it is always so. Thirty years is just the right age for the stage of life at which Joseph then arrived; at thirty a man emerges from the darkness and wilderness of the time of preparation into active life; it is the age of fruition and fulfilment. Thirteen years, then, passed from the time when he entered Egypt a seventeen-year-old lad to the day when he stood before Pharaoh. There can be no doubt of it. But how many of them were spent in Potiphar's house and how many in the grave? The established tradition leaves it open; a few non-committal phrases are all we have to help us clear up the dates within our history. How shall we interpret them? What shall we conclude was the real division of the time?

The question seems inept. Do we know our story or do we not? Is it proper and suitable to the nature of story-telling that the narrator should openly reckon dates and facts according to any deductions or considerations whatever? Should he appear at all, save as anonymous source of the tale which is being told or is telling itself, in which everything is by virtue of itself, so and not otherwise, indisputable and certain? The narrator, according to this view, should be in the tale, one with it, and not outside it, reckoning and calculating. But how is it with God, whom Abram thought into being and recognized? He is in the fire but He is not the fire. Thus He is at once in it and outside it. Indeed, it is one thing to be a thing, quite another to observe it. And yet there are planes and spheres where both happen at once: the narrator is in the story, yet is not the story; he is its scene but it is not his, since he is also outside it and by a turn of his nature puts himself in the position of dealing with it. I have never tried to produce the illusion that I am the source of the history of Joseph. Before it could be told, it happened, it sprang from the source from which all history springs, and tells itself as it goes. Since that time it exists in the world, everybody knows it or thinks he does — for often enough the knowledge is unreal, casual, and disjointed. It had been told a hundred times, in a hundred different mediums. And now it is passing through another, wherein as it were it becomes conscious of itself and remembers how things actually were with it in the long-ago, so that it now both pours forth and speaks of itself as it pours.

It tells, for instance, about the apportionment of the years between Joseph's sale to Potiphar and the lifting up of his head. And this much is certain: that the Joseph who went down into the prison was far from being the lad Joseph whom the Ishmaelites led before Petepre's house; that much the larger part of the thirteen years was passed in that house. I might state the fact categorically, but prefer merely to inquire how it could have been other-wise. Joseph was, from a social point of view, a complete cipher when as a seventeen- or eighteen-year-old youth he came among the Egyptians; and his career there must

have embraced the whole time of his stay. For it was not
on the second or the third day of it that Potiphar set the
Shabirite slave over the whole of his property and left
it in Joseph's hands. It took some time before the master
was even aware of Joseph's presence — and the same
is true of certain other persons of importance to the issue
of events. Moreover, that swiftly mounting career to the
great height he reached must even so have stretched into
years, in order to be the schooling in administration and
economics which we are led to consider it.

In a word: Joseph stayed with Potiphar for ten years,
and became a man of twenty-seven, a Hebrew " man,"
as it is said of him, by some even a Hebrew servant, which
sounds rather distorted and exaggerated, considering that
in practice he had long since ceased to be a servant. We
cannot tell or define the precise point at which he ceased
to be so — as little now as we could have done then. In
legal fact Joseph remained a servant, a slave, even at
the time of his greatest honour and actually until the
end of his life. For we read of his being sold, and of his
being sold again, but nowhere at all of his being freed.
His phenomenal career ignored the legal fact of his
status, and after his swift elevation it no longer came in
question. Even in the house of Petepre he did not long
remain a slave in any strict sense of the word; his rise to
Eliezer's position of stewardship by no means occupied
the whole of his time there. One thing is certain, that
seven years were enough; another, that it was only the
remaining three which were dominated and overshad-
owed by the emotions of an unhappy woman and which
brought in their train the termination of the decade. The
tradition does, by its very vagueness in the matter of time,

indicate that the trouble did not begin at once or even very soon after Joseph's appearance; that it did not coincide with his rise to power, but only commenced after he had reached his height. " After these things," it says, " it came to pass "; in other words, after its own account of Joseph's rise to a position of the highest trust. That unhappy passion, then, must be thought of as lasting three years — quite long enough for the actors in it! — before the final catastrophe.

The results of our examination of this part of the story are borne out by the other half. We have calculated that the Potiphar episode occupied ten years of Joseph's life. Accordingly, there are three years left for the period in prison. No more and no less; and certainly it is not often that fact and probability coincide more nearly than in this case. For what could be more illuminating, more inevitable, than that Joseph lay three years in the prison, no more and no less, corresponding to the three days which he lay in the well at Dothan? We may even go so far as to assert that he suspected it beforehand, or even knew it, and measuring it by all that he held fitting, significant, and in the divine order of things, was convinced that nothing else was possible — confirmed therein by a destiny which took a perfectly inevitable line.

Three years — and not only that it was three, but also that it could not be otherwise. The tradition fixes with extraordinary precision and detail the way in which the three years were divided: it shows that the famous episodes of the chief baker and the chief butler, Joseph's elegant fellow-prisoners, upon whom he waited, fell in the first year. " At the end of two full years," it says,

"Pharaoh dreamed," and Joseph interpreted unto him his dreams. Two full years after what? Opinions might differ. It might mean two years after he became Pharaoh — that is, two years after the accession of that Pharaoh who dreamed the riddling dreams. Or, on the other hand, it might mean two years after Joseph had interpreted the dreams of the butler and the baker, and the latter, as we know, had been hanged. But it would come to the same thing in the end: Pharaoh dreamed his dreams two years after the episodes of the imprisoned courtiers, and also two years after he had become Pharaoh. For during the time Joseph spent in prison, at the end of the first year, to be precise, it came to pass that Amun-hotep, of his name the Third, united himself with the sun, and his son, the Dreamer, set upon his head the double crown.

Thus we see that there is nothing wrong about the story, but that all the evidence agrees concerning the ten and three years of Joseph's life until he was thirty; the true and the actual are one.

IN THE LAND OF THE MODERNS

PART of the game we play with life consists in the relations of human beings one to another. Take two people who have just exchanged their first glance — what could be slighter, what could be more unconscious, tenuous, distant, and casual than the bond between them? And yet it may be destined to take on, some unimaginable day, a character of burning intensity, a frightful and breathtaking immediacy. Truly this game, and the innocence of the players, may well be the subject of head-shaking and pondering on the part of the forewarned observer.

There knelt Joseph, a little round mound, beside the dwarf called Shepses-Bes, on the paving of the court and peered curiously through his fingers at the priceless, utterly unknown presence which swayed past him in its gilded chair adorned with lions' heads, only a few paces away. This underworldly product of culture, civilization's height, roused in him no other feeling than a respect strongly tinged with critical disapproval, no other thought than perhaps something like: " Ha ha, that must be the mistress — Potiphar's wife, who is supposed to tremble for his safety! Where does she belong — is she friend or foe? One cannot tell from her looks. A very great Egyptian lady. My father would disapprove of her. I am more lenient in my judgment; on the other hand, I am not to be dazzled." That was all. And on her side it was still less. As she swayed past she turned her jewel-crowned head for a second to the place where they did reverence. She saw them and saw them not — so idle and unseeing was her glance. She probably recognized the dwarf, for she knew him; perhaps the faintest shadow of a smile showed in her enamel-lengthened eyes and just deepened the corners of her sinuous mouth. Even that is doubtful. The other figure she did not know, and scarcely noticed it. He looked a little odd, because of the faded cloak the Ishmaelites had given him, and also his hair had not an Egyptian cut. Did she see it? She must have done so. But he could scarcely have penetrated her lofty consciousness. If he did not belong here, the gods knew where he did belong and that was quite enough; she, Mut-em-enet, called Eni, thought far too much of herself to consider the question. Did she see how beautiful and well-favoured he was? Why ask? Her seeing was no seeing; she never thought, it was hidden from her, that here was any occasion for the use of her eyes. Not the shadow of a suspicion visited either, of what was to happen, whither a few years was to bring them both. That the reverential little bundle over there on the ground was one day to be her one· and all, her ecstasy and anguish, the single morbid content of her mind, which should distract its sense, make her commit mad acts of folly, destroy all the dignity, self-control, and order of her days — the woman dreamt not of it. What tears she would bring him to, with what uttermost danger she threatened his brideship of God and the garland of his head; that through her folly he would come in peril of losing his God — all this the dreamer could not dream, though the sight of her lily arm hanging down from her chair might have given him to think. The onlooker, knowing the tale as it fell out in all its hours, may be forgiven if he pauses a little, shaking his head, and assumes the ignorance of those who are in the story and not outside it.

He puts aside the indiscretion which made him lift the curtain of the future, and confines himself to the hour of the reigning feast, which lasted seven years, the years of Joseph's incredible rise in the house of Petepre, from that moment when, after the litter had swayed past them, the fool Bes-em-heb whispered to Joseph there in the court: " We must cut your hair and dress you as others are dressed — " and led him to the barber in the servants' quarters; who, jesting the while with Bes-em-heb, cut Joseph's hair in the Egyptian fashion, so that he looked like the wayfarers along the canals. Thence they took him to the wardrobe room, where the apron skirts were kept, and issued to him Egyptian clothing out of the stores: the livery of Petepre for best and for common wear; so that at last he looked like a child of Kemt, and even his brothers, at first glance, might not have known him.

These seven years, then, were a repetition and imitation of the father's life in the life of the son; corresponding to the period in which Jacob turned from a landless fugitive to a man weighed down with possessions, and an indispensable partner in Laban's enterprises, which by the power of the blessing were swollen with prosperity. Now it was Joseph's turn to make himself indispensable — and how did he do it? Did he find water, as Jacob did? It would have been utterly superfluous. There was abundance of water on Petepre's estate, not only in the lotus-pond in the pleasure-garden, but also in square basins sunk in the ground among the orchards and vegetable-gardens. They had no connection with the Nourisher, but supplied the estate from subsoil sources. No, there was no need of water. Nor of domestic well-being of any kind. For if Potiphar's house was not a house of blessing — and indeed it proved despite all its dignity to be rather a house of tribulation and folly — yet it abounded in material prosperity, to an extent which made it wellnigh impossible for anybody to give it increase or to play the rôle of blessing-bringer in any such sense. It must suffice that the owner should one day come to the conviction that if he put his affairs into this young stranger's hands all would be well and himself not need to trouble further, or act otherwise than befitted his lordly station and ways. So that the blessing displayed itself above all in the establishment of trust; and Joseph's natural dislike of betraying such confidence in any point — above all in the most personal and delicate — was to prove to the blessing-bearer a mighty bulwark against betraying his compact with God.

Yes, this was Joseph's Laban-time. Yet there were great material differences, and things fell out quite otherwise for the son. For in repetition there is always change, as in the kaleidoscope the bits of coloured glass shape ever different patterns. Life in its play produces changing patterns out of the same material, and the constellation of the son, formed of the same little glass splinters as the father's, yet showed a new form. The parallel of the kaleidoscope is instructive; for in how much richer, more involved and varied patterns did the son's life shape itself! He is a later, more difficult and dangerous " case," this Joseph; a son, probably cleverer and flightier than the father, yet more interesting, difficult, painfuller; scarcely even is the pattern of the father's life recognizable in that of the son who repeats it. How much richer it is, how much more complex, more dangerous! Where for instance is the figure and concept of Rachel, that pure and classic fundamental? — and what extraordinary and hazardous arabesque instead! Of course, we see what is coming, what is already present because it happened when the story first told itself, and is only not yet come to pass because we give due heed to later introduced laws of time and sequence. It exerts a powerful, uncanny fascination; our lively curiosity — of a peculiar kind, indeed, since it already knows, and interests itself only in the telling — tempts us ever and anon to anticipate the hour. Thus the double sense of the " once upon a time " practises its magic upon us; future is past, and what happened long ago now plays itself out again in the clear-cut present.

What we can do, in order to put reins to our impatience, is to extend somewhat our notion of the present; to include in it somewhat larger entities of sequence, and make of them a sort of loose coincidence in time. And the period we have in hand is quite suited to such a procedure — the years, that is, in which Joseph became first Petepre's body-servant and then his head overseer. They even demand such treatment, because there were circumstances which — quite contrary to probability — contributed to his success, and not only so but exercised an influence afterwards; and these played a part — like an all-pervasive atmosphere — even in the beginning, so that one cannot even discuss the early stages without bringing them in.

Our source, after confirming the fact of Joseph's second purchase, promptly states that " he was in the house of his master the Egyptian." Certainly, there he was — where else? He had been sold into that house and there he was — the tradition seems to assert the known and to be redundant. But let us be sure that we understand it. To say that he " was " in Potiphar's house means that he remained there, which is a new fact and one to be emphasized. After he was bought, Joseph *remained* in Potiphar's *house;* that is to say, he escaped, by God's will, the imminent danger of being sent to field labour, where he would by day have fainted in the heat, by night have shaken with cold, and might easily, under the lash of a barbarous overseer, have ended his days obscurely and in want, uncherished, unadvanced.

The sword hovered over him; we must wonder that it did not fall. It hung loose enough. Joseph was an alien sold into Egypt, a son of Asia, an Amu boy, a Shabirite or Hebrew; we must realize the contempt felt for such in this most arrogant of lands before we pass on to explain the influence which weakened and counteracted it. We have seen that Mont-kaw was tempted for a second or so to regard Joseph more or less as a god; but that does not mean that — certainly in the beginning — he did not think of him more rather than less as a man. For of course he did. The denizen of Kemt, whose forbears had drunk from the waves of the sacred river, at home in an unsurpassable land crowded with temples, statues, and writings compelling from old time, where once the sun-god in person had been king, was too expressly aware of his status as " man " to have much esteem left over for non-Egyptians, such as Negroes from Kush, Libyan pig-tail-wearers, and Asiatic louse-beards. The conception of uncleanness and abomination was not an invention of the seed of Abram, and by no means peculiar to the sons of Shem. Some things they held in common detestation: as for instance the pig. But to the Egyptians the Hebrews were themselves an abomination — it went against them to break bread together; indeed, some twenty years later, when Joseph, God consenting, had become to all intents and purposes an Egyptian, he had foreign barbarians served separately when such sat at his table, in order to keep himself in countenance with his own.

This was the position in Egypt respecting the people of Amu and Haru. And such was the view taken of Joseph himself when he first came. So that it is really a miracle that he remained in Potiphar's house and had not to perish in the fields — or rather it is to be marvelled at; for a miracle, a wonder-working of God in the full sense of the word, it was not. What actually came in play was the human — matters of taste and custom, influences which, as I said above, weakened and even abrogated the effect of the fundamental tradition. Not that the latter was not vocal. It spoke, indeed, in the voice of Dudu, spouse of Djeset, who demanded that Joseph be sent to field labour. For Dudu was not only a man — or a manling — of great and solid dignity; he was also spokesman and defender of the sacred and traditional in all its strictness; he was fundamentally pious, and withal, as a party man, he held with a school of thought which, committed by every consideration of state, ethics, and religion to an organic and militant unity, had to dispute its position against less limited and reactionary views. This school, so far as Petepre's establishment was concerned, had its seat in the house of women, more precisely in the apartments of the mistress, Mut-em-enet. For a familiar guest in those apartments was a certain man whose rigid personality made him the centre and nucleus of the traditional view: this man was Beknechons, the first prophet of Amun.

We shall speak of him later. For it was only after some time that Joseph first heard of the man; indeed, he only gradually gained insight into the situation hinted at above. However, he would have needed to be much less acute than he was, much less quick in sizing up advantage and disadvantage, not to have gained some inkling of essentials, even in his first conversations with the servants of the house. His method was to behave as though he already knew as well as anybody the inner mysteries and secrets of the country. His Egyptian sounded quaint and amusing in the ear of the natives and he made no haste to regularize it; but his choice of words was both lively and judicious, as he talked about the " rubber-eaters " — glibly adopting the popular name for the Nubian Moors whom he had seen crossing the river to audience on his arrival; or repeated the carping words of the gentlemen at the levee. They would not, he said, succeed in undermining the prince-prefect of Kush, for the latter had cut away the ground under their feet by the surprisingly lordly tribute with which he had rejoiced the heart of Pharaoh. All this made them laugh much more than if he had told them something new; and the way they made merry over his strange speech, even admiring it and listening to the Canaanitish words with which he helped himself out, shed even now some light upon the problem of advantage and disadvantage.

For they tried, as best they could, to speak as he did, mixing into their sentences scraps of Akkadian or Babylonian as well as words from Joseph's own linguistic sphere. He divined, long before he could know it for a fact, that they were imitating the elegant attitude of their masters; and that these in turn did not ape the foreigner of their own motion, but because they wished to copy the manners of a still higher sphere — namely, the court. Joseph grasped the situation, as I have said, long before he could actually know it. He smiled to himself as he did so. These little people, so absurdly vain because they were brought up on Nile water and born in the land of " men," the only true birthplace of the gods, would have laughed to scorn the slightest doubt cast upon the superiority of their civilization over that of any of the surround-

ing countries. They were full to overflowing with the
martial glory of their kings, their Ahmoses and Thut-
moses and Amen-hoteps, who had conquered the earth as
far as the contrary-flowing Euphrates and advanced their
boundary-stones to the northern Retenu and the deserts
and bowmen of the farthest south. And then, secure as
they were, they were weak and childish enough to be
openly envious of his Canaanitish speech, and that it was
his mother tongue; and against all reason and sense to
regard it as meritorious that he could speak it.

Why? Because Canaanitish was fashionable. And
why fashionable? Because it was foreign and strange.
But the foreign and strange was of no value and worthless? Yes, of course. But in spite of that it was fashionable; and this inconsequential esteem rested, in their
own opinion, not on weakness or childishness but on
liberality of thought. Joseph felt this — he was the first
person in the world to feel it, since the phenomenon now
appeared for the first time in the world. It was the freedom of thought possessed by people who had not themselves conquered those wretched foreign lands, but had it
done for them by their forbears, and now took leave to
make liberal thought the mode. The example was given
by the great. The house of Petepre the fan-bearer made
that clear to Joseph; for the more he saw, the plainer it
became that most of its treasures came from the port —
in other words, were importations. In fact, they came in
large part from Joseph's own sphere, in a narrower or a
more extended sense: from Syria and Canaan. That was
flattering; at the same time he found it a little undignified.
For on the leisurely journey from the Delta to the house
of Amun he had had ample occasion to admire the na-

tive skill and craftsmanship of Pharaoh's country. Potiphar's horses were Syrian stock — it was indeed better
to get them from Syria or Babylonia, for the Egyptian
strain was poorish. But his chariots as well, and that very
one with its wheels inlaid with stones like fireworks, were
imported too. Then his cattle came from the land of the
Amorites — which could be nothing else than a freak
of fashion, considering the beauty of the domestic breed,
with its lyre-shaped horns — the mild-eyed Hathor cows
and the strong bulls from whose number Merwer and
Hapi were chosen. Pharaoh's friend carried an inlaid
walking-stick from Syria, and from Syria came the beer
and the wine he drank. The jugs that held them came
" from the port " as well; likewise the weapons and
musical instruments which adorned his rooms. Orna-
mental vases almost the height of a man stood in painted
alcoves in the northern and western hypostyle halls and
on both sides of the dais in the dining-hall; the gold they
were made of came doubtless from Nubian mines, but the
vases were shaped in Damascus and Sidon. A reception-
and banqueting-hall, entered by stately doors from the
court itself, lay in front of the family dining-room; in
it Joseph was shown other vases, somewhat eccentric in
shape and decoration, from Edom, the Goat Mountains;
they brought to mind Esau, his foreign uncle — he, too,
was obviously the fashion here.

So were the gods themselves of Emor and Canaan:
Baal and Astarte. They were considered very elegant;
Joseph could tell by the way Potiphar's people took it
for granted that they were his, asked about them, and
paid them compliments. It seemed a feeble sort of broad-
mindedness, because after all in the imagination of the

people the relations between the powers of the various countries were incorporated in the gods and were only the expression of their personal life. Indeed, what was the thing itself, and what their picture? What the reality and what the paraphrase? Was it just a manner of speaking to say that Amun had conquered the gods of Asia and made them tributary, when the actual fact was that Pharaoh had subdued the kings of Canaan? Or was the latter only an unreal and sublunary expression for the former? Joseph knew that you could not distinguish. The thing and the image, the actual and the non-actual, formed an inextricably interwoven whole. But that was just why the folk of Mizraim were abandoning Amun, not only when they flattered Baal and Ashteroth but also when they interlarded the tongue of their own gods with fragments of the speech of the children of Shem and said " *seper* " for scribe and " *nehel* " for river because the Canaanitish words were " *sofer* " and " *nahal*." It was indeed a free-thinking spirit which underlay these fashions, whims, and habits — and free-thinking against Egyptian Amun. The issue of it was a much less thoroughgoing distaste for the Semitic and Asiatic — in his estimating advantage and disadvantage Joseph booked this fact on the credit side.

Thus he took note of fluctuations and variable currents of thought and opinion, growing, as I said, more able to judge them with each day that he lived and observed the life of the land. His master, Potiphar, was a courtier, one of the friends of Pharaoh; it was not hard to guess that this loose tolerance of foreign ways, this rebellion against Amun, displayed in Potiphar's life and habits, had its source over there in the West, beyond the " *nehel*," in the Great House. Had it, Joseph wondered, to do with Amun's warrior hosts, the lance-bristling temple troops which had shoved him to the wall in the Street of the Son? With Pharaoh's displeasure when Amun, too powerful already as the established god of the state, competed with him on the military side as well?

What strange, far-reaching considerations! Pharaoh's irritation at the presumption of Amun or his temple became perhaps the final reason why Joseph had not to go and labour in the fields, but might remain in his master's house, and came on the fields much later, in the capacity not of labourer but of overseer and administrator. The situation, which made the boy profit from considerations of so lofty and far-reaching a kind, pleased the young slave Osarsiph and made a bond — aside from that through his present master — with the Highest. But something else rejoiced him even more: a more pervasive atmosphere in this world to which he had been transplanted. He detected it as he sniffed for advantage or disadvantage with that pretty if rather thick-nostrilled nose of his, and it was an air in which he was as much at home as a fish in water. For the prevailing atmosphere — to put it in an old phrase — was *fin de siècle*. It was that of a society composed of descendants and heirs, already remote from the patterns of the founding fathers whose victories had put their successors in the frame of mind to regard the conquered as elegant. It appealed to Joseph, for he himself was late, too, in time and in his soul, a very good specimen of a descendant, volatile, witty, difficult, and interesting. So he felt like a fish in water, and filled with lively hope that by God's help he

would do honour to Him and to himself and go very far
in Pharaoh's land.

THE COURTIER

DUDU, then, the married dwarf, acted as a defender of
tradition and a partisan of the good old times; he spoke
in Amun's name when he advised Mont-kaw to send the
new Shabirite slave to work in the fields, for that he came
from the enemies of the gods and was no fit person for the
house. He stood waving his stumps of arms and sending
his deep voice up to reach the ear of Mont-kaw. But
the steward seemed disinclined to remember what Dudu
was talking about or to whom he referred. An Amu boy?
Bought from the Minæans? Named Osarsiph? Oh yes,
yes. And after having thus given the other a lesson in
the careless and forgetful attitude proper to such a theme,
he expressed surprise that the keeper of the wardrobe
should give it any thought, much less waste words on it.
He did so for the sake of propriety, Dudu replied. It was
offensive to the people of the estate to break bread with
such a one. The overseer simply denied that they were
so fastidious, and mentioned the case of a Babylonian
female slave named Ishtarummi, with whom the others in
the house of women got on very well. " Amun! " said
the keeper of the wardrobe, naming the name of the conservative deity and looking severely, even almost menac-
ingly up at Mont-kaw. It was on Amun's account, he
said. " Amun is great," replied the steward, with an ill-
concealed shrug. " Anyhow," he added, " I may send
the new slave to the fields. I may send him, or I may not;

but if I do, it will be on my own motion. I like not those who try to throw a noose over my thoughts and lead them on a string."

In a word, he sent the spouse of Djeset about his business; partly on the ground that he could not stand the dwarf, but also on a ground that had backgrounds as well. The ground for his disinclination was the dwarf's pompous respectability, which rubbed him the wrong way; but the background was his own honest devotion to his master, Petepre, which sustained a sense of injury at Dudu's pretensions. All this will become clear later on. But ill will against Dudu's self-righteous personality was not the only reason why Mont-kaw turned a deaf ear to his words. The steward had a liking for the other dwarf, Beauty — less, perhaps, for himself than because he was an agreeable foil to Dudu. But he had snubbed him likewise when he appealed to his superior in the opposite sense. Good, beautiful, and wise is the desert youth, darling of the gods, that was what Bes had whispered. He, Bes, by name the beautiful, but in fact not such a one, had seen the truth, with the unerring penetration of his dwarf senses; the overseer should see to it that Joseph be given tasks, whether in the court or outside it, which would give employment to his qualities. But here too the steward had pretended absent-mindedness and then irritably refused to give any thought to the problem of employment for the chattel which partly by chance and partly by good nature he had acquired. There was no hurry, and he, Mont-kaw, had other things to think of.

That was reasonable enough, for the steward was weighed down with cares, and his kidneys gave him much trouble. The reply was convincing, the dwarf had nothing to say against it. But the truth was that the steward pretended, to himself and others, forgetfulness of Joseph because he was ashamed of the equivocal thoughts and impressions which he, a practical man, had had at first sight of the slave; when he had been half inclined to take him for a god, the Lord of the White Ape. He had felt ashamed, and that was why he wished to forget and not be persuaded by the importunities of others to act in line with his own impressions. He refused alike to send his purchase to the fields or to think of using him in the house; refused, in short, either to act or to think of acting, in either or in any direction. The good man did not perceive, he tried not to see, that precisely in doing nothing he was acting on his first impressions. And the bottom of his restraint was fear; it arose, just among ourselves, from the feeling which is the bottommost one in the world and thus lay at the bottom of Mont-kaw's soul: the feeling of expectancy.

Thus it came about that Joseph, garbed and barbered like an Egyptian, spent weeks and months without work; or at most in some light and desultory occupation on Petepre's court; in which he was not very noticeable, for there were plenty of loiterers and bystanders besides himself. And in a way he was pleased and satisfied to have no notice paid him — that is, not prematurely, or until it could come about in proper and dignified fashion. He did not want to begin his career in a false or unreal way, by being drawn into some one of the trades practised in the courtyard and being lost for ever in that obscure activity. He guarded himself against such a fate, keeping himself from observation at critical moments. He would sit and chat with the gate-keepers on their brick bench, making them laugh with his Asiatic expressions. But he avoided the bakery; such marvellous triumphs of the baker's art were there achieved as would put his uncommonly good pancakes quite in the shade; nor did he call attention to himself in the booths where they made sandals, or paper, or mats of woven palm, or pottery, or furniture. He was warned by an inward voice that it would be foolish to play the part of ignorant apprentice — foolish, and prejudicial to his later career.

On the other hand, there was no harm in making lists and doing accounts now and then for the laundry or the granary; and for this his knowledge of writing soon became adequate. At the bottom he would sign with flourishes: " Written by the young foreign slave Osarsiph, for his master the great Petepre; may the Hidden One give him long life! Likewise for Mont-kaw, the steward set above all, greatly skilled in his office; for whom he implores from Amun ten thousand years of life beyond his life. Written on this and this day of the third month of Akhet, the time of the flood." In such terms, recreant to the practice of his own land, did he express himself, in the consciousness of his blessing, and in sure trust that God, seeing his situation and the need of making himself loved, would not take them ill. Such lists and signatures came to the eye of Mont-kaw; he saw them at odd times and made no sign.

His bread Joseph ate with the people of Potiphar, in the servants' house; drank beer with them and passed the time of day. Soon he could chatter with the best — or even better; his gifts inclining him to use his tongue rather than his hands. He listened to their idiom and took it in his mouth, first to talk but later to give orders. He learned to say: " As true as the king liveth! " " By Khnum, the great, Lord of Shab! " He learned to say: " I am in the greatest joy of the earth " and " He is in the rooms beneath the rooms " — in other words, on the ground floor. Of an angry overseer he said: " He raged like the leopard of Upper Egypt." In telling a story, he trained himself to give great prominence to the demonstrative pronoun, this being the custom of the country; to say: " And when we came before this impregnable fortress this good old man said to this officer: ' Look at this letter! ' And when this officer looked at this letter he spake: ' By Amun, these strangers may pass! ' " His hearers enjoyed it hugely.

Several feast-days fell in each month, not only calendar but also seasonal, as when Pharaoh cut a swath of grain to open the harvest; there was the anniversary of his accession and that of the unification of the two lands; the day when they set up the column of Osiris, with masques and sistrum-playing. There were the days of the moon and the great days of the Triad, Father, Mother, and Son. And on all such days there was roast goose and beef in the servants' house, and Joseph's small-sized patron, Bes, brought him all sorts of dainties and sweetmeats from the house of the women: grapes and figs, cakes baked in the shape of cows lying down, and fruits in honey. " Take it, young sandman," he would whisper, " it is better than leeks to your bread, and your little friend brings it to you from the tables of the shut-in ones, after they have feasted. For they grow far too fat with their munching and crunching, and are nothing but cackling stuffed geese before whom I dance. Take it all, then, that the dwarf brings you and may it do you good; the others have not such food."

"And is Mont-kaw yet mindful of me in the way of my advancement?" Joseph would ask, after thanking the dwarf for his offerings.

"Not much as yet," Bes would answer shaking his head. "He is deaf and asleep where you are concerned and will not be reminded. But the dwarf is at work to bring your ship into the breeze, let him see to it. He is thinking how best to make it come about that you shall stand before Petepre — and it shall come to pass."

It was Joseph who had urged upon Bes-em-heb the necessity of his coming to stand before Petepre, in some way and at some time; but the thing was almost impossible to bring to pass, and the dwarf could only go about it by small stages. Attendance on the master, even of a general kind, and much more the personal service, was firmly held in jealous hands. It was a pity that Joseph had not been granted duties in the stables: feeding, currying, harnessing and unharnessing Potiphar's Syrians. But never once had he succeeded in leading out the fiery pair — not even for Neternakht the driver, to say nothing of the master himself. That would have been a step in advance — but it was impossible. No, for the present it would not be his to speak with the master, but only to hear his servants speak about him; to question them of their lord and the way matters stood in the house, and to keep a watchful eye wherever possible on the service of the master. The latter enterprise had to do above all with Mont-kaw, and he had begun putting it into effect on the very day he was bought.

And each day the same scene repeated itself, he saw

and heard it. Mont-kaw flattered the master. His lips
ran over with praise, and moisture stood in his eyes as he
sang pæans to the dignity and riches of his lord; he never
failed to laud and marvel at his boldness and virility, his
control of his steeds and prowess as hunter, whereat all
the world about him trembled. And all this he did — Joseph felt certain — not for his own sake and not to curry
favour, but on the master's account, and thus by no means
in a lickspittle spirit. Mont-kaw seemed a very decent
man: not cruel to those below nor cringing to those above
him; his adulation of the master was only to be taken in
a good sense, as an expression of his genuine love, his
desire to bring by sweet words comfort to the soul of his
lord. Such was the impression Joseph got, strengthened
by the faint smile, at once gratified and melancholy,
which appeared on the lips of Pharaoh's friend as he
listened to the words of praise, this tower of a man, who
yet in all other ways was so unlike Reuben. And the
more Joseph understood the situation in the house, the
more clearly he felt that Mont-kaw's bearing toward his
master was only an example of the relations of all the
other members of the family. They were all very gracious, very respectful, and delicately considerate of each
other, displaying a mutual politeness which was a support, no doubt, but made an impression of exaggeration
and strain: so Potiphar to his wife, the lady Mut-em-enet,
and she to him; the exalted parents in the upper storey
to Petepre their son and he to them; they in turn to their
daughter-in-law Mut, and she to them. Their dignity and
self-confidence, supported by outward circumstances of
the very best and by their own behaviour, seemed after
all not to be on a very firm footing; there was some-

thing hollow about it. Therefore they the more strove to strengthen by all this tact and courtesy each other's self-respect. If in this house of blessing there reigned an atmosphere of uneasiness which even had its comic side, in this it consisted; if there was a weight of care, herein it lay and showed itself. It gave itself no name, but Joseph guessed it: the dignity was a sham.

Petepre had many titles and honours. Pharaoh had lifted up his head. Many times the Highest at his window, in presence of the royal family and the court, had flung down upon him the gold of favour, while the populace had applauded and made ceremonial leaps of joy. Joseph heard about it in the servants' house. The master was called fan-bearer on the right hand and friend of the king, and lived in well-founded hope of one day becoming " unique friend of the king " — there were very few with this title. He was captain of Pharaoh's guard, head executioner, and commandant of the royal prisons. Or rather he bore the title of these court offices, for they were empty or nearly empty honours. Actually — so Joseph was told — it was another man — an upper officer named Haremheb, or Hor-em-heb, a rough soldier and lieutenant-colonel — who commanded the body-guard and presided over the executions. Very likely he had to render account to his titular head and the honorary commander of the prisons, but only as a matter of form. Certainly it was lucky for this fat towering Reuben of a man, with his high voice and melancholy smile, that he had not to administer justice by mangling the backs of criminals with five hundred blows, or, as the expression went, " bringing them to the house of execution and martyrdom " to " put them in corpse-colour." It would

have been most unfitting and repugnant to him. Yet
Joseph was given to understand that much gilded per-
turbation and recurrent vexation might grow out of such
a state of things.

For Potiphar's offices and honours, symbolically represented by the staff he carried in his small right hand,
once a bludgeon and now degenerated into a pine-cone,
were a dignified fiction, which not only Mont-kaw but all
his world about him combined to sustain for the sake of
his self-respect. Yet secretly, half-unconsciously, he
knew them for what they were: for unreality and hollow
pretence. And just as the pine-cone formed the symbol of
that pretence, so, Joseph felt, was Potiphar's whole state
a symbol of a more far-reaching hollowness, that had not
to do with offices, but with the man's own natural dignity
as a man.

Joseph knew, he had memories not personal to himself
which instructed him, that social conventions, the traditional conceptions of honour, avail but little against the
dark and silent knowledge in the depth of the soul, which
will not be deceived by daylight fictions. He thought of
his mother. Yes, strange though it was, while he explored
and pondered on the situation of his purchaser and master, Petepre the " man " of Egypt, his thoughts turned to
her, the lovely one, her trouble and bewilderment. He
knew about it; it was a chapter of his prehistory and tradition — besides, Jacob had often told him stories of that
time when Rachel, great though her willingness, was unfruitful by decree of God, and Bilhah had had to be
brought in and had given birth upon Rachel's knees. Joseph could see that puzzled smile upon the face of her rejected by God: a smile of pride at her maternal dignity,

which yet understood that this was a sham and a conception of honour upheld by human standards but not
founded in her own flesh and blood. It was half a joy and
half a pretence; countenanced by usage, but at bottom a
detestable sham. He called these recollections to his aid
as he thought of his master's position and pondered over
the conflict between the conscience of the flesh and the ex-
pedient honoured by usage. Certainly Potiphar had
many more and richer compensations than Rachel had
had. He was wealthy. His existence was brilliantly
adorned with precious stones and waving ostrich plumes;
kneeling slaves attended his ways, his house was full of
treasures, his women's house of the twittering and cackling, lying and sweet-eating apanage of a lordly life, with
the lily-armed Mut-em-enet as his chief and lawful wife.
All this redounded to his dignity and availed mightily to
uphold it. And yet far within, where Rachel had been
aware of her secret shame, he knew that he was not captain of the bodyguard, but only its titular head. Otherwise he would not have needed the flattery of Mont-kaw.

He was a courtier, a chamberlain and servant of the
king. A very highly placed one, overwhelmed with honours and possessions, yet a courtier in the full sense
of the word; and the word " courtier " had a slightly
malicious tinge, or rather it was used in two related
senses which flowed together. It was a word not used
today in its original — or not only in its original —
meaning, but in a transferred one which kept the original
one as well, so that in a quite honourable and respectful
way it was malicious, and contained an innuendo which
flattered in two directions: with reference both to dignity
and to the lack of it. A conversation heard by Joseph —

not overheard but listened to quite openly and in the
course of his duties — taught him much about all these
matters.

THE TASK

IT was ninety or a hundred days after his entry into this
elegant and distinguished household that Joseph, through
the good offices of Sa'ankh-Wen-nofer-Neteruhotep-em-
per-Amun, the dwarf, was given a task. It was an easy
and rewarding one, if also a little burdensome and painful to carry out. He was lounging as usual in Potiphar's
courtyard, willy-nilly waiting his hour, when the dwarf
came running, in his crumpled finery, with the felt cone
of ointment cocked on his head, and announced in a
whisper that he had something for him, a piece of good
luck worth hearing, and leading to advancement. He
had got it from Mont-kaw, who had said neither yes nor
no, but simply suffered it. No, he was not to stand before
Petepre — not yet. " But hearken, Osarsiph, what you
are to do and how fortune smiles by the dwarf's contrivance, who has kept you in mind and brought it about:
today at the fifth hour after midday, after their nap, the
exalted parents from the upper storey will come to the
pleasure-garden, and there, sheltered from sun and wind,
will enjoy the coolness of the water and the peace of their
great age. They love to sit there hand in hand in two
chairs, alone in this hour of repose save for a dumb
waiter who shall kneel in a corner with a salver of refreshment to comfort their spirits when they are tired
from their peaceful sitting. You are to be the dumb
waiter, Mont-kaw has commanded, or at least has not

forbidden it, so you shall hold the salver of refreshment.
But you must not budge as you kneel with your burden,
not even to blink your eyes, else you might disturb their
rest with your too much presentness. You must be entirely the dumb waiter and like a figure of Ptah, for so are
they used to have it. Only when the exalted brother-
sister pair give sign of fatigue, then you must set yourself
briskly in motion, still on your knees, moving very carefully without stumbling or spilling anything on your
clothing, and bear them the delicacies to be a cordial to
them. When they are satisfied, then you must kneel backwards swiftly into your corner and take care for your
body, not to pant or do aught to disturb or give sign of
your presence, but to become at once the dumb waiter as
before. Can you perform all that? "

"That can I," Joseph replied. "Thanks, little Bes,
all that will I do, precisely as you have said, and even
my eyes shall be as though glass, that I may look like an
image, without presence more than the space of air which
my body takes up. So nothing shall I be. But in all my
stillness my ears shall be open wide, unseen by them,
the exalted brother-sister pair, when they speak before
me and name by their true names all the household
matters, and I shall become master of them in my mind."

"Very good," answered the dwarf. "But conceive not
that it will be simple to play for so long a space the dumb
waiter and image of Ptah, or to haste to and fro upon
your knees. It would be well for you to practise by yourself. The dish of refreshment will be dealt out to you by
the scribe of the sideboard; not in the cook-house, but in
the provision-chamber of the house of the master. They
will have it ready. Enter through the gate of the house

into the entrance-hall and turn left by the stair toward
the private room of trust which is the bedchamber of
Mont-kaw. Cross over diagonally and open the door on
the right, leading into a long corridor-chamber, full of
provisions so that you will see it is the store-chamber.
There you will find the scribe who will give you all needful. That you must carry most heedfully across the garden to the summerhouse, a little time before the appointed hour, that you may be already in your place
when the exalted ones come. You are to kneel in your
corner and hearken. When you hear them approaching,
stir no eyelash more, or even scarcely breathe, until
when they seem fatigued. Do you understand your service now? "

" Perfectly," Joseph replied. " There was once a
man's wife turned to a pillar of salt because she looked
back at the place of destruction. Such will I become in
my corner and with my dish."

" I know not the tale," said Neteruhotep.

" One day I will tell it to you," Joseph responded.

" Pray do, Osarsiph," murmured the dwarf, " in reward for the service which I have procured you. And
repeat to me again the tale of the serpent in the tree, and
how the pleasant one slew the unpleasant one, and the
story of the far-seeing man and his ship like a chest.
Also the tale of the saved sacrifice, and the smooth one
whom his mother made rough with skins, and later in the
darkness knew the false bride."

" Yea," replied Joseph, " ours are good tales to hear.
But now I go, to practise running to and fro and up and
down on my knees, noting the shadow on the clock that
I make myself fine in time for my service and fetch the

refreshments from the provision-room and perform all
as you have said."

He did accordingly; and when he thought himself
perfect in running he anointed and preened himself, put
on his best clothes, the under apron-skirt and the longer
upper one that was transparent, tucked in the little shirt
of darker, unbleached linen, and failed not to adorn
breast and brow with garlands for the honour of the
service to which he was called. Then he glanced at the
sun-dial, in the open space surrounded by the master's
house, the house of women, the cook-house, and the
house of the servants; and went through the wall and the
gate into the vestibule of Potiphar's dwelling, which had
seven doors of red wood with fine wide bands of decoration above them. The roof was supported by pillars
likewise of polished red wood, with stone bases and
green capitals. The floor had a design of the heavens
with its constellations, containing hundreds of figures:
lion, hippopotamus, scorpion, serpent, goat, and bull
stood in a circle with many figures royal and divine, and
the ram, the ape, and the crowned falcon.

Joseph crossed the hall and by a door beneath the
stair leading to the rooms above the rooms he entered
into the private room of trust which was the nightly place
of him above the house, Mont-kaw the steward. Joseph
himself slept among the others, on the floor in the servants' quarters; he looked curiously round at this private
room. The bedstead was of elegant form and rested on
the claws of beasts; it was covered with skins and the
head-board had pictures of the gods that preside over
man's sleep: mis-shapen Bes, and Ipet the pregnant
hippopotamus. There were chests, and stone washing-

things, lamp-stands and a bucket for coal. He thought
to what high position of trust he must rise here in Egypt
to achieve such comforts as these. The thought brought
him back to his service, and passing on he came to the
long provision-chamber, so narrow that it needed no
columns or supports to the roof. It ran the whole western length of the house, abutting not only on the dining-
room and reception-hall but on the third or western
pillared hall; for besides this and the eastern one there
was another or northern hall, of such rich and superfluous extent was the structure of Petepre's house. This
long corridor, however, was, as the dwarf had said, lined
with rows of shelves full of dishes and provisions: fruit,
cakes, loaves of bread, boxes of spice, basins, beer-skins,
long-necked wine-jugs in beautiful stands, with flowers to crown them. It was Khamat, the lanky scribe,
whom Joseph encountered here, rummaging and reckoning among the stores with his reed pens behind his ear.

"Here you are," said he, "greenhorn and know-
nothing from the desert! You have made yourself fine
indeed. You like it well in the land of men and of the
gods? Yes, you are permitted to attend upon the exalted
parents — I have it written upon my tables. Most like
it was Shepses-Bes who procured you the service; how
else would you have come by it? But he was anxious for
your purchase and screwed up your price to a fantastic
sum. For how can you who are a calf have the value of an
ox?"

"Take heed to your words," Joseph mentally addressed him; "for one day I shall most certainly be set
above you." But aloud he only said:

"Be so good, Kha'ma't, scholar of the book-house,

who can read and write and make magic, as to give this unworthy petitioner the refreshment for Huia and Tuia, the venerable parents, that I may have it ready for them as dumb waiter in the hour of their exhaustion."

" I must, I suppose," the scribe replied. " Your name is on my list and the fool has brought it about. But I foresee you will spill the drink on the feet of the exalted pair and then you will be taken off to be refreshed in your turn, until you are exhausted too and he that gives it you as well."

" Praise be to God, I foresee quite otherwise," Joseph replied.

" Do you indeed? " asked the lanky Khamat, blinking. " And after all it is your affair, not mine. The refreshment is here and is written down: the silver bowl, the little gold jug full of pomegranate juice, the little gilt cups, and five sea-shells with grapes, figs, dates, doum fruit, and little almond cakes. You will not steal or even nibble them? "

Joseph looked at him.

" You will not, then," said Khamat, in some confusion. " So much the better for you. I merely asked, though I thought at once you would not like to have your ears and nose cut off — and moreover it is probably not your way. It is only," he went on, for Joseph was still silent, " because it is said that your former owners condemned you to the punishment of the well for certain shortcomings — I know not what, they may have been slight and had to do not with matters of mine and thine but with questions of wisdom — I cannot tell. And I have heard that the punishment availed to cleanse you; so that I only thought it right to put a warning question. . . ."

"What am I saying?" he thought to himself. "Letting my tongue run on like that! I am a surprise to myself, to find that I am irresistibly tempted to say all sorts of other things which should not be urgent, but are, all the same."

"My office obliged me," he said, "to ask as I asked. It is my duty to assure myself of the honesty of a servant whom I do not know; and for my own sake I must do it too, for mine is the fault if any of the gear is lost. And I do not know you, your origins are dark — at least in so far as it is dark in a well. Back of that they may be brighter; but the name they call you — Osarsiph, is it not? — seems in its last syllable to say you are a foundling from the rushes and rode round in a rush basket until a water-carrier drew you out; such things come to pass now and then in the world. However, it is possible that your name has another meaning, I cannot tell. For in any case I asked as I did because it was my duty — or if not absolutely my duty then according to custom and in a manner of speaking. For that is the way and it is the tradition that one speaks thus to a young slave, as I spoke, and calls him, as I did, a calf. I would not say you are actually and in fact a calf, how could that be? Rather I spoke but according as all speak. Nor do I actually expect and foresee that you will spill the pomegranate juice on the feet of the exalted parents. I only said so to be gruff, as is the custom in such cases, and spoke not the truth. Is it not a strange thing in the world that a man will hardly ever say what is his own, but that which he thinks others would say, and speaks after pattern and scroll?"

"The dishes and what is left of the drink and food,"

Joseph said, " I will bring back when my service is
done."

" Good, Osarsiph. You can go straight through the
door at the end of the store-room instead of through
the private room of trust. Then you will stand before the
wall and the little gate in it, and beyond are the gardens
and flowers and you will see the pond and the smiling
pleasure-house."

Joseph went out.

" Well," thought Khamat, left behind, " how I did run
on, God help me! What this Asiatic will think of me is
past finding out. Had I but spoken as others do and
according to pattern and scroll! Instead of that I felt
all at once I must utter some uncommon truth, and gab-
bled quite against my will till my cheeks burn to think
of it. By the aard-vark! When he appears next before
me, I will be as gruff with him as the best of them! "

HUIA AND TUIA

JOSEPH meanwhile had passed through the little gate
in the ring wall and found himself in Potiphar's garden, where the finest sycamore trees, date-palms and
doum-palms, fig, pomegranate and persea trees stood in
rows on the greensward. Paths of red gravel ran across
the grass. Half hidden among the trees, on a terraced
mound, stood the gaily painted summerhouse, open toward the square basin of water bordered with papyrus
reeds. On that green mirror swam bright-feathered
ducks, and a light bark floated among the lotus blossoms.

Joseph, with the dishes in his hands, mounted the steps
to the kiosk. He was familiar with these elegant and

aristocratic surroundings. Beyond the pond the plane-tree avenue was visible, leading to the double-towered gate on the south side of the ring wall, which gave direct entry to Potiphar's flourishing estate. The orchard, with its little runnels full of subsoil water, continued from the east edge of the pond, and then came the vineyards. And there were fields of the loveliest flowers, on either side of the plane-tree avenue and about the summerhouse on the mound. The carrying of all the soil needed to make the original desert blossom like the rose must have cost the children of the house of bondage much labour and sweat.

The little building, quite open on the side next the pond, was flanked by white columns fluted in red, and furnished most charmingly. It was a dainty little retreat, adapted alike for solitary contemplation and enjoyment of the garden's loveliness and for intimate intercourse — perhaps of two people, as the draughtboard on a little stand seemed to indicate. Gay paintings covered the white background of the walls, partly floral decorations consisting of garlands of corn-flowers, yellow persea, grapevines, red poppies, and the white petals of the lotus flower; but partly too of spirited natural scenes: there was a troop of asses so lifelike that one thought to hear them bray; a frieze of high-chested geese, a green-eyed cat peering from among reeds; stalking cranes of the most delicate rust-red colour; people slaughtering and carrying poultry and legs of beef in a sacrificial train. All this was so excellently carried out; so blithe and light-hearted and playfully mocking was the relation of the painter to his subject, so bold and faithful at once his hand, that involuntarily one would find oneself exclaiming: " Yes, yes, what a jolly cat, what a haughty

crane!" And yet the whole seemed elevated into a sphere
both more vivid and more austere, an æsthetic heaven as
it were, a celestial realm of good taste. Joseph as he
scanned these things could give no name to that which
none the less he perfectly well understood. This was
culture which smiled down upon him from the walls; and
Abram's late descendant, Jacob's youngest son, a little
worldly as he was, leaning to youthful curiosity and
youth's glorification of freedom, rejoiced in the sight —
always with a silent reservation and a thought of the too
spiritual-minded father, who would have objected to all
this picture-making. "It is charming to the last degree,"
he thought; "admit it, old Israel, and revile not this
achievement of Kemt's children, this taut and worldly
and smiling effort, in the very flower of good taste — for
perhaps it might even be pleasing in the sight of God
Himself! I feel friendly toward it and find it exquisite
— despite the consciousness in my blood that probably
the real and important thing is not to carry nature's
handiwork into the high heaven of good taste but rather
the urgent need of care for God and the future."

Thus Joseph to himself. The furnishings of the little
house were in the same heavenly good taste: an elegant
long couch of ebony and ivory, resting on lions' claws,
spread with panther and lynx skins and strewn with soft
cushions; roomy armchairs with backs of gilded leather
stamped in fine designs, full of embroidered cushions
and with fat foot-stools to match; bronze incense-stands
giving off priceless savour. This interior, so comfortable, domestic, and inviting, was at the same time a
chapel and place of worship; for on a raised platform at

the back were offerings of flowers and little silver teraphim with the crowns of gods on their tiny heads; while
various cult objects showed that their rite was observed.

So then Joseph knelt down, to be in readiness, in the corner by the entrance, setting his burden on the mat before
him, to rest his arms. But before long he hastily lifted it
and stiffened his pose, for Huia and Tuia were scuffling
in their beak-toed sandals across the garden, each supported on the arm of a child servant. The two little maids
had arms like thin sticks, and mouths that hung foolishly
open. For the brother-sister pair would have only such
to wait on them. These then helped the old people up the
terrace and into the house. Huia was the brother and
Tuia the sister.

" First before our lords," old Huia ordered in a husky
voice, " and to bow before them! "

" Just so, just so," old Tuia agreed. She had a large,
pale oval face. " Before our gods first of all, that we
may pray their leave, before taking our ease in our
chairs, in the peace of this summerhouse."

And they had the children lead them over before the
teraphim, where they lifted their withered hands and bent
still more their bended backs — for age had bowed and
buckled the spines of both. Huia, the brother, had an
unsteady head; it shook a good deal up and down as well
as sometimes sidewise. Tuia's neck was still steady. On
the other hand, her eyes had retreated in her face till
they were a mere pair of blind colourless slits; a fixed
smile sat on her large face.

After the parents had prayed, the little maids led them
to the chairs which stood ready in the foreground of the

little house, and let them sink cautiously down. They took their feet and set them on the foot-stools, which were laced with gold cord.

"There, there, there!" Huia said in his hoarse whisper, for other voice he had not. "Go now, maidservants, for ye have done your duty, our feet are set and our bones rest, and all is well. Let be, let be, I sit — and thou too sittest, Tuia, bed-sister of mine? Then all is well, go until we call you and stay away, for we want to be by ourselves to enjoy the sweet hour of late afternoon and early evening, as the light rests upon reeds and duckpond; and to look across the avenue to the towers of the gate in the strong wall. We want to be quiet, and sitting thus seen and heard by nobody to talk to each other in the familiar phrases of old age."

Meanwhile Joseph, with his dish, was kneeling in his corner, diagonally opposite to them and quite near. But he well knew that he was nothing but a dumb waiter, in presence like a piece of furniture and no more; with glassy eyes he gazed past their old heads.

"Go, little maids, obey the mild command," said Tuia. In contrast with her brother's she possessed a clear, soft voice. "Go, and wait just so near and so far that ye shall hear our hands clap when we call you. For if weakness should come over us or death surprise us we will clap our hands in sign that you are to come and let the soul-birds to flutter out of our mouths."

The little maids prostrated themselves and went. Huia and Tuia sat beside each other in their chairs, a beringed old hand of each clasping the other's on the inside arm. They wore their grey hair, the colour of much-tarnished silver, just alike: it fell in thin strands from the scantily covered head, over their ears nearly down to their shoulders. But sister Tuia had made an attempt to twist the strands together by twos and threes into a sort of decoration, which did not come to much because of the thinness of the hair. Huia, on the other hand, had a little beard of the same dull silver on the under side of his chin. And he wore gold ear-rings that showed through his hair, while Tuia's old head was crowned with a broad band in a petal design in black and white enamel, which one would have liked better on a younger head. For we feel that beautiful things belong to youth and freshness and jealously grudge them to a head which is already nearly a skull.

In other respects too, Petepre's mother was elegantly dressed: her pure white robe was cut like a shepherd's cape at the neck and girdled with a beautiful ribbon embroidered in bright colours, its lyre-shaped ends hanging nearly to her feet. A wide necklace of the same black and white enamel as her head ornament covered her age-shrunk breast. In her left hand she held a bunch of lotus blossoms and carried them now and then to her brother's nose.

" Smell them, my treasure," she said. " Sniff the sacred flowers, lovely gift of the swamp! Comfort thyself with their scent of anise, after the tiring walk from the upper storey to this peaceful spot."

" Thanks, twin sister and bride," old Huia answered hoarsely. He was well wrapped in a mantle of fine white wool. " Enough, let be; I have smelt and I am refreshed. Thy health! " said he, bowing over her like a stiff old nobleman.

" And thine! " she replied. Then they sat silent

awhile, blinking into the beauty of the garden, the bright perspective of pond and avenue and flowery meadows, with the towered gate at the end. And old brother Huia blinked even more anciently than his sister-bride, with weary eyes, like lights gone out. He chewed ceaselessly with his toothless jaws, and his little beard bobbed evenly up and down.

Tuia did no such mumbling. Her large face was calm, the head a little on one side, and the little cracks of eyes seemed to share in her permanent smile. Very likely she was skilled at raising her husband's spirits and bringing him back to awareness of the world about him; for she said:

" Yes, my little old bullfrog, here we sit, and the silver gods are good to us. Our slim young maids have settled us dutifully in the cushions of these fine chairs and slipped away, so that we are alone together like the divine pair in the mother's womb. Only in our hole it is not dark, and we may feed upon its pleasantness — the pretty pictures and the well-made furniture. Lo, they have set our feet on broidered foot-stools, as a reward for having trod the earth so many weary years, all four together. But if we lift our eyes we can see the beautiful disk of the sun spreading its bright wings above the entrance to our hole, flanked by cobras, Horus, lord of the lotus, son of the dark embrace. The shapely alabaster lamp by the sculptor Mer-em-opet they have set on a stand to our left and in the right-hand corner kneels the dumb waiter with dainties in his hands prepared for our desire. Hast thou yet desire, my bittern? "

Frightfully hoarse came the brother's reply:

" I desire already, dear mud-lark; but I mistrust my

mind and palate, lest it is they that desire, and not my stomach, which might rise up against food with cold sweat and deadly anguish if I feed it before time. It is better we should wait, until we are weary of sitting and have actual need."

"Thou'rt right, buttercup," answered she, her voice sounding very full and soft after his. "Check thy appetite, that is wiser, thou wilt still live long nor will the dumb waiter run away with the cordials. Look, he is young and pretty. He is as choice as all the other things with which they surround our old eyes. Garlanded is he like a wine-jug, with tree blossoms, flowers from the reeds, and flowers from the beds. His pretty black eyes gaze past thine ear, they look not on the place where we sit, but at the background, and thus into the future. Dost thou understand my play with words?"

"It is easy to understand," old Huia strained his voice to croak. "For thy words point to the purpose of this charming little hut, where for a while the dead of the house always lie, behind us, in front of the silver ones in their shrines, on well-shaped trestles, after they have been disembowelled, after the doctors and embalmers have filled them with nard and rolled them in bandages and before they are borne in their ship up the river to Abdu, where He Himself lieth buried, and been given their splendid burial such as that they make for Hapi and Merwer and for Pharaoh, and are shut up in their good eternal dwelling and its columned rooms where their own life smiles at them in colour from all the walls."

"Right, my swamp-beaver," Tuia rejoined. "Thy mind is clear and clearly hast thou grasped the play of my words, as I also can understand thy meaning in a trice, whatever the figure thou clothest it in, for we play on each other's minds, being an old brother-sister pair, who have played together all the games of life: first those of childhood and then those that a man and a woman play together. Thy old mole takes no shame to say it, for we are here alone in the house and are as one."

"Yes, yes," said old Huia, with apologetic haste. "For our life was life together, from the beginning unto the end. We were much in the world and among the people of the world, for we are nobly born and near the throne. But at bottom we were always alone together in the little house, the house of our brother-sisterhood, as we are in this one here: first in the mother's womb, then in the house of childhood and in the dark room of marriage. Now we two old folk sit here and gaze at the dainty decorations of this little house, so lightly built, our refuge for a day. But the eternal refuge awaiteth us in the pillared cave in the West, which shall shelter us through all time, through unnumbered jubilees, while the dreams of life smile down upon us from the dark walls."

"Right, my good house-wren," Tuia agreed. "But is it not strange that at this hour we still sit here in our chairs in the front of this little temple and talk to each other — yet in but a little while we shall be resting at the back on lion-footed trestles, in our wrappings, with feet pointed up, and have our faces outside once more, with the little god-beard on our chins: Usir Huia and Usir Tuia, and above us sharp-eared Anpu will bend?"

"Very queer, no doubt," croaked old Huia. "But for myself I see it not so clearly and shrink from the strain on my head, for it is tired. But thine is still strong in thoughts and steady on thy neck. That makes me misgive, lest thou in thy freshness might not depart when I do, but sit in thy chair while I take the narrow path alone."

"Have no fear, my king-fisher," answered she. "Thy little old mole will not leave thee alone; and shouldst thou breathe thy last before her a draught of physic will congeal the life in her veins and we shall still be together. For I must certainly be at thy side after death, to prompt thee in the reasons and justifications at the judgment."

"Will there be judgment?" asked old Huia uneasily.

"We must expect it," answered she. "So the law teaches. But there is doubt whether it still hath full authority. There are laws which are like old houses: they endure and stand upright but no one lives in them any more. I have questioned Beknechons, Amun's great prophet, how it may be in the hall of the judging goddesses, with the scale for the weighing of the heart and the hearing in the presence of Him of the West, at whose side sit the two-and-forty frightfully named. Beknechons's words were unclear. The law stands, so he told thy mole. For all standeth to everlasting in the land of Egypt, the old as well as the new set up beside it, the land being thick with laws, images, and buildings, with living and dead, and one moves among them in decency and propriety. For the dead is the more holy only in that it is dead, the mummified truth, to be preserved everlasting to the people, even though it is forsaken by the spirit of the newly taught. Thus spoke Beknechons the wise. But he is very much the servant of Amun and zealous for his god. The king of the lower regions, with the fan and crooked staff, about him he troubles less, and the teachings and tales that are told about him he cares for but little. He may call them a forsaken building and mummified truth; but there is no certainty that we must not come before them, as the common folk believe, to declare our innocence and have our hearts weighed in the scale, before Thoth absolve us of the two-and-forty sins and the Son take our hands to lead us to the Father. We must reckon with the chance. And therefore must thy wise little old owl be at thy side, in death as in life, to take the word in her mouth when we stand before the throne and explain our deeds to the frightfully named, lest thou forget the reasons and thy head fail thee at the great moment. For my little buck-bat is even now sometimes cloudy in his mind."

"Do not say so!" Huia burst out more hoarsely than ever. "For if my head is tired and foggy, it is because I have pondered so long and hard upon the reasons and the explanation. But even a foggy mind may talk of the matters which make it foggy. For was it not I who thought and spoke in the sacred darkness of the sacrifice and the atonement? That canst thou not deny; it was I, for I am the man, thy brother-husband and the begetter, between us two; dark indeed in the holy darkness of the nuptial chamber, but not too dark or foggy in his mind that he could not light up the ancient darkness with the idea of making part payment to the holy new law."

"Have I denied it?" Tuia replied. "Nay, that thy old bride denies not at all: truly it was her old knave of dark corners who first begot the idea of drawing a line between the holy old and the splendid new, in other words the worldly, which mayhap may be the order of the new day. We might have to reckon with it, and so it behoved us to make offering and atonement. For thy old mouldwarp saw it not," she said, turning her large face this way and that as the blind do; " I was reposing in the holy old, and unable to understand anything of the new order."

" Not so," Huia contradicted her, croaking. " For thou didst see it as soon as I brought it up. Thou art quick to receive, if not to invent; and thou hast well understood thy brother's plan and his concern over the new order and the age. How else shouldest thou have agreed to the sacrifice and the payment? And when I say agreed, the word is not enough; rather I had but to tell thee my worry concerning the age and the order of the day, and thou camest of thyself on the idea of consecrating the dark son of our holy wedlock to the splendid new time and of withdrawing him from the old."

" How canst thou say so? " the old woman asked, bridling. " Thou crafty old corncrake, to say that it was I who had the idea; thou wilt be putting it off on me when we stand below before the king and the frightfully named! What a sly old fox! For at most I but understood and conceived, after thou, the man, hadst begot — as I received from thee our Horus, our little son-of-the-dark, Petepre the courtier, whom we turned into a son of the light and vowed him to the lordly new according to thy own notion, which was from thee, though I brooded and bore it as Eset the mother. And now cometh the judgment; and when we stand before the judge and it may prove that our deed was wrong and false, thou wilt make it seem that not thou but I conceived and bore it, of myself alone! "

" Stuff and nonsense! " he answered, in an angry croak. " It is well and good we are alone and no one can hear the folly thou art prattling. For have I not myself said that I was the man, and that I lighted our darkness with the idea? How canst thou then put on me the meaning that begetting and bearing are the same — though they are, indeed, in the swamps and the black river mud, where the mother-stuff breweth and giveth itself to its own embrace and fructifieth in the darkness; but not in the world above, where it is so that the man must visit the woman."

His voice gave out, he coughed and mumbled with his jaws. His head shook violently.

"Might it not, dear old mother-frog," he said, "be time to summon the dumb waiter to refresh us? Thy green frog feels worn out with all this thinking and his strength is sapped by the effort to make clear the motives and the justification."

Joseph, still staring like a lifeless image past their heads, made ready to run on his knees. But the occasion passed over, for Huia went on:

"Yet it is probably excitement and not real weariness that bringeth me in mind of food; which then my stomach, being unsettled, might reject. For there is nothing in the world more upsetting than these thoughts about the age and the order of the day. They are most important of all, save only that a man must eat, for of course that comes before everything else. Yet so soon as he is full, and free of that care, he thinks of holiness, and asks if it is holy still, not already despised, and a new era begun, so that he must hasten to suit himself to it and appease it with consecration and sacrifice, to save his life. Now we, brother-sister pair that we are, are rich and well born, and need have no thought for food, having everything of the best. So there is nothing more important for us or more upsetting than this very matter. Long indeed hath thy old croaker's head shaken, being troubled by it; we may so easily make a serious blunder, in trying to set things right and atone. . . ."

" Be quiet, my buck-rabbit," said Tuia, " and shorten not thy life without need. If there is judgment and the law still stands, then will I speak for us both and frankly explain the deed of atonement, that the gods and the frightfully named ones shall understand and not reckon it to the two-and-forty misdeeds, and Thoth shall acquit us."

" Yes," Huia answered her, " it will be well for thee to speak, for thou hast it more in thy mind and art not so upset; because thou hast it from me and only understood and received it, so thou canst better put it in words. I who begot it might be confused and stammer in my excitement before the judges, so that we lost the game. Thou shalt be the tongue for us both; for the tongue, as thou well knowest, hath two natures in the slippery-slimy darkness of the womb and standeth for both sexes, like the swamp and the brewing mud which embraceth itself, before the time of the higher order, wherein the man visits the woman as is fit."

" But thou didst visit me well, as man to wife," said she, with a delicate gesture of modesty, moving her large sightless face to and fro. " Long and oft it had to be, before blessing came and the sister was fruitful to thee in wedlock. For our parents had vowed us to each other in our earliest youth, but many cycles passed before our brother-sisterhood was fruitful in a son. Then brought I to thee Petepre, the courtier, our Horus, the beautiful lotus, Pharaoh's friend, in whose upper storey now we the exalted live out our latter days."

"True, true," old Huia agreed. "So was it, as thou sayest, in all properness and even holiness, and yet after all there was a catch in it in our secret thought, and a hidden care which paid heed to the time and age and strove to fit in with the order of the day. For we, male and female, begot in propriety, but we did so in the dark chamber of our sister-brotherhood. And the embrace of brother and sister — is it not after all a self-embracing in the depths and so not far removed from the brewing mother-stuff, hated by the light and the powers of the new order?"

"Yes, so hast thou told me, as my husband, and I took it to heart. I may have taken it amiss of thee to call our embrace a brewing of the swamp, when it was pious and honourable even to holiness, in harmony with the most refined custom and well done in the sight of gods and men. Is there then anything more pious than to imitate the gods? For they all beget upon their own blood and embrace in wedlock their mothers and sisters. It is written: 'I am Amun, who hath made pregnant his mother.' So it is, for each morning the divine Nut beareth the radiant one, but at midday, become a man, himself begets with his mother the new god. Is not Eset sister, mother, and spouse to Usir? Even in the beginning and before birth, in the wrapping of the mother's womb, the exalted brother-sister pair embraced each other, and dark it was, and slippery-slimy, as in the house of the tongue and the depth of the swamp. But holy is the darkness, and highly honourable in the sight of men is this pattern of marriage."

"That sayest thou, and sayest with right," he responded, in his hoarse, labouring voice. "But in the darkness the wrong brother-sisters embraced each other too, Usir and Nebthoth, and that was a great mistake. So the light avenged itself, the glorious light, to whom the mother-dark is hateful."

"Yes, so speakest and spokest thou as husband and master," she retorted, "and art of course for the glorious, the lordly and new, while I as mother and wife stand more for the holy, for the pious old custom, and thy views made me sad. We are noble old folk, and near the throne. But the high consort, was she not nearly always Pharaoh's sister, after the divine pattern, and precisely as sister destined to be the wife of the god? He whose name is a blessing, Men-Kheper-Re-Thutmose, whom should he have embraced as the mother of God if not Hatshepsut, his exalted sister? She was born to be his wife and they were divine flesh. Man and wife shall be one flesh, and if they are that from the beginning, then the marriage is propriety itself and no brewing-up of the depths. Thus was I born for thee, for a bond and in the bond, and we were destined for each other by our noble parents from the day of our birth because they surely guessed that the brother-sister pair had embraced each other already in the womb."

"I know naught of all that, and can certainly remember not at all," he answered hoarsely. "We might just as well have fought in the womb and kicked each other, for at this stage people have no thoughts. Even outside it we sometimes quarrelled, as thou knowest, though of course not kicked each other, for we were well brought up and very respectable in the sight of gods and men, living happily in harmony with the best traditions. And thou, my mouldwarp, wast content in thy soul, like a sacred cow with satisfied countenance, especially after thou wast fruitful to me with Petepre, our Horus, as my sister, mother, and spouse."

" So it was," she nodded pensively. " Blissfully satisfied was I, blind mouldwarp and satisfied cow, in the caul of our happiness together."

" But I," he went on, " was man enough, in the days of the strength of my mind, and according to my sex close enough to the lordly in the world, that I could not be satisfied with the pious old views. I had enough to eat, and so I thought. Yea, I remember, the twilight of my mind lifts a little at this moment, so that if I now stood before the judgment of the dead, I could speak. For we lived after the pattern of gods and kings, in full harmony with pious custom and with the approval of men. And yet there was a thorn in my flesh and a care concerning the vengeance of the light. For light is lordly, in other words manly, and hateful to it is the brewing up of the mother-darkness, to which the manner of our begetting was still near and knit to it by its umbilical cord. For lo, one must cut the cord, so that the calf may free itself from the mother-cow and become a bull of the light. Which teaching prevaileth, and whether there be judgment after we breathe our last is not the important thing. Important is only the question of the age and whether the thoughts by which we live are still the order of the day. That alone is of import, after hunger is appeased. But now there is come into the world that which I divined long since: that the male principle will tear the umbilical cord between him and the cow and set himself as master over the mother-stuff on the throne of the world, and found the order of light."

"Yea, so hast thou taught me," answered Tuia. "And satisfied as I was in the sacred darkness, yet I took thy idea to my heart and bore it for thee. For the woman loveth the man and so she taketh his thoughts even though they are not like hers. The woman belongs to the holy and old, but for the sake of her husband and master she loveth the lordly new. And thus we came to the sacrifice and the atonement."

"So we did," agreed the old man. "And today I could explain all that clearly before the king of the lower world. We wanted to withdraw our Horus, whom as Usir and Eset, brother-sister pair, we begot in the darkness; withdraw him from the dark kingdom and dedicate him to the purer light. That was our partial payment to the new age, upon which we agreed. And we asked not his wish in the matter but did with him as we did, and perhaps it was a mistake, yet a well-meaning one."

"If it was," said she, "then are we both guilty, for we concocted it together, to do thus with our son of the darkness; but thou hadst thy thoughts about it and I mine. For as mother I thought not so much about the light and the propitiation as of our son's greatness and honour on earth. I would make of him a courtier and chamberlain by thus preparing him; a royal official, destined by what we made him to be an honorary captain, and to have Pharaoh gild with the gold of favour the man devoted to his service. Those were, I confess, my thoughts, which made atonement to my heart for the atonement, though I found it very hard."

"It was but in the order of things," he said, "that

thou hast taken my idea in thy own way and added to it in thine, so that out of the whole grew our deed, which we did in love to our little son, since he had yet no views of his own. I too was glad at the advantage which flowed to the dedicated boy in thy thoughts as a woman. But mine were the thoughts of a man and turned toward the light."

"Aha, little old brother," said she; "I fear that he has only too much need of the advantages which flowed to him. Perhaps we shall have to speak of them not only at the judgment, but before our son as well. For however tenderly respectful his treatment of us, however high and dear he holds his parents, yet I think and sometimes fear to read in his bearing that secretly he is not glad that we pruned him into a courtier without asking his consent, and before he was able to defend himself."

"That," Huia hastened to say hoarsely and with some heat, "would be grumbling against the exalted parents in the upper storey! For his duty is to reconcile us with the age, it was for that we dedicated him; and what he gets in return is enough to make everything good, so that he need not find fault or pull a long face. Nor do I think he does, least of all at us, for he is by nature and spirit a man, and thus related to the lordly new; I cannot believe but that he consents to his parents' act of atonement and wears his consecrated state with pride."

"Surely, surely," she nodded. "And yet, old man, thou'rt not sure thyself that the cut with which we severed the cord between him and the mother-darkness was not a cut in the wrong direction, after all. For did he, by being so consecrated, become a bull of the sun? No, he is only a courtier of the light."

"Repeat not my own scruples after me," he reproved her hoarsely. "Anyhow they are not of the first importance. The first concern is that about the age and the order of the day, and the act of atonement. It is in the nature of atonements that they may turn out badly and leave something not quite atoned for."

"Surely, surely," she said again. "And doubtless he hath, our Horus, rewards of the most flattering kind, and his compensations as sun-chamberlain and honorary official to the lordly are magnificent indeed, no question of that. But there is Eni too, our little daughter-in-law, Mut-em-enet the beautiful, Potiphar's chief wife and head of the house of the secluded ones. Sometimes an old woman and mother like me has thoughts about her too. She behaves with most loving respect toward us; yet I suspect that in the depth of her soul she harbours a faint secret grudge against us because we made a courtier of our son so that he is not really in her sight a captain of the guard but only bears the title. Trust me, she is woman enough, our Eni, to sulk over it; and I am enough of her kind to read it in her face when she thinketh herself unwatched."

"Nonsense," Huia rejoined. "It would be ingratitude itself for her to cherish such a grudge as that in her exalted breast. For she has compensations, and even supercompensations, more than Petepre himself; and I cannot bear to believe that she is gnawed by the worm of envy for earthly things when she has the blessings of the divine, bearing the title of bride of Amun and dweller in the house of his consort at Thebes! Is it nothing, is it a slight thing, to be Hathor, spouse of Re, and to dance before Amun with others of her order, in the close-fitting garment, and to sing to the beating of the tambourine, the gold cap on her head, with the horns, and the disk of the sun between them? No, it is no slight thing, but a compensation of the highest and most glorious kind, which she has as spouse of the courtier our son. All this her kin well knew, when they gave her to him as his chief and true wife when both were but children and there could be no thought of marriage between them according to the flesh. And it was good so, for an honorary marriage it was and has remained."

" Yes, yes," responded Tuia. " So it had to be. Yet when I think of it as a woman, I find it hard: brilliant indeed and of great honour by day, but an affliction by night. Mut is she called, the wife of our son, Mut in the valley of the desert, a mother-name from ancient times. But mother can she and may she not be, on account of our son's consecrated state; and I fear that she lays it up against us, taking it ill despite all the gentleness she shows."

" She must not be a goose," scolded Huia, " not a bird of the water-sodden earth. That she shall hear from me, our daughter-in-law, if she sulks. I do not like to hear thee take her side against our son, simply because thou art a mother and a wife. Thou dost offence to Horus our son. And even more to the woman-nature for which thou thinkest to speak, for thou degradest it in the world, as though one could never see it in any other image than that of the ever pregnant hippopotamus. Truly thou art by nature a mole; and it was I by my man's nature gave thee the thought of the new age and the part payment. And yet thou couldst never have received it nor understood it, nor come to terms with the act of atonement, if there were no link between the woman's nature and the purer and more lordly one, so that it had no share in it at all. For must it be that the black pregnant earth is ever the woman's image and portion? By no means: the woman may in all dignity appear likewise as the chaste priestess of the moon. I will let her know, thy Eni, that she must not be a goose. As our son's chief and true wife she is counted among the first women of the land; to his greatness she oweth it that she is friend to Queen Tiy, the wife of the god, and is herself a god-wife of Amun's southern house of women and belongeth to the order of Hathor, whose head and first woman of the harem is the wife of Bekne-chons the great prophet. So great indeed are her spiritual compensations that she is in short herself a goddess, with horns and sun-disk, and a white moon-nun in her spiritual state. Is it not quite fitting that her earthly marriage is honorary and her spouse on earth a dedicated atonement and a courtier of the light? All that seemeth to me most excellent, and let me tell thee, it is what I would have said to her, if she hath not understanding for the fitness of it!"

But Tuia answered, shaking her head:

"I cannot tell her, for she gives no occasion to her mother-in-law for such a rebuke, and would be amazed if I were to do thy errand and tell her she is a goose. She is proud, our Eni, as proud as Petepre, her husband and our son. Neither of them knows aught but the pride of their day, neither moon-nun nor sun-chamberlain. Do they not live in happiness and self-respect in the sight of day, in harmony with the best society and pleasing in the sight of man? What need they know but this their pride? For if they knew more, they would not admit it or confess it to their own souls, but only continue to pay honour to their pride. How shall I take the word 'goose' from thy lips and give it to our daughter-in-law? For she is no goose; she is proudly conscious of being set apart for the god, and her whole being is scented with the bitter fragrance of the myrtle. When I speak of ill feeling and of affliction I have not the day in mind nor the honours of the day, but the silent night and the mother-darkness, where it is no use to scold and call names. Thou hast sometimes been afraid of the vengeance of the light because of our marriage in the darkness; I sometimes as a woman fear the vengeance of the mother-darkness."

Here Huia began to snigger. The sound startled Joseph a little, so that he stirred the slightest bit and for a moment lost his impersonality as dumb waiter. His gaze forsook the background for a flash and sought the old pair, to see if they had noticed. But they had not; absorbed as they were in their talk they gave him as little heed as they did the alabaster lamp made by the sculptor Mer-em-opet, that stood in the other corner. He turned away his gaze and once more looked past Huia's ear into the background. But his breath went fast, after all that he had listened to, to hear old Huia still laughing his old-man laugh — it sounded uncanny.

" He he! " went old Huia. " No fear, the darkness is dumb and knoweth naught of anger or revenge. Son and daughter-in-law are proud and know naught of mumps and dumps, nor yet ill feeling against the parents who treated them thus and made a barrow of the little boar when it could hardly walk and had no ideas at all. He he! No fear! Mumps and dumps are well shut down in the dark, and even if they stuck their noses out into the light they would be bound by the rules of decorum to be

gentle and polite to their exalted parents, however much
we may have played them a trick in the past to our own
advantage. He he he! Twice bound, doubly sure, doubly
sealed, nothing to be done against the parents so snug in
the upper storey! "

Tuia at first seemed uneasy as she listened; but she was
gradually convinced, and joined in his laughter till her
blind eyes went quite shut. There sat the old pair in their
stately chairs and chuckled together, with their hands on
their stomachs, their shoulders stooped, and their heads
drawn down between.

" Yes, he he! Thou art right," Tuia chimed in. " Thy
old mole can understand the joke: we played a trick on
our children, but we are doubly safe against their wrath.
That was cautious and crafty. And glad am I that my old
frog is merry and hath forgot his fear of the judgment in
the halls of the dead. But feelest thou now no desire to be
refreshed, no exhaustion, so that I should summon our
dumb waiter to fetch up his dainties? "

" Not at all," replied Huia. " I feel not the slightest
weariness, rather our hour of talk has given me new life.
Shall we save our hunger till the hour of the evening
meal, when the exalted family gathers in the dining-room
and we elegantly hold the lotus blossom to each other's
noses? Let us clap that our servants may come and support us as we walk in the orchard, for my old limbs feel
desire to stir."

And he clapped. The little maids came running, their
mouths open foolishly in their zeal. Each offered a spindling arm to a parent, helped them down the terrace and
away.

Joseph fetched a deep breath and set down his burden

on the floor. His arms were nearly as lame as when the Ishmaelites had drawn him out of the well.

"Certainly these are fools before the Lord," thought he, "these exalted little old parents! What a glimpse have I had into the painful secrets of this house of blessing, may God pity it! Thus we see that to live in the highest heaven of good taste doth not save one from the most arrant blunders. How I should like to tell my father of this exalted idiocy! Poor Potiphar!"

And he lay down on the mat to rest his tired limbs before carrying the refreshments back to Khamat.

JOSEPH CONSIDERS THESE THINGS

HE was excited and dismayed by what he had overheard, and during this time it preoccupied his thoughts. For the exalted parents he felt a lively disgust, only held in check by the need for politeness and reverence, not in the least by the darkness of ignorance. For neither his anger at the irresponsible stupidity of those old people in the sight of God, nor his abhorrence of their smug satisfaction at being secure against all reproach, was lacking in any element of clear-sightedness toward himself.

It did not escape him that what he had heard possessed instructive implications for him, the descendant of Abram; and he would not have been Joseph had he not been ready to profit by them. The experience was calculated to broaden his view and warn him not to regard his own immediate spiritual home, the world of his fathers and its preoccupation with God, whose nursling and pupil he was, as something all too unique and incomparable. Not Jacob alone had cares in the world. Care was every-

where among men; everywhere the anxiousness to be sure
one understood this problem of the Lord and the times —
though it might lead here and there to the most dubious
expedients, and indeed Jacob's inherited thoughts of God
might afford the subtlest test one could apply to a possible
decline of custom and tradition from the will and influence of the Lord.

And anyhow it was just here that error lay closest to
hand. One did not even need to think of Laban, left
clinging to the primitive, nor of the little son in the jar.
There every kind of awareness of the problem had been
lacking, even though the practice had already gone far
to become an abomination. But precisely the developed
sensitivity for such changes could easily lead one astray.
Had not Jacob's painful misgivings in the matter of the
feast tempted him to destroy feast and custom root and
branch just because of their roots, which drew their nourishment from the unclean soil? The son had had to beg
him to spare the feast, the tree that spread its shade and
tossed its tip in the air, which like the Lord had risen out
of the earth, but must wither if one uprooted it. Joseph
was for sparing, he was not for uprooting. He saw in
God — who after all had not always been what He was
— a God of sparing and of passing over; not even in the
case of the deluge had He proceeded to extremes or
hewed at the root of mankind, but had put the idea of the
ark into the head of an exceeding wise man. Wisdom and
passing over: these seemed to Joseph related thoughts,
which might exchange their garb and even had a name in
common: goodness. God had tempted Abram to offer
Him his son; but then He had not taken him, introducing
a ram, in a most edifying way. The tradition of these

people here, in however exalted kingdoms of taste they moved, was lacking in such good stories. There was some excuse for them, repulsive as they were with their sniggers over the blundering trick they had played on their children. To them, too, instruction had come from the spirit of the father, in the shape of an uncertainly moving rumour, itself still very much having its being in the darkness, that one must emerge and escape from the stage of the traditionally sacred and come over into the light. They had received the instigation to the sacrifice. But how like Laban they were in their clinging to the old! For precisely to cling was what they hoped to do, by dint of making sacrifice to the new. But no ram had appeared to these God-forsaken ones, that might turn into a ram of light; the sacrifice had been their trembling little son, Potiphar.

Yes, one might truly call that a God-forsaken way of dealing, a gross lack of skill in going about to propitiate a new and splendid age. For an approach to the spirit of the father, thought Joseph, did not lie in taking things out by the roots; and there was truly a great difference between consummate double-sexedness and its utter abrogation in the courtier. For the double-sexed powers united both male and female glory in themselves; like the image of the Nile with one woman's breast and one man's; or like the moon, that was wife to the sun and yet male to the earth, sending the ray of his seed to beget the bull on the cow. The relation of all this to the status of courtier was, in Joseph's mind, as two to nothing.

Poor Potiphar! For a cipher he was, in all the splendour of his fiery chariot-wheels and his greatness among the great of Egypt. His young slave Osarsiph had a

cipher for a master, a Reuben-tower without the strength
or the fallibility, a broken sacrifice, neither accepted nor
rejected, a neither-nor, not human nor divine; very proud
and stately in the light of day, yet poor indeed, and in
need of all the support and flattery that could accrue from
outward circumstance — and especially from the devotion of Mont-kaw.

Joseph considered that devotion afresh in the light of
his new understanding, and did not hesitate to find it
worth imitating. So it was: on the ground of the insight
he had gained while playing the dumb waiter he resolved
to be " helpful," as Mont-kaw was helpful, to his Egyptian master; nor did he doubt that he would exceed the
measure and quality of the other's service. For thus, he
told himself, would he best be helpful to another master,
and that the Highest, in the task of prospering the young
slave Osarsiph in the land to which he had been transplanted.

Here in the interest of truth we must warn the reader
lest he level against Joseph the reproach of being coldly
calculating. That would be precipitate and censorious.
The situation was too complicated for such moral judg-
ments. For Joseph had long been watching Mont-kaw,
the oldest servant of the house, realizing that he was a
good man, whose obvious flattery of his master deserved
a better name and must be called a service of love. And
the conclusion followed that Potiphar, the honorary captain of the guard, must be worthy of such love — a conclusion confirmed by Joseph's own observation of his
master. This great man of Egypt was a noble, fine and
sensitive soul; and kindly, too, in the slave's opinion.
True, he took pride in making others tremble for his

sake; but considering his status as a sacrifice to certain mistaken conceptions of the spiritual, that probably ought to be allowed him, Joseph thought.

We see that it was not when Joseph began to serve Potiphar, but actually before it, and in his own heart, that he defended him and espoused his cause. In the first place, the Egyptian was his lord, to whom he had been sold, and highest of his sphere. And Joseph's conception of his relation to him included, by right of his tradition, an element of loyal forbearance, which was applicable not only in the higher but in the lower sphere, and to some extent to earthly conditions and immediate surroundings. We are to understand that the idea of the Highest bore within it a conception of unity that was favourable to interchange and a certain equalization as between the higher and the lower. This was reinforced by the idea of " helpfulness " — the thought that he, Joseph, by serving Potiphar as did Mont-kaw, would best be " helpful " to the wide designs of the Highest who sent him his dreams. And other considerations as well came to make his relations with the Highest to a certain extent colour his attitude toward the master of the fiery wheels. He had seen Petepre's smile, melancholy, proud, and yes, grateful, in answer to the flatteries of Mont-kaw. He had seen the helpless loneliness it expressed. It sounds childish; but Joseph found a resemblance, equally appealing to his pity, between the solitary remoteness of God the Father and the isolation from the human lot of this tower of a man, this mutilated Reuben, however behung he was with the gold of favour. Yes, God too, the Lord, was lonely in His greatness; and Joseph's blood and his memory spoke in the realization that the isolation of a wifeless and childless God had much to do with the jealousy of the bond He had made with man.

Joseph knew the peculiar happiness which loyal service can give the lonely; the quite peculiar pain which lack of it can mean. He did not of course fail to see that God, after His nature, had nothing to do with procreation or death, for that He was both Baal and Baalat; the great difference between two and nothing did not for a moment escape him. Yet I but express in words what he certainly felt, when I say that these intuitions of loving and sparing were dreamily at one in his heart when he resolved to keep faith with the cipher in its need as he did with the needy Two.

JOSEPH SPEAKS BEFORE POTIPHAR

AND now we come to that decisive first meeting and conversation between Joseph and Potiphar, in the orchard. It has not been described in any of the sources; none of the accounts, Oriental or Occidental, in prose or verse, so much as dream of it. It is in the same case as countless other corroborative details which this version may boast of bringing to light and embodying in the accepted tradition.

We know that it was again Bes-em-heb, the mockvizier, to whom Joseph owed the long-desired and in the result decisive meeting; even though the dwarf could not actually arrange for it but only prepare the ground. And the preparation lay in bringing it to pass that the young slave Osarsiph, heretofore lounging superfluous about, with but occasional occupation, was one fine day given a job as gardener in Potiphar's garden. Not, of course, as head gardener; for the head gardener was a certain Khun-Anpu, son of Djedi, nicknamed Red-belly, because that part of his body was burnt by the heat and hung down like a setting sun over the apron round his middle. He was a man about the age of Mont-kaw, but lower in station, though possessing dignity and competence in his calling: well-versed in the lore of plants, both for purposes of decoration and gain, and also on their medicinal side. Thus he was not only forester, gardener, and florist but also apothecary and barber-surgeon; master of the arts of decoctions, draughts, salves, clysters, juices benign and malign, cataplasms and emetics, which he prepared at need for man and beast, though of men it was only the servants for whom he prescribed, since the masters had a severe professional physician from the temple of the god. — Khun-Anpu's bald spot was red too, for he scorned to cover it, and wore a lotus blossom behind his ear, as the scribes did their pens. Bunches of all sorts of herbs hung out of his apron, roots and shoots, which he snipped off or dug out as he moved among his plants; shears, chisel, and a little saw hung from his waist and clanked as he went. He was stout, with a red face screwed up in an expression not at all unfriendly; his nose was knobby; his mouth, likewise wried, whether in satisfaction or the opposite one could not tell, was covered with irregular, unshaven hairs like little rootlets; they added to the earthy aspect of Red-belly's blinking, sunburnt face. His short forefinger, brownish-red and soilencrusted, when he held it up to threaten some malingerer, looked like nothing so much as a freshly dug beet.

Little Bes, then, had approached the gardener on the subject of the foreign slave. He had told him in a whisper

that the stranger was gifted and skilled from childhood
up in the knowledge of growing things; that before he
was sold he used to tend his father's olives in the wretched
Retenu, and out of love for the fruit had quarrelled with
his fellows because they had thrown stones at the trees
and crushed the olives too roughly in the press. Likewise
had given the dwarf to understand that he had inherited
a sort of charm, a lucky hand as it were, of twofold nature, from heaven above and from the earth beneath;
which was just what a gardener needed and therefore
Khun-Anpu might take the boy among his underlings as
at present he was a loss to the household, being idle. It
was dwarfish wisdom that spoke, and those who hearkened had never regretted it.

Thus spoke the mock-vizier, having in mind Joseph's
desire to stand before the master and knowing that employ in the garden would give him the best opportunity.
For like all the great of Egypt the fan-bearer loved his
well-watered grounds, the like of which he hoped to
possess and enjoy in the life after life. At various times
of day he would rest there or walk up and down, talking
with the labourers if the mood took him. Not only with
Red-belly, their overseer, but with the workers as well,
hoers and water-carriers. On this circumstance the dwarf
rested his hopes, and they were well founded.

Thus Joseph was put to work by Red-belly; and it was
in the orchard that he received employment, more precisely in the palm garden, which ran from south of the
house to the edge of the pond, giving place to vineyards
on the east, near the court. But the palm garden was a
vineyard too, festoons of vine hung between the tall
feathered columns, with merely openings here and there

that one might pass through. The garlands were heavy with grapes, and the date-palms bore each year a crop of many hundreds of litres; the sight of their combined fruitfulness was a paradisial delight to the eye — no wonder, then, that Petepre loved his palm garden, with its basins of water sunk here and there in the ground, and often had a couch spread for him there, that he might listen at the same time to the breeze whispering in the crown of the palm trees and the voice of the reader or the scribe making a report at his side.

Here then it was that the son of Jacob found employ, of a kind both evocative and painful, since it called up memories of a dear and now frightfully lost possession: the veil, the coat of many colours, his and his mother's *kuttonet passim*. Among its embroideries had been one he had noticed when for the first time he saw the shimmering bridal garment draped from his father's arms, in Jacob's tent. It was a sacred tree, and on either side a bearded angel was fructifying it by touching it with the cone of the male flower. Joseph performed now the work of these two genii. The date-palm is diœcious; and the task of pollinating the fruit-bearing trees with the pollen of those which produce pollen-sacs instead of blossoms with pistil and stigma is performed by the wind. However, man long ago took over the job and practised artificial pollination, cutting off the blossom of the non-fruit-bearing tree and bringing it into contact with the blossom of the fruitful ones. It was this which the genii of the veil had been doing to the sacred tree, and just this was Joseph now called on to perform. Red-belly, son of Djedi, head gardener to Potiphar, assigned him to the task.

He did so by reason of Joseph's youth and the supple-
ness of his years. For it is a task not easy to perform; it
takes agility in climbing, daring and a steady head to do
the office of the wind. With the help of a padded rope,
encircling his body and the trunk of the palm, the climber
with his wooden vessel or little basket must work himself up the pollen-bearing tree using what stumps and
knots he can find for foothold, till he reach the crest,
throwing up the rope each time from the height at which
he had arrived, with the motion of a driver who gives
his horses the rein Arrived at the top, he cuts off the
panicles and puts them in his basket, then glides down
the trunk. Then one after another he mounts the trunks
of the fruit-bearing trees and everywhere puts the seed-
bearing panicles to " ride " — that is, to hang down inside the ovary-bearing flower-stalk, which will then produce the pale-yellow fruit; these can soon be picked and
eaten, though the ones grown in the hot months Paophi
and Hathyr are the really good ones.

Khun-Anpu with his earth-encrusted beet of a finger
pointed out to Joseph the pollen-bearing trees, of which
there were only a few, for a single one could pollinate
some thirty of the fruit-bearing kind. He gave him the
rope, which was very stout and of the best quality, made
not of hemp but of strands of reed thoroughly soaked and
beaten. He supervised the tying of it round Joseph and
the first tree, for he was responsible, should the master
lose the price of the new slave by his falling and dashing
out his bowels. He soon saw that the lad was clever: he
scarcely needed to be tied, but swarmed up the trunk in
a way to put a squirrel to shame, and reaching the top
performed the business with care and intelligence. Khun

soon left him to himself, promising other work in the
garden and saying that he might in time become a proper
gardener if he did well this work and produced early and
abundant fruiting of the pollinated trees.

Not only was Joseph ambitious for the credit of his
God; but also he found pleasure in the skilled and daring
operation. He performed it with great zeal, bent on sur-
prising Khun by his quickness and thoroughness — in
general, indeed, this was the effect which Joseph sought
to produce upon all men. He worked all day, and then
another into the evening. At sunset when beyond lotus-
pond, city, and river the sky unfolded the almost un-
bearable splendour of its daily crimson and tulip red,
he was alone in the garden among his trees, or rather in
them, setting the last of his panicles to " ride " by the
swiftly failing light. He was sitting in the crown of a
tall, swaying trunk dealing with the fruit-bearing blossoms when he heard whispering and footsteps beneath
him, and glancing down saw Beauty, the dwarf, looking
like a mushroom from that height. The manikin waved
with both arms and cupped his hands to his mouth.
" Osarsiph! " he loudly whispered. " Osarsiph! He is
coming! " Then he vanished.

Joseph hastened to leave his employ, and slid down
the tree faster than he had climbed up. There, sure
enough, Potiphar was approaching from the pond, between the festoons of vine, with a little train. An erect
white figure in the sunset glow, with Mont-kaw beside
him a step to the rear, Dudu, the guardian of the jewel-
house, and two scribes rather farther behind, with Bes-
em-heb, who had stolen back to their side.

" Lo," Joseph thought, with his gaze upon his lord,

" there he walks in the garden in the cool of the eve."
And when the group drew near he flung himself at the
foot of his tree and laid his forehead to the ground, with
his hands stretched toward the master, palms out.

Petepre stopped and looked down at the arched back-
bone in his pathway. His train paused with him.

" To your feet," he said briskly but in a mild voice.
Joseph with one swift motion obeyed. He stood close by
the shaft of the palm, in humble posture, his hands
crossed at his throat, his head bent. His heart was exceedingly ready and alert. It had come: he stood before
Potiphar. Potiphar had stopped. He must not move on
too soon. Everything depended on his staying. What
question would he ask? One, it was to be hoped, which
required an answer of some length. Joseph waited, his
eyes cast down.

" Are you of the household? " he heard the high crisp
tones inquire.

For the moment the opportunity afforded was small.
Only by the manner and not the matter of the reply could
he arrest the master's attention and persuade him not
to move on. Joseph murmured:

" The great master knows all. I am the least and lowest of his slaves. He counts him happy who is even the
least and lowest of his lord."

" Only fair," he thought. " He surely will not go on
yet. No, he must ask why I am here at this hour. And I
must answer prettily."

" You are one of the gardeners? " the mild voice, after
a brief silence, went on above his head. He replied:

" My lord knows and sees all, even as Re, who gave
him. Of his gardeners I am the least."

To that the voice:

" But why do you linger in the garden after the time of leaving, when your fellows do honour to the hour of rest and take their meal? "

Joseph bowed his head still lower above his hands.

" My lord presides over the hosts of Pharaoh, he is greatest among the great of the land," he said appealingly. " He is like Re, who rides across the heavens in his bark with his train. He is the steersman of Egypt guiding the bark of state after his will. He is next to Thoth, who judges without distinction of persons. Bulwark of the poor, may his mercy fall upon me like to the satisfaction of the hungry. Like a garment to cover the naked may his forgiveness come upon me that I lingered at my work among his trees until the hour when he walks in the garden and was a stumbling to his path."

Silence. Perhaps Petepre was exchanging glances with his companions as they listened to this well-turned prayer, spoken in rather harsh pronunciation, indeed, but apt in phraseology and though formal yet not without a note of real sincerity. Joseph could not see whether Potiphar looked at his train, but he hoped so and waited. His sharp ears seemed to catch a faint laugh as Potiphar replied:

" Zeal in office and industry at late hours call not forth the master's wrath. You may breathe in peace. For it seems you love your task and are skilled in its performance? "

Here Joseph thought best to lift his head and raise his eyes. Those deep, black Rachel-eyes met in their upward gaze the master's mild and even sad ones, long-lashed, and brown like the doe's; veiled with pride, yet good-humouredly searching, they looked into Joseph's own. Potiphar stood there, tall and fat and most elegantly clad, his hand on the rest of his tall walking-staff, a little way below the crystal knob on its end; pine-cone and fan he held in the other hand. The bright-coloured faience of his necklace was in a pattern of flowers. Leather gaiters protected his shins; leather, papyrus, and bronze were the sandals he stood in, the points of which ran between his great and second toes. His finely shaped head was bent as he listened, and from the top of the brow dangled a lotus flower.

"How shall I not love the gardener's art," answered Joseph, "and be zealous therein, my lord, when it is pleasant in the eyes of gods and men, and the work of the hoe exceedeth in beauty that of the plough as well as many others if not the most? For it is an honour to the man, and many chosen ones practised it in ancient time. Was not Ishullanu gardener to a great god and found favour in the eyes of the daughter of Sin, and brought her daily blossoms and made her table smile? I have heard of a child whom they exposed in a basket of rushes, but the stream bore him to Akki the water-carrier, who taught the boy the art of gardening, and to Sharuk-inu, the gardener, Ishtar gave her love and her kingdom. And another king, Urraimitti of Isin, changed places in jest, I have heard, with Ellil-bani his gardener and set him on his throne. And lo, then Ellil-bani sat there and himself remained king."

"Well, well," said Petepre and cast another smiling glance at Mont-kaw, who was shaking an embarrassed head. So were the scribes, and most of all Dudu, the dwarf. Only little Shepses-Bes wrinkled his face with delight. " But whence have you all these tales? Are you from Karduniash, then? " the courtier said, in Akkadian, meaning Babylonia.

Joseph answered in the same tongue: " It was there my mother bore me, my lord. But 'twas in the land of Zahi, in a valley of Canaan, that your slave grew up, among his father's flocks."

" Ah! " was all he heard Petepre say. The master liked to speak Babylonian, and a certain poetic timbre in the reply, vaguely like a quotation, particularly in the phrase " his father's flocks," arrested him — and embarrassed him at the same time. An aristocratic dread of evoking intimacy, of hearing things that did not concern him, conflicted with a curiosity already quite lively and a desire to hear more from these lips.

" But you speak not badly," he said, " the tongue of King Kadashmansharbe." And falling back into Egyptian: " Who taught you the fables? "

" I read them, my lord, with my father's oldest servant."

" So you can read, then?" asked Petepre, glad to express legitimate surprise and not wishing to hear more of the father and the eldest servant, or that the father had a servant at all.

Joseph bowed his head, not merely inclined it, but rather as though he admitted guilt.

" And write? "

The head went lower still.

" What work was it," the other asked after a moment's hesitation, " which made you linger? "

" I was putting the blossoms to ride, my lord."

" Ah! — and is that a male or female tree behind you? "

" It is a fruit-bearing one, my lord, it will bear. But whether one should call that male or female is uncertain — people disagree. In Egypt they call male the fruit-bearing tree. But I have spoken with folk of the isles of the sea, Alashia and Crete, and these call the fruit-bearing ones female and male the unfruitful which only bear pollen and are barren."

" This is a fruit-bearing one, then," the captain of the guard said shortly. " And how old is the tree? " he asked, since such a conversation could have but one purpose, an examination into Joseph's proficiency.

" It has blossomed for ten years, my lord," he replied with a smile. He spoke with a certain enthusiasm, partly out of his quite genuine feeling for trees, but also because it seemed useful. " And it is seventeen since its planting. In two or three years it will bear full crops and be at the height of its yield. Even now it bears close to two hundred *hin* of the best fruit every year, of great beauty and size and a fine amber colour. That is, of course, if it is pollinated by hand, instead of leaving it to the wind. It is a tree glorious among your trees," said he with a burst of enthusiasm, laying his hand on the slender shaft, " male in the pride of its growth and strength, so that one feels inclined to call it so, as do the Egyptians; but on the other hand female in its fruitful yield, according to the speech of the people of the islands. In short it is a godlike tree, if your servant may unite in the word what is divided on the tongues of the peoples."

" So," said Petepre teasingly, " you can talk of the

nature of the divine as well! Do you worship trees at home? "

" No, my lord. Under trees, perhaps, but no more. We have reverent thoughts of trees, it is true; there is something sacred about them, and they say that they are older than the earth itself. Your slave has heard of the tree of life, with power to produce all living things. Shall one call that all-creative power male or female? Ptah's artists at Menfe and Pharaoh's here, who are fruitful of forms and fill the world with beautiful images: is their power male or female, begetting or bearing, which produces their works? We cannot tell, for the power is of both kinds, and the tree of life must have been hermaphrodite, two-sexed, as trees mostly are, and as Kheper is, the sun-beetle, who conceives himself. Lo, the whole world is divided in twain, and we speak of male and female and cannot even agree in distinguishing between them, discussing whether the fruitful tree is male, or the barren. But the bottom of the world and the tree of life are neither male nor female, rather both in one. And what does that mean? It means they are neither. Virgin are they, like the bearded goddess, and are father and mother at once to the thing they beget, for that they are above sex and their power of giving has naught to do with being torn in twain."

Potiphar was silent, supporting his towering figure on his beautiful staff and gazing on the ground in front of Joseph's feet. He felt a warmth in his face, his breast, and all his limbs, a sort of dim stirring; it held him to the spot and would not let him go; and yet this man of the world knew not how to continue the conversation. His aristocratic dread of intimacy had made him avoid the subject of the young slave's personal life; now another sort of shyness seemed to bar this avenue as well. He might have gone, and left the young foreigner standing by his tree; but that he could not do nor did he wish to. He hesitated, and in the pause were heard the pompous accents of Dudu, the dwarf, spouse of Djeset, who took upon himself to say:

"Were it not better to proceed toward the house, my lord? The fire of heaven pales and at any moment a chill may blow up from the desert, giving him without a coat a cold in the head."

To Dudu's annoyance the fan-bearer heard him not at all. The warmth he felt closed his ears to the dwarf's sensible warning. He said:

"A thoughtful gardener are you indeed, O Canaanitish youth." And returning to the word which had stamped itself on his mind he said: "Were they numerous, your father's flocks?"

"Very numerous, my lord. The land could scarce bear them."

"Your father, then, was a man without care?"

"Save his care for God, my lord, he knew none."

"What is the care for God?"

"It is enlarged throughout the earth, my lord. With more or with less blessing and well-being it is cherished by all the world; but especially was it from old time laid upon my people, so that my father, a king of his flocks, was also known as a prince of God."

"A king and a prince, you call him? Then you lived in great well-being in the days of your childhood?"

"Your servant," answered Joseph, "may say that he anointed himself with the oil of gladness in his childhood

and lived as of high rank. For the father loved him more
than his brethren and made him rich with the gifts of his
love. He gave to him a sacred garment where were woven
many of the great lights and signs. A dissembling garment it was and a coat of reversion, handed down from
the mother's side, and he wore it in her place. But it was
torn from him by the fang of envy."

Potiphar had not the impression that he was lying.
The youth's eye gazed into the past, the earnestness of his
words spoke for him. There was a certain hesitation and
vagueness which might be ascribed to his foreign tongue,
and the details he gave were convincing.

" How then did you come — " the other began to ask.
He wanted to put the question delicately, and began
again: " How did your present then grow out of your
past? "

" I died the death of my life," answered Joseph, " and
a new one was vouchsafed me in your service, my lord.
Shall I weary your ear with the circumstance of my story
and the stages of it? I must call myself a man of sorrow
and joy. For the favourite was driven into the desert,
into misery, he was stolen and sold again. He drank
deep of suffering after his joy. Grief was his bread. For
his brethren hated him and in their hate they laid snares
about his steps. They dug a grave before his feet and
thrust his life into the pit so that darkness became his
dwelling."

" Do you speak of yourself? "

" Of the least of your servants, my lord. Three days
he lay in bonds to the lower world, so that truly he stank,
for he had fouled himself like a sheep with his own filth.
Then came travellers with souls of mildness; they raised

him forth in the goodness of their hearts and freed him from the maw of death. They stilled with milk the new-born and gave him a garment for his nakedness. But after that they brought him before your house, O Akki, great water-carrier, and you made him to be your gardener in the goodness of your heart and to be a helper of the wind among your trees; so that his second birth may be called as strange as his first."

" What of his first? "

" Your servant hath blundered with his tongue. My mouth had no will to speak what it spoke."

" But you said your birth was strange."

" It escaped me, great lord, as I spoke before you. It was virgin."

" How can that be? "

" Lovely was my mother," Joseph said, " and Hathor had sealed her with the kiss of loveliness. But her body was closed for long years so that she despaired of her motherhood and no man could expect to see her loveliness bear fruit. But after twelve years she conceived and bore, with unnatural pains, what time the sign of the Virgin rose in the east."

" Do you call that a virgin birth? "

" No, my lord, if it displease you."

" One cannot call it a virgin birth only because your mother bore you in the sign of the Virgin."

" Not therefore alone, my lord. One must consider further circumstances, the stamp of loveliness upon her brow, and that for so many years the womb of God's handmaid was closed. All this together with the sign of the Virgin makes it up."

" But there is no virgin birth."

" No, lord, as you say it."

" Or is there, in your way of thinking? "

" Many thousand times, my lord," said Joseph joyously. " Many thousand times it comes to pass in the world, which is sundered in sex, and the universe is full of begetting and giving birth that is exalted high above sex. Does not a moonbeam bless the body of the cow awaiting the bull and she bears Hapi? Does not old wisdom teach us that the bee is created out of the leaves of the trees? Then there are the trees, themselves the care of your servant, and their mystery, wherein creation plays her game with sex, putting it together into one, and dividing it among them according to her whim, and in one case one way and another, so that no one knows name and order of their sex, or if it is actually one, and the peoples disagree. For often it happens not at all through the sex that they propagate, but outside of it: not by pollination or conception but by shoots or runners or because they were planted; and the gardener sets out shoots but not kernels of the palm, that he may know whether he is growing a fruit-bearing or a barren one. But if they are propagated by their sex, then sometimes pollen and conception are put together in their blossoms and sometimes divided among the blossoms of the same tree, but sometimes also among different trees in the garden, the fruitful and unfruitful, and it is the business of the wind to carry the seed of the pollen trees to those of the conception. But when one considers, is it thus truly a begetting and a conceiving in sex? Is not that which the wind does, already quite like the begetting of the moonbeam upon the cow — already a middle stage or transition to a higher kind of begetting and a virgin birth? "

" It is not the wind that begets," Potiphar said.

" Say not that, O my lord, in your greatness! Often, so I have heard, the sweet breath of Zephyr visits the birds, before the close time is at hand. For it is the breath of God's spirit, and the wind is spirit; and as Ptah's sculptors fill the world with beautiful forms, and no one can tell whether their activity is to be called male or female, because it is both and neither, or in other words is virgin-fruitful — so too is the world full of fructifying and bringing forth without sex, from the fructification of the breath of God. The father and creator of the world is God. He creates all living things, not because they are brought forth from seed, but the unbegotten in other ways lays a source of fruitfulness within matter, which changes it and alters it into the manifold. For all the manifold shapes of things were first present in the thoughts of God, and the word, borne by the breath of God, is their begetter."

It was a strange scene, one never before enacted in the Egyptian's house or court. Potiphar stood leaning on his staff and listening. On his fine features the expression of tolerant irony which they habitually sought to wear struggled with a gratification strong enough that it might be called joy or even happiness. It was in fact so strong that one may scarcely speak of its struggling with the irony, since joy obviously took the upper hand. Beside him stood Mont-kaw with the little wedge-shaped beard, steward of the house, staring with his little inflamed eyes with the great puffy tear-sacs underneath; incredulous, dazed, grateful, and with appreciation which was nearer to wonder, he looked into the face of this bought slave, this lad, who was doing something which love had taught himself to do for their noble master, and in a higher, finer, and far more effective way. — Then behind him was Dudu, spouse of Djeset, most self-righteously enraged, because the master had been deaf to his warning, and prevented from entering fresh objection and interrupting the interview by Potiphar's complete absorption in Joseph's words. The puppy was obviously cutting a good figure, and the dwarf proportionately disadvantaged. It seemed to him that the things the slave was saying — shameless, really not allowable things, which Potiphar was drinking in as though they were the water of life — detracted in some way from his own dignity and were calculated to weaken it and his influence over certain of the small and certain of the great. As for the small, there was Beauty, the midget, his face wrinkled with delight at his favourite's success, fairly swollen with satisfaction because the lad had known how to improve his chance and prove that he had a right to it. Then there were the two scribes, to whom nothing of the kind had ever happened before in their lives, and who had ceased to smile, instructed by diligent study of their master's face and that of Mont-kaw, as well as by their own impressions of what they had heard. And beside his tree, before this group of listeners, stood Joseph, a smile on his lips, and perorated most enchantingly. He had long since abandoned the humble posture which at first had constrained him, and stood in easy grace, accompanying with pleasing and eloquent gesture the words which flowed unsought from his lips, as with blithe seri-

ousness he discoursed upon the higher procreation and
the fruitful power of the breath of God. In the gathering
twilight, among the columns of this temple grove he
stood there, not unlike an eager child, in whom God
speaks to His own glory, loosening his tongue that it may
give forth doctrine to the amazement of the doctors.

"There is but one God" — so he went joyously on —
"but of godlikeness there is much in the world, and of the
virtue of giving which is neither male nor female but
lifted above sex and has naught to do with dismember-
ment. Let me, O lord, as I stand before thee, sing with
lively tongue of that giving virtue. For mine eyes were
opened in a dream and I saw as it were a great and blessed
house, in a far land, its courts abounding in weal, with
buildings, gardens, granaries, and shops, men and cattle
in number like the sands of the sea. There thrift and prosperity ruled, sowing and reaping came to pass, the oil-
mills rested not, wine gushed from the vats and the
presses, rich milk from the udders of kine, with golden
sweetness from the honeycomb. But by whom did all this
move in its appointed ways, and who was the source of this
well-being? Ah, it came to pass through its master and
head, and through him who owned it. For all went at his
beck and nod, and all was moved by the breath of his nostrils. He said to one: Go! and he went, and to another: Do
this! and it was done. And without him would have been
no life, but all would have withered and perished. From
his fullness all fed, his manservants and maidservants,
and praised his name. Father and mother was he to the
house and to all the estate, for the glance of his eye was
like the moonbeam which fructified the cow and it gave
birth to the god, and the breath of his mouth like the wind

that bears the pollen from tree to tree, and out of the lap of his presentness gushed all beginning and prospering, as the golden honey gushes from the honeycomb. Thus dreamed I, far from here, of that virtue of giving so that I perceived that there is a fruitfulness and a begetting which is not earthly after manner or sex and not of the flesh but of the spirit and of God. Lo, the people dispute whether the fruit-bearing tree or the pollen-bearing one be male, and they agree not. And the reason therefor is that the Word is spirit and in the spirit things contend. I saw a man — frightful was he to you, O my lord, splendid in his might and terrible in the strength of the flesh, a giant and a son of Enak, and his soul was of neat's-leather. Then went he out against lions, smote the wild ox, the crocodile and rhinoceros, and laid them all low. And they asked him: ' Have you no fear? ' and he answered and said: ' What is fear? ' For he knew it not. But another child of man saw I in the world, tender of soul as in flesh, and he was afraid. Then he took shield and spear and spoke: ' Come on, my fear! ' And smote the lion, the wild ox, the crocodile, and the rhinoceros. Would you now, my lord, try your servant and think to ask him which of these men one should call by the name of man before the other — it might be that God would put His answer in my mouth."

Potiphar stood leaning on his staff, so that he stooped a little. He felt a pleasant warmth in his head and limbs. Such a sense of well-being, it was said, came to those visited by a god in the guise of a wayfarer or beggar or some acquaintance or relative, and they held speech together. For it was by this they knew him or at least received happy intuition. The peculiar sense of well-being which streamed through them was a sign that he with whom they spoke might indeed be a wayfarer or beggar, a friend or relation, a fact to be taken account of by their sober sense and treated accordingly, but yet — considering that peculiar sense of well-being — to be thought of at the same time in the light of other and far-reaching possibilities. That all things may coincide in time is of their very nature and essence; realities wear each other as disguises, the beggar is not less a beggar because a god has put him on. Is not the river a god, in the shape of a bull or of a wreath-crowned man-woman with one breast of each sex; did it not make the land and does it not nourish it? Which does not forbid one to hold a common-sense attitude toward the water of the river, impersonal as itself: to drink it, to ride on it, to wash one's clothes in its stream. And only the sense of well-being as one drinks and bathes may suggest a higher point of view. The border-line between the earthly and the heavenly is fluid; and one need only fix one's eye upon a phenomenon for it to break up in diplopy. Again, there are stages and pre-stages of the divine: half-gods, transitional existences, intimations. In the things which the youth by his tree had uttered about his previous life, much was familiar, much teasingly allusive and monitory, much might be taken in a literary light. Even so it was hard to say how far it rested upon assimilation and deliberate arrangement and how much upon objective elements: traits which characterized the life of beneficent presences, beings by nature deific, consoling, saving and redeeming. The young gardener knew these traits, he had made them spiritually his own and knew how to bring his personal promptings in life into harmony with them.

That might be an effect of his allusive intelligence; but Potiphar's striking sense of well-being spoke for the fact that the things themselves bore it out. He said:

"I have tried you already, my friend, and you have stood the test not badly. Of course there can be no talk of virgin birth," he added, in a pleasantly instructive and admonitory tone, "simply because your birth was in the sign of the Virgin. That you can well see." He said this out of a sound sense of the practical side of things, and, as it were, not to let the god know that he knew him. "Go now," said he, "and take your rest with your fellows, and with tomorrow's sun take up your work again among my trees." With that he turned away, smiling and red of face, but after two paces brought his train to a halt again and instead of turning back beckoned Joseph to his side.

"What is your name?" he asked. He had forgotten to do so before.

Not until after a pause, which could not have been for reflection, Joseph, looking up gravely, replied:

"Osarsiph."

"Good," responded the fan-bearer, short and crisp, and hastened his steps. Crisp too were his words (Bes the dwarf heard and reported them to Joseph before an hour was out) when he told his steward Mont-kaw as they went:

"That is an exceptionally clever slave there. Certainly the trees are in good hands with him. But you will scarcely be able to keep him at such work for long."

"You have spoken," answered Mont-kaw, and knew what he had to do.

JOSEPH MAKES A PACT

NOT idly have I introduced this conversation, of which
elsewhere we have no record, word for word, with all its
ins and outs, just as it came to pass. For it was the point
of departure for Joseph's career in Potiphar's house; its
immediate sequel was that the Egyptian took him for his
body-servant, and later set him over his house that he
might put all that he had into his hands. The news of it
has ridden us swiftly into the heart of the seven years
which raised the son of Jacob to new heights before casting him down to a new death. For in this test which he
had passed he showed his understanding of the painful
secret of the blessing-house whereinto he had been sold:
the need for mutual forbearance, tact, and flattering
service to uphold its hollow dignity. And not only had
he shown his understanding, but also his ability to perform the needed service better and more skilfully than
anyone else.

Such was in particular the experience of Mont-kaw,
who found himself so far outrun by Joseph's incredible
skill in his loyal endeavours for the health of their noble
master's soul. I would expressly add, to the honour of
the steward's good heart and to point the difference between love and flattery, that he felt no pang of jealousy,
but only joy. Indeed, it did not need the master's hint
to decide him, after the encounter in the garden, to raise
the slave at once out of the obscurity of his lowly state
and put him in the way of higher testing. Long since, we
knew that what had held the steward back was secret
shame at those thoughts which had crossed his mind when

Joseph stood before him with the roll — thoughts like to those which stirred in Potiphar during the talk in the garden.

Hardly had the next day's sun seen Joseph after his morning meal at work in the garden as Khun-Anpu's underling and helper to the wind, when Mont-kaw summoned him to come before him and announced decided changes in his employ. He found it good to say that these were overdue, and even in a sort to chide Joseph for the delay. How strange men are, and how they will twist the facts in their minds! The steward was pleased to be gruff; making announcement of his subordinate's good fortune in the odd form of a reproach, as though he had been guilty of lingering out by his own acts an untenable situation.

He received the Hebrew slave in that part of the court which lay near the stables, between the women's house, the kitchens, and the servants' quarters.

" Ah, there you are," said he, as Joseph saluted. " Well that at least you come when you are called. Do you think it can go on like this for ever and you can play about in tree-tops to your days' end? You think falsely, let me tell you. But now we shall string the lute with other strings, for your days of idleness are over. You are to come into the house for service, with no more ado: wait upon the masters in the dining-room, hand the dishes, and stand behind the chair of Pharaoh's friend. You will not be asked if it likes you. Long enough you have played the laggard and run from the higher service. And your looks? Full of bark and dirt from the garden are your skin and linen. Go cleanse yourself. Get a silver apron from the stores for your waiter's service,

and for your hair a fitting garland from the gardeners.
Or how else then did you think to stand behind Potiphar's
chair? "

" I did not think to stand there," Joseph replied, very
low.

" It goes not after your thinking. And adjust your
thoughts further to this: after the meal you shall read
aloud from the book-rolls to the master, for he will try
you, before he sleeps, in the northern columned hall,
where it is cool. Can you acquit yourself? "

" Thoth will aid me," Joseph made bold to answer,
trusting in the indulgence of Him who had snatched him
away to the land of Egypt, and speaking as Egyptians
speak. " But who is it who may read unto the master till
now? " he added.

" Who till now? Amenemuia it was, scholar of the
book-house. Why would you know? "

" Because for the sake of the Hidden One I would step
before no one's steps nor injure any man's boundary-
stone by taking away his office, which is his pride."

Mont-kaw was most pleasantly impressed by this
unexpected thoughtfulness. Since yesterday — and perhaps before — he had a clear idea that the capacity and
calling of this young man to rival others for office in the
house went further than perhaps even he himself suspected, further than to the office and person of Amenemuia the reader — and much further still. Thus he was
pleased with Joseph's delicacy, quite apart from the fact
that he belonged to those Reuben-natures which find their
joy and the dignity of their souls in being " fair and
just "; in other words, take pleasure in reconciling their
own view with those of the higher powers, even if that

involve their own dismissal. Mont-kaw was this kind of man and acted accordingly, perhaps because he was not quite well and often troubled with his kidneys. But I repeat that Joseph's tact gratified him. What he said was:

"You are full of consideration in your relations with men. But let Amenemuia's honour and promotion be his affair and mine. For such consideration is but another name for meddlesomeness. You hear."

"Has the most exalted commanded it?"

"What the overseer commands is a command. And what did I command this minute?"

"To go and cleanse myself."

"Then do it."

Joseph bowed low and retreated backwards.

"Osarsiph!" said the steward in a gentler voice and Joseph returned.

Mont-kaw put his hand on his shoulder.

"Do you love the master?" he asked, and his small eyes with the large tear-ducts beneath them looked searchingly into Joseph's face.

The question was strangely moving, and fraught with memories familiar to Joseph's thoughts since childhood. Just so had Jacob asked, drawing his favourite to his knee; with just such painful searching had the brown eyes with the pouches beneath them looked into the face of the child. Involuntarily he answered in the formula which is the right reply to this ever recurring question, and the giving of which did no offence to its inner nature:

"With my whole soul, with my whole heart, with my whole mind."

The steward nodded his satisfaction, just as Jacob had done.

"That is right," said he. "He is good and great. Yesterday in the date orchard you spoke commendably before him — as not everybody could have done. I saw well that you can do more than say good-night. There were errors in it, as when you spoke of a virgin birth, only for that it occurred in the sign of the Virgin — but one may forgive the errors of youth. The gods gave you subtle thoughts and loosened your tongue to utter them, so that they wreathe and wind as in a dance. The master had his good pleasure therein and you are to stand behind his chair. But also you shall be with me in my comings and goings as my pupil and apprentice, that you may gain insight in house and court and field, the business and supplies, and shall in time be my assistant, for I have much trouble in the world and very often am not too well. Are you satisfied?"

"If I am certain to take no one's place behind the master's chair and at your side," Joseph said, "then truly am I glad and thankful, if also not without a slight timidity. For between ourselves who am I, and what can I do? My father, who was king of his flocks, had me taught to write and speak, but in other wise I might anoint myself with the oil of gladness, and I know no trade, neither cobbling nor paper-making nor pot-throwing. How then shall I dare to go amongst those who sit and know their task, one this, the other that, and I take upon myself the overseeing of them?"

"Think you that I can make shoes and paper?" asked Mont-kaw. "Or pots, or chairs and coffins? It is not needful nor would anyone ask it, least of all those who can. For I am of different birth from theirs and from another stock, with a head for the general; and thus I have become overseer. The workmen in their shops inquire not what you can do, but rather who you are, that is another sort of ability, and made for overseeing. Who can speak before the lord as you can do, and rhyme your subtle thoughts to subtle words, shall not sit stooped over detail, but walk abroad at my side. For in the word and not in the hand is command and oversight. Have you something to object or carp at in my opinions? "

" No, great steward. I agree and am grateful."

" That is the word, Osarsiph! And it shall be a word between me and you, the old man and the young, that we shall understand each other in our service and in our love of our master the noble Petepre, Pharaoh's captain of the guard, and make a pact between us for his service, which each shall hold to the end of his life, so the death of the elder shall not dissolve the bond; but the other shall keep it over his grave, as his successor and son, who protects and justifies his father in that he protects and justifies the noble master in bond with the dead. Can you see that and does it please you? Or does it seem fanciful and strange? "

" By no means, my master and overseer," Joseph replied. " Your words are after my mind and understanding; for long have I understood such a bond, which one makes with the master as with one another in his service, and I could not tell what were more familiar in mine eyes and less strange. By my father's head and Pharaoh's life, I am yours."

He who had bought him kept still one hand upon the

lad's shoulder and now with his other took both of Joseph's in his.

"Good," said he. "Good, Osarsiph. Go then and cleanse yourself for the personal and the reading service of the master. But when he has done with you, come to me that I may teach you to know the economy of the house and to oversee it."

5

THE MAN OF THE BLESSING

JOSEPH IS READER AND BODY-SERVANT

WE know the behaviour of servants, the smiling and casting down of eyes, when one of their number, least and least-considered among them, is with apparent favouritism lifted up beyond their ken. They smile, look at each other and then down; are disconcerted, envious, spiteful, yet on the other hand cautious and apparently acquiescing with enthusiasm in the whim of the ruling powers. These looks, these smiles Joseph now encountered every day; for the first time on that morning in the garden when he was sent for to Mont-kaw — he, the climber of trees — and always after that. For this was the beginning, and his head was now lifted up in manifold ways. He became Potiphar's personal servant, his master gradually put all that he had into the Hebrew's hand, just as we are told; and all that was prepared for, and the germ of it lay, in the words of Mont-kaw and the pact he made; was implicit in it as is the slow-growing tree in the seed, needing but time for its unfolding and fulfilment.

Joseph, then, received the wreath and the silver apron which formed the livery of the dining-room servants — and which, it need hardly be said, became him to a marvel. For so must they look who might wait upon Petepre and his family at table; but this son of a lovely mother stood out among them of course, by reason of a superior brilliance which was not mere charm, rather a union of physical and spiritual parts in which both were enhanced.

He was given his place behind Petepre's chair on the dais, or rather at first beside the stone platform opposite, along the narrow side of the room, where the wall was covered with flags and a bronze jug and beaker were set. For when the illustrious family entered for their meal, from the northern or the western hall, they mounted this platform and water was poured over their hands. It was Joseph's part to pour the water over Potiphar's small white hands, which were ornamented with seal and scarab rings, and to hand him the scented napkin to dry them. While Potiphar did this, Joseph had to hasten with swift foot across the matted floor with its bright embroidered runners to the dais where the chairs were placed: those for the exalted parents from the upper storey as well as for their son and the mistress Mut-em-enet. Behind Potiphar's chair he stood, and served the latter with viands handed him by other silver-clad waiters. He did not run to and fro to fetch or take the platters, but others gave him and he offered to Pharaoh's friend, who thus received from his hand all that he ate and drank.

The dining-room was high and bright, although the light came not from outdoors but through the adjoining rooms, particularly through the seven doors of the western outer hall and the windows above them, which were of fine open-worked stone slabs. But the walls were very white and gave back the light; painted friezes ran round them under the ceiling, which was also white and crossed by many sky-blue beams, supported by wooden columns painted blue, with round white bases and bright-coloured capitals. These sky-blue columns were a delightful decoration, and delightfully decorative, full of gaiety and abundant ornament was everything else as well, in this room where Potiphar daily ate his meals. The dining-chairs were ebony and ivory, adorned with lions' heads and filled with embroidered down cushions. Along the wall stood lamp-stands and incense-tripods in elegant shapes, standing basins, ointment-jars and broad-handled wine-jars in holders, wreathed with flowers; these and all the other appurtenances of the dining-room glittered and gleamed. In the centre of the room stood a capacious buffet, piled high, like Amun's sacrificial table, with food — far more than the exalted family could possibly consume — which was handed to the waiters by servants in attendance: roast goose, roast duck, joints of beef, loaves of bread and cake, vegetables, and lavish display of melons, cucumbers and Syrian fruits. Amid the eatables towered a costly centre-piece, a New Year's present from Pharaoh to Petepre, in the shape of a little gold temple standing among exotic trees with apes clambering in their branches.

A hush prevailed in the hall when the family sat at table. The servants' bare soles were inaudible on the matted floors, and the speech of Petepre and his kin was infrequent and soft-voiced from mutual respect. They bent tactfully toward each other, and in the pauses between courses held to each other's noses a lotus flower, or some dainty morsel to each other's mouths. Their mutual gentleness was exquisite, it was almost painful. The chairs were placed by twos, with free space between; Petepre sat with his mother, and the lady Mut beside old Huia. When Joseph had first seen his mistress as she swayed past him in her carrying-chair, she had worn her own hair, in locks like a poodle's, thick-dusted with gold. But often she wore a wig, of blue, blond, or brown hair coming down far on her shoulders, made into tight little rings and set with corkscrew curls underneath. Atop was a close-fitting wreath. The wig was shaped rather like the head-cloth of a sphinx; it came out in a heart-shaped curve over the white forehead, and a few strands or tufts, with which she sometimes toyed, hung down on either side over the cheeks, making a singular frame to that singular face, in which the eyes were at war with the mouth, they being slow in movement, sombre and stern, while the mouth was sinuous as a serpent, the corners of it chiselled very deep. The bare white arms were notable near as far; as they moved among the dishes, modelled and polished as by the hand of one of Ptah's artists, one might well call them divine.

Pharaoh's friend took much food into his shapely mouth — after all, he had to nourish a mountain of a man. And many times during the meal the beaker had to be replenished from the long-necked jug. Probably the wine was cordial to his self-esteem and made him believe that despite Hor-em-heb he himself was a real and actual captain of the guard. But the mistress — about whom hovered a slender and decorative female slave, in flowing spider-web garb, so thin that she was as good as naked, and it was well that Jacob the father could not see her — Mut-em-enet, that is, displayed but small appetite and seemed to sit there because it was the thing to do. She took a single bite, idly, hardly opening her mouth, into the breast of a roast duck, then tossed it into the basin. The exalted parents, waited on by their silly little maids, for they tolerated no adult attendance, only picked and poked at their food; they too seemed to sit there as at a ceremony, for a mouthful or two of bread and vegetable sufficed them, particularly old Huia, who had to be careful lest his stomach revolt and throw him into a cold sweat. Bes-em-heb, the unmarried dwarf, sat sometimes and munched on the step of the dais, at the masters' feet; though actually he took his meal at a sort of officials' table, with Mont-kaw himself, Dudu, warder of the jewel-house, Red-belly, the head gardener, and a few of the scribes; in other words, the upper staff of the house. Joseph, called Osarsiph, the Shabirite slave, was soon to join them. At times the mock-vizier, in his crumpled finery, would perform comic dances round the great centre buffet. In a corner there cowered nearly always an old harp-player, touching the strings with warped and withered fingers and murmuring rhapsodical incoherent songs. He was blind, as befits a bard, and could soothsay a little, though but haltingly and unclear.

Such was the daily scene. But often too the chamberlain was with Pharaoh in the palace of Merimat, across the river, or attending the god in the royal bark up or down stream to inspect quarries and mines, estates and waterworks. On such days no dinner was served; the blue salon was empty. But when the master was present and with many manifestations of mutual fine feeling the meal had come to an end, the exalted parents betook themselves to their upper storey, and their daughter-in-law the moon-nun retired to rest in her own apartment, in the master's dwelling, separated from her consort's by the great columned northern hall, or went under escort in her lion-chair to the women's house. Then Joseph followed Potiphar into one of the adjoining halls, spacious airy rooms with paintings along three of their walls and the fourth side open save for supporting columns: either the northern, extending in front of the dining- and reception-rooms, or the western, which was still better, because it looked out on the garden, the trees, and the little summerhouse on the mound. The former, however, had the advantage of giving the master an eye upon the court, the storehouses, and the stables. Besides, it was cooler there.

In both rooms were many splendid things, regarded by Joseph with the mixture of admiration and contempt which he kept for the manifestations of high civilization in this land whither he had been snatched. They were presents, tokens of Pharaoh's regard for his chamberlain and titular head of his troops, like the exquisite little gold temple in the dining-room. They were hung on the walls or disposed on chests and shelves: statuettes in silver and gold, ivory and ebony, of the royal donor Neb-mat-Re-Amenhotpe, a fat, thickset man, in various costumes, crowns and head-dresses; bronze sphinxes likewise representing the god; all sorts of statues of animals — a herd of running elephants carved in ivory, squatting apes, a gazelle with a flower in its mouth; costly vessels, mirrors, fans, and whips. But above all there were weapons, in large number and variety: axes and daggers, scale armour, and shields covered with hide, bows and arrows and bronze sickle-shaped swords. It was strange that Pharaoh, who though the successor of warriors was in his own person no man of battles but a builder and prince of peace, should have showered such profusion of warlike implements upon a favourite — and that favourite, that Reuben-tower of a man, himself not at all constituted to let the blood of rubber-eaters and sand-dwellers.

Among the furnishings of the hall were handsome decorated bookcases. Petepre stretched his bulk upon a light day-bed, which looked more fragile than ever beneath his weight; while Joseph went up to the shelves to read out the titles to his master. Should he unroll the adventures of the shipwrecked sailor upon the island of the serpent or the tale of King Khufu and that Djedi who could put a head back on after it had been cut off; or the true and apposite story of the conquest of the city of Joppa by the stratagem of Thuti, the great general of His Majesty Men-Kheper-Re-Thutmose III, who had five hundred soldiers carried into the town in sacks and baskets; the fairy-tale of the king's son to whom Hathor prophesied that he would come to his death by means of a crocodile, a serpent, or a dog — what would the master prefer? The choice was large. Petepre had a varied library arranged in the cases of the two halls; consisting in part of lively and amusing fables and conceits like the "Fight of the Cats and the Geese"; in part of stimulating dialectic like the polemic between the scribes Hori and Amenemone, texts and tracts in religion and magic in obscure and artificial language; lists of kings from the times of the gods down to the foreign rule of the shepherd kings, with dates and reigns of each son of the sun, and annals of remarkable historical events such as important jubilees and extraordinary tax-collections. He possessed the "Book of Atmen," the

book " Of That which is in the Underworld," the book
" May the Name Flourish," and a learned topography of
the Beyond.

Potiphar knew all his books. When he listened to
reading, it was to hear again the well known — as one
listens to music. Such an attitude toward his choice was
the more natural because in the great majority of these
writings the interest lay very little in the matter or
the story and very much in the charm of style, the choiceness and elegance of the phrasing. Joseph read, with
his feet drawn up under him or standing at a sort of
liturgical reading-desk. He read capitally; was fluent,
exact, unaffected, moderately dramatic, with such natural command of words that the most involved literary
style had a happy conversational ease. Literally he read
himself into the heart of his listener; and when we seek
to understand his swift rise in the Egyptian's favour we
must by no means leave out of account these reading
hours.

Moreover Potiphar often dozed off early in the hour,
lulled by the measured, agreeable voice, the level, practised tone. And often he interrupted with lively interest,
corrected Joseph's pronunciation, called attention to the
excellence of a rhetorical flourish, criticized what he had
heard, or if the meaning were obscure, discussed it with
Joseph and was much taken with the lad's penetration
and expository gift. His personal feeling for certain
literary products came out by degrees, for instance a
preference for the " Dispute with His Soul of a Man who
is Tired of Life." This as time went on he had read to
him over and over; in yearning, rhythmical accents death
was compared to many fine and good things: the recovery

from sore illness, the scent of myrrh and lotus blossoms, to a seat under shelter of a sail on a windy day; with a cool drink on the shore, a "way in the rain," the home-coming of a sailor in a ship of war, the return to house and home after long imprisonment — and many other things devoutly wished for. Like all these, said the poet, was death to him. And Potiphar hearkened to the words as they were shaped by Joseph's lips, as one hearkens to music as familiar as loved.

Another piece of literature which enchanted him, so that he must hear it over and over from Joseph's mouth, was the sinister and frightful prophecy of encroaching disorder in the two lands, ending in complete anarchy, an awful reversal of the order of things, when the rich should be poor and the poor rich, when the temples should be desolated and the service of the gods utterly neglected. It was unclear why Petepre liked to hear this account. Perhaps only for the shudder which he might enjoy while reflecting that the rich were still rich and the poor still poor, and that they would remain so if one avoided disorder and sacrificed to the gods. He expressed himself on the poem as little as he did on the " Dispute with His Soul " or the so-called " Songs of Rejoicing," upon whose honeyed words and love-lorn lamentings he preserved silence. These romances told of the joys and sorrows of a poor little fowler maid who went mad for love of a youth, cooing after him and longing that she might be his wife and his arm for evermore lie in hers. In honeyed tones she mourned that he came to her not by night so that she was as one lying in her grave, for in him alone was healing and life. And it was all a mis-take; for he too lay in his bed and mocked the doctor's skill with his sickness, which was but love. But then she found him upon his bed and no longer did they grieve each other's hearts but made each other the first people in the world, roving hand in hand hot-cheeked through the flowery garden of their joy. From time to time Petepre had these cooings read aloud. His features never moved, only his eyes went slowly to and fro in the room as he listened with cold attention; and never did he express liking or disliking for the songs.

But once after many days he did ask Joseph how he liked them; and so for the first time master and servant came again upon the theme and touched lightly once more upon the subject of their talk in the palm garden.

"Very good," Potiphar said. "You utter the songs with the very mouth of the fowler and her lad. You prefer them, then, before all the rest?"

"I seek, my lord," answered Joseph, "to win your pleasure with my reading, and whatever I read, it is the same."

"That may be. But your effort might in one case more than another be supported by the spirit and heart of the reader. For one subject may be nearer to him than another. I will not say that you read this better than other things. But that need not mean that you do not like better to read it."

"To you, my lord," Joseph said, "to you it is a joy to read them all."

"Yes, yes. But I would hear your judgment. You find the songs beautiful?"

Joseph put on a consummately lofty and critical air.

"Very nice," said he and pursed his lips. "Very

pretty certainly, and every word of it dipped in honey. Yet perhaps a little too simple — just a trace."

" Simple? But the writing itself, which so completely expresses the simplicity, and in so masterly fashion brings out the pattern, just as it always is between human beings, will persist to endless jubilees. Your years call you to judgment, whether these words are not the very pattern of the pattern itself."

" It seems to me," said Joseph with great detachment, " that the words of this fowler maid and her bedridden youth do perfectly convey the simplicity of the pattern and make it convincing."

" Only that? " asked the fan-bearer. " I reckoned on your experience. You are young, and beauty sits upon your countenance. Yet you speak as though for your part you had never walked with such a fowler maid in such a garden."

" Youth and beauty," Joseph replied, " may also signify a sterner adornment than that with which that garden crowns the children of men. Your slave, O master, knows an evergreen which is a symbol of youth and beauty, and yet is an adornment for a sacrifice. He who wears it is reserved, and whom it adorns is set apart."

" You speak of the myrtle? "

" Of the myrtle. I and mine name it the herb touch-me-not."

" Do you wear that herb? "

" My seed and stock, my lord, we wear it. Our God has dedicated Himself to us, and is our blood-bridegroom in all jealousy, for He is solitary and on fire for our loyalty. And we for our part are the bride of His loyalty, consecrate and set apart."

" What, all of you? "

" In principle all, my lord. But among the heads and friends of God in our race God chooses out one who shall be especially dedicate to Him in the adornment of consecrated youth. To the father it is indicated that he shall bring the son as a whole offering. If he can, so he does. If he cannot, then is it done to him."

" I do not like," Potiphar said, tossing on his bed, " to hear that something is done to someone that he will not and cannot have. Speak, Osarsiph, of other matters."

" I can at once better what I said," responded Joseph; " for there is a consideration and mildness which obtain in the whole sacrifice. While it is commanded, it is also forbidden and made a sin, so that the blood of a beast shall intervene for the blood of the son."

" What do you mean? Made what? "

" A sin, my lord. Made a sin."

" What is that — sin? "

" Just this, my lord: what is demanded and yet forbidden, ordered but accursed. We, almost alone in the world, know what sin is."

" That must be a heavy knowledge, Osarsiph, and to my mind a painful contradiction."

" God suffers, too, for our sin, and we suffer with Him."

Potiphar asked: " And when the fowler maiden wandered in the garden, was it, as I begin to surmise, a sin in your sense? "

" It hath a strong smack of it, my lord. Since you ask me, certainly yes. I cannot say that we especially love it, though we ourselves have doubtless also produced such songs. The garden — I will not go so far as to say that to us it is the land of Sheol. It is not an abomination but a dread, a dæmonic kingdom where an accursed command has play, full of the jealousy of God. Two animals lie at the gate: the name of one is shame, of the other guilt. And out of the branches looks a third and its name is mocking laughter."

"And now," said Petepre, "I begin to understand why you have called the song simple. Yet I cannot but think that it stands strangely and dangerously with a people to whom the pattern of simplicity is sin and mocking laughter."

"It has its history with us, my lord, it has its place in time and events. The pattern comes first, then recurs in many ways. There was a man and friend of God, and his love to his lovely one was strong as his love to God, and this tale of the fathers was of a pattern-like simplicity. But God in jealousy took her from him and plunged her into death, and she came forth to the father in another form, as a son, in whom he now loved his lovely one. Thus death made out of the beloved a son in whom she lived and who was a youth but by the power of death. But the love of the father for him was a love changed through that bath of death — love no longer in the form of life but of death. Thus my lord can see that in the story things went in different ways and less according to the pattern."

"The youthful son," said Petepre with a smile, "was doubtless the same of whom you went so far as to say that his birth was virgin, only because it happened in the sign of the Virgin."

"Mayhap, my lord, you are in your goodness inclined," Joseph answered, "after what I have said, to

soften the reproach, or even graciously to withdraw it —
who knows? For as the son is only a youth through death,
the mother in the sign of death, and as it is written, at
evening a woman, but in the morning a man — cannot we
then with some justice, considering everything, speak of
a virgin birth? God has chosen my seed, and all of us
bear the sacrificial adornment of the bride. But one in
particular wears it and is set apart for special zeal."

" Let it be as it is, my friend," said the chamberlain.
" For our talk has led us a long way, and from the simple
into the complex. If you will and greatly desire it, I will
soften the reproach, and reduce it almost to nothing at all.
But read me something else! Read me the night journey
of the sun through the twelve houses of the nether world
— I have not heard it for long, though there are in it, to
my memory, many fine sentences and choice phrases."

And Joseph read the journey of the sun through the
nether world, with good taste and discrimination, and
Potiphar was entertained and much sustained thereby.
The word " sustained " is in place, for by the voice of the
reader and the excellence of the matter to which he subdued it, was sustained the sense of well-being with which
the previous conversation had filled the listener. He was
sustained, as the flame on the stone of sacrifice is sustained by nourishment from below and fed with fresh
fuel from above. It was a sense of well-being, amounting
to confidence in himself or in the person of his servant,
which the Hebrew slave seemed always to know how to
impart to Pharaoh's friend. This twofold confidence of
Potiphar in Joseph, and its growth, were of high importance; and for that reason it seemed good to reproduce
the above conversation in detail — even though, like the

confrontation in the palm garden, it is unknown to earlier versions of our story.

Other such conversations there were, of course, which went to strengthen Potiphar's confidence and his preference for Joseph, to an extent which finally led to his servant's exaltation. We cannot reproduce them all. It is enough to have characterized by some striking instances his methods of " flattering " his master and being " helpful " to him, in the sense of the bond which he had made with the good Mont-kaw. I may use the word " method " without fear of chilling the reader's sympathies, since he already knows that in Joseph's way of dealing with his master there existed the same mingling of calculation and sincerity which characterized his relation to another isolated Being of a far more exalted sphere. Moreover, we are entitled to doubt whether sheer sincerity, unassisted by calculation and a good technique, would ever achieve practical results — for instance in inspiring a sense of well-being in another person. Confidence among human beings is rare. And in gentlemen of Potiphar's bodily habit, titular officials with titular wives at their sides, there is usually a fundamental vague jealous mistrust of everybody not constituted like themselves. So then nothing could be so calculated to rouse in them the unfamiliar and thus so much more gratifying feeling of self-respect, as the discovery that a member of the enviable outer world wears the rue, so to speak; in other words, the garland in his hair, which comfortably cancels out all his other disquieting characteristics. It was method, it was calculation that caused Joseph to let Potiphar make this discovery. But if anyone feel inclined to take offence at this, let him make use of the advantage he has in that he already knows the story we are telling, and remember that Joseph in the hour of temptation did not betray the confidence so engendered, but kept the faith and was true to the pact with Mont-kaw which he had sworn by the head of Jacob and incidentally also by the life of Pharaoh himself.

JOSEPH FLOURISHES AS BY A SPRING

So now, when he was free of his service with Potiphar, he went with the steward, whom already he called father, as his aid and apprentice about the estate, among people smiling and casting down their eyes; and learned how to oversee. Mostly there were other attendants as well: like Khamat, the scribe of the buffet, and a certain Meng-pa-Re, scribe of the stables and prisons. But these were people of but average gifts; pleased to be equal to the claims of their narrow field and speciality, and to keep order among gear and accounts, men and beasts, to the steward's satisfaction. They took no thought for those wider and higher spheres which require a head for the general; nor of improving themselves to be fitted for such; they were slack creatures who preferred to write down to dictation; it would never have occurred to them that they might be born to overseeing and government, and just for that reason they certainly were not. For let a man once have the idea that God has special plans for him, which he must further by his aid, and he will pluck up his heart and strain his understanding to get the better of all things and be their master, though the sum of them be as vast as it was in the prosperous establishment of Petepre at Wese in Upper Egypt.

For they were many and various. And of the twofold achievement, that Joseph became Potiphar's soothing and indispensable body-servant, and that afterwards the master put all that he had into his hand, the second was incomparably the harder part. Mont-kaw, who initiated Joseph into the work, was right in his oft-repeated saying that he had a hard time in the world. For a man with a good head for the general there was probably too much drudgery, and Mont-kaw suffered with his kidneys as well. It is easy to see that he was glad of the chance to acquire a strong young assistant and to train him for his successor — indeed, he must have been quietly looking for one for some time.

Petepre, the friend of Pharaoh, titular commandant of the palace troops and chief executioner, was a very rich man — richer, and rich in much grander style, than Jacob at Hebron. And he always grew richer, for he was highly paid as a court official and the constant recipient of the royal largesse, and also his property bore and bred for him without stint. Indeed, it came to him only partly by inheritance, being itself, especially the landed property, a gift of the god to his favourite, and continually increased and fed from the same source. He had little acquaintance with it in any active sense; applying himself exclusively to the maintenance of his physical bulk by eating, his mental by the books he had read aloud to him, and his manly self-respect by hunting in the marshes. Everything else he left in the hands of his steward; and when the latter as in honour bound sub-

mitted the accounts for inspection, he would glance at
them indifferently and say:

"Very good, old man. I know you love me well, and
do your work as well as you can, and you can very well
indeed. What does it say here about the wheat and spelt?
Is that right? — but yes, of course it is. I am convinced
that you are as good as gold, and devoted to me body and
soul. How could it be otherwise, considering your nature
and the baseness it would be to do me wrong? Out of love
for me you make my affairs your own; very good, I leave
them to you for the sake of your love; in your own affair
you will not come short out of carelessness or worse.
Besides, the Hidden One would see it and you would
have only torment from it in the end. Your accounts are
correct, you may take them again with my thanks. You
have no longer a wife, nor children — for whom should
you disadvantage me? For yourself? You have not
good health; your body indeed is strong and hairy, but
inwardly a little worm-eaten, you have often a yellow
face; the tear-glands under your eyes grow larger — you
will probably not live to a great age. Why then should
you offend your love to defraud me? Heartily I would
that you should live to grow old, for I know not whom
I could trust like you. What doth Khun-Anpu, our
barber-surgeon, think of your health? Have his medicines helped you? I have no understanding for these
things, I am healthy myself though not so hairy. But if
he does not know how to help you and so your state grows
worse, we will send to the temple for a physician. True,
you are of the servant class, and Red-belly should do for
you in illness, yet you are dear enough to me that I
would procure you a learned man from the book-house

if your body require. Thank me not, I would do so for the sake of your love and because your accounts are so clear and right. Here, take them again, and go on in your accustomed way."

Thus Potiphar to his house-steward on these occasions. For he took nothing upon himself. His aristocratic nature, its unactuality made him shun the practical realities of life, confiding as he did in the love and care which those about him had for his sacred and fleshly person. Certainly, he had good ground to trust Mont-kaw, for the steward really loved him and did him loyal service, making him richer and richer with the most disinterested care and caution. But suppose it had been otherwise, and this man who had all in his hands had robbed him, so that he and his had come to want? He would have had himself to blame and would have deserved to be reproached for his indolent over-confidingness. Yes, Potiphar presumed all too much upon the deeply motivated and tender devotion which those about him had to pay to his peculiar constitution and sacred person as courtier of the sun. We should all have had to agree to the justice of this charge.

Thus he was responsible for naught, save his eating and drinking; but the hardship for Mont-kaw was the greater in that his own affairs were involved with those of his master. As pay for his services he received supplies — corn, bread, beer, geese, linen, and leather — in much greater quantity than he could eat up or wear out. He had to take them to market and exchange them for durable goods to increase his permanent holdings. The same was true in general of his master's property, both that produced on the estate and that which came from without.

The fan-bearer stood high on the list of Pharaoh's beneficiaries; a rich and constant stream of rewards and superfluities flowed out upon his titular and unreal existence. The good god gave him every year quantities of gold, silver, copper, clothing, yarns, incense, wax, honey, oil, wine, vegetables, corn, and flax; birds caught by the fowlers, oxen, and geese; yes, even armchairs, coffers, mirrors, wagons, entire wooden ships. All this was only in part used on the estate; and the same was true of the estate's own produce, the household goods and the fruits of garden and field. Most of it was taken to market up or down river and sold in exchange for other wares or for metal worked and unworked, which then went to swell Potiphar's treasury. And these operations, combined with the actually producing and consuming economy of the estate, necessitated much book-keeping and careful oversight.

Provisions had to be rationed out to the servants and workers: bread, beer, and barley or lentil porridge for work-days, for feast-days geese. The women's house had a separate domestic economy which had to be supplied and accounted every day; the raw materials had to be given out to the bakers, sandal-makers, paper-stickers, brewers, carpet-weavers, carpenters, potters, weavers, and spinners, and their finished wares to be apportioned where needed, or stored, or marketed. The same was true of the crops and the produce of orchard and garden. Potiphar's live-stock had to be kept up and taken care of: the horses which drew his chariot, the dogs and cats with which he hunted. The dogs were large and fierce, and he used them when he hunted in the desert; the cats were of a jaguar kind, for bird-hunting in the marshes. Some head of oxen were kept on the estate, but the most of the herds were pastured on an island in the middle of the river, somewhat upstream toward Dendera and the house of Hathor, which Pharaoh had likewise given him as a mark of affection. That comprised five hundred square rods of ploughland, each of which produced twenty sacks of wheat, twenty sacks of barley, and forty baskets each of onions, garlic, melons, artichokes, and gourds. Multiply that by five hundred, and one can see the amount of work and account-keeping entailed! There was a separate steward for it, the overseer of the harvest and the barley, who filled the measures pressed down and running over and measured the wheat for his lord. Actually the man expressed himself thus, in epigraphical style, about his performance; yet the responsibility was not his, but Mont-kaw's. All the accounts went through his hands; for the sowing and reaping, the oil-mills, the wine-presses, the herds and flocks — in short, for all that such a prosperous estate produces and consumes, brings in and sends out. And he had to go out on the fields too and see that things were going well; since he to whom they and everything else belonged, Potiphar the courtier, was not used to supervising anything or disturbing the delicate insubstantiality of his state with any care at all.

So it was fortunate that Joseph after all did go out to the fields — at the right time and under the right auspices, not the wrong ones. For he went not as a labourer, as Dudu, the married dwarf, in his conservatism had wanted and tried to bring about, before he had had the chance to stand before Potiphar. Instead with tablet and pen he accompanied Mont-kaw, to learn the business of overseeing; went down-river with him in a sail-boat with rowers, to Potiphar's island. Mont-kaw sat stiff and solemn between the carpet hangings of his little niche, like the travelling grandees whom Joseph had seen during his first voyage; he himself, with the other scribes, sat behind. The boat was well known, and people as it passed them said:

"There goes Mont-kaw, the steward of Petepre, to inspect his master's estate. But who is the strikingly pretty lad among his train?"

Then they would disembark to walk over the island, inspect the sowing or reaping, have the cattle driven up, and strike terror to the heart of him who " let the measure run over " — while the culprit looked his astonishment at the youth to whom the overseer was showing everything, introducing it, as it were, and bowing above him as he talked. And Joseph, fully aware that the man before him might have been his slave-driver and swung the lash over him had he come out too early to the field, spoke to him privily and said:

" Have a care that you do not let the measure run over to your own gain, my man. For we should see it at once and you would be in a hole."

He used an expression native to his home, not familiar here, but by that so much the more impressive to the startled scribe of the harvest.

At home Joseph accompanied Mont-kaw on his round among the workers sitting at their benches. He examined their work, listened to their reports of the foremen and scribes and the explanations of Mont-kaw for his benefit; and he congratulated himself on not having displayed his ignorance and earned their contempt; that would have made it much harder for them to accept him as a man

endowed by nature to be a supervisor. It is hard enough
for us to make ourselves into that for which we were
created and to arrive at the height of God's purpose for
us, even when that may not be in itself a very lofty goal.
And God's purposes with Joseph were lofty indeed, and
follow them he must. He sat and did sums and accounts
in the business of the estate; with figures and statements
before him, he kept his mental eye fixed upon the realities which they represented. And he worked with his
father Mont-kaw in the special room of trust, and the
steward marvelled at the swiftness and penetration of
his understanding, the power possessed by this pretty
head of grasping facts and their relations, of suggesting,
even, improvements on his own account. For instance,
the garden produced such large quantities of sycamore
figs that they disposed of them in the city, and particularly in the quarter of the tombs, where there was a great
demand for them to furnish the offertory tables and as
ceremonial food for the dead; and one day it occurred
to Joseph to have the potters make imitation fruit in the
natural colours, which would serve the purpose of the
funerary offerings quite as well as the actual fruit. And
as the purpose itself was magic, these symbols answered
to it even better than reality, and very soon the magic
figs were in great demand. They cost the producers little
or nothing and could be made in great quantities, so
that the making soon became a flourishing branch industry in Potiphar's house, occupying many work-people
and contributing substantially to the proprietor's income,
though of course the sum was small in comparison to the
whole.

The steward Mont-kaw was grateful to his young aide

for understanding so well how to keep the bargain they had struck for the sake of their noble master. Not seldom, as he watched the boy's single-minded endeavour and the sagacious purposefulness with which he conquered the manifold detail of his work, he felt afresh those equivocal sensations which had assailed him when Joseph for the first time stood before him, roll in hand, and moved him so strangely.

Soon he was able to relieve the pressure by sending his young pupil on business trips and to market in his place: downstream toward Abdu, the abode of the mangled one, yes, even to Menfe, and upstream to the Elephant Isle. Joseph became the master of the bark, or rather not of one but of several, which carried Potiphar's wares: the beer, the wine, the vegetables, hides, linen, earthenware, and castor oil, the latter of two kinds, the coarser for lamps, the finer for inward lubrication. Soon those who saw him said:

" There goes Mont-kaw's assistant, from the house of Petepre. He is an Asiatic youth, of beautiful countenance and very shrewd; he takes goods to markets, for the steward trusts him, and with right too, for he has magic in his glance and speaks in the speech of men better than you or I, and gains favour for his wares as for his person, and can obtain prices to gladden the heart of Pharaoh's friend."

Thus or something like it spoke the sailors of the Nehel as they passed. And it was true; for blessing abode by Joseph's endeavours, he had the most engaging way with the merchants in village and town, and his words were a joy to hear, so that there were crowds about him and what he had to sell and he brought back better profit to the overseer than the latter could most likely have got himself or anybody else. But Mont-kaw could not often send him on journeys of any duration, for Petepre was displeased when his servant was absent from the dining-room, when another poured water over his hands or gave him dish and cup; or if he must take his nap without hearing Joseph read aloud. Yes, only when we realize that his service to Potiphar continued alongside his task of learning to manage the estate, can we measure the claims which were made at this time upon his energies and powers. But he was young and full of zeal, as of high resolve to attain the height of God's purpose for him. Already he was no longer the least of these here below; already there were those who bowed before his steps. But there must be much more than this; for the sake of his God he was filled with the idea that not some but all must bow — all, with exception of One, the Highest, whom alone he might serve. Such was now the fixed and unchanging principle which guided the life of the descendant of Abram. How it would come about he did not know or conceive. The important thing was to walk with courageous and willing steps the road God set under his feet, to look as far ahead as it is given man to see, and not to startle though the way were steep, for the steeper the more certainly it pointed to the highest goal.

So he chafed not at the struggle to master the details of the business and to make himself every day more in-dispensable to Mont-kaw, as well as to keep the pact with regard to Potiphar, his good master and the highest in his immediate circle, devoting himself as his servant and reader and establishing himself in Potiphar's confidence as he had done by the conversation in the orchard and

the discussion about the garden and the fowler maiden.
It took much skill and understanding to do this, to reach
and help the master in his innermost soul and nourish
his self-esteem with a warmth more cordial than the wine
he poured for him at table. And even this was not all.
For to conceive the sum of Joseph's efforts for master
and steward one must add that he had every evening to
say good-night to Mont-kaw, and every night in different
phrases. For that service he had originally been bought;
and Mont-kaw had been too favourably impressed with
the first instance to forgo the pleasure in the sequel. He
was a poor sleeper, as the pouches under his eyes be-
trayed. Only hardly did the overburdened brain relax
from the occupations of the day and find the good highway to slumber. The kidneys too were bad and helped
to make the transit difficult. So that he could well use a
few sweet words and mellifluous murmurings at the end
of the day. Thus Joseph might never neglect to come before him at night and drop soothing speech in his ears
— which, besides everything else, had to be prepared
during the day, for it must have comeliness of form.

"Greetings at evenfall, my father," he would say, with
lifted hands. "Lo, the day is lived out, it has closed its
eyes, weary of itself, over all the earth stillness has come.
Hark, how strange is the stillness! There might sound a
stamping from the stable, or a dog give tongue, only to
make the silence more profound. It reaches with soothing into the souls of men, it makes them slumbrous;
while over city and country, fertile and desert land are
kindled the wakeful lamps of God. The peoples rejoice
in the timely coming of the night, for they were weary;
they rejoice that morn shall open their eyes again when

sleep has washed them. Truly God's works are grateful
to man! For imagine that there were no night; that the
burning road of his toil glared endless and uniform before him. Were it not a horror and a quailing? But God
has made the days and to each set its limit, so that we
unfailingly reach it at its hour; the grove of night invites
us to pious repose; with outstretched arms, head sinking
back, with open lips and blissfully closing eyes we enter
into its priceless shadow. Yet think not, dear my master,
on your bed, that you must rest, but rather that you may,
then the great boon of peace will come. Lie then, my
father, outstretched on your couch and may sweet sleep
fall upon you and over you, fill your soul quite with exquisite repose, that freed from care and cark you may
breathe it in as resting upon the breast of God!"

"Thanks, Osarsiph," said the steward; and his eyes
were filled with tears, as they had been that first time by
broad daylight. "May you rest well too! Yesterday you
spoke perhaps a trace more sweetly, but yet today's
words were full of consolation like poppy-seed, and will
help me even better against wakefulness. Strange, your
distinction — that I may but must not sleep — strange
and appealing. I mean to think of it and it will stead me.
Yet must I wonder at the way your words fall from you
like a charm: 'Upon you, over you, fill your soul
quite . . .' — but that you can probably not tell yourself. — And so good-night, my son!"

AMUN LOOKS ASKANCE AT JOSEPH

SUCH were the many and varied demands made upon
Joseph at this time; he must not only satisfy them but

take care that his good fortune be not laid up against him. For the smiling, the downcast eyes with which men mostly greet such a rise to power hide much ill will, which must be mollified with tact, shrewdness, and consideration, thus adding another to the many claims upon his judgment and alertness. Joseph flourished as by a spring; and it is wellnigh impossible for one in his position to avoid encroachment on another's field, and damage to another's boundary-stones. His advancement is inevitably bound up with detriment to another's; he must devote a good part of his understanding to reconcile with his own existence the outshone and overthrown. Before the time in the pit Joseph had been without sensitivity for these things. The view that everybody loved him more than they did themselves closed his eyes. In death and in his Osarsiph life he was cleverer, or, if you like, shrewder, for cleverness does not shield one from folly, as witness Joseph's case. The delicate compunction he had displayed to Mont-kaw about Amenemuia, his predecessor in the reader's office, was in the first instance directed toward Mont-kaw himself, in the consciousness that it would please him, even taking into consideration that the steward was by nature inclined to cheerful abnegation. But even for Amenemuia Joseph did all he could, addressing him so courteously and modestly that the scribe was quite won over and felt himself repaid by his successor's charming friendliness for the fact that he had ousted him from office. For Joseph, hands on his breast, put into moving words his pain at the decision and the master's whim, which must be held sacred but which to his knowledge he had done nothing to bring about. His best excuse was his sincere conviction that Amenemuia, scholar of the book-house, and a son of the black earth, could read aloud much better than himself, Osarsiph, who could but mangle the Egyptian tongue. But it had come about in the orchard that he had had to speak before the master, and in his embarrassment told him all sorts of things about trees, bees, and birds as they came into his head. They had oddly enough pleased the master to such a disproportionate extent that with the swift decision of the great and mighty he had come to a resolve which by now he probably saw was not to his own advantage. For ever and often he held Amenemuia up to his new reader as an example, saying: " Thus and so spoke and pronounced Amenemuia, my former reader, and so must you do, would you win favour in my sight, for I am spoilt to begin with." Joseph had endeavoured so to do, and as it were had life and breath only from his predecessor. Probably the master would by now have recalled his command, if it were not that the great would never admit that they had spoken too soon or given a mistaken order. He, Joseph, had realized the unspoken regret and sought to assuage it by saying: " You must, my master, give Amenemuia two feast-day garments and that excellent post as scribe of the sweetmeats and the revels in the house of the women, then will your mind be relieved and mine too on his account."

All that was of course balsam to Amenemuia's wound. He had not known that he was such a good reader; mostly the master had gone to sleep soon after he opened his mouth. He told himself that since he had had to leave to find it out he must perforce be satisfied with his congé. Likewise his successor's pangs of conscience did him good in his very soul, as also the master's supposed regret; and when he did actually receive the fine garments and the excellent post of master of revels in Petepre's house of women, in evidence that Joseph had spoken for him, he bore no malice at all, but conceived that he had been most charmingly treated.

It was of course nothing to Joseph to get for others good posts, since he himself, with God, aimed at supervision of them all, if as yet from afar, and dealt with all the problems at Mont-kaw's side. The same thing happened again with a certain man named Merab, who had formerly accompanied Petepre when he went bird-hunting and fish-spearing. For now it was Joseph who enjoyed these masculine pleasures attendant on his lord; and that must truly have been a thorn, a poisoned one at that, in Merab's side. But Joseph took away the sharpness and the sting, speaking to Merab as before to Amenemuia and procuring him presents and a good post — that of head of the brewery — so that he was Joseph's friend instead of his enemy, and went about saying: "Of course he is from the wretched Retenu and of the desert fly-by-nights; but a fine chap is he none the less, with the most charming ways, that one must admit. By All the Three! He still makes mistakes in speaking a man's tongue; but in some wise is it so that if one must give way before him one does it with pleasure and one's eyes light up. Explain it as you will and you can only blunder thereby — but it remains the fact that one's eyes light up."

Thus Merab, a quite common man of Egypt. It was Sa'ankh-Wen-nofer-and-so-forth, little "Beauty," the dwarf, who whispered it all to Joseph, how the superseded one had spoken to the people of the courtyard. "Well, then, all is well," Joseph had answered. But he perfectly knew that not everyone spoke thus. He had got over the childish illusion that everybody must love him more than themselves; he fully understood that his rise in the house of Potiphar, irritating in itself, was further offensive in that he was a foreigner, a sand-dweller and of the Ibrim. He knew that he must treat the situation with the utmost tact. And here we come back to those inner contradictions and factions which reigned in the land of ancestors and among which Joseph's career was run: certain religious and patriotic funda-mentals which went counter to that career and had al-most succeeded in sending him out untimely to the field; likewise certain factors of an opposed kind, free-think-ing, tolerant — or one might say degenerate and capri-cious — which favoured his rise. These things concerned the steward Mont-kaw simply because they concerned his master the courtier. But why did they concern Petepre? Because they concerned the court. Because the court was angry at Amun in his temple and at his oppressive power, the latter-day embodiment of patriotic conservatism and the bondage of tradition, and because the great at court inclined to and cultivated another god and worship — and it was already suspected which god that was. It was the worship of Atum-Re at On in the Delta, that very old and mild god with whom Amun had put himself on a par — not courteously but with violence, calling himself Amun-Re, sun-god and god of the empire. Both of them were the Sun-in-his-Bark, Re and Amun, but in what un-like sense and in what different way! Joseph had had proof on the spot, in converse with the blear-eyed priests of Horakhte, of the god's blithe, many-sided, and edify-ing sun-meaning; he knew of his desire to extend, his

tendency to associate himself and reach understanding
with all possible popular sun-gods, with Asia's youths of
the sun, who went forth like a bridegroom out of his
chamber, rejoiced like strong men in their race, and were
mourned in their setting with the laments of women. Re,
it appeared, would have no more great distinction among
them, just as Abram in his time would perceive none
between his god and Melchizedec's El Elyon. He was
called Atum in his going down, very lovely and lamen-
table; but of late, out of lively speculation by his learned
prophets, he had given himself a like-sounding name for
his universal sunship — not only for his going down but
for morning, midday, and evening all together: he called
himself Aton — with a peculiar intonation noted by all.
For he thus assimilated his own name to that of the youth
mangled by the boar and bewailed by the flutes in Asia's
gorges and groves.

The sun-meaning of Re-Horakhte, with its foreign associations and inclination to a lively universalism, was
well received at court. Pharaoh's wise men found it good
to practise themselves in its thought. But Amun-Re at
Karnak, Pharaoh's father in his rich and mighty temple,
was just the opposite of Atum-Re. He was rigid and strict,
hostile to every sort of wide-ranging speculation, averse
to foreign influence, abiding by unarguable custom and
the sacred traditional. All this though he was much
younger than he of On. The ancient of days was here
flexible and blithe, the new unbendingly conservative —
and that was confusing.

But even as Amun at Karnak looked askance upon the
growing esteem in which Atum-Re-Horakhte was held at
court, so also, Joseph felt, the god looked askance at him,

Potiphar's foreign body-servant and reader. Weighing favour against disfavour, he soon deduced that the sun-meaning of Re favoured his course, while that of Amun did the opposite — also that this situation, too, demanded exercise of tact.

His closest contact with Amun, the embodiment of the god in Potiphar's house, was the wight Dudu, keeper of the jewels. It had been clear from the beginning that Dudu loved him not as himself but even considerably less; unspeakable trouble did Jacob's son have through all these years with the pompous creature. In every way, with the most punctilious courtesy, he sought to win and reconcile the dwarf, as also by attentions to her whose arm went about him, Djeset his spouse, who had place of authority in the house of the women; and his two overgrown and ugly sons, Esesi and Ebebi. He painfully avoided every slightest affront to Dudu's boundary-stones. Surely it would have been easy, standing in such cordial relations with Petepre, to push Dudu aside and take his office. The master would have liked nothing better than to draw him even closer into his personal service. It is as good as known that he offered Dudu's post to Joseph unasked — and certainly, as Joseph saw, and had inferred also from the loyal steward's attitude, he simply could not bear the arrogant dwarf. But Joseph declined — meekly but firmly; in the first place, busy as he was with learning to oversee, he could take on nothing more; but in the second, on which he laid stress to Potiphar, he could not and would not bring himself to tread on the worthy manikin's toes.

But one would think the dwarf might have been grateful. He was not — in this respect Joseph had given himself to false hopes. The enmity evinced by Dudu from the first day, nay, from the first hour, for he had tried his best to prevent him being bought, was not to be softened or won by any politeness. And if we wish to get an insight into the foundations and motivations of all these events, we shall not be satisfied to explain Dudu's dogged dislike as the ill will of a partisan of Egypt against a foreigner and his increase in Potiphar's house. We must quite certainly bring in those peculiar talismanic powers by virtue of which Joseph had known how to be " helpful " to the master and to win favour from him. Of these Dudu had had proof, of a kind peculiarly offensive to the dwarf, injuring him as they did at once in his exaggerated personal dignity and in values which sustained the pride and the self-esteem of his dwarfish existence.

This too Joseph perceived. He knew that his oration in the palm garden had wounded the deepest sensibilities of one hearer in the same measure as it had worked healing to the other's; that, without meaning to, he had somehow encroached on the domain of the married dwarf. This was why he had been so gracious to Dudu's wife and her brood. But it did no good. Dudu showed his dislike whenever he could, especially by casting up at him — from below — the reproach familiar in the stern old code, that of being a stranger, a Shabirite, and as such unclean. At table, when the upper servants of the house broke bread together, among them Joseph and the steward Mont-kaw, Dudu, pursing his upper lip till it stuck out like a thatch, insisted that the Hebrew be separately served; and when the steward and the others tried, in the sun-sense of Atum-Re, to make light of the matter, he held to the strict letter of the Amun-observance, withdrew from the abomination, spat toward the four quarters of the heavens, and drawing a circle round about him, practised charms and exorcisms against the pollution, quite obviously actuated by the wish to be offensive to Joseph.

If he had only stopped at that! But Joseph soon learned that the worthy Dudu actively worked against him and tried to drive him away. He got it fresh and hot from his little friend Bes-em-heb; for the latter, thanks to his minute size, was extraordinarily clever at peeping and hearkening in the right places, and simply a master at hiding in holes which could never have occurred to a full-sized man. Dudu was a dwarf too, by nature adjusted to the scale of the dwarf world; he too should have shown himself less clumsy and defenceless than ordinary mortals. But it might be true, as little " Beauty " asserted, that his marriage into the full-sized world had blunted the edge of his finer perceptions — perhaps by dint of the same virtue which had made him capable of contracting it. In any case, he let himself be tracked down and spied upon by his despised little colleague, who soon learned how Dudu went about to hinder Joseph's growth. The road led into the house of the secluded, it led to Mut-em-enet, Potiphar's chief wife; what the dwarf said to her she repeated, sometimes in his presence, but oftener alone with a certain mighty man who went in and out in Petepre's house of women and in her private rooms as well: Beknechons, the first prophet of Amun.

We know from the lips of Potiphar's mischief-making little old parents the close relation in which Joseph's

mistress stood to the temple of the wealthy state god and
the house of Amun-Re. Like numberless women of her
social standing, for instance Renenutet, wife of the overseer of the bulls of Amun, she belonged to the aristocratic order of Hathor, whose protectress was the exalted
consort of Pharaoh and its present leader the wife of the
head priest of the god's temple at Karnak; in other words,
of the pious Beknechons. The centre and spiritual home
of the order was the beautiful temple by the river, called
Amun's southern house of women or simply the harem;
connected by the amazing avenue of rams with the great
temple at Karnak, and now in process of enlargement
by Pharaoh with a vast and towering columned hall.
The honorary title of the members of the order was
" harem-wife of Amun "; and accordingly the " mother "
of the members, the wife of the high priest, was called
" first of the women of the harem." But why were these
ladies priestesses of Hathor, when Amun-Re's great consort was called Mut or mother, and Hathor, the cow-eyed,
beautiful of countenance, was the wife of Atum-Re, the
lord of On? These were the refinements and subtle statesmanlike balancings of the land of Egypt! For as it
pleased Amun on political grounds to put himself on a par
with Atum-Re, so Mut, the Mother of the Son, did the same
with all-compelling Hathor; and Amun's earthly harem-
women, the ladies of the best society of Thebes, followed
her example: each one of them was Hathor, the mistress
of love, in her very person; at the great feasts of Amun,
wearing the narrow garment, the mask of the bride of the
sun, the gold cap with the cow-horns and crescent moon,
they made music and danced before him, singing as well
as ladies in high society can sing — for they were not

chosen for their voices, but for their riches and aristocratic birth. But Mut-em-enet, Potiphar's lady wife, had a charming voice, and taught the others, among them Renenutet, wife of the keeper of the bulls, to sing. She had a high place in the women's house of the god, her rank in the order was next to its head, whose husband, the great prophet Beknechons, was her friend and trusted intimate and went in and out of her house.

BEKNECHONS

JOSEPH had long known that forbidding man by sight; had repeatedly seen him on his visits to the house of women and sympathized with the anger in Pharaoh's soul at sight of Beknechons's pomp and state. Troops of the god, with spears and clubs, ran before his carrying-chair as it swayed on long poles upon the shoulders of four times four shiny-pated temple servitors. At its sides were bearers with ostrich-feather fans and another troop followed behind — as though the god Amun himself were going a progress in his bark. Criers ran in front of the train with staves, filling the court in advance with their loud insistent shouts, so that the people hurried up, and he who was set over the house, if not Petepre himself, came to receive the great guest on the threshold. Petepre avoided these occasions, but Mont-kaw was always on hand and on sundry of them Joseph had already stood behind him, attentively fixing the great man with his eye. For here was the embodiment, the highest and remotest, of the hostile sun-doctrine, as Dudu was its smallest and closest to hand.

Beknechons was of goodly stature and bore himself

haughtily, his torso strained upwards from his ribs, his shoulders thrown back, his chin thrust up and out. His head was impressive: egg-shaped, with a never-covered, smooth-shaven poll, and characterized by the sharp and deep-cut furrow between the brows. It was a permanent furrow, losing none of its severity when he smiled, as he sometimes did, condescendingly, or as a reward for some particular obsequiousness. His face, likewise meticulously shaven, was clean-cut and immobile, with high cheek-bones and furrows as deeply graven as the one on his forehead, about the nose and mouth. He had a way of gazing past men and things, which bespoke not merely arrogance but a thoroughgoing rejection of the modern world, a denial and condemnation of the whole course of life, for centuries or even millennia back. And his raiment, though costly and fine, displayed a priestly conservatism, being fashioned after a mode whole epochs earlier in time. Beneath his outer garment, which began under his shoulders and fell to his feet, could plainly be seen the simple, narrow, brief loin-apron, cut in the manner of the first dynasties of the Old Kingdom. To even more remote and thus presumably more pious times belonged the priestly leopard-skin which was draped round his shoulders, with the head and fore-paws hanging down his back, the hind-paws crossed on his breast, where likewise he wore other insignia of his state: a blue scarf, and a complicated gold ornament with rams' heads.

The leopard-skin was clearly an unwarranted presumption, for it belonged to the insignia of the head priest of Atum-Re at On and not at all to the servants of Amun. But Beknechons was just the sort of man to decide for himself what was fitting for him; and nobody, not even

Joseph, failed to understand why he wore the primitive
and sacred skin. It signified that Atum-Re had been absorbed in Amun, that he was but a manifestation of
the Great One of Thebes, to some extent his subject —
and not only to some extent. For Amun — that is to
say, Beknechons — had succeeded in making Re's head
prophet at On take the honorary title of a second priest
of Amun at Thebes; the superior status of the high priest
was thus made evident, also his right to the insignia of
the other's office. Even at On, Re's own seat, he had
managed to prevail. For he not only called himself
" Head Priest of all the gods of Thebes," but also assumed the title of " Head Priest of all the gods of Upper
and Lower Egypt," and was thus the first of the first in
Atum-Re's own house. Why should he not wear the
leopard-skin? Not without awe could one look at this
man, in view of all that he represented. And Joseph had
come to enough understanding of Egyptian affairs that
his heart misgave him as he thought how Pharaoh made
him wax ever more in girth and pride by endless gifts
of goods and treasures, in the pleasing fancy that it was
his father Amun to whom he gave them — and, in a
sense, also to himself. Joseph — for whom Amun-Re
was only an idol, like another, though he kept it to himself: sometimes a ram in his chamber, again a doll-like
image in his chapel shrine, whom they took riding in his
bark on the Jeor because they knew no better than so
to do — Joseph made sharp and clear distinction which
Pharaoh failed to make: he found it not good and not
wise of the god to let his suppositious father wax fatter
and fatter; they were higher cares which beset him when
he saw Amun's greatest disappear into the house of the

women. And they transcended, in his statesmanlike mus-
ings, his concern for his own welfare, although he knew
that it was being threatened by the talk going on inside.

He knew from little Bes, his first patron in Potiphar's
house, that Dudu had complained of him more than once
to Mut, the mistress. The midget, hidden in unlikely
places, had been present at these scenes and made such
detailed report to Joseph that the latter could fairly see
the keeper of the robes, standing in his starched apron
skirt before his lady, pompously sticking out his upper
lip and gesturing indignantly with his stumpy arms as he
sunk his voice to its deepest note and sent up to her ears
his plaint over the annoyance and the offence. The slave
Osarsiph, for so he mysteriously chose to call himself,
the Shabirite lout and scum of the desert — verily it was
a scandal, said Dudu, and a malignant sore, the way he
waxed in favour in Potiphar's house. Surely the Hidden
One saw it with displeasure. Not alone that he had been
bought, against the dwarf's advice, for far too high a
price, a hundred and sixty deben, of some worthless pedlars from the desert, who had stolen him from a prison
grave; not alone that he had been taken into the house,
through the contrivance of the jester Shepses-Bes, the unmarried dwarf, a fellow not worth a rotten nut. But instead of sending the foreign hand to field labour, as
sensible folk had advised the steward, the latter had let
him lounge about the court and he had come to stand
before Petepre in the palm orchard, and the rascal had
turned it to his advantage in a way that could only be
called shameless — and even that was too mild. He had
filled the master's ears with the rankest and most insidious jargon, which was an affront to Amun and a blas-

phemy against the sun. And the exalted master had been
taken in, had been criminally bewitched, so that he had
made the slave his waiter and servant, while Mont-kaw
treated him like a son, or more correctly like a son of the
house, who was learning to administer it because he was
the heir, and plumed himself as the overseer's assistant
— a scabby Asiatic in a house of Egypt! He, Dudu, permitted himself most humbly to call the mistress's attention to this abominable state of things, at which the Hidden One might be so wroth as to avenge himself for this
corrupt free-thinking upon those who committed and
suffered it.

"What said the mistress?" asked Joseph after hearing. "Tell me exactly, little Beauty, repeating if you
can her very words."

"Her words," the little man replied, "were these:
'While you were speaking, steward of the jewel-house,'
she said, 'I have tried to think who he is whom you have
in mind, and what foreign slave you accuse in your
words; but I searched my memory in vain. You could
not expect me to have all the servants in my eye and thus
understand at once the sense of your words. But in time
it came to me, that he of whom you speak is the youth,
still young in years, who now for a while has filled my
husband's cup. Vaguely I can recall the silver apron
if I try.'"

"Vaguely?" repeated Joseph, with some disappoint-
ment. "How can I be so vague to our mistress, when I
stand each day beside her and the master at table, and
the favour I have found in his eyes and Mont-kaw's cannot have escaped her? I wonder therefore that she must
search so long and make such effort before she guessed

to whom Dudu's spiteful words referred. What more did she say?"

"She said," went on the dwarf, "she said: 'Why do you bring me all this to reproach me, keeper of the wardrobe? For you will call down Amun's wrath upon me; have you not said he would be enraged at those who suffer the offence to be? But if I know naught, I suffer naught, and you might have spared me and not made me to stand in danger by my knowing.'"

Joseph laughed at this and gave it great praise. "What a capital answer, what a shrewd reproof! Tell me more of our mistress, little Bes! Repeat all to me with exactness, for I am sure you listened well."

"It was that spiteful Dudu," the dwarf went on, "who said more, justifying himself and saying: 'I have told the mistress, not that she may suffer the evil, but may do it away. For out of love for her I have made occasion that she may serve Amun, by telling the master that the unclean slave must be sent away out of the house. Now that he is bought he should be sent to the fields, instead of making himself master here and setting himself above the children of the land.'"

"Very hateful," Joseph said. "A bad, spiteful speech. But the mistress, what did she say to that?"

"She answered," little Beauty responded, "and said: 'My solemn friend, it seldom happens that it is vouchsafed to the mistress to speak in confidence with the master. Think of the formal manners of our house and do not dream that it stands between him and me as between you and her who is your spouse and familiar, Djeset your wife, who puts her arm about you. She comes in simple confidence and speaks of all her concerns and yours and may also decide your mind to this or that course. For she is a mother, having borne you two sightly sons, Esesi and Ebebi, so that you are bound in gratitude to her and have all reason to give her your ear and heed her words and wishes. But what am I to the master and what cause has he to hearken to me? For his self-will is great, his mood unhearing; I am powerless before him with my reminders.' "

Joseph was silent, looking thoughtfully over his little friend's head as the dwarf sat with wrinkled anxious face supported on his hands.

" Well, and the wardrobe master, what answered he? " Jacob's son probed again after a while. " Did he reply and enlarge himself yet more? "

That the dwarf answered in the negative. Dudu had preserved a dignified silence; and the mistress had added that she would speak as soon as might be with the head priest. For as Petepre had advanced the foreign slave after the latter had spoken with him concerning sun-matters, it was plain that they were here dealing with religion and the state, which were the affair of Bekne-chons, the great prophet of Amun, and her confessor and friend. He must be told; she would pour into his fatherly heart, to her relieving, all that Dudu had told her concerning the offence.

So far the dwarf's information to Joseph. But the latter recalled afterwards how Bes-em-heb lingered, sitting beside him in his comic costume, the cone of ointment perched on his wig, his chin in his hands, sombrely blinking.

" What are you frowning at, Beauty in the house of

Amun? " he had asked. " Why do you brood over these things? "

The other answered in his cricket chirp:

" Oh, my Osarsiph, I brood because it is not good that the spiteful gossip speaks of you to Mut the mistress — how little good it is, and how great harm! "

" Of course not," Joseph replied. " Why do you tell me that, when I know of myself that it is evil and even dangerous? But behold, I have no care because I trust in God. Has not the mistress herself admitted the weakness of her power over Petepre? It would take more than a word from her to send me to the field, so have no care! "

" But how shall I be quiet," whispered Bes, " when there is danger still, of another kind, if Dudu open your mistress's eyes and enlighten her concerning you? "

" Who can understand that? " Joseph cried out. " Not I indeed, for your prattle is like so much gibberish to me. Danger of another kind — what sort of dark saying is it you whisper there? "

" I whisper, I whisper my fear and foreboding," he heard the dwarf say. " I murmur my dwarfwise cares, of which you, being of the full-grown race, as yet have no notion. The old gossip intends evil; but it may turn out that he has done well, yet only too well, so that in the end it is worse than before, much worse than he thought to make it in his spite."

" Take it not ill, little man, that I understand not one word of your words, for they have no sense. Good, evil, only too well and yet much worse — and that is but little language and dwarfish nonsense, and try as I may, I understand it not."

" Then why has your face turned red, Osarsiph, and why are you vexed — as you were before when I said that the mistress knew you but vaguely? My dwarf-wisdom would have you remain ever vague to her; for the danger is doubly a danger if the accursed gossip opens her eyes with his malice. Ah! " the manikin said, and hid his head in his arms, " the dwarf is afraid, he is terrified in face of the foe, the bull whose fiery breath scorches the field."

" What field? " Joseph asked, with wilful want of understanding. " And what sort of fiery bull? You are not in your right senses today nor can I give you reason. Go get yourself a soothing drink from Red-belly, it will cool your head. I go to my work. Can I help it if Dudu complain of me to the mistress, however dangerous it may be? But you see my trust in God, and need not be disturbed. Yet take heed always to let no word escape you of that which Dudu speaks before the mistress, and even more what she says to him, and report it to me with exactness. For it is important that I should know."

Such had been the course of their conversation; Joseph later recalled it, and how the dwarf had displayed such fear. But had it been merely his trust in God, and nothing else, which made Joseph receive with relative blitheness the news of Dudu's unfriendly activities?

Up till then, to the mistress he had been, if not precisely air, still a vacant shape, like a dumb waiter in the service of Huia and Tuia. Dudu's ill will now altered the situation. For when at table Joseph handed the dish to his lord or filled his cup and her eye fell upon him, it was not mere chance, not as though it rested on an object in the room, but she looked at him as a person, with associations and backgrounds to give food for thought, whether pleasant or otherwise. In a word, his mistress, this great lady of Egypt, had begun to heed him. Of course, in an idle and cursory way; it would be too much to say that her eyes really rested upon him. But for the space of a second perhaps, they sought him out — very likely as the thought crossed her mind that she must speak to Beknechons; and Joseph behind his eyelashes took note of such moments. Despite all the attention he must give to serving Petepre, not one of them escaped him — though only once or twice did he let it happen that the moment was mutual: that the two pairs of eyes, the mistress's and the servant's, actually chanced to meet — hers blankly, haughtily, with stern insistence, his with startled respect, then veiling their gaze to look humbly down.

That happened after Dudu's talk with the mistress. Before, it had not — and between ourselves Joseph found it not altogether unpleasant. To some extent he saw progress in it and was tempted to be grateful to Dudu. And next time he saw Beknechons enter the house of women he found it agreeable to realize that they would be talking in there of him and his advancement — there was a certain satisfaction or even joy connected with the thought, though mingled with however much misgiving.

Of this talk too he got a report from the mock-vizier, who had been present in some crack or cranny and heard it all. First the priest and the lady of the order of Hathor had discussed religious and ritual matters as well as those of a personal and social nature — they had made tongue, as the children of Kemt said (the expression was a Babylonian one); in other words, exchanged the gossip of the metropolis. When the talk veered round to Petepre's house the mistress took occasion to put before her

spiritual adviser Dudu's complaint and the improprieties
centring in the Hebrew slave to whom the courtier and
his steward had shown such signal and sensational favour.
Beknechons nodded as he listened, as though her words
confirmed his general gloomy expectations and con-
formed only too well with the morals of a time which
had forfeited so much of the righteousness that had held
sway in those epochs when the apron was worn short and
tight as Beknechons wore it. A bad sign, certainly, he
had said. A sign of the loose times and the neglect of the
ancient piety; all very fine in the beginning, but getting
lost in the wilderness, rending the most sacred bonds,
sapping the strength of the lands till no more awe before
their sceptre lived on the coasts, and the kingdom fell
to decay. And the high priest forsook the subject of
Dudu's complaint, said Bes, to enlarge upon higher
themes, questions of power and statesmanship, waving
his hands about in the air. He spoke of Tushratta, king
of Mitanni, and the need of using Shubbilulima, king of
Hatti in the north, to check his encroachments; but only
just enough, Shubbilulima must not succeed too well.
For if warlike Hatti were to bring Mitanni completely
under its rule and overrun the southland with arms, it
might become a danger to Pharaoh's Syrian possessions,
descended to him from the conqueror Men-Kheper-Re-
Thutmose. In any case it was on the cards that Hatti,
urged by its savage gods, might some day, avoiding Mitanni, overrun the land of Amki on the sea, between the
cedar ranges and those of Amanus. Yet he was opposed
on the world chess-board by Abd-Ashirta the Amorite,
who as Pharaoh's vassal held the region between Amki
and Hanigalbat, on purpose to set limits to Shubbilulima's

southward advance. But this the Amorite would do only
so long as his awe of Pharaoh remained greater than his
fear of Hatti; failing that, he would assuredly betray
Amun and make common cause with Shubbilulima. For
they were traitors one and all, these vassal kings of the
Syrian conquest, just as soon as they dared, so that everything depended on their fear, theirs and that of the Bed-
ouins and migratory hordes of the steppes, who without it would fall upon the fertile land and lay Pharaoh's
cities waste. In short, there were many cares; many
considerations admonished Egypt to keep itself nerved
and sinewy if it wished to preserve awe for its sceptre
and the kingdom for the crown. To that end it must be
stern of morals and pious as in ancient time.

" A mighty man," Joseph opined after listening to the
speech. " For besides being a man of God and a shiny-
pate before the Lord, who should be a good father to his
children and put out his hand to them that stumble, he
has a head for things of the earth and for political affairs
— one has to admire him for it. But just between ourselves, little Bes, he ought to leave the running of the
kingdom and the terror of the tribes to Pharaoh in his
palace, who is set in his place to that end. Certainly it
was thus between temple and palace in the days which he
praises so highly above these. But our mistress, did she
answer nothing to his words? "

" I heard," said the dwarf, " how she answered, saying: ' Ah, my father, is it not true that in the past, when
Egypt was pious and strict in observance it was also small
and poor; nor were its boundary-stones set among vassal
peoples either southwards beyond the cataracts to the
Negro lands or eastwards to the river that floweth the

wrong way? But out of the poverty have riches come, and out of the smallness a great kingdom. Great Wese and both the lands teem with foreigners, the treasures pour in, and all is changed. But do you not rejoice at all over the new that grew out of the old and is its reward? From the tribute of the peoples Pharaoh offers richly to Amun, so that the god can build to the height of his desire, so that he increases like the river in spring when it is already at high-water mark. Must not my father then approve the course of things since the times of their early piety?' "

" Very true," Beknechons had, according to the dwarf, made answer. " Very justly does my daughter speak concerning the problem of the lands. For thus it stands: the good old times bore within them the seed of the new — that is, the kingdom and the riches of the kingdom — which in its turn bore within it the loosening, the relaxing, and the loss. What shall be done that the blessing not become a curse, and the good not be rewarded with evil? That is the question; and Amun, lord of Karnak, answers it in this wise: the old must become lord in the new, the strict and sinewy be set over the kingdom that looseness not go too far and the reward of strictness be lost. For not to the sons of the new but to the sons of the old pertains the kingdom and belong the crowns, the white, the red, the blue, and the crown of the gods as well! "

" Strong! " said Joseph, after he had taken it in. " A strong, uncompromising speech is this you have heard, little Bes, thanks to your want of size. I am alarmed by it, if at the same time not surprised. For I have always known ever since I saw his troops for the first time in the

Street of the Son, what was in Amun's heart. So our mistress just spoke a little of me and it sent Beknechons off into all those high matters and they forgot all about me. Did you hear that they came back to me at all? "

Only just at the end, Shepses-Bes told him. When he left, the high priest had promised to take Petepre to task as soon as he could and put him on his guard, for the sake of the traditional morality against the foreign slave whom he had so favoured.

" Then must I tremble indeed," said Joseph, " and be in sore fear that Amun put an end to my growth in the land; for if he is against me, how then shall I live? It is very bad, for if I go now to field labour, after the scribe of the harvest hath bowed before me, it will be worse than if I had gone in the first place; and I should perish of heat by day and of cold by night. But do you think that it will be given to Amun to deal thus with me? "

" So stupid am I not," whispered back the dwarf. " I have not wasted my dwarf-wisdom by marriage. True, I have grown up — if I may put it thus — in the fear of Amun. But I have long known that you have a god with you, Osarsiph, stronger than Amun and wiser than he; and never will I believe that He will give you into his hands and permit him in his chapel to set limits to your growth that He Himself has not set."

" Well, then, little Bes, be blithe! " cried Joseph, giving the other a slap on the shoulder, but gently so as not to hurt him, " and concerning me be of good cheer. For after all I have the ear of the master and can put him on his guard too when we are alone, against things which perhaps are dangerous for Pharaoh too. Then will he hear us both: Beknechons and me. The high priest will speak to him of a slave, and the slave of a god; and we shall see to what he inclines his ear — to what, I say, to what subject, and not to whom. But you, my little friend, be watchful, and hide your wisdom for me in cracks and crannies if Dudu should complain of me again to the mistress, that I may come to know his words and hers."

And thus it was. For it is certain that the keeper of the wardrobe did not rest with one tale-bearing to Mutem-enet, but from time to time in conversation with her came back to the foreign slave from the prison pit and the gross favour shown him in Petepre's house. The little jester was always at his post and faithfully brought back the tale of Dudu's doings. Yet even had he been less watchful, Joseph would have known whenever the married dwarf had complained; for then one of those moments would come in the dining-room. And when for days there had been none, so that Joseph was cast down, their renewal, and that stern inquiry directed not as though at an object but a person, made him realize that Dudu had been with her again, and he would say to himself: " He has reminded her, and it is a danger! " But when he said it he also meant: " How pleasant! " and in a way was grateful to Dudu for calling him to the mistress's mind.

JOSEPH BECOMES VISIBLY AN EGYPTIAN

No longer evident to the father's eye, but in his place very much alive and alert, Joseph lived on in the Egyptian world, lived into it, one might say; for he went in harness to its claims, and they were heavy on him who as a lad in his first life had known no tasks and had no demands laid upon him, but spent time according to his whim. Here he was the more active in that he now strove to rise to the height of God's purpose for him; his head was full of figures, facts, and things, all sorts of business details, and more than that involved in a web of human problems and relations which always required most delicate handling, the threads of which led to Potiphar, to the dwarfs, to Mont-kaw, to God knows whom else in the house and outside it — in constant functioning, in short, of a kind that his early home, where Jacob now was, and the brothers, would never dream of.

That home was far away — farther than seventeen days, farther than Jacob had been from Isaac and Rebecca when he lived and looked into the Mesopotamian light of day. Nor had they any idea or been able to form any picture of how their son lived or what his problems were; and from their day he in his turn was estranged. Where a man lives, there is his world: a narrow circle of life, work, and experience. The rest is vague. Though men were always inclined to shift their centre, to let the known sink into the mist and look into a different day. Naphtali's urge was strong upon them, to run off into the mist, to report strange news to those dwelling there who know only their own, and to take back home something worth the knowing. In short, there was always traffic and intercourse. Even between the widely separated places of Jacob's land and Potiphar's, there always had been, time out of mind. Was not the man from Ur accustomed to change his horizon, had he not been to the land of mud, though not so far into it as Joseph; had not his sister-bride, Joseph's ancestral grandmother, dwelt for a time in the house of women of that Pharaoh who then glittered in his horizon not at Wese but farther north, nearer to Jacob's sphere? Always there had been contacts between that sphere and Joseph's present one; for the darkly beautiful Ishmael had taken to wife a daughter of the black earth, and from the marriage the half-Egyptian Ishmaelites had sprung, called and chosen to bring Joseph down hitherwards. And many like them traded between the rivers to and fro, and apron-skirted messengers had gone about, a thousand years and more, with letters written on bricks carried within their garments' folds. But if this Naphtali-nature had always been, yet now in Joseph's time it was as never before a regular, customary, and developed thing; for the land whither he was snatched and where he lived his second life was definitely a land of descendants: no longer piously self-sufficient and strict as Amun would have it be, but worldly and seeking the pleasures of the world; so that if a Come-hither Asiatic lad had but a cunning gift at saying good-night and could add two and two, he could become the body-servant to a great Egyptian and goodness knows what besides!

No, there was no lack of communications between Jacob's place and his darling's. But he whose affair it was to use them since he knew his father's abode but his father knew not his, for whom it would have been easy, as a great steward's right hand, and so skilled in all arrangements, to have arranged opportunity for this too; he did not do it, he did it not for many years. The reasons have long since become clear to us, and nearly all of them are comprehended in the one word: expectancy. The calf bleated not, it kept still as death, it did not let the cow know to what field the man had brought it; for in agreement with the man, it demanded expectation of the cow as well, however hard it might be for her; for needs must the cow consider her calf to be dead and mangled.

Strange, and confusing too it is, to think that Jacob, the old man back there in the mist, all this while held his son for dead — confusing, in that on the one hand one would like to be glad for him because he was mistaken, and on the other one grieves for him precisely because of his mistake. For there are, we know, certain consolations for the death of a beloved one, though they may be of a sufficiently hollow and desolate kind; and so we may feel a double pity for that sorrowing old man: first because he held Joseph for dead, and second because he was not. The father-heart lulled itself — no doubt with a thousand pangs, but yet with a gentle sense of soothing — in the security of death. It imaged his son as treasured up in death, unchangeable, inviolable, needing no more care, eternally the seventeen-year-old boy who had ridden off on white Hulda. And all this was a mistake, not only the affliction but also the consolation which gradually surmounted it. For Joseph lived, and was exposed to all the chances and changes of life. He was snatched away, but not snatched out of time; he did not remain seventeen, but waxed and riped in the place where he was, got to be nineteen and twenty and one-and-twenty; certainly he was still Joseph, but the father would not have known him, at least not at the first glance. The stuff of his life was altered, while still wearing its triumphantly successful shape; it ripened and became a little broader and firmer, less a youth and more a young man. A few years more, and of the fabric of that Joseph whom his Rebecca-father kissed at parting little will be left — as little as though death had dissolved the flesh. Only, since it was not death but life that changed him, the shape to some extent remained. Not so faithfully or exactly as death would have preserved it in the spirit, and did, illusorily, in Jacob's mind. After all, in this matter of content and form, whether it is death or life that removes the loved object away from our eyes is perhaps not so important as we are prone to think.

Likewise we must consider that the substance of Joseph's life, by which among all the changes and chances of his maturing youth its form was preserved, was drawn from quite another sphere than the one which would have fed it had he remained under Jacob's eyes; and the fact influenced its form as well. He was nourished by the airs and juices of Egypt, ate Kemt's food; the water of her river moistened and swelled his tissues and cells, her sun irradiated them; he dressed in the linen from Egypt's flax, trod her soil, receiving from it the impulse of her silently shaping powers; took in with his eyes every day the evidences shaped by the hand of man, the expression of her fundamental, all-embracing, decisive character; lastly, he spoke her speech, and it gave to his tongue, his lips, his jaws another shape than that they would have had. Very soon Jacob the father would have said to him: " Damu, my seed, what is it with thy mouth? I know it no more."

In short, Joseph as he grew became visibly an Egyptian, in form and manner; quickly, easily, unnoticeably, because he was a child of the world, pliant in body and mind, likewise very young and soft when he came into the land, and thus the reshaping of his person after the local type happened readily and painlessly, the more that physically he had, from God knows where, something Egyptian about him — the square shoulders, the slender limbs; and mentally because it lay in his tradition, it was natural to him, to live a stranger among the " children of the land." Even at home he and his, the children of Abram, had always been *gerim* and guests, long settled and well adapted, it is true, but with an inner reserve and looking with detachment upon the easygoing Baal-abominations of the real children of Canaan. So now Joseph in Egypt. As a child of the world he found it simple to conform and to practise detachment at one and the same time, for the one made the other easier and drew out the sting of his fear lest he be disloyal to Him, Elohim, who had brought him into this land, and upon whose countenance and indulgence he might reckon, though Joseph were to comport himself in all ways as an Egyptian and become a child of Hapi and subject of Pharaoh — always excepting the silent reservation. Thus to be a child of the world meant that he might blithely adapt himself to Egypt's children and move among them, consenting to the high culture of the land; yet all the while he might feel that they were the children of the world, at whom he gazed, benevolently but apart, and ever aware of the mocking spirit in his blood at sight of their decorative and detestable folk-customs.

The Egyptian year laid hold upon him and whirled him round with itself in the ebb and flow of nature and the rhythmic recurrence of its feasts — of which one or other might be regarded as the first: the New Year's festival at the beginning of the inundation, a day rich

in hopes and incredibly tumultuous, a fateful day for
Joseph, indeed, as we shall presently see; or the recurrent celebration of the accession of Pharaoh to the throne
— when the rejoicing populace renewed the hopes which
were bound up with the original day, the beginning of
the new dynasty and era: when justice should banish injustice, and life be lived amid laughing and amaze. Or
indeed any other of the recurrent feasts, for they were
many.

Joseph had first set eyes upon the Egyptian scene at
the time of the ebb, when the land had emerged and the
sowing had been done. Then he had been sold, and gone
on further into the year and round with it: the harvest
came, which in name lasted into the flaming summer and
the weeks which we call June, and then the diminished
stream, amid reverential jubilation, began to swell and
climbed slowly out of its banks; closely observed and
measured by Pharaoh's officials, for it was of the first
and last importance that it should rise properly, not too
wildly and not too weak, that Kemt's children might have
to eat, and the tax-gatherers make it possible for Pharaoh
to build. Six weeks the river rose and rose, the Nourisher
of the Land, quite quietly, inch by inch, day and night,
while men slept and, sleeping, trusted. And then, about
the time when the sun was most blazing, and we should
have written July, in the second half, which the children
of Egypt called the moon of Paophi, the second of their
year and in their first season, which they called Akhet,
the river swelled mightily, overflowed the fields on both
sides far and wide, and covered the land — that strangely
and uniquely conditioned land, which had not its like
in the world and which now to Joseph's wonderment and

laughing, when he first saw it, was changed into a sacred lake, out of which high-lying towns and villages stood up, connected by causeways. The god stood there and let his richness sink, and his nourishing mud, on all the fields, until the second or winter season, Peret; then he began to bate and retire — " the waters returned from off the earth continually," as Joseph reminiscently put it to himself; so that beneath the moon of our January they flowed in the old bed, but continued to shrink until summer. It was two-and-seventy days, the days of the two-and-seventy conspirators, the days of the winter drought, that the god pined and died; up to that day when Pharaoh's river conservancy announced that it was rising and a new year of blessing took its beginning. It might be moderate, it might be abundant; Amun send there should not be famine or a scant yield for the tax-gatherers, so that Pharaoh could not build!

Time went very fast, Joseph discovered, from New Year to New Year — or from that moment when he came into the land till the same came round again, reckoning in the Egyptian seasons as he now did, the flood, the sowing, and the harvest, each adorned with its proper feasts, in which Joseph took part — with reserve, and confiding in indulgence from on high; he must indeed do so, and wear a pleasant face, for these heathen celebrations were involved with the economic life of the land. In Petepre's service and as the representative of Mont-kaw he could not avoid the fairs and markets which were bound up with the religious features of the feasts, since always trade springs up wherever men come together in numbers. There were always markets in the fore-courts of the temples of Thebes, on account of the thank-offerings; but likewise up and down the river were many places of pilgrimage and the people streamed together in great hordes wherever a god held his feast, adorned his temple, possessed oracular wisdom, and promised, along with spiritual refreshment, crowds and booths and general mass jollification. It was not Bastet only, the she-cat of the Delta, held a feast — of which Joseph had heard so much that was unedifying. Every year there was a popular excursion from near and far to the ram of Mendes, Djedet in the people's mouth; it was even more jocund than Per Bastet's feast; for Bindidi the ram, racy and rank as he was, stood closer to the temper of the folk than the she-cat, and during the festivities publicly cohabited with a virgin of the country. But the reader may be assured that Joseph, who went down to the feast on business, did not seek out the sight; being occupied, as the steward's confidential man, solely with the marketing of the paper, tools, and vegetables which he had brought.

There was much in the land, and the customs of the land, particularly the feast-day observances — for the feast is the great hour of the traditional, the hour when it comes uppermost and glorifies itself — at which, in all his worldliness, mindful of Jacob, he did not look; or at most with a very detached eye. He did not love the people's love of drink; recollections of Noah prevented him, as well as the picture in his soul of his sober, pondering father. His own nature too, though bright and merry, was averse to drunken disorder. For the children of Kemt knew no better than to drink themselves drunk on every occasion, with beer or wine; men and women alike. Wine flowed freely at all the feasts, and they and their children could drink four days on end and be good for nothing at all. Moreover, there were special feasts of drinking, like the great beer-feast which commemorated the legend of Hathor the mighty, the lion-headed Sakhmet, how she had raged among mankind to destroy them and was only prevented from blotting out the race of men by Re, who with a most clever stratagem made her drunk on red blood-beer. On that day the children of Egypt drank beer in quite insalubrious quantities, a dark beer called *khes,* very powerful; beer with honey, foreign and home-brewed, the latter mostly in the city of Dendera, seat of Hathor, whither one made pilgrimage to the feast and it was actually called " Place of Drunkenness " as the seat of the goddess of drunkenness.

To all this Joseph paid little heed, and only drank a little, symbolically and socially, to the extent demanded by his business. And some of the practices at the great feast of Osiris, lord of the dead, at the time of the shortest day, when the sun died, he also, for the sake of Jacob, regarded with but very distant eye. The feast itself, however, with the ritual performances proper to it, interested him very much and he followed them attentively. For they told again the story of the passion of that mangled and buried and risen god; presented by priests and people in very beautiful masques, faithfully reproducing both the terror and the jubilation of the resurrection, whereat the populace leaped on one leg with joy. Along with this came a deal of primitive foolishness and antique survivals of which nobody any longer knew the meaning: as that various groups of men belaboured each other, one group representing the " folk of the city of Pe," the other the " folk of the city of Dep," and both cities were now entirely unknown. Or a herd of asses was driven round and round the city with mocking shouts and blows from cudgels. A certain contradiction lay in the fact that they treated with blows and contumely a creature which stood to them as a symbol of phallic readiness, for actually the feast of the dead and buried god was likewise a commemoration of the rigid readiness of the male, which tore the mummy-wrappings of Osiris so that Eset the female vulture received from him the avenging son. At this time of year in all the villages there took place processions of women carrying a phallic emblem as long as an ell, which they made to move by means of strings. Thus the worship contradicted the maltreatment; and the reason was after all clear. For on one side this erection and procreation was a matter of dear life itself, and of fruitful continuance; but on the other, and more strikingly, it was a feast of death. For Usir was dead when the vulture conceived from him; the gods were all erected in death; and just among ourselves that was the reason why Joseph, with all his personal feeling for the feast of Usir, the mangled one, did not look on at some of the rites, but averted his head even inwardly speaking. What sort of reason was that? Well, it is hard to talk about so delicate a matter, when one knows and the other does not yet see — and that is the more pardonable in that Joseph himself hardly saw it, and only darkly and partially took account of what he did see. A faint, almost unconscious sense of guilt was stirring in him, guilt on account of disloyalty to the " Lord " — interpreting the word on whatever plane one choose. Remember that he thought of himself as dead and belonging to the kingdom of the dead, wherein he grew; remember moreover that name which he had ingeniously and somewhat presumptuously chosen. After all, the presumption was not so great: Mizraim's children each one of them, even the least, had long had the right to become Usir when he died, and unite his name with that of the mangled one, as Hapi the bull became Serapis in death. The association meant: "To be dead in God," or "To be as God." But just this, to "be God" and to be "dead," brought up the subject of the bandage-rending erection; and Joseph's half-unconscious guilty fear was connected with the intuition that certain moments — for which Dudu was responsible — now beginning to play a rôle, half of fear, half of joy, in his life, were, however remotely, yet perilously connected with that godlike rigidity of death and with disloyalty.

There, it is out. With all possible restraint it has been revealed why Joseph did not care to look on at the popular customs of the feast of Osiris or the processions of women or the cudgelled asses. But he took a good look at much else, in city and country, during the feasts that punctuated and adorned the Egyptian year. Once or twice as the years went on he saw Pharaoh, for it came about that the god made his appearance: not alone at the window of audience when he threw down the gold of favour upon favourites, in the presence of his elect, but when he came forth in brilliance from the horizon of his palace and beamed in full splendour upon all the people, who as one man hopped for joy upon one leg, according to prescribed form and also because they loved it from their hearts. Pharaoh was short and stout, Joseph noted, his colour was not very good, at least not when Rachel's son saw him for the second or third time; his facial expression, too, reminded him of Mont-kaw when his kidneys troubled him.

Amen-hotpe III, Neb-Mat-Re, did in fact begin to fail in the years which Joseph spent in Potiphar's house and grew great therein. In the judgment of the skilled priests from the temple and the sorcerers from the book-house he displayed in his physical condition a growing inclination to rejoin the sun. To control this tendency was beyond the power of the priests of healing, for it had all too much natural justification. In Joseph's second year the divine son of Thutmose IV and the Mitannic Mutemweia celebrated his jubilee, the so-called Hebsed: that is, it was thirty years since amid innumerable ceremonies, exactly repeated on each anniversary, he had set the double crown upon his head.

It had been a regal and splendid life, as good as free from wars, weighed down, as with a golden mantle, by hieratic pomp and the cares of government; but set off by the pleasures of the chase, in commemoration of which he had issued scarabs; and made splendid above all by his love of building, which he had been able to gratify in full measure. Now all that lay behind him; his nature was as active in decline as Joseph's in upbuilding. In his early days the majesty of this god had only suffered from toothache, an affliction which he treated by the usual method of chewing balsamic sweetmeats, and often had to receive audience in the throne-room with a great lump in his cheek. But since the Hebsed (when Joseph saw him drive out) his bodily ailments were of a more deep-seated kind. Pharaoh's heart fluttered, or beat too quick against his chest so that it took away his breath. His secretions carried matter which the body should have retained but could not because it was breaking down; later it was not only the cheek that was thick and swollen, but the legs and belly. It was at this time that the confrère and correspondent of the god, who was likewise a god in his own sphere, King Tushratta of Mitanniland, son of Shutarna, the father of Mutemweia, whom Amenhotpe called his mother — in short, his brother-in-law from the Euphrates (for he had received from Shutarna the Princess Gulichipa into his house of women) — his brother-in-law sent him a magic image of Ishtar, with safe-conduct from his far-away capital to the palace at Thebes. For he had heard of Pharaoh's affliction and in his own case found the image efficacious for slighter ailments. The whole city, yes, all Upper and Lower Egypt from the borders of Nubia down to the sea, spoke of the arrival of this image in the palace Merimat, and in the house of Potiphar almost nothing else was talked of for days. But we know that Ishtar of the Road was unavailing, or unwilling to relieve more than temporarily Pharaoh's short breath and swollen limbs — to the satisfaction of his domestic sorcerers, whose gifts of healing were not much help either, simply because the tendency to rejoin the sun was stronger than all else and slowly got its way.

Joseph saw Pharaoh at Hebsed, when all Wese was abroad to see the god drive out, in the course of the ceremonies which lasted the whole day. There were investitures, accessions, coronations, purificatory baths assisted by priests in masks representing various gods; incensing and primitively symbolical procedures, at first within the palace, in the presence of the great of the land, while outside the populace by dint of drink and dance made themselves believe that from this day forth time should renew itself from the foundations and an age of peace, justice, and prosperity, of laughter and universal brother-hood, take its beginnings. This glad conviction had been ardently bound up with the original accession, a genera-tion before, and renewed more faintly and fleetingly on each recurrence. But at Hebsed it sprang up in freshness and festal power in all their hearts, the triumph of faith over knowledge, the cult of an expectation which no ex-perience can banish from the heart of man because it was implanted there from on high. — But Pharaoh's progress when at midday he betook himself to the house of Amun to make sacrifice, was a public spectacle, and many people, including Joseph, awaited it in the West, before the gate of Pharaoh's palace, while other crowds lined the route which the royal train was to take through the city, especially in the great ram-sphinx avenue, the sacred way of Amun.

The royal palace, Pharaoh's great house — from which in fact Pharaoh took his name, for the word means " great house," though on the lips of the children of Egypt it sounded rather differently, just as in the case of Potiphar and Petepre — Pharaoh's great house, then, lay at the edge of the desert at the foot of the gleaming colourful cliffs of Thebes. It stood inside a great ring wall with ar-moured gates, which also included the exquisite gardens of the god and, laughing amid flowers and exotic trees, the lake which by command of Amenhotpe glittered east of the garden for the delectation of Tiy, his consort.

The populace outside, though they strained their necks, could see little of the bright splendours of Merimat. They saw the palace guards before the gates, with wedge-shaped leather leaves over their apron kilts, and feathers in their storm-helmets; they saw foliage lit by the sun and waving in the wind; saw airy roofs hovering upon coloured columns, long, many-coloured streamers fluttering from gilded poles; they sniffed the Syrian odours from the beds of the invisible gardens, and these accorded well with the idea of Pharaoh's godship, since sweet odours are thought of as accompanying the divine. But now the expectation of the eager, good-natured, lip-smacking, dust-swallowing crowd before the gate was to be fulfilled. Just as Re's bark reached the zenith a cry burst out, the guards at the gate raised their spears, the bronze doors between the standards flew open upon the sphinx avenue strewn with blue gravel, which ran through the garden. And upon that avenue Pharaoh's train appeared, dashing out through the gate directly into the throng, which swept back and gave way with shouts that were part joy, part fear. Men bearing staves laid into the crowd to make a path for the chariots and horses, with loud cries of " Pharaoh! Pharaoh! Take heed to your heart! Turn away your heads! He drives out — room, room for his driving out! " And the reeling rout made way, it hopped on one leg, it rolled like a wave in a storm, stretched up its thin arms into Egypt's sunlight, madly kissed hands. The women waved their wailing infants on high, or with heads flung back offered their breasts in both hands, while the air throbbed with exultation and yearning as they filled it with cries of " Pharaoh! Pharaoh! Strong Bull of your mother! Lofty in feathers! Live a million years! Live to eternity! Love us! Bless us! We love and bless you with fierce ardour! Golden falcon! Horus! Horus! Re you are in your members! Kheper in his true shape! Hebsed!

Hebsed! Turn of the ages! End of trouble! Beginning of joy!"

A popular jubilation like that is moving, it clutches at the heart, even of him who does not quite belong and is inwardly detached. Joseph shouted a little with the rest, he hopped a little too, with the children of the land; but chiefly he looked on, with silent emotion. What moved him was the sight of Pharaoh: he saw the Highest, coming forth out of his palace like the moon among stars, and his heart beat responsive to that old legacy, now a little weakened by his cosmopolitan understanding, which bade him serve the Highest, whom alone man shall serve. Long before he had stood even before the next-highest, Potiphar, he had, we know, already bent his thoughts upon still more absolute and final embodiments of that idea. We shall see that even now his eager spirit did not pause.

Pharaoh was wonderful to behold. His chariot was pure gold, naught else — gold wheels, gold sides, gold axles; and covered with embossed pictures, which, however, one could not see because the whole car flashed and glittered so, as it reflected the midday sun, that the eye could scarcely bear it. The wheels and the hoofs of the steeds whirled up thick enveloping clouds of dust so that it was as if Pharaoh came on in flame and smoke, frightful and glorious to behold. You expected nothing less than that the stallions too, Pharaoh's great First Team, as it was called, would breathe fire from their nostrils; so they danced, so their smooth muscles shone, so wild they were, in their ornamented harness, with gold breast-plates, and gold lions' heads on their crests from which coloured ostrich plumes stood up and nodded. Pharaoh drove himself; he stood alone in the chariot of cloud and fire, the reins in his left hand; with his right he held the lash and crook, the black and white one, in a sort of ritual position, slantingly upon his breast just underneath his jewelled collar. Pharaoh was already rather an old man, one could tell by his sunken mouth, the tired look in his eyes, and his back, which seemed a little stooped beneath the lotus-white linen of his upper garment. The cheek-bones stood out in his gaunt face and it looked as though they were rouged. All sorts and kinds of charms in the shape of stiff emblems and variously knotted and looped ribbons hung down from his hips under his garment. His head was covered to behind his ears and down to his neck by the blue crown set with yellow stars. But on the brow, above Pharaoh's nose, the poison-cobra reared, glittering with coloured enamel, Re's talisman.

Thus, without looking to left or right, the king of Upper and Lower Egypt drove past before Joseph's eyes. Tall ostrich-feather fans swayed over him; the soldiers of his bodyguard, archers and shield-bearers, Egyptian, Asiatic, and Negro, hurried under standards beside the wheels and officers followed in cars covered with purple leather. Then all the people gave another adoring cry, for after the officers came another single chariot, with gold wheels whirling up the dust, and in it a boy eight or nine years old, likewise under ostrich-feather fans, driving, too, with weak bebraceleted arms outstretched. His face was long and palish, the full, raspberry-coloured lips smiled with charming shyness at the yelling populace, the eyes were half-open, from pride or sadness. That was Amenhotpe, the godlike offspring, heir to the throne and crown, when he who drove in front of him should have decided to mingle with the sun: Pharaoh's only son, child of his old age, his Joseph. The recipient of all these plaudits had a thin, childish torso, nude save for the arm-rings and jewelled necklace. His apron kilt of pleated gold stuff came high up in the back and down to his calves; in front, where the gold-fringed draw-string hung, it was scooped out, exposing a drum-shaped paunch like a Negro child's. On the boy's brow the serpent reared, as on the father's; his close-fitting head-dress of gold stuff enveloped his head and came together at the back like a knot of hair, while the youth-lock of the kings' sons hung in the form of a broad fringe over one ear.

The populace shouted at the top of their lungs to this engendered but not yet risen sun, the sun below the eastern horizon, the sun of tomorrow. " Peace of Amun! " they shouted. " Long live the son of the god! How beautiful you are in the bright places of the sky! Youthful Horus in the childhood lock! Rich-enchanted falcon! Protector of the father, protect us! " — They still shouted and adored when after the rabble in the wake of the morrow's sun followed another fiery chariot with high sides; behind the driver, as he leaned over the rail, stood Tiy, consort of the god, Pharaoh's chief wife, the lady of the lands. She was small and dark of countenance, with gleaming eyes lengthened by paint, a firm and delicate nose with a pronounced curve; a smile sat on her full curling lips. Anything as beautiful as her head-dress there could not be on earth; it was the vulture cap, the whole bird, made of gold, covering her head with its body and outstretched head, while the pinions hung down in splendour over cheeks and shoulders. On the bird's back a ring was fastened, from which rose a pair of high, stiff plumes, converting the cap to a divinity's crown; while in front on the brow, besides the featherless head and crooked beak of the bird of prey, was likewise the uræus, fanged and erect. Here were the very signs and insignia of godhood — it was too much, the people could not but greet them in ecstasy, and quite beside themselves shriek out: " Eset! Eset! Mut, heavenly mother-cow! Mother of God! You who fill the palace with love, sweet Hathor, pity us! " They cried out to the princesses too, who stood embraced in their own chariot behind the driver bent to his steeds; to the ladies of the court, driving by twos, with the fan of honour in their hands; and to the friends of Pharaoh, the unique and only friends, who attended his levee. Thus the Hebsed procession moved among the crowds from the house Merimat to the river where the gaily coloured boats lay ready, and Pharaoh's bark " Star of the Two Lands "; and the god, the goddess, and their offspring, with all the court, were set across to the eastern shore and driven by other teams through the city of the living, attended by the plaudits of the throng in all the narrow streets and from all the house-tops. And they drove to the house of Amun and the great incensing.

Thus then Joseph had seen Pharaoh, as once in the court of his house he, the bought slave, had seen Potiphar, first of his sphere, and thought how he could come to stand before him. At his side he now stood, thanks to his shrewdness in discourse; but we know that even then his thoughts outran the moment, secretly anticipating a connection with distant and final manifestations of the highest; his audacity even envisaged a still further goal. But how could that be — was there than the highest a higher

still? Certainly, when one has in one's blood a feeling
for the future — that is to say, for the highest of the morrow. During the exultations of the throng, which Joseph,
with a certain reserve, had shared, he had observed
Pharaoh in his fiery chariot with sufficient care. But his
inmost and uttermost curiosity had for its object not the
old god but his successor, the lad with the lock and the
sickly smiling mouth, Pharaoh's Joseph, the next sun.
He gazed after the narrow shoulders and gold knot of
hair, the thin, armleted arms, as the lad drove by. Him,
not Pharaoh, he had in his mind when the procession had
passed and the crowds followed to the river. With the
little coming one his thoughts were concerned; and it
might well be that his opinion was that of the children of
Egypt; for they had cried out more fervently at sight of
him than when Pharaoh himself passed by. For the future is hope; and in the goodness of God time is given to
man, that he may live in hope. Joseph had need still to
grow mightily in his station before the hope of standing
before the highest, or at his side, could have the smallest
prospect of fulfilment. So then with reason it was that, as
he watched the feast of Hebsed, his gaze passed over the
present highest into the future and rested on the not yet
risen sun.

ACCOUNT OF MONT-KAW'S SIMPLE PASSING

SEVEN times had the Egyptian year carried Joseph with
it in its round; four-and-eighty times the planet that he
loved, to which he was kin, had gone through all its
phases. Of the material substance of Jacob's son, that in
which he was clothed when the father blessed him and

sent him from him, nothing at all was left. He wore, so to speak, a new earthly garment, in which God had arrayed his life; of the old, of that worn by the seventeen-year-old youth, was not one thread remaining. For he walked in one woven of Egyptian stuff, in which Jacob would only doubtingly have known him. The son would have had to reassure him, saying: It is I, Joseph. Seven years had passed, in sleeping and waking; in thinking, and feeling, in doing and being done by; passed as days pass; that is, neither fast nor slowly, but simply passing; and in his age he was now four-and-twenty, a young man, very beautiful in form and feature, son of a lovely one, a child of love. His bearing, by reason of his activities, had become more serious and assured; his voice, the one-time childish pipe, had grown more resonant as he moved among the workmen giving directions or as Mont-kaw's mouth transmitted all his orders; for Mont-kaw's mouth he had been now all these years, or one might have called him his eye, his ear, or his right hand. The work-people, however, spoke of him simply as the steward's "mouth," for so in Egypt they called a man through whom orders are transmitted. In Joseph's case the word was doubly apt, for the youth spoke like a god, a gift most pleasing, yes, a laughing delight to Egypt's children, and they knew that it was by that gift of shrewd and comely speech, such as was beyond their own powers, that he had made his way, or at least opened his way, to the favour of the master and Mont-kaw.

Mont-kaw by now trusted him in everything — administration, accounts, oversight, and business. When the tradition states that Potiphar put all that he had into his hand and knew not aught he had save the bread that he did eat, it refers, in the last analysis, to a delegation of power, from the master to the steward, and from the steward to the purchased slave with whom he had made a pact in love and loyalty to their lord. And the master and his house might be glad that it was Joseph and no other on whom the delegation finally fell and who in the end took over the economy of the house, for he oversaw it with the utmost of loyalty and ability, for the sake of the Lord and His far-flung plan; thinking day and night on the advantage of the house; so that, in the words of the old Ishmaelite and consonant with the name he had chosen, he not only provided but also increased it.

As for the reason why Mont-kaw, toward the end of this period of seven years, had entrusted Joseph more and more with the oversight of affairs, until he finally gave them all into his hands and withdrew into the private room of trust — of that anon, and only a little farther on. For first I must say that Dudu, despite all his malicious striving, did not succeed in barring the way to Joseph's happy advance — which finally, and before the seven years were out, had set him over all the other servants, even above the rank and dignity of Potiphar's undersized keeper of the jewel-caskets. Dudu's office was indeed a dignified one, and he owed it, certainly, to his sterling quality, his honesty and dwarf-worthiness. It brought him into close contact with the master and would have afforded occasion for confidence and the exercise of influence against Joseph, but that Potiphar could not abide the little man, whose pompous dignity went against him. He did not feel justified in taking away his office, but he kept him as removed as possible, setting subordinates between them for the service of the robing-rooms, so that

to Dudu fell only the care of the garments, jewels, am-
ulets, and orders. He saw the dwarf only for brief con-
ferences. Thus Dudu could not easily come to speech
with Potiphar, certainly not to that speech which he would
gladly have made with reference to the favourite and the
offence of his growing favour in the house.

Even though he had had the chance he would not have
dared to speak — at least not before the master himself.
For he well knew Potiphar's dislike for him, the serious-
minded dwarf; it rested on the concealed sense of superiority which he neither could nor would deny, as well as
on his partisanship for Amun's sun-power; he knew that
his word availed little before Potiphar. Why should he,
Dudu, spouse of Djeset, expose himself to a rebuff? No,
he preferred a roundabout way: he would act through
the mistress — to her he often complained, and at least
she listened with respect — and through Beknechons, the
mighty man of Amun; he, when he visited the mistress,
could be warned against the advancement of the Shabirite, so offensive to ancient traditions. And he instigated
Djeset, his full-sized wife, who was in Mut-em-enet's service, to talk to her mistress in the same sense.

But even industry will not always bring success; if
Djeset had not been fruitful to her spouse it would have
been a case in point. Here, at least, his striving bore no
fruit. It is true, that one day Beknechons, in Pharaoh's
antechamber, took Petepre to task, diplomatically, for
the annoyance suffered by the pious of his household
through the advancement of the impious there, and ex-
postulated with him in fatherly wise. But the fan-bearer
did not take it in, he could not remember, he blinked and
seemed absent; and Beknechons, owing to his flair for

greatness, was incapable of pausing for more than a minute upon small domestic details. He soon passed over into more exalted spheres and harangued the four quarters of the heavens as he held forth upon problems of state, speaking of the foreign kings Tushratta, Shubbilulima, and Abd-Ashirta — and upon these high themes the conversation expended itself and died. As for Mut, the mistress, she had not brought herself as yet to speak to her husband on the subject. She knew his unhearing obstinacy; moreover, she was not used to talking over matters with him, their intercourse consisting altogether of tender and exaggerated expressions of concern; it did not occur to her to make any demands upon him. These were sufficient grounds of excuse for her inaction. But in our eyes it is also a sign that even at that time — that is to say, toward the end of the seven years — she was indifferent to Joseph's presence and had no motive for wishing to have him sent away. The time when she would want him removed from her sight and hearing was still to come for this woman of Egypt; it came at the same time with that fear of herself which yet she was too proud to know. And another strange something would come to pass at the same time — the time when she realized that it would be better for her to see Joseph no more and turned to Petepre to get him sent away: it was that Dudu had been converted to the Shabirite and become his partisan. For he began to flatter him and be obsequious to him, to such an extent that a change of rôles seemed to have taken place between the dwarf and his mistress; the latter appeared to have assumed the former's hatred and the dwarf to praise and belaud the youth in her hearing. Both attitudes were entirely specious. For at the moment when the mistress would have wished that Joseph was not there, she could no longer do so, and deluded herself in thinking that she did. But Dudu, who had quite a glimmering of it, acted in malice, hoping the more to injure the son of Jacob by being comradely with him.

But I shall speak of this a little later. For the event which brought about these changes — or upon which they followed — was the sore illness of the steward Mont-kaw, Joseph's ally in the service of the master — sore for him, sore for Joseph, who so clung to him that he almost made a matter of conscience of his sufferings and death; and distressing to all sympathizers of the simple but intuitive man — even though these might have insight into the necessity of his destined passing. For we are obliged to see the hand of destiny in the circumstance that Joseph had been brought into a house whose steward was devoted to death; and so in a sense his passing was sacrificial. Fortunate that he was a man whose soul inclined to resignation, a readiness which in another place I have attributed to his trouble with his kidneys. But it is quite possible that the latter was only the physical constitution corresponding to his spiritual state, actually the same, distinguished from it only as the word is distinguished from the thought, and the word-sign from the word — so that in the book of the steward's life a kidney would have been the hieroglyph for the word " resignation."

Why should we concern ourselves with Mont-kaw? Why do I speak of him with a certain emotion, though unable to say much more of him than that he was known to be a man simple — that is, modest — and upright — that is, both practical and good-hearted? A man who trod the earth of Egypt and the land of Kemt, late or early according as one takes it, at the time when life among its manifold shapes brought just him and no other forth, but early enough in all its lateness that his mummy has long since been dust and scattered to the four winds. A practical son of earth who did not imagine himself to be better than life and had no use for higher or speculative matters; not out of inferiority, but out of modesty, although in his secret depths he was quite accessible to higher promptings — indeed, it was these which made him play a rôle, a not inconsiderable one, in Joseph's life. Figuratively speaking, he did very much what Reuben had one day done: he retreated three steps before Joseph, bowed his head, and turned away. It needs no more than this rôle given him by destiny to make us owe him a lively sympathy. Aside from which, and for his own sake, I like to dwell upon the figure of this man, simple yet sensitive as he was, and pervaded by an unassuming melancholy; it has a sympathetic, spiritual claim upon us — he would have called it magic — which makes me like to conjure it up out of its ancient dust.

Mont-kaw was the son of an under official of the treasury of the Montu temple at Karnak. When he was five years old his father, whose name was Akhmose, had dedicated him to Thoth and put him into the school attached to the administration of the temple of Montu, the falcon-headed god of war, where the rising generation of officials was brought up, on short commons, strict discipline, and plenty of canings, for the view obtained that a pupil had his ears on his back and heard when he was beaten. The pupils were of varied origins, aristocratic and middle-class; besides the discipline, they received the fundamentals of a literary education: the word

of god, otherwise writing, the art of the reed, the gift of a
good style, and the necessary equipment for a career of
learning as well as for that of official scribe.

Akmose's son did not want to become a scholar; not
because he was not clever enough, but because he was too
modest; resolved from the beginning to dwell within the
sphere of the respectable average and not at any price
to depart beyond it. It happened almost against his will
that he did not, like his father, spend his days as a writer
of documents in the office of Montu's temple, but became
overseer to one of the great. It was his superiors and
masters who recommended him thither and got him the
excellent post, out of the regard they had for his gifts
and his modest demeanour. At school he received only
the inevitable canings, which fell to the lot of even the
best pupils, in order to make them hear. For he early
gave evidence of his head for the general by the quickness
with which he mastered the great gift of the ape, the art
of writing; the care and neatness with which he wrote out
in long lines in his roll the copy before him, consisting of
ancient rules of propriety, style-forming models, didactic
poems, admonitions, and praise for the writer's craft,
and covered the reverse side with calculations about
sacks of corn, and notes for business letters. Almost
from the beginning he had been set to work on the practical business of administration, more on his own initiative
than that of his father, who would gladly have made of his
son something better than he was himself, a priest perhaps, a magician or star-gazer; whereas from boyhood
Mont-kaw in his modesty had decided for the practical
side.

There is something peculiar about this sort of inborn

resignation which takes the form of honest capacity and quiet toleration of the hardships of life, where another nature would shatter the heavens with loud remonstrance. Mont-kaw married rather early the daughter of one of his father's colleagues with whom he fell in love. But his wife died in her first childbirth and the infant with her. Mont-kaw lamented her loss most bitterly, without being greatly astonished or rebellious at this blow from the hand of fate. He did not try for happiness a second time, remaining a widower, and solitary. He had a sister married to a bazaar-keeper at Thebes; he visited her sometimes, when he had a holiday, of which he never took many. After finishing his education he worked at first in the offices of the temple adminstration, later became steward to the chief priest and after that to the great household of Petepre the courtier, where he had for ten years wielded his office with firm but good-natured authority, at the time when the Ishmaelites relieved the overburdened man in his service to his beloved master by bringing him an assistant — and at the same time a successor.

He had early perceived that Joseph was destined to follow after him — for he was, in all his assiduous simplicity, a man of intuition. We may almost say that the simplicity itself, the selfless resignation, was a product of the same intuition: in other words, of the illness lying dormant in his powerful frame. The very working of it, silently breaking down his physical morale, but refining the spiritual, was what made possible the subtle impressions which he received at first sight of Joseph. At that time he already knew the nature of his ailment. Red-belly, the barber-surgeon, had told him plainly, diagnosing from the symptoms of frequent dull pressure in his back and left side, irregular pains in the region of the heart, frequent giddiness, sleeplessness, poor metabolism, and excessive urination, that he suffered from degeneration of the kidneys.

This ailment is often insidious in its nature; strikes its roots during early life and then has periods when it seems to be arrested or even cured, only to evince its hidden progress later on. Mont-kaw could remember that when he was twelve years old he passed blood-impregnated urine — but only once, and then not again for many years, so that he had really forgotten the alarming symptom. It happened again when he was twenty, together with the above-mentioned manifestations, the headache and giddiness culminating in violent nausea. That too passed; but since then he had quietly and grimly wrestled with intermittent attacks, which would leave him free for months or even years, to take possession of him again with greater or less violence. The modesty which was their source came out often in profound fatigue, physical and mental weariness and indifference; he made a practice of sticking to his tasks throughout, heroically and in silence, being treated by medical science, or what passed as such, with blood-letting. His appetite was satisfactory, his tongue clean, the skin excretions in good order, and his pulse fairly regular; the physicians therefore did not consider his condition serious until one day his ankle-bones displayed whitish swellings full of a watery fluid. When it was drawn off, the relief to his vascular system and his heart made one regard the symptom as favourable, because it was the disease coming out and being got rid of.

He had indeed, with the help of Red-belly and his herbal treatments, got through quite tolerably the decade before Joseph's arrival, with but few interruptions to his activities; though that was very likely to be ascribed more to his own modest strength of purpose, holding in check the slow process of decay, than it was to Red-belly's homely remedies. He had his first really severe attack very soon after Joseph came; with such dropsy in hands and legs that they had to be bandaged; throbbing head-ache, badly upset stomach, and even a dimming of the vision. Probably it had begun during the bargaining with the Ishmaelite and the examination of his goods. At least we may surmise it; for it seems as though his sensi-tiveness to Joseph's looks and the emotion he showed at the test good-night greeting indicated a morbidly height-ened receptivity. But the converse might also be true: that the all too gentle words had affected his spirit to soften it and make it a more ready prey to the evil power assailing it. I am tempted to harbour the misgiving that Joseph's good-night addresses, however soothing to the steward, were actually unfavourable to the will to live which struggled in his depths with the fell disease.

The attack was responsible too for the fact that Mont-kaw paid no attention to Joseph in the beginning. It lamed his initiative. But it passed, like others of greater or less severity, thanks to Khun-Anpu's blood-lettings, leeches, arbitrary decoctions of animal or vegetable na-ture, and abdominal compresses made of old pieces of writing soaked in warm oil. Recovery — or apparent recovery — ensued, and reigned over large spaces of the time during which Joseph was growing up to be his first assistant and chief " mouth." But in the seventh year of

Joseph's time Mont-kaw caught a cold at the funeral of a relative, his sister's husband (the bazaar-keeper in fact), and it opened the door wide to dissolution, which then ensued.

This "catching" death and being "carried off," through standing in a draughty hall to pay last honours to the deceased, was a frequent phenomenon then as now. It was summer, and very hot, but, as often in Egypt, at the same time very windy, a dangerous combination, for the air fanning over the perspiring flesh cooled it too rapidly. The steward, overwhelmed with business, had lingered at home until he was in danger of being late for the services; he sweated as he went, and when he was ferried across the river in the train of the funeral bark he shivered in his thin clothes. Then he stood by the little grave in the rock which the bazaar-keeper, now united with Osiris, had acquired with his savings. Before its modest portal a priest in the mask of Anpu held the mummy upright while another performed with the calf's foot the mystic ceremony of the opening of the mouth; and the little group of mourners looked on, their hands upon their ash-strewn heads. The cold dank air that breathed from the vault was not very good for Mont-kaw. He came home with a cold in his head and catarrh of the bladder. Next day he complained to Joseph of feeling queer and heavy, and of the effort it was to move his limbs; he was overtaken by a sort of numbness which forced him to give over work and take to his bed. The head gardener attended him and set leeches to his temples, to relieve the intolerable pains in his head, which were accompanied by severe nausea and semi-blindness; but an attack of apoplexy supervened.

Joseph, when he saw the purposes of God with Mont-kaw, was greatly shocked. He came to the conclusion that it would not be a crossing of the divine purpose but merely putting God to the test to try all human means of combating the disease. He persuaded Potiphar to send at once to Amun's house for a learned physician; and Red-belly, offended, yet at the same time relieved from a responsibility the weight of which he knew enough to realize, retired from the field.

The medical man from the temple did indeed reject most of Red-belly's measures; but the distinction between his and the gardener's was, in the eyes of all the world, his own as well, more of a social than a medicinal kind: the latter were for the people and for them might do very well; the former for the upper classes, where the treatment was of a more refined kind. The doctor from the temple rejected the ancient documents soaked in oil with which his predecessor had covered the belly and loins of the patient, demanding in their place linseed poultices on good handkerchiefs. Likewise he stuck up his nose at most of Red-belly's popular cure-alls, which had been invented by the gods themselves for Re when he was old and ailing. They consisted of from fourteen to seven-and-thirty separate disgustingnesses: lizard's blood, ground pigs' teeth, sweat from a pig's ears, the milk of a woman in childbed, various sorts of excrement such as antelopes', porcupines', and flies', human urine, and more of the same kind. But there were other ingredients more to the physician's liking, which he also prescribed, without the disgustingnesses: honey and wax, henbane, small doses of opium, bitter bark, bear-berries, natron, and ipecacuanha. The doctor also concurred in the use of

the gardener's cherished remedy, the chewing of castor-
oil berries with beer; and in his use of a root rich in resin
with a strong purgative effect. But he declared that the
drastic blood-lettings, which Red-belly performed nearly
every day to control the agonizing pain in the head and the
mist in the eyes, must be discontinued or only performed
with great reserve; he could tell by the patient's pallor
that the temporary relief was too highly paid for by the
loss of certain nourishing and stimulating properties in
the blood.

The dilemma was probably an impossible one; for
obviously it was precisely the indispensable but impoverished and infected blood that carried insidious inflamma-
tions and overwhelmed the body with various morbid
manifestations, either by turn or at the same time; all of
them, as both physicians were aware, having their source
in the originally diseased kidney. Thus Mont-kaw, without regard to the name or nature of this or that distressing
phenomenon, suffered one after another or at the same
time from inflammation of the chest, the peritoneum, the
lungs, and the pericardium; from brain symptoms such
as vomiting, blindness, congestion, and spasms. In short,
death attacked him with all its weapons and on every side,
and it was only a wonder that he resisted for weeks after
he took to his bed, and in part overcame the supernumer-
ary ailments from which he suffered. He was a stout in-
valid; but however sturdily he defended his life — he had
just to die.

Joseph realized this, while Khun-Anpu and the learned
man of Amun still hoped to save the steward. He took it
much to heart; not only on account of his attachment to
the good man, who had shown him so much kindness and

in whose mingled destiny he sympathized, finding him one of those " glad-sorry " men, the Gilgamesh type, favoured and disfavoured at the same time. No, it was also and particularly because he had pangs of conscience over his sufferings and death. They were obviously ordained to his own advantage and growth, poor Mont-kaw was a sacrifice to God's plans; he was put out of the way, that was plain and clear, and Joseph would have liked to speak to the author of the plans and say: "What Thou here dost, O Lord, is exclusively thine own idea and none of mine. I must say plainly that I will have naught to do with it, and that it happeneth on my account must not, I hope, mean that I am to blame for it — in all humility I must beg to be excused." But it did not help him, he still felt guilty for the death of his friend and perceived that if there could be any talk of responsibility in the affair it fell upon him, whom it advantaged, God being blameless. " That is just it," he thought to himself: " God does all, yet has given us a conscience, and we become guilty before Him because we are guilty for Him. Man bears God's guilt; and it would be no more than right if one day God were to make up His mind to bear our guilt. How He, the holy and blameless, could do that is hard to say. I should think He would need to become a man to that end."

He did not stir from the bedside of the suffering sacrifice throughout the four or five weeks of struggle against the death that came on in protean shape. So guilty did he feel. He tended the afflicted man day and night; he sacrificed himself, as one says, and here would say it with justice, for he offered himself in return, to the extent of offering up his own sleep and physical well-being. He set up his cot beside the sick man's in the special room of trust, and hour by hour did the needed service: warmed the compresses, gave the medicines, rubbed in the lotions, gave him to inhale the vapour of powdered herbs heated on stones, as prescribed by the doctors, and held his limbs when attacked by spasms. For as his end approached, the steward so suffered from these that he cried out under death's torturing grip — for death seemed not to expect that he would yield himself and so laid violent hands upon him. Especially when Mont-kaw tried to sleep death interfered, sending such potent cramps as almost to wrench the sufferer bodily from the bed — as though to say: " What, thou wouldst sleep? Up with thee, to thy end! " This was more than ever the place for Joseph's soothing good-nights; he employed them skilfully, murmuring in the steward's ear that now he would surely find the path into the land of peace for which he yearned, find and tread upon it; nor would his left arm and leg, carefully bound up for him by Joseph with strips of linen, snatch him back again to day and anguish.

That was true, and sometimes efficacious. But Joseph himself was alarmed to see that his invocations to peace and repose helped only too much — for the steward, wakeful for so many years, inclined now to stupor, so that the gracious path became a dangerous one, embarked on which the wanderer might forget to return. He must sing no more lullabies, but try to rouse the patient to the things of earth, and his will to live with tales and anecdotes out of that copious store, extensive in time and space, which Joseph, thanks to Jacob and Eliezer, had commanded ever since he was small. The steward had always loved these tales of his assistant's first life, his

childhood in the land of Canaan, of his lovely mother
who had died by the way, of his father's wilful tenderness
for her and for his son, so that they were one in the festal
garment of his love. He knew of the brethren's furious
jealousy, of the sin of overweening blind self-confidence
which had weighed down Joseph; of the mangling and the
pit. The steward, of course, like Potiphar and all his
house, always thought of that region where Joseph had
spent his youth as a land far off, dusty and indescribably
wretched; which one forsook, naturally, when destiny
transplanted one into the land of men and gods. He was
as little surprised or critical as anybody else that the
Egyptian Joseph made no effort to resume contact with the
barbaric world of his youth. But he enjoyed hearing of
that world, and during his last days it was his dearest and
most soothing distraction to lie with folded hands and
listen to his young nurse unfold the memories of his clan,
in the charming way he had, so thrilling, so blithe and
impressive all at once. He told of the rough and the
smooth and how even in the womb they had fought each
other; of the feast of the blessing and the betrayal, and
the flight of the smooth man to the nether world; of the
wicked uncle who exchanged his children on the bridal
night; how the cunning rogue tricked the stupid one,
taking a leaf from nature's book and so got back his own.
Shuffling here and there: the trickery of the first-born
and the blessing, exchange of brides, exchange of possessions. Exchange of the first-born and the beast, on the
offering-table; of the beast and the son, who looked like
the beast as he bleated and died. All these illusions and
transformations fascinated the hearer and held him rapt;
for what is more charming than illusion? And a light

played to and fro, back and forth, between the teller and his tale; illusory light, illusory charm, illusory magic of charm, fell upon him from the tales he told, and he himself in his turn lent to them the same from his own person — from him who had worn the veil of love in turn with his mother, from him who in the eyes of Mont-kaw had always possessed an agreeably teasing and mischievous charm, from the first moment when the boy had stood before him with the roll in his hand and by his smile tempted the steward to confuse him with the ibis-headed one.

Mont-kaw could scarcely see at all now, he could not tell how many fingers when Joseph held them up. But he could still listen and be lured by the sound of strange tales murmured sweetly at his bedside, away from that path of heavy slumber to which he was drawn by the poison in his blood. He heard about the ever present Eliezer who with his master had smitten the kings of the east and toward whom the earth had sprung when he rode on the bridal journey for the saved sacrifice; of the bride by the well who had dismounted from her camel and veiled her face in the sight of the wooer; of the wild and beautiful son of the desert who had tried to persuade the cheated red one to kill his father and eat him. Of the original wanderer, the father of them all, and what had one time befallen him and his sister-bride, here in this very land of Egypt. Of his brother Lot, the angels before his door, and the extraordinary shamelessness of the Sodomites. Of the sulphurous rain, of the pillar of salt, and what Lot's daughters did out of care for the continuance of the human race. Of Nimrod at Sinear and his arrogant tower. Of Noah, the second first man, called the exceeding wise one, and his ark. Of the first man himself, made out of clay in the garden of the east, of the she-man made of his rib, and of the serpent. From this great heritage of tales Joseph gave with wit and eloquence of his best, sitting by the bedside of the dying man — to assuage his own remorse and to hold the other in the land of the living for yet a little while. But Mont-kaw too was seized with the epic vein and began to talk in his turn, having them prop him up in the cushions and in the unease of oncoming death feeling for Joseph to touch him as though he were Yitzchak in the tent.

" Let me see with seeing hands," he said, his face lifted to the ceiling, " if you are Osarsiph my son, for I will bless you before my end, mightily strengthened to the blessing by the tales with which you have so richly fed me. Yes, it is you, I see and recognize you as do the blind and there can be no doubt here, for I have but one son whom I can bless and you are he, Osarsiph, whom I have come to love in the course of the years in the place of the little one whom the mother took with her in her hour — for he was suffocated, she being built too narrow. By the way? No, for she died at home, in her chamber in childbed, and I dare not call her agonies more than human, yet frightful they were, and cruel so that I fell on my face and begged the gods for her death, which they granted her. The boy's death they granted too, though I had not begged for that. But what would the child have been to me without her? Olive Tree was she called, daughter of Kegboi, the treasury official. Beket was her name and I was not bold enough to love her as the man of the blessing made bold to love his lovely one of Naharin, your mother — I did not dare. But she was lovely too, unforgettably lovely in the adornment of her silken eyelashes which dropped over her eyes when I spoke to her, words from my heart, words of songs which I never presumed to attempt, yet which at that time, that beautiful time, my words became. Yes, we loved each other, despite the narrowness of her build, and when she died with the child, I wept, wept many nights for her, till time and work dried mine eyes — dried them quite and I wept no more at night; but the tear-sacs, and their smallness, they come, I think, from all those nights — I do not know, it may be, and may not, for I am dying and my eyes are going with which I wept for Beket, it will be all the same in the world whether it was or not. But my heart was empty and desolate, since my eyes were dried; and it grew small like my eyes, and despondent for that it had loved in vain so that there was room only for resignation in it. Yet the heart must cherish something besides resignation; it yearns to throb for some care tenderer than profit and use. Petepre's house-steward was I and his oldest servant and had no thought save for his house that it might flourish. For he who has given up is good for service. And lo, that then was a thing for my shrunken heart to cherish: service, and tender helpfulness to Petepre my master. For who is there more needing than he the service of love? He takes no affairs to himself, he is strange to all affairs and not made for business. Strange, delicate, and proud he is, the honorary official, and cannot face any business, so that one must pity him, for he is good. Has he not come to me and visited me in my illness? He has taken trouble to come hither to my bedside while you were at work, to ask after me, the sick man, in the goodness of his heart, though it is plain that he feels

strange and shy before illness too, for he is never ailing
— though a man would be puzzled to call him healthy
or believe that he will die — I can scarcely believe it,
for one must be healthy to be ill and live to die. But can
that lessen one's care for him, and the need of upholding
his sensitive dignity? It is rather the other way. My
heart cherished this care, above and beyond profit and
use: to devote itself to the service of upholding his dignity and addressing his pride, as well as I knew how. But
you, Osarsiph, know how, incomparably better than I,
for the gods have given subtlety to your mind, and greater
pleasingness than mine, who lack it either because I was
too dull and dry or because I did not dare to attempt the
highest nor had confidence to do so. Therefore I have
made a pact with you for this service, which you will keep
when I die and am no more. And when I bless you and
make over to you my office as steward of this house, then
must you vow to me upon my death-bed that you will not
only cherish the house and the business according to the
best of your wits, but also faithfully keep our loving bond
and do service of love to Petepre's soul and shield and
justify his dignity with all your skill — far indeed from
ever doing him offence or from being tempted to shame
him with word or deed. Can you solemnly promise me,
Osarsiph, my son? "

"Solemnly and gladly," Joseph answered to this dying speech. "Have no care, my father! For I promise
you to be helpful to his soul with careful loyalty according to our pact, and keep faith with his need; and will
think of you, if ever temptation should befall me to inflict
upon him the peculiar pain which disloyalty is to the
lonely. You may rely upon it."

"It calms me much," said Mont-kaw, "though the feeling of death disquiets me greatly, as it should not do; for nothing is commoner than death, and especially of a simple man like me, who always avoided higher things. For I die no higher death and will make over it no ado, as little as I made over my love to my little Olive Tree, nor emboldened myself to call her childbed pains more than human. But yet I will bless you, Osarsiph, in the room of my son, not without solemnity, for the blessing is solemn, not I — therefore bow yourself beneath my groping hand. House and court make I over to you, my true son and successor in the steward's office to Petepre the great courtier and my master, and resign in your favour, which gratifies my soul; yes, this joy death brings me, that I can resign, and joyfully am I agitated by death, for it is joy and naught else that I feel. But that I leave all to you is by the will of the master, who among all his servants points with his finger to you and chooses you in my place as his steward when I am dead. For when he came to see me of late in the goodness of his heart and looked helplessly at me, I talked it over with him and begged him that he would direct his finger upon you alone and name you by your name when I am made god; that I might go hence with quiet mind as regards the household and all the business. ' Yes,' said he, ' it is well, Mont-kaw, very well, old man. I will point to him with my finger, if you really do die, which would grieve me sorely. Yes, I will point to him and no other, that is certain, and let anybody try to persuade me, he will find my will like iron or black granite from the quarries of the Retenu. He himself has said that of such quality is my will and I had to agree with him. He moves me with a feeling of confidence, very

pleasant indeed, even more than you yourself have done
in your lifetime; often have I thought that a god is with
him or even several gods, who make all to succeed which
is in his hands. And he will be less likely to go behind
my back than even you in all your uprightness, for
he has knowledge of sin in his heart and wears in his hair
something like a garland of sacrifice, which is a charm
against sin. In short, it is settled, Osarsiph shall be set
over the house and take all things upon himself with
which it is impossible I should concern myself. I will
point to him with my finger.' Those were the master's
words, I have remembered them exactly. So then I bless
you, only after he hath blessed you himself, for so it ever
is: one blesses always the blest and wishes the joyful
joy. The blind man in the tent blessed the smooth one
only because he was already blest and the rough one was
not. One can do no more. Be then blessed, as blest you
are! Your spirits are blithe, and you measure yourself
boldly against higher things; you are blithe to say your
mother's pains were more than human and your birth
was virgin — though your reasons for that are probably
not sound. But those are the signs of the blessing, which
I possessed not and so cannot bestow; but I can bless you
and wish you joy as I depart. Bend then your head lower
beneath my hand, my son, the head of the aspiring beneath the hand of the meek. To you I make over household, house, and fields in Petepre's name, for whom
I administered it; their riches give I to you, the fat of
these lands, that you may preside over shops and stores,
the fruits of the gardens, the herds great and small, the
island farm, the accounting and trade; I set you over
sowing and harvest. kitchen and cellar, the master's table,

the needs of the house of women, the oil-mills, the wine-presses, and all the servants. May I have forgotten nothing! But you, Osarsiph, do not forget me, when I am made a god and like Osiris. Be my Horus, who protects the father and justifies him. Let not my tomb inscription be blurred, and support my life! Tell me, will you see after it that Min-neb-maat, the master of the bandaging, and his assistants make of me a good mummy, not black, but a beautiful yellow, for I have put aside all things needful thereto; that they consume it not themselves, but salt me well with natron and use fine balsam to make me eternal, styrax, juniper wood, cedar gum from the port, mastic from the sweet pistachio shrub, and fine bandages next the body? Will you take care, my son, that my eternal shell is well painted, and covered within with writings, without crack or cranny? Promise me to take care that Imhotep, priest of the dead in the West, does not divide among his children the fund I have set aside with him for my sacrificial offerings of bread, beer, oil, and incense, but that it remain whole and your father be for ever provided with food and drink on feast-days. It is dear and good that you promise me all this with reverent voice; for death is a common thing, yet bound up with great cares, and a man must secure himself on many sides. Put too a little stove in my chamber that the servants may roast a joint of beef. And add an alabaster goose, and the wooden likeness of a wine-jug, and also plenty of your sycamore figs. I like to hear you reassure me as to all that, in your reverent words. Put too a little ship with rowers beside my coffin, for I might have need of it, and let other apron-boys be with me that they may take my place when He who is over the West calls me up to work upon his fruitful fields, for I had ever a head for the general, and knew how to oversee, but not to drive the plough nor ply the sickle. Ah, with how many cares is death surrounded! Have I forgotten aught? Promise that you will be mindful of what I forget — for instance, take care that they should lay the beautiful jasper scarab upon the place of my heart, the one which Petepre gave me in his goodness and on which is written that my heart shall not rise up as witness against me in the scale. It is in the right hand of the coffer in a little box of yew-wood, together with my two necklaces, which I bequeath to you. — Enough, I will make an end of my dying speech. One cannot think of everything and there is still much unrest which death brings in its train, and only ostensibly the need to take care for it doth so. The very thought, the uncertainty as to how we shall live after our parting is itself more a form assumed by the unrest; but that is what my thoughts are none the less — thoughts of unrest. Shall I perch on the trees, a bird among birds? Shall I be this or that at will: a heron in the swamps, a beetle rolling his ball, a lotus chalice on the water? Shall I live in my chamber rejoicing in the offerings purchased from my fund? Or shall I be there where Re shines by night and where all will be just as it is here, heaven as on earth, river, field, and house and I shall be Petepre's eldest servant as I always have been? I have heard it one way and I have heard it another, and all ways at once, when one thing probably stands for another and all is but a figure of our unrest, which dies away in the gentle drowsiness that calls upon me. Let me down again in the bed, my son, for my strength is gone, I have spent the last of it in the provision for death and in the blessing. I will give myself to sleep, which murmurs drowsily in my head; but before I yield myself, I should like quickly just to know whether I shall meet again my little Olive Tree, who perished away from me — whether I shall meet her again on the Nile in the West. But before all comes the fear lest in the last moment, when I would fall asleep, the cramp will snatch me back. Tell me goodnight, my son, as you know how to do, hold my arm and leg and conjure the cramp with soothing words! Perform once more your delicate office — for the last time! Yet not the last; for if on the Nile of the transfigured all is as it is here, then, Osarsiph, you too will be again at my side as my apprentice and every night give me your evening blessing sweetly phrased as is your gift to do. For you are blest and can give blessing, whilst I can but wish — I can speak no more, my friend! I have done with my speech. But believe not that I cannot hear you still! "

Joseph's right hand lay on the wan hands of the dying man, with the left firmly supporting the thigh.

" Peace be with you! " he said. " Rest, rest, my father, beatified through the night! Lo, I keep watch over your limbs, that you may carefree tread the path of consolation. You need not to be careful for aught, and thinking that may be blithe. Not about your limbs, nor the cares of the house, nor yourself and what will become of you and how it may be in the life after this life. For just so is it, that all this is not your affair nor care and you need not to have unrest about it but may leave all as it is, for somehow it must be, since it is, and however it is has been well cared for; but you, who have had so much care, are done with care and may quietly repose and be cared for. Is that not gloriously soothing and happy? And is it not with must and may as ever it was when I bade you good-night and told you not to think that you must rest but only that you may? Lo, you may! All toil and moil, all heat and heaviness are past. No anguish more, no wrestling struggle, nor terror of cramp. No bad medicines, no burning poultices, nor sucking leeches on your neck. The dungeon of your sore trouble opens its door, you can come out and stroll strong and hale down the path of consolation, which leads you deeper with each step into the ways of peace. At first you will go through vales you know, those which each eve received you when I said good-night; you have still some heaviness and scantness of breath, of which you are scarce aware; they come from your body, which I hold here in my hand. But soon — you will not know the crossing — you will gain the meadows with light tread, where no distress from afar can hang on or plague you even unaware, for all at once you are free of all doubt or care as to how it will be with you or what become of you, so that you are amazed how they could once have so concerned you; for all is as it is and in the most natural way, the most right and best, in happy harmony with itself and with you, since you are Mont-kaw to all eternity. For what is, is, and what was shall be. Did you doubt in your heaviness if you would find your little Olive Tree in the blessed fields beyond? You will laugh at your little faith, for lo, she is at your side — and why should she not be, since she is yours? And I too shall be with you, Osarsiph, the dead Joseph, as I am called for you — the Ishmaelites will bring me to you. For ever you will come across the court with your little wedge-shaped beard, your ear-rings, and the tear-sacs under your eyes, which may have come from the nights of quiet weeping for your Beket, your Olive Tree; and you will ask: ' What men are these? ' And will say: ' Be so good — dost think I can listen to your chattering all the days of Re? ' For since you are Mont-kaw, you cannot fall out of your rôle nor look before the people as though you believe I was nothing else but Osar-siph, the bought slave from afar, for secretly you will know, with silent intuition, from the other time, who I am and whose bow I draw, that I prepare the way of the gods my brothers. Farewell, then, my father and chief! In light and in lightness shall we see each other again."

Here Joseph closed his lips and ceased to speak; for he saw that the steward's ribs and his belly were still and that unaware he had passed through the vale and reached the meadows. He took a feather, which he had often held before his eyes to tell if he could still see it, and laid it on his lips. But it stirred not. The eyes he needed not to close, for the steward had peacefully shut them himself as he fell asleep.

The doctors came and salted and embalmed the body of Mont-kaw, forty days long, then it was wrapped and laid into a coffin which fitted it exactly. Then, a bright-coloured Osiris, he might lie some days at the back of the garden-house in front of the little silver gods. Then he took a voyage downstream, to the sacred tomb of Abdu, to visit the Western Lord, before in modest pomp be-taking himself to the rocky grave-chamber set aside in the mountains of Thebes.

But Joseph never thought of this father of his without feeling tears in his eyes. Then they were strangely like the eyes of Rachel, when they filled with impatient tears at the time when she and Jacob waited for each other.